Natural Rhythm

Tamzin took a deep breath, as Ray had instructed, but it didn't help. Tears were threatening again.

'Fran,' she said. 'I don't know how to tell you this, but Sophie's not here.'

'Not there?' said Fran. 'What are you saying?'

'She wasn't in the playground when I called the kids inside. Nobody knows where she went. I was hoping you might have ... I'm pretty sure she didn't get out of the front gate by herself because the lock was secure, but she's just nowhere to be found. If she had got out somehow, she wouldn't have tried to walk home, would she, do you think? Or gone to Davy, or —' She was babbling. She knew she was babbling.

For a moment the line was so dead Tamzin thought they had been cut off. Then Fran said, in her low, husky voice, 'I don't think I can take any more, Tamzin. If something's happened to Sophie, I don't know what I'll do.'

Alison Lowry is Publishing Manager of Penguin South Africa and lives in Johannesburg with her two daughters. Natural Rhythm *is her first novel.*

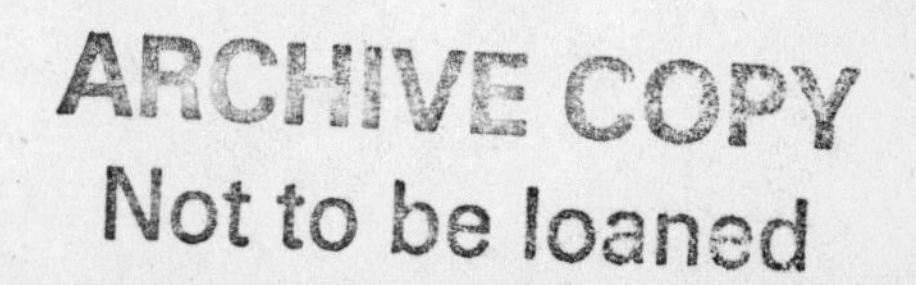

Natural Rhythm

Tamsin took a deep breath, as Kay had instructed, but it didn't help. Tears were threatening again.

'Fran,' she said. 'I don't know how to tell you this, but Kay's not here.'

'Not here,' said Fran. 'What are you saying?'

[illegible]

Nobody knows where she went. I was hoping you might have [illegible] pretty sure she didn't get out of the front gate by herself because the lock was broken, but she's just nowhere to be found. If she had got out somehow, she wouldn't have tried to walk home, would she, do you think? Or gone to [illegible], or — She was babbling. She knew she was babbling.

For a moment the line was so dead Tamsin thought they had been cut off. Then Fran said, in her low, [illegible] voice, 'I don't [illegible] Tamsin, if something's happened to [illegible] I don't know what I'll do.'

[illegible] *Memoirs of* [illegible] South Africa and lives in [illegible] *Natural Rhythm* is her first novel.

ALISON LOWRY

Natural Rhythm

Mandarin

A Mandarin Paperback
NATURAL RHYTHM

First published in Great Britain 1993
by William Heinemann Ltd
This edition published 1994
by Mandarin Paperbacks
an imprint of Reed Consumer Books Limited
Michelin House, 81 Fulham Road, London SW3 6RB
and Auckland, Melbourne, Singapore and Toronto

A CIP catalogue record for this title
is available from the British Library
ISBN 0 7493 1375 7

Printed and bound in Great Britain by
BPCC Paperbacks Ltd
Member of BPCC Ltd

For R.A.L.
who gave me the words

Prologue

The 13th of September would always be a significant date in Fran Phillips' memory. It was the day her daughter Sophie was born. It was also the day Laurike Malan had died in detention.

One image had haunted her for a long time afterwards, had taken the edge off her joy: while she had lain anaesthetised, placid and expectant, offering up her swollen belly to the precision of the surgeon's blade, Laurike had chosen another kind of blade with which to change her life – a razorblade kept hidden in the heel of her shoe. She had pushed aside the damp black curls and drawn a neat line across her own throat. While the arrival into the world of the newborn baby had been greeted with joy and wonder, at the same time, on the other side of town, another life, once so precious to her, had ebbed stickily away on to the cold, hard floor of a prison cell. Birth and death. A life for a life.

She'd not known, of course, about Laurike until that evening, when she'd seen the headlines: FIRST WHITE WOMAN TO DIE IN DETENTION. In the ward around her it was visiting time. Husbands sat on beds, close and intimate. Conversations were full of bonhomie and bursts of laughter. Window-sills stiff with cute cards and fruit in coloured cellophane cages.

Davy'd been late. She'd heard his sneakers squeaking on the lino all along the corridor and she turned her face to the doorway as he entered. His eyes took in the newspaper lying on the bed and he crossed quickly to her, walking lightly on the balls of his feet, as if afraid of waking a hundred slumbering infants. He kissed her on the forehead.

'I've just come from her folks,' he said. 'The kid's with them.'

'How are they taking it?'

'Fairly stoically, I suppose, although Oom Bram was looking exhausted. May was holding up all right. There were a lot of people there, so I didn't stay. The funeral's on Friday.'

'I should be up by then. We must go.'

Davy took her hand, shifting his chair closer to the bed. 'How are you feeling? How's the baby doing?'

'I'm fine and she's lovely.' Fran's face relaxed a little. 'Are you sure you like the name?'

'Mm. Sophie Phillips. Suits her. Can I go and gaze adoringly at her on my way out?'

'I'm sure they won't mind. Davy –'

'What?'

'She must have been so ... lonely, so afraid, to have ... '

He squeezed her fingers. 'I know,' he said. 'Oom Bram said he was able to see her about a month ago. He said she was depressed and was on some medication.'

Davy had left with the rest of the fathers. He'd looked so young, in his jeans and T-shirt and long, springy hair. The girl on the other side of her had a stockbroker for a husband, the one across the way an insurance salesman. You could tell they'd come straight from their offices, sober-suited, proud new dads. All working towards their time-share deposits. She'd longed, then, for their Kensington cottage, her warm, book-lined study, Van Morrison singing 'Tupelo Honey' in the background. She'd felt tired and sore.

There had been a thousand people at the funeral, and – unusual at that time – the green, black and gold of the ANC flag draped over the coffin. There were banners from the South African Communist Party, and more black mourners than white. Youths in MK uniform had carried blown-up photos of Laurike on placards on the tops of poles. 'They'll have my head on a spike yet,' Laurike had said to Fran just a month before her arrest. Prophetic,

Laurie, thought Fran, but wrong side, wrong circumstances.

Laurike's six-year-old son, François, Fran's godson, had held tightly on to his grandmother's hand at the graveside, and thrown rose petals on to the coffin. Afterwards they'd sat for almost an hour in a traffic jam getting away from the cemetery and she'd had to feed Sophie in the car. It was all a long time ago now. Laurike had been dead five years. François was at school in Swaziland. And Sophie – Sophie, oh Sophie ...

Laurie, thought Fran, but wrong side, wrong circumstances.

Laurie's six-year-old son, François, Fran's godson, had held tightly on to his grandmother's hand at the graveside, and thrown rose petals on to the coffin. Afterwards they'd sat for almost an hour in a traffic jam getting away from the cemetery and she'd had to feed Sophie in the car. It was all a long time ago now. Laurie had been dead five years. François was at school in Switzerland. And Sophie – Sophie, oh Sophie . . .

One

'My penis has fallen off!'

The children giggled and pointed. Tamzin came to the rescue. 'I did tell you not to touch it,' she said, carefully picking the little clay model up off the floor. 'We'll go on with sex education tomorrow and get these guys sorted out then. Never mind, Simon. You can give him a new pecker.' She ruffled the small boy's spiky blond head and laid the clay figure back on the window-sill in the sunshine. A whole row of mud-coloured figurines stared through the glass into the playground. Two were in advanced stages of pregnancy; two were babies lying on their backs, and the rest were very clearly fathers, if their enthusiastic protuberances were anything to go by. Tamzin's playschool teaching methods were unorthodox, to say the least, some would have said eccentric, but she had a loyal following nevertheless.

It was nine a.m. on 1 September, the first day of spring. The children had all been out in the garden stripping the trees of blossoms, and the classroom was bright with their colour and scent. Every available plastic container was crammed with blooms.

'Looks like a bloody funeral parlour in here. What's going on?'

'It's *spring!* Don't you *know!*' yelled Thabo Thekiso, jumping down the steps and into the garden. He spread his arms and zoomed off and out of sight.

'Jess. Come in,' said Tamzin. 'Have you got time for a coffee before we start?'

'Thanks, but no. I found a bratlet's lunch-box out on the path. Any idea whose?'

Tamzin gave her an odd look. 'Isn't it Glenda's?' she said.

'Oh, God, so it is. I'll put it in her locker, shall I? Oh, hello, Cassandra. Are we on for tennis on Friday? You playing, Tam?'

Cassandra Symons paused in the doorway. She wore black calf-length boots and a black leather miniskirt. Her legs were an even milk chocolate. She held a pile of egg boxes in her arms. She came into the room and waited while Tamzin cut chewing-gum out of somebody's hair and smiled up at her.

'Excuse me if I don't get up,' she said. She had a pile of black wool on her lap. 'We're making Michael Jackson wigs,' she explained. 'To go with the guitars we did last week. Starting early for the Christmas concert – be warned.'

Cassandra smiled faintly. 'Egg boxes,' she said. 'You do collect this kind of thing, don't you? My maid saved them for you. Can I put them down somewhere?' She looked vaguely about. The solid gold charm bracelet clinked on her wrist. Tamzin and Jessica exchanged a look.

'Great. Thanks.' Tamzin swept aside some coloured paper to make room on the table, while Jessica looked at the boxes thoughtfully.

'You could do beans in them, couldn't you?' she said. 'You haven't done beans yet... '

They watched Cassandra hitch her Kenyan grass bag over her shoulder and walk away up the path. Ruefully, Tamzin looked at her own pale, end-of-winter legs. Bermuda, was it, they tried to remember. Or just Madagascar this time? Or maybe, Jessica suggested uncharitably, Cassandra had a sun lamp somewhere in that mansion of hers. Jessica blew a kiss at her children and strolled to the gate while Tamzin got ready for the day.

Tamzin Jones was the owner of Rosepark playschool. She was small and compact with the kind of solid figure that would be called dumpy in middle age. Now, at twenty-four, she still looked like a child herself, a Lucy Abbott illustration, with round rosy cheeks, wide nut-brown eyes and copper curls which bounced about her face, unchecked by the yellow satin ribbons she wore.

She walked barefoot down the steps to where the children were playing on the grass. Petra was making a tunnel in the sandpit, as usual allowing no one within spitting distance. Doing a quick head-count with her eyes, she realised she was one short. Sophie. She clapped her hands. 'Come on in, guys. Everyone inside. Last one in's a skuzbucket.'

One last go on the slide for Rosalie, sand to be brushed out of Petra's long fair hair, and they were all in, wriggling and tumbling about on the carpet, waiting for the story they knew was coming as the first activity of their day.

Tamzin cast another eye over the group. Still no Sophie. She'd seen her arrive with Fran, quite early that morning. Fran had been in a rush and hadn't had time to stop for a chat. Sophie had made for the jungle-gym, but Tamzin couldn't recall seeing her after that. She glanced at the lockers. The blue and white striped suitcase was in its place. She felt an unpleasant churning beginning deep in the pit of her stomach as her mind swiftly eliminated possibilities. Could someone have left the gate open? Impossible – it was on a very safe hinge which automatically swung closed. Besides, it was too high up for a child to reach, even a child as agile as Sophie on the jungle-gym. And why would Sophie want to go out into the road anyway? Mind you, she'd been a moody child since her father had left home. She was unpredictable at the moment.

Tamzin turned to the children. 'Where's Sophie?' she asked. 'Anyone seen her? She was playing on the jungle-gym earlier. Glenda? Jason?' Those who looked up shook their heads. 'Come on – somebody must have been playing with her.' Petra looked at Tamzin but offered nothing. Rosalie was showing Simon Fleming her belly button.

Trying to control the rising panic she felt, Tamzin went to the door and looked out into the quiet spring morning. One swing moved gently back and forth in the breeze. She called Sophie's name loudly, echoed by Thabo, who had squeezed under her arm to stand on the step below. There was no answer, only the barking of the dog next door, and the faint noise of traffic on the main road a block away. She half-walked, half-ran up the path to the gate. It was firmly closed. She went out on to the pavement and stared distractedly up and down the road. The next-door gardener was sweeping up leaves in the road. Tamzin crossed over to him, describing Sophie as she went. But he was already shaking his head before she reached him. He'd probably learnt from experience that it was easier to plead ignorance to white people's problems than to get involved. She ran back inside, pure fear clutching now at her stomach. Please be there, she prayed silently as she neared the classroom. Please let her be there. But Sophie Phillips was not there.

Tamzin made a quick tour of the playground, the sandpit, the wendy-house. The only sign of life was Boris, the school's big black witch's cat, who stretched himself lazily on the roof of the wendy-house and then jumped down to rub himself against her legs. She checked behind the azaleas running along the back fence, and even pushed her head through the broken section to look into the disused and overgrown service lane behind the house.

She would have to call Fran. And the police. Glancing at her watch, she was surprised to see that it was already nine thirty. In the classroom she could tell that the children were disturbed. Whatever she did, she knew she must not frighten them.

'OK, you lot,' she shouted above the noise. 'I'm going to make some phonecalls up at the house.' The children looked up at her, puzzled by the odd tone to her voice. She tried to speak calmly. 'You may all have your juice early today and play outside for a while longer ...'

With shrieks of delight and much tripping and shoving, they pushed past her and scrambled out into the garden. Up in the office the telephone on the desk rang shrilly just as she was reaching out a hand to it. Tamzin jumped back with a cry, her heart pounding.

'I know, I know, I know. I'm not supposed to call you during school hours, but I thought the little fiends might be having a pee break or something. How are you, my sweet? Since it's officially the first day of spring, I thought we might indulge in a bottle of chilled white and a picnic hamper – pâté and french bread – on my patch of lawn this afternoon. To celebrate my daffodils. Tammy? You there, honey chile?'

'Ray. Something terrible's happened. Sophie's missing.'

'Missing? Fran's and Davy's Sophie? What do you mean, missing?'

Tamzin told him. She started to cry.

'Take it easy,' he told her. 'Take a few deep breaths. Have you searched the garden – could she have fallen off something, perhaps have knocked herself out? Have you talked to Fran? Perhaps she came back to fetch her for some reason?'

'I've looked everywhere. There's no sign of her. And Fran would surely have said something if – I was about to call her when you rang. Should I get the police, do you think?'

'I suppose so,' Ray said slowly. 'But wait till I get there if you like. I'm on my way.'

Fran worked mornings at the Village Bookshop. She picked up the phone on the second ring.

'Tamzin,' she said. 'What ... is Sophie all right? I'm sorry I had to rush off this morning, but I had to be here early – we're stocktaking. I wanted to mention that Sophie'd had another bad night and I thought she might be below par today. She's a bit insecure at the moment, I'm afraid. I hope she isn't being a pain?'

Tamzin took a deep breath, as Ray had instructed, but it didn't help. Tears were threatening again.

'Fran,' she said. 'I don't know how to tell you this, but Sophie's not here.'

'Not there?' said Fran. 'What are you saying?'

'She wasn't in the playground when I called the kids inside. Nobody knows where she went. I was hoping you might have ... I'm pretty sure she didn't get out of the front gate by herself because the lock was secure, but she's just nowhere to be found. If she had got out somehow, she wouldn't have tried to walk home, would she, do you think? Or gone to Davy, or –' She was babbling. She knew she was babbling.

For a moment the line was so dead Tamzin thought they had been cut off. Then Fran said, in her low, husky voice, 'I don't think I can take any more, Tamzin. If something's happened to Sophie, I don't know what I'll do.'

Fran Phillips was a hippie. She'd always been one. The flower-child movement of the sixties had merely coincided with her lifestyle. She'd been wearing loose cotton dresses and leather thong sandals since she was fifteen, and the long auburn hair which cascaded, rippling, about her face she still held back, on occasion, with a raffia-weave headband. She seemed to float through life like a Botticelli angel. She would have been amazed to be labelled trendy in the nineties. Her favourite denim mini-skirt she'd had since school and the baggy men's sweaters she wore over her long print dresses on chillier days were just that – two cast-offs from her father, and one she'd picked up on a park bench.

She stood with the phone in her hand beside the till.

'Is this the latest Paul Theroux?' a man said to her, holding the cover to face her. 'Miss?'

Fran put the phone back in place. It didn't seem quite to fit the cradle and it slipped off, banging on to the counter. She fumbled with it, frowning.

'Miss?'

There was a queue behind the man now. A child was trying out the ballpoint pens on a pile of Garfield books.

'Are you the only one serving here?' a woman in the queue called out.

Davy. She had to call Davy. Fran picked up the receiver again and started to punch in the digits. She stopped. What was Davy's number? Where would he be at this time of the day?

'Excuse me! Are you in charge here? Who's in charge here?'

The manager of the bookshop came hurrying through from the offices at the back of the shop. 'Fran?' he said. 'What's going on?'

'I can't remember the number.' Fran turned her face to him. She was stabbing at the digits on the telephone with her right hand, seemingly at random, not looking at what she was doing.

Her face was pale and there was a sheen of perspiration on her forehead. 'I can't remember Davy's number,' she said. 'I have to call Davy. Sophie's missing from the school. I have to call –'

The manager took the phone out of her hand. Apologising over his shoulder – 'Someone will be out to attend to you right away' – he led Fran to the office. He had to push her through the doorway and make her sit down. A secretary, looking stricken, held out a glass of water.

'No,' she said, pushing it away and slopping water on to a stack of Beatrix Potter mobiles. 'I can't … I have to … ' She jumped to her feet where she stood, rocking slightly, looking bewildered. Then she reached for her car keys hanging on a hook on the wall. 'I'm sorry,' she said. 'I'm going to the school. I've got to find Sophie.' And then she was gone, and running through the shop and out into the mall. The manager stood nonplussed, as he watched her cut her way through the morning shoppers and saw their heads turn with annoyance and alarm. The secretary drank the water.

Once in her car and queueing at the parking ramp, Fran began to calm down. She held her hands steady on the wheel. She put Sophie in the front of her mind, focusing on her features.

'Mommy?' Sophie was standing in the doorway to her bedroom.

Fran put on the bedside lamp. 'What is it?'

She was standing on one leg, rubbing up and down her shin with the foot of the other. Her small feet were pale as feathers in the darkness. Fran held out her arms. 'Come,' she said. 'It's cold. Come and snuggle with me for a bit.'

'Where's Davy?' Sophie had never called her father Daddy.

'Sophie –'

'It was me what ate the ice-cream in the fridge.'

'What?' Fran was fighting off sleep.

'Davy went away because I was naughty. It was me who ate the –'

'Oh Sophie. You know that's not why Davy went away. You know how much he loves you. He comes to see you all the time. You know that.' She stroked her daughter's hair and was glad of the warmth of her body curled into hers.

Sophie was falling asleep. She could sense her breathing

slowing. Her eyelids were slits, opening, closing, like a kitten's. She had a musky smell and Fran buried her face in her neck and drank it in greedily. They fell asleep together, tightly curled like shells, until the alarm clock woke them at dawn.

Once on the highway Fran put on her hazard lights and drove in the fast lane at 120 km an hour. She drove automatically, skilfully, weaving in and out of the traffic with grim sureness. She switched on the radio and turned it up loud, letting the music slam through her head and ricochet round the Morris like gunfire. She tried to remember Tamzin's exact words. Had she said Sophie had actually run away, or that she thought she had run away? Whatever she'd said, Tamzin had got it wrong. Sophie would never have run away from school. School was her security. Her friends were there. Tamzin was there. She was looking forward to Thabo's party in the afternoon. It was Davy. It must have been Davy with a day off, going over to surprise her and take her to a movie or to Gold Reef City for a treat. He would have called her sooner or later to tell her, before Fran was due to pick Sophie up. He would also have cleared it with Tamzin. Tamzin was so scatterbrained she had probably forgotten. Davy had probably called to say he was coming. He probably ...

She was there. And there was a yellow police car, the kind with a wire grille across the back seat and a police dog slavering in the back. This one was empty and its windows were open. There was a crumpled newspaper on the front seat.

Fran ran down the path along the side of the house. The uneven bricks of its paving were mossy and slippery. Tamzin was waiting for her.

'Where is she? Have you found her?' Fran said. 'Is she hurt?'

The sound of children's voices, shouting, high pitched, came up from the playground. Fran turned her head sharply, but Tamzin shook her head. Her eyes were red-rimmed. 'Sophie's not there,' she said. 'I ... I called the police. They want to talk to you. Davy called –'

'Sophie's with him?'

'No. Someone from the bookshop called him for you. He's on his way.' Fran felt a pain in the centre of her chest, as if someone was squeezing her ribs together, squashing the air from her lungs. She shrugged away the hand Tamzin put out to her and squared her shoulders. She walked with Tamzin to the office. There were two policemen in the room. They held out their hands and shook hers. One of them, a man in a baggy suit, looked down at his hand. There was a smear of blood on his palm. He took Fran's hand again and opened it, and she stared down at her palm where her car keys had cut into the flesh. Blood oozed in a jagged cut along her heart line. 'I'm sorry,' she whispered, ashamed. She folded her arms.

'I'll use the phone in the other room,' Tamzin said to nobody in particular, 'to call the other mothers.'

Fran sat in a chair and began to answer questions. She felt somehow as if she had left her body, in the way that people who've been pronounced clinically dead sometimes claim to do. She saw her bent head, the faint stripe of her centre parting, and the whiteness of her arms at her sides. She was astonished at how little she knew about her daughter.

'Height?' The policeman paused. 'Weight?'

Fran could answer neither question with accuracy. She felt she was failing Sophie already. What sort of mother didn't know these elementary things?

Clothes? A sundress, with flowers on it, smiling, and bumble bees. Yellow and red and green.

Hair colour? Red, like mine, only curly and bright and all over the place. Bouncing in the wind in the egg and spoon race at the Five Freedoms Forum picnic last month.

Any distinguishing features? A gurgling laugh, low in her throat like water from the rusty tap in Mary's farmhouse. A gruff, helpless chuckle when Davy held her feet and tickled them till they curled and scrabbled to get away. Dabs of freckles on the bridge of her nose and across her cheekbones. A pout second to none when she was angry ('Put your lips back, Sophie.' That was Jessica). A birthmark shaped like Madagascar on her left calf, or was it her right? A map of blue veins showing through the parchment skin of her stomach. Was that enough to go on?

Articulate? Friendly? How would she react to strangers? Would she talk to a black man?

Fran swallowed hard. These men were trying to help. She had to co-operate. Sophie talked slowly. She was thoughtful, serious, curious. Capricious sometimes, flirtatious on occasion. Strong in spirit, stubborn – and yes, she would talk to a black man. Fran felt panic fluttering in her chest. How was she to answer? How could she be of use to Sophie now?

She could hear a child's voice out in the garden, calling 'So-phie! So-phie!' and she sprang to her feet. The policeman in the suit held up a hand. 'I have a man out there,' he told her. 'He would tell us if she were there.'

Fran never cried in front of people, not even in front of her friends. She was strong. She could cope. Even when Davy walked out on her and Jessica had turned up with a plastic dustpan and brush 'to pick up the pieces', not even then had she cried. But now, with this stocky, untidy man, who took her by the shoulders and guided her back down into the chair, she felt her jaw tighten unbearably and her vision blur. She tried to get up again and found no strength in her legs or arms. So she sat where she was and felt the tears well up and out of her eyes and her nose run wet and salty on to her upper lip.

Gloria Mkhize heard the front door slam and listened to Gail Fleming's high heels clip-clopping along the path to the garage, where Alpheus had just finished washing and polishing the sleek cream Lancia. She heard the engine start up, then roar into life as the car pulled out and into the road. She turned on the radio in the kitchen, looking at the sinkful of last night's dirty dishes with distaste. Baby James, sitting in his high chair with lumps of oatmeal porridge on his face and pyjamas, banged his spoon cheerfully. 'Mama, Mama!' he said.

Gloria beamed back at him. 'Yes,' she said. 'Who's your mama, hey, Baby James? You got two mothers, I think.' She wiped his face gently with the dish cloth and lifted him down to the floor. Since Gail had decided to take a job, Gloria had to look after James for most of the day. When Gail whirled in after picking Simon up at school, it was 'Gloria – where's my pink blouse? Haven't you ironed it yet?' 'Gloria – I'm expecting people over for bridge. Make us some scones, please.' 'Gloria – please take the children to the park. My head is splitting.'

Last night Gail had hosted one of her tedious dinner parties and Gloria had spent all afternoon chopping vegetables into tiny, inexplicable pieces. This morning, when she had let herself in at the back door, there was a small dish of leftovers put to one side, covered with silver foil, and Gail was slopping round the kitchen in a dressing-gown eating a bowl of trifle. She waved vaguely at the leftovers with her spoon. 'Have some of this for your lunch, Gloria,' she said. 'But keep a bit over for the dogs, all right?'

While James played with a basket of toys on the carpet, Gloria made the beds, emptied ashtrays, scrubbed rings off baths and hung up Gail's discarded clothes. As she hoovered in time to Brenda Fassie on the radio she saw a pearl ear-ring lying on the carpet, and she hoovered that up too. 'Nothing sucks like Electrolux, hey, Jamie,' she said. The silky material of the shirt Gail had worn for the man-catching dinner party was creased and stained with a dribble of red wine. Gloria tried it on over her uniform, looking carefully at her reflection in the mirror from all sides. Then she put it in a basin to soak. As she moved off to start on the children's rooms, the telephone rang.

It was Simon's teacher from Rosepark school. 'Is Mrs Fleming at home?' she asked.

Gloria put on her maid-answering-telephone voice. 'No, Mam,' she said. 'The madam she gone to wuk.' But the teacher's voice was anxious and friendly at the same time so Gloria relented and found the number quickly of the estate agent where Gail currently dabbled in property.

'Thank you,' the teacher said.

'Is everything all right at the school?' Gloria asked, thinking of Simon.

'Oh, yes,' said the teacher. 'Thank you again.'

Gail was putting the finishing touches to her nails when Tamzin's call came through. She held the receiver gingerly, blowing gently on her hand as she listened to Tamzin's story. Although she didn't say so, she imagined Tamzin was over-reacting, but she promised to get to Rosepark as soon as she could. Waiting for the lift, she caught sight of her reflection in the black perspex nameboard nailed to the wall opposite the lift doors. She paused to look critically at her carefully layered silver-blonde hair. It was time for highlights again. She blew a mock kiss at her reflection and pouted coquettishly.

'Going down?' drawled a voice behind her and she whirled round, cheeks flaming. The lift doors were open and a couple of post-office technicians, festooned with telephone cable, grinned out at her. One had a Mickey Rourke stubble and a slow, unattractive smile. 'You can go down on me, baby,' he murmured.

Ansie Barker moved to the sink to fill the electric kettle. Her eyes wandered round the spacious kitchen and, as usual, a feeling of immense satisfaction washed over her. She and William had bought this house four years ago because they had fallen in love with the garden full of old established trees and a herb garden laid out in traditional pattern. The house itself had been in an advanced state of disrepair and they had had their work cut out for them. The oregon pine floors had been covered with maroon carpet tiles, dotted with burn holes from years of cigarettes, and the smell of cat pee was almost ineradicable. It had taken a lot more out of them to restore than they or their bank manager had anticipated, but gradually the shabby old house had been completely transformed. They'd ripped up the carpeting, sanded the floors and polished and sealed them. Now they glowed with a rich, warm colour, highlighted by Ansie's precious rough-woven rugs, bought on holiday one year in Lesotho. But the kitchen was always Ansie's favourite room.

She sat down now at the wooden table with her mug of tea. The ringing of the telephone broke into her thoughts.

'Ansie? It's Tamzin. Something's happened here. No, don't worry, Petra's fine. But, if it's not inconvenient, do you think you could come and fetch her early today?'

'You mean right now, don't you? Yes, of course, but what's the problem?'

'It's Sophie. She's vanished.'

As she passed the Smiths' old place in Cumberland Road, the property which backed on to the Barkers' house, Ansie noticed that the 'For Sale' sign had been removed and replaced with a 'Sold' one. She wondered idly whether the new owners would have any children. Petra could do with some friends. She was much too *afsydig*, too introspective, for a child her age. Children right next door would be sure to be good for her. She thought of Fran's daughter, Sophie, the cheerful little redhead with the ready smile.

Petra seldom mentioned her friends at school and never seemed to want to invite them home in the afternoons, but she'd enjoyed having Sophie over once or twice when Ansie was helping Fran out. What could have happened to her?

Father Henry McBride put a match to his pipe, then leaned back in the low-slung garden hammock and stretched out his legs. From the open door of the convent kitchen he could hear the sounds of preparations for the afternoon's party. Miriam was excited and it was her voice he could hear rising over that of Sister Joseph as they went about buttering rolls for hotdogs and popping corn and whatever else one did for these affairs.

He shook open his copy of the *Weekly Mail* which he hadn't had time to read yet, but his attention was distracted by the strident squabbling of a trio of mynah birds in the magnolia tree above his head. There were long-tailed mousebirds in the tree too; they loved the magnolia. He only felt that spring was truly here when he saw them in the garden.

The sun was making him sleepy. He felt a little bit guilty too, sneaking off here in mid-morning when he had plenty of things to do in his office, and he knew he ought to be preparing for his meeting with Gwen Sutherland of the Black Sash about the memorial service coming up at the cathedral. But the sun was warm, the breeze gentle. He pushed a toe into the ground and set the hammock in motion.

'You dropped your pipe, Father.' Mbekhi was brushing sand off and holding it out to him. 'And your paper's flying all over the garden. Oh – I'm sorry. You're sleeping.'

'No, no, Mbekhi. Just closed my eyes for a moment. The glare.'

'Oh, I see. Well, the school phoned. They want us to fetch Thabo early today. Shall I go, or will you?'

'I wonder why? Nothing wrong, I hope. You go, Mbekhi, do you mind? I've got an appointment later on this evening and I'm ill-prepared. Here, let me see those? Are they spring onions – my, they're coming along nicely, aren't they?'

Smiling, Mbekhi tucked the paper under his arm and held out a hand to the priest. Together they strolled in the direction of the kitchen.

'Mbekhi, where are my onions?' Miriam looked up sharply as they entered, arm in arm.

'Don't worry, Ma, I have them. And we'll have carrots soon, too.'

'You made a good choice for head vegetable gardener, Father,' beamed Sister Joseph, wiping at her shiny forehead with the grubby sleeve of her habit. 'Any news yet about a job?' She looked anxiously at Mbekhi, then at his mother. 'Miriam?'

'No, nothing yet.' Miriam answered for him. She washed vigorously at the mud on the onions. Water splashed noisily in the sink.

'Well. I'm going to fetch Thabo.' Mbekhi went quickly through the parlour and out the front door. McBride watched him vault lightly over the low wall, raise a hand in greeting to a man in the street and walk up the road and out of sight.

Mbekhi was a remarkable young man. It hadn't been easy getting a Matric at school in Soweto over the past few years, what with the unrest and the boycotts in the townships. Mbekhi would have had his Matric at sixteen under a normal education system, but now, just turned nineteen, he was sardonic. 'What's the difference,' he said. 'Bantu education. I couldn't get a job anyway, even if I wanted one.'

Miriam worried about him. They all did. Mbekhi had turned down the opportunity at the height of the unrest to complete his education at the convent's brother school. He returned to Soweto each term, when the schools were functioning, that was, and he stayed with his uncle and family in Diepkloof. Mostly he came to the convent at weekends to be with Miriam and Thabo, but lately his appearances had been sporadic and his explanations for his absences vague. He'd come home this weekend, the first in a while, because it was Thabo's fifth birthday and he'd promised to help Miriam with the party. Thabo was a favourite at the convent, spoilt rotten by the sisters and the bigger girls. And Henry McBride, of course, who loved Thabo like a son.

McBride took the stairs two at a time, calling out over the banisters as he went, 'I've got a Black Sash woman coming to see me this evening. Moustache. Big hips.'

The two women exchanged glances.

'Kaftan,' said Sister Joseph.

'Sandals,' said Miriam. 'Hokay, Father.'

McBride spent half an hour looking through his notes for his sermon on Sunday and then ten minutes with the newspaper. There was new pressure building for further investigation into the activities of the government-sanctioned hit squads. It appeared that former members of these recently exposed units of death were believed still to be active and, to back up the claim, there was an unconfirmed report of a diary said to be in the hands of the ANC which belonged to one of these former members and which listed a number of new 'targets', so-called enemies of the State, whom it was planned would be eliminated. As serious, perhaps even more so, was the alleged link between this man and a senior government minister who was rumoured to have financed these sinister activities. At a particularly delicate stage of the negotiation process, such information, if it were true, could be dynamite in the hands of the opposition.

McBride felt frightened. This was not the struggle he knew. He thrust his fears aside when he heard the front door open downstairs and he went down to greet Thabo and Mbekhi. They were standing in the hallway, looking up at him.

'I'm having jelly at my party,' Thabo informed him gravely. 'Sophie's not coming. Sophie's lost.'

Jessica was changing Edwina's nappy when the phone rang. 'Will you get that, Anna?' she called out. She examined her daughter's nappy rash through a magnifying glass.

Anna appeared in the doorway. 'It's Tamzin at the school, ma,' she said.

'I wonder what she wants. Are the kids all right, did she say? Take over here a sec, Anna.' Anna grabbed Edwina's waving legs in one hand and slipped a nappy beneath her bottom in a swift, practised movement, while Jessica picked up a half-eaten apple from the top of the cupboard and strolled down the passage to the telephone.

'Tammy, what's up? Sorry – I've got a mouthful of Granny Smith.' She listened intently for a moment, groping behind her for a stool that should have been there but wasn't. 'Oh, Christ. Yes, of course. I'll be there straight away. Don't cry, Tam. I'm sure there's an explanation. She'll turn up. Fran's on her way, is she? Oh, Jesus, I hope ... She's been through such a lot lately. I know. Oh good. Ray's always a help in a crisis. Look, is there anything else I can ... OK, I'm on my way.'

Backing her car out of the driveway, and pretending she hadn't seen the remains of a KitKat which Edwina must have been sitting on in her car-seat and which had caused her, unnecessarily, as it turned out, to change a nappy on the floor of the supermarket that morning, Jessica tried to remember when it was that she and Fran had last sat down together for a real talk. They always seemed to be rushing past each other these days, saying 'We must get together soon ... ', 'I'll give you a ring ... ', so what with one thing and another it had been a long time since they'd had one of their old heart-to-hearts. Fran hadn't been playing much tennis at Cassandra's lately either, she reflected. Since Davy'd left she'd kind of cut herself off from her regular friends. She knew she should be making more of an effort to be supportive. God, if something really had happened to Sophie, Fran would go out of her mind.

Jessica hooted impatiently at an old man in a hat doing sixty in the fast lane, and stuck her tongue out at him as she sped past. Turning into Franklin Avenue, she pulled up at the playschool gate, noting with a shiver the yellow police car parked on the other side of the street. She could hear the crackle of its two-way radio through the open window. Fran's Morris Minor was there too, and as she locked her door Ray drew up behind her. She waited for him at the gate, taking in with slightly guilty pleasure the strong brown arms and the thick mane of dark hair that hung almost to his shoulders. Tamzin had said he was growing it for Rasputin, the part he was playing in his new play. Ray was quite famous, in a local sort of way.

'It's been far too long, Jessica Tucker,' he said. 'How are you, girl?'

Girl, thought Jessica. I wish.

Ray's eyes were worried, though, and the arm around her shoulders gripped her tightly. 'Tammy's called in all the mums, I see,' he said.

Inside the house they found a sober group. Fran was slumped in a chair, a tissue in her hand. She looked smaller, shrunken somehow. Her face had no colour at all. Tamzin had been crying again, judging by her red eyes and the lines of mascara down her cheeks. Ray went to her side, where she was talking to a policeman in uniform. When Fran saw Jessica she struggled to her feet. They were neither of them demonstrative people and they stood now, facing each other, hands by their sides. Then Fran felt her control break and she collapsed into Jessica's arms. Jessica stroked her back.

'Oh, Jessie,' Fran said. 'I'm so afraid.'

'Where's Davy?' Emotion made Jessica's voice abrupt.

'On his way. He'll be here any minute, not that there's any point now. We might as well just go home, the police say. They'll let us know.'

The men were preparing to leave, gathering notebooks, nodding to the women.

'We'll be in touch, Mrs Phillips. Rest assured, we'll be doing everything we can. We have your number. I suggest you keep within reach of your telephone and try to leave the line open.' The policeman had a kind face and tufts of gingery hair in his ears. Patches of sweat showed under the armpits of his shirt. Fran, holding Jessica's hand, caught a sickening whiff of sweet aftershave. Blue Stratos. As they watched the men walk away, she felt a wave of pure misery engulf her. They were abandoning her. They were abandoning Sophie. And she wasn't used to feeling that way about policemen. The emotion confused her. While they were in the office, with their official forms and sharp, direct questions, it seemed at least that something was being done. Now the prospect of simply going home to an empty house and just *waiting*, was unbearable. Where was Davy? He had always been there when she needed him. Had that changed too? She was vaguely aware of Ansie, putting out a hand in sympathy, and of Jessica standing close by, frowning and biting her nails.

She could see Mbekhi Thekiso shepherding Thabo up the path from the playground. It all seemed so unreal. She felt as if she were in the middle of some ghastly case of mistaken identity. This sort of thing didn't happen to people she knew; one read about them in the papers. Sophie would slip in in a minute, curl a thin arm round her thigh and smile round the room. She had waved to her only a couple of hours ago, hanging upside down on the jungle-gym. 'Look at me, Mom! Look what I can do!' Were those to be Sophie's last words to her?

Then Tamzin was standing in front of her, her eyes downcast. 'Fran –' Her voice was a whisper, a thin, pathetic vapour. 'This is all my fault. I can't tell you how awful I feel. I'll never forgive myself ...'

'Save it, Tamzin.' Fran heard her voice come out as a harsh, rasping, unpleasant sound. She saw everyone look at her, startled. But she couldn't help herself. 'Spare me the self-recrimination. What do you expect me to say – "That's OK, these things happen"?'

Tamzin's face crumpled as if she'd been struck and she put her hands over her eyes like a child. Ray came up behind her and put his arms round Tamzin's shoulders. She seemed to wilt back against his chest as if physically hurt. Fran wanted to hurt them both. How dare they unite against her? How dare they wash their hands of this?

And then Davy was there. Glancing round at the tense faces, he came to her in a moment. He held her up with his slender hands. He was a tall man, long-waisted, in faded jeans and sloganed T-shirt. He wore a single copper bangle on his wrist, where it had made a dark green band on the skin.

Tamzin broke from Ray's hold and left the room abruptly, and Fran watched her run, stumbling, in the direction of the playschool classroom. Ray, meanwhile, had taken command again. Outlining the facts, such as they were, to Davy, he gave off an air of authority which went some way towards defusing the stifling atmosphere in the room. Fran heard nothing of what was said. She allowed Jessica to sit on the edge of her chair while they waited, and then to take her arm and move her like a sleepwalker through the garden and up to the school gate. They stopped to wait for Ansie, who was rounding up the children. They came slowly up the path, trailing a string of jerseys, drawings and bumping suitcases. Fran turned once to stare down the garden at the classroom and thought she saw Tamzin step back from the window. She also saw Jessica hesitate, looking unsure. Fran waited listlessly. Tamzin was not her concern. Cassandra's two children, Jason and Rosalie, were waiting for their mother at the gate. Rosalie's eyes were magnified behind her thick glasses. 'Is Sophie going to come back to school?' she asked Fran. Fran looked down at her. She wanted to push her face in.

'We don't know,' Jessica answered quickly, herding her children in front of her. 'But we hope so, don't you?'

'She's naughty to run away,' Jason said. He could be a pompous child, rather like his father.

'We don't know that she ran away,' said Ansie, glancing nervously at Fran, who stared back at her impassively. 'We don't know what happened. Nobody seemed to see where she went. Are you *quite* sure you didn't see her go anywhere?'

Jason shook his head. Davy took Fran's hand and pulled her into the road. 'Come on,' he said. 'Let's get out of here.' In the middle of the road Fran stopped again, as if she had just run out of steam, and Davy had to pick her hand up again and lead her like a child.

'Tam—zin!' It was Ray, and the sound of his voice started them all moving properly again. Fran felt a cloud of anger swirl swiftly round her head. Tamzin had Ray to comfort her. He would probably make her tea and tell her it wasn't her fault.

'I'll drive your car,' said Jessica. She held out her hand for the keys.

Fran put her hands in her pockets. 'I'm fine,' she said. 'I can drive myself.'

'Fran –' Davy said. He, too, was in shock. He ran his hands through his hair. Fran thought someone should probably drive him. She could feel her muscles stiffening up again, as if all her joints were seizing. Even talking was becoming difficult. She had better go before she had to be airlifted home in a helicopter.

'I'll drive myself,' she said again, turning stiffly round to Jessica. 'But you can follow me if you like.'

Two

Jessica sent her children home with Ansie. She, Fran and Davy drove away from the school in convoy. Fran felt like a novice behind the wheel, grating gears, hugging the edge of the road, driving very slowly. For some reason an incident from her childhood, unrelated to anything, lodged suddenly in her mind the way things do. She'd been about twelve years old. It was a Sunday morning in Cape Town, a rare cloudless day at the end of winter. The family had been to Mass. Fran was wearing a blue woollen suit which she'd thankfully grown out of rather quickly and given away. Her mother brought toasted buns and tea on to the front stoep where her father sat in his shirt-sleeves reading the Sunday papers. Fran was day-dreaming on the steps, leaning her back up against the rough brick of the wall. She'd had a kitten at that time and it sat on her lap kneading her thighs with its paws, pulling threads in her skirt. An ordinary Sunday morning, nothing in particular to do, nobody caring much either way, when round the corner an ambulance suddenly appeared. It moved slowly and they could see the driver peering at the numbers on the gates of the houses in their road. He stopped outside No 6, where the Edwardses lived. Fran's mother paused in the pouring of tea, the heavy brown pot motionless in her hand. 'Poor Dilys Edwards,' she murmured. 'I suppose they've come for her.'

Fran watched as two men carried a stretcher up the path. A few minutes later they came out again, and this time she could see Mrs Edwards' head joggling down the path between them. Mr Edwards, awkward, was trying to hold her hand and he almost tripped and fell as he hobbled clumsily alongside. Everyone in the neighbourhood knew that Mrs Edwards had cancer. Fran's mother went in to see her twice a week and help wash and change her. She never came home from the hospital after that morning and Mr Edwards had moved away shortly afterwards. Tea and toasted buns on a warm Sunday morning, and Dilys Edwards going off to die. Fran had played checkers with her father in the sunshine.

She found her hands were slippery on the wheel. She looked in the rear-view mirror and saw Davy's car turn the corner. Davy had never been very good at facing up to things, even he admitted that. She had always been the problem-solver in their marriage (or thought she had). When he wasn't working putting somebody else's music together, he was lost in his home-built studio in their garage in Kensington. Fran still had to park in the street outside because Davy hadn't removed his equipment, but she didn't resent it, not yet. The real world didn't often impinge where Davy was concerned, but when it did, he would recoil, poised for flight, tense and watchful as a hare. Now his daughter was missing and Fran recognised the stance.

Missing. Fran felt bitter bile rise in her throat and she swallowed hard to try to dislodge the knot of terror that was threatening to choke her. It astounded her that people could be going about their normal daily business outside of this car – doing their shopping, going to the bank. She saw two schoolgirls sitting at a bus shelter comparing notes while her entire life was in danger of falling to pieces, with nothing in it ever the same again.

Fran parked the Morris and stood waiting for the others. She looked already in mourning, with a loose black skirt and baggy jacket. Her cloud of auburn hair blew wispily about her face from beneath a black beret. Davy looked very tense. He held the gate open while she watched and waited for Jessica. They went up to the front door, no one touching or speaking. Fran raised her key to the lock. The blood on her palm was a stiff, crusty line. She found her hands shaking so much that the bunch fell from her grasp. She and Davy both bent down at the same time to retrieve it, bumping their heads. Fran found herself quite unable to stand up again. She looked as if she had no bones in her legs. She sat on the cement of the stoep and cried long streams of tears. They came up out of her grey eyes and spilled and spilled. Her thin shoulders shook. Davy knelt beside her, while Jessica stepped past them, picked up the keys and opened the door. Davy led Fran to the bedroom. Guiding her gently over to the bed, he slipped off her shoes and laid the beret on a chair.

'Jessica's making tea,' he said. 'Lie down for a moment – you're shaking. Here, let me cover you up.'

Fran lay staring at the ceiling, her mind numb. She turned her head and Sophie's smile seemed to mock her from the framed photograph on her dressing-table. The tears came again, oozing past her eyelids, warm as blood. Then Davy was back, a cup of tea in his hand. He set it down beside her and sat next to her on the bed, feeling for her hand. His fingers were ice cold.

'Where's Jessica?' asked Fran.

'In the lounge,' Davy said. 'She won't go home.'

Fran smiled faintly.

'We've always taught Sophie never to wander off by herself,' Davy said. 'Get into strangers' cars, stuff like that.' His voice was loud in the silent room. Fran wasn't sure he was talking to her.

'I know,' she said miserably. 'I can't think that she would. She's got so much sense. It's completely unlike her.'

'How's she … I mean, has she been OK lately? Not sick or anything?'

'She hasn't been sleeping very well. She wakes up nearly every night and crawls into bed here. It's been more traumatic for her than I expected, frankly.'

Davy sighed. 'I know, I know. She's too young to understand.'

'Give her another thirty years and she might.'

'Please, Fran, this isn't the time … I don't feel up to this now. I need to get my head together.'

Musician talk. Cop-out language.

Jessica came into the room. She looked at the telephone

beside the bed. Black, inanimate, it squatted there, obstinately silent. She walked across and picked up the receiver. She held it to her ear. 'Just checking,' she said severely.

Davy got up and walked restlessly around the room, picking things up and putting them down again. He crossed to the window and stared out into the garden. A postman came whistling down the road, kicked out at a dog barking at his heels, and put a brown envelope in the letterbox. As Davy stood watching, a motorcycle drew up at the kerb and a man jumped off and removed a spangled crash helmet. He bent to look into his small side mirror. He smoothed down his hair, cupped a hand to smell his breath. The helmet had made an indentation into the hair at the back of his head like a contour path round a hillside. He had a camera bag over one shoulder.

'Someone's coming up the path,' Davy said. Fran leapt off the bed and joined him at the window. The ring at the door startled them all. Jessica was there before either of them.

'Ivor Sampson, *Sunday Times*.' The man took a step forward. 'May I come in?'

'What for?' said Jessica.

'We've heard the Phillips child has run away from school – and there could be a story in it ...'

Fran stared at him, frozen.

'Get the fuck away from here.' Davy's voice was low. 'Take your fucking camera and fat, slimy body and run before I break your nose.'

'But –'

Davy slammed the door. He was flushed and breathing hard. 'Bloody press. Bloody vultures. Don't they have any sense of fucking decency?'

'Nope,' said Jessica.

This time it was Fran who steered Davy back to the bedroom, while Jessica paced the narrow hallway like a soldier. Fran, through half-closed eyes, saw her peep round the doorway, where she and Davy lay together on the bed, side by side on their backs. Like corpses in a suicide pact, she thought absurdly. They held hands, slackly.

It was late afternoon when the insistent ringing of the telephone woke them. Fran reached for the instrument first, her head muzzy with sleep, heart knocking painfully in her chest. 'Yes, who is it?' she said anxiously.

'Franny? It's Jim. I heard about Sophie. Can I come over?'

'Oh, God.'

'Fran?'

'How did you hear?'

'It's in the paper. Are you all right?'

'Not really. But Davy's here. And Jessica.'

'Can I come over? I'd like to.'

Fran could see Davy in the mirror, lacing up his shoes. He made leaving signs at her and she frowned. She was conscious of a pin-point of pain at the base of her skull.

'Let me come over and make you supper. Davy too.' Jim didn't like Jessica and the feeling was mutual.

Fran didn't have the energy to deal with Jim's persistence. 'Come if you want to,' she said. 'But I'm not hungry.'

She went to the door with Davy. Jessica, too, was leaving. Fran felt empty of all emotion as she kissed her.

'I'm going to drive around for a bit,' Davy said.

Fran nodded. The streetlights were coming on. Lights shone in neighbouring houses. She could hear somebody's TV. And somewhere out there, she thought to herself as she watched first Davy's tail-lights then Jessica's disappear, is my child. She shuddered and turned back inside. She went into the kitchen. All her limbs felt stiff and wooden and her mouth was dry and unpleasant tasting. On the kitchen table, beside a pile of pamphlets about next Sunday's memorial service, was a small gift-wrapped parcel, tied up with a red bow. Thabo Thekiso's birthday present. Sophie had picked them out herself: a red pickup truck and a blue beach buggy. She thought briefly of the party. All the other kids from Rosepark would have been there, and their mothers – except Jessica, of course – all talking about Sophie, speculating, exchanging horror stories. She scraped back a chair and held the parcel in her hands, smoothing the ribbon mechanically with finger and thumb, feeling the seep of tears begin again. One thing she'd pushed to the back of her mind came at her now like a sudden blow – the voice on the telephone only a few days before. *Watch your back*, it had said. *We know who your friends are*. She'd gone through the motions, reported it, but had not given it excessive thought. She was used to death and other threats, or as used to them as anyone could ever be. It went with the territory, as they said in the Rambo comics. Now, suddenly, she felt a moment's pure terror. Sophie. Would they have hoped to get to her through Sophie?

Just then she heard footsteps on the stoep and a light knock at the front door. Again her heart leapt, but it was only Jim.

Jim Walton qualified as an 'old family friend', literally the boy next door, but without the attractive connotations. He and Fran had grown up together in Cape Town. They'd played marbles together and long-jump, and sevens. Inseparable as toddlers, they had grown apart in their teens and after Jim had gone into the navy and Fran to university, they saw little of each other. Jim's father had died in a car accident when Jim was thirteen. He had been coming home from an evening meeting and had swerved to avoid an overtaking car; he lost control of his own vehicle and crashed into a tree. Dead on impact, they said. Pissed as a newt, said Fran's father. Jim had been left with his mother, who began almost immediately to make a career of grief and ill health.

Fran experienced a faint rush of irritation when she opened the door to see Jim's large anxious face. Immediately she felt sorry for him and annoyed with herself. It was no secret that Jim had a huge crush on her. It had irritated Davy in the beginning, when he had appeared on their doorstep with his new job in Johannesburg, and thereafter had proceeded to arrive, uninvited, at weekends and odd evenings for a drink and, more often than not, a free meal. Fran treated him as she had always done, like a younger brother, and tried not to let his puppy-like devotion and mournful brown eyes get to her.

'He's quite harmless, Davy,' she would say, many times. 'But he hasn't made any friends here yet and he has precious little social life with his mother and her arthritis. Let's try to be kind to him. It's not much to ask.'

He stood on the doormat now, a bottle of wine in one hand, newspaper in the other. 'I didn't know whether you would want to see the paper, but I brought it anyway,' he said hesitantly.

'Oh, let me have a look.' She sighed. 'Come inside. Go into the lounge.' Jim never did anything unless directed. Fran moved him about like a chess piece, but absent-mindedly today, as if her mind wasn't on the game. The story had made the front page. There was a picture of Rosepark's front gate and one of Davy from an old album cover. 'Tamzin Jones, who runs Rosepark playschool, was said to be too distraught to talk to anyone,' she read aloud. 'Apparently Sophie Phillips (4) had been at the school earlier in the morning, but was not with the rest of the children when they were called in to class. Police are investigating. Sophie is the daughter of ANC activist Fran Phillips and well-known Johannesburg musician David Phillips.' Fran threw the paper to one side and took the glass Jim was offering her. 'Labels,' she said dully. 'Cheers.'

They sat in silence. Then 'Got any eggs?' Jim asked. 'I make a decent omelette.'

'I know,' Fran said. 'But I'm not hungry. You go ahead.'

Jim was already heading for the kitchen. Fran pulled the curtain aside and stared out into the darkness. 'Davy's driving round the streets,' she said. 'I should be with him.'

Jim had found a spatula and pan. He put his head round the door. 'Buck up,' he said. 'I'm sure the police are doing all they can.' Fran could see an unattractive film of perspiration on his upper lip. She looked away.

'I keep going over and over it.'

'She'll turn up, Franny, you'll see. Look, I'm going to rustle up something to eat anyway. It'll do you good.'

Feeling too worn out to protest, she let him carry on. She watched his large, ungainly body through the kitchen door. There were folds of fat across his shoulders, pulling at the seams of his shirt. Fran felt sorry for him. He tried so hard to be acceptable. She took hold of the neck of the wine bottle and topped up her glass. She imagined the liquid tumbling over the knot in her chest, whittling away at it like a river over a pebble. In the kitchen Jim began to whistle through his teeth – 'Oh Chitty, you Chitty, pretty Chitty Bang Bang ... '

Jessica scooped up a mixture of playdough and sausage with a damp cloth and wondered whether life was worth it. Andrew was trying to force a hairclip between the wheels of a toy train, whose pistons were pumping feebly, prior, she suspected, to ceasing forever. She'd last seen Glenda playing outside in the dogs' water-bowl, ladling teaspoons of sand into it from the garden. And the baby – where the fuck was the baby! Emptying the contents of the cloth into a potted palm without a twinge of guilt, she strode down the passage expecting the worst. Visions of infants blowing bubbles in nappy buckets, turpentine sneaked out of unlocked cupboards, fingers sizzling in wall sockets ... She glanced at her watch: it was getting late and Ben not home yet.

'Edwina!' she called, listening for an answering echo, and hearing none. 'Oh, God, there you are.'

The baby was curled up, thumb in mouth, fast asleep in Martha's basket. Martha, looking distinctly put out, was lying beside it. Jessica stooped to pick Edwina up. She carried her down the passage to her room, picking dog hairs off her Babygro as she went. She lowered her gently into her cot and drew the curtains, pausing to look out at the moonlit garden. She could see the first stars appearing – 'twinkle-littles', Glenda used to call them.

'Thomas the train broke, mama.' Andrew was standing behind her. 'You must buy new bashtrees.'

'I don't think new batteries will resurrect him. And,' said Jessica, studying the graunched pistons, 'I think Thomas is fucked, if you want my candid opinion.'

'Oh,' said Andrew gravely. 'But if you buy new bashtrees –'

'No,' said Jessica. 'Watch my lips. Thomas is broken. New batteries won't help. Look here, this piece that's all twisted and bent? That's where you stuck the hairclip in after I told you not to. That's why he won't go. Batteries have nothing to do with it.'

'Why?' said Andrew.

'Oh, ask your father,' said Jessica.

An hour later Ben still wasn't home and Jessica remembered that it was his squash night and toots with the lads. She wished she had asked him to bring home take-aways as the prospect of cooking a meal was daunting. She felt an urgent need to put her feet up and open a beer. She wondered why she was so tired and washed out. It was probably worrying about Fran. And she was still trying to kick the flu she seemed to have had for weeks. It was quite true what they said: once the kids started playschool they brought home every virus and bug.

She opted for a long soak in a hot bath. She turned on the taps, poured in some Mr Plod bubblebath and let the bathroom steam up as she slowly shed her clothes. Standing naked in front of the full-length mirror, she took a long, calculating look at her thirty-three-year-old body. She'd read a novel once where the heroine had always bathed by candle-light. Romantic, she'd thought at the time, as the book had implied. Bullshit, she realised now. The reason was that candle-light had the edge over fluorescent when it came to bulges and flab. The bright tube above the mirror highlighted the droop to the breasts, the silvery stretchmarks on her stomach and hips. Still, if she stood back a little and tried to ignore the crow's feet, the violet blue eyes and rich, thick brown hair that hung heavily to her shoulders still recalled another time, and the mouth was generous and full. Her legs, perhaps, were not as entirely unmarked by time as when she'd been chosen Rag Queen – was it fourteen years ago – at university, but they were still worth more than a passing glance.

Sinking back into the warm water, she cupped her breasts in her hands, rubbing the nipples softly between finger and thumb. She felt an answering tingling warmth spread throughout her body, and her lips parted slightly as she closed her eyes and let her mind drift.

Half an hour later, the bath water cool, Jessica heard Ben's car and got out of the bath quickly. She wrapped herself in a towel and shook her hair loose. She switched on the front veranda light and opened the door before Ben could get his key to the lock. He looked spruce and almost handsome, and only a little drunk. She felt an unaccustomed wave of affection for him as he bent to kiss her cheek. He smelt of whisky and she turned her head. Squash kit was dropped on the floor. He was looking at the headlines in the evening paper over her shoulder.

Jessica made scrambled eggs, whipping them to a froth in a glass bowl. Metal clashed on glass. Plates on their laps, they watched the news on TV.

'Something awful happened at Rosepark today,' said Jessica during a commercial break.

'Mm?' Ben didn't take his eyes off the small screen.

'Sophie Phillips disappeared. She must have got out of the gate somehow and just – went missing. The police were there and everything. Fran is beside herself. So was Tamzin, as you can imagine.'

'That so?' murmured Ben, groping blindly for his beer can. His jaw chewed rhythmically.

'I'm leaving you. You can have the kids,' said Jessica.

She called Fran before she washed the dishes. There was no news at all. Fran didn't want to talk. She wanted to keep the line open.

'Chaos!' beamed Father McBride. 'Absolute chaos. I'd say it was a great success, wouldn't you, Sister?'

Sister Joseph raised her eyes and sighed. 'If you're judging by the mess, Father,' she replied. 'Mess equalling success, that is.'

They looked around them. The birthday party had been held in the church hall, the eats and drinks set out on trestle tables. Now the floor was littered with popped balloons, trampled popcorn, bits of dropped hotdogs and biscuits with the cream licked off. There was wrapping paper ripped from presents. There were stains on the wooden floor.

'Ah – and who's this? The birthday boy himself.' McBride bent tenderly over the small boy sprawled out the length of two folding chairs. One plump arm hung limply off the edge, the new shorts and shirt a mess of ice-cream and juice. He stirred in his sleep, murmuring something unintelligible. McBride stooped and gathered him up in his arms and tiptoed through to the kitchen where Miriam was busy stacking dishes.

'I was getting to him,' she said.

'The little chap's worn out,' he whispered. 'I'll take him straight off to his bed, shall I?'

Miriam nodded. She put out a hand and touched her son's soft cheek. 'Have you seen Mbekhi, Father?' she asked. 'He promised to help me clear up here.'

McBride shook his head. 'I'll keep my eyes open,' he said. 'Will you give me a shout when the Sutherland woman arrives?'

It would soon be dark outside and a brisk wind blew the kitchen curtains about. Side by side, not talking much, Sister Joseph and Miriam Thekiso set about clearing away the party debris.

Up in his small, untidy office, Henry McBride settled himself at his desk. He had just lit his pipe, sat back and inhaled deeply when Gwen Sutherland's forthright knock made him lift his head.

'Come in, come in,' he said, rising hastily and extending a hand. 'Gwen – take a seat.'

Gwen Sutherland was a square, heavy-breasted woman in her fifties. She wheezed asthmatically after two flights of stairs.

'Beautiful evening, Father,' she puffed, lowering her Swazi-kaftaned buttocks into an easy chair. 'There's no doubt that spring is well and truly here at last. All we need now is a spot of rain. Mind you, *your* garden is looking lovely.'

'That's thanks to our green-fingered Mbekhi Thekiso,' said McBride. 'The son of our excellent cook downstairs. He's taken on the horticulture portfolio and a fine job he's making of it. But you haven't come to talk about gardening. It's the memorial service for the Boksburg boys, right?' Seven black youths, among a group of returned exiles, spending an afternoon in a park in Boksburg, had been gunned down in cold blood by a group of white men, who had first chased them across the grass in a white *bakkie*. The *bakkie* had then sped away and no arrests had been made, no witnesses come forward. This was a not unusual pattern in the country at the moment, especially in the more conservative areas. And it was a pattern already being met with alarming apathy. Self-styled assassination squads, in clumsy imitation of the slick, professional death squads exposed not long ago, were taking the law into their own hands with increasing frequency and daring. But these days, not even the Boksburg Seven were big news.

'May I?' Gwen shook a cigarette out of a squashed pack of Camels and McBride steered an ashtray towards her through the papers on his desk. He patted pockets for a lighter but she forestalled him by taking a cheap plastic one from her bag.

'We discussed it briefly on the phone last week, but I thought we should run through the schedule together now so as to avoid any confusion on the day. We're expecting quite a large crowd, as you know – and of course the Bishop has managed to fit us in, which is a coup. It's also the anniversary of the death in detention of Laurike Malan, so emotions may be running fairly high.'

'I suppose the boys in blue will be in evidence?'

'Of course. They're supposed to be there for our protection these days, remember. Anyway, we don't anticipate any trouble. Their image can't afford it right now and the right-wingers will stay away this time; they've done their damage. Still, the police always do have a provocative effect ... ' McBride could have sworn there was a touch of nostalgia in her tone.

'Proceedings begin at nine o'clock, do they?' McBride put on his glasses and searched surreptitiously for the letter he'd received in the mail.

'That's right. That is, we're asking that everyone be seated by nine. The actual service will begin at nine thirty. You and Father Justinian will be assisting the Bishop, if that's all right? Bram Malan will read the lesson, and Patience Mkhize will say a few words.'

'And the procession – you mentioned something about a procession ... ' He wished he'd paid more attention to the letter. He had a feeling that the folded square of paper serving as a mat for his coffee mug might be what he was looking for.

'I was coming to that.' Gwen pressed her cigarette butt into the ashtray. Her fingers were stained yellow with nicotine. 'We're asking all the participating parish priests to suggest that those of their congregations attending bring along some spring flowers. After the service there will be buses, for those who wish to go, which will take us to Alexandra and we'll proceed on foot from the entrance to the township to the Laurike Malan Centre, where the flowers will be laid round a sort of memorial plaque to be unveiled.'

'And there will be no problem in spite of the trouble in the area?' There had been some ANC-Inkatha skirmishes in the township of late, resulting in a heavy army presence and an after-dark curfew.

'You mean will we be allowed in?' She shrugged expressively. 'I think so. Permission for the march hasn't been granted yet, mind you, but we see no reason why it shouldn't be. Things seem to have quietened down.' She smiled conspiratorially. 'Anyway, the homosexuals are marching in Hillbrow at the same time. Personally, I think that's where the trouble will be.' She stood up. 'So we can count on your support as usual, Father?'

McBride smiled. His weather-beaten face broke into creases. 'You know you can, Gwen. And the Sash is to be congratulated on organising the service. I shall do my best to involve my parishioners in this one – it's close to my heart. They're an apathetic lot, I'm afraid, most of the time, but I'll try to get them thinking. And I've got some of Mbekhi's freesias lined up for my own contribution.' He walked Gwen Sutherland to the door, where they shook hands. Then McBride walked across to the chapel in the darkness, his hands behind his back and his head bowed. He would have to pull something out of the bag this Sunday if he was to motivate his sluggish congregation to get themselves involved. Rosepark was a fairly large parish and his parishioners mostly in the upper income bracket. He could guess how the majority of them voted, but their liberal dispositions didn't go much further than voting moderately left and paying their servants slightly more than the minimum wage. When it came to making any sort of personal effort they turned vague and uneasy, and reaction to these hit-and-run raids was strangely mixed.

Try as he might, though, McBride couldn't concentrate on the service this evening. He could think only of Fran and Davy Phillips. He knew the family well. Fran was a Catholic, too, and active in the End Conscription Campaign and a regional branch of the ANC, for which she wrote or edited news-sheets and press releases. She had spent many hours with him after her separation from Davy, trying to make sense of it all. And now this. What a desperate tragedy if something had happened to her child. He wanted to drive over to see her before it got too late.

The chapel was silent. It smelt of wax polish and incense. The priest slipped into a pew, knelt and bowed his head in prayer. After a short while he became aware that he was not alone. Looking round, he saw Mbekhi in shadow sitting hunched up in a pew near the wall. His face was in his hands, the close-cropped head motionless. McBride turned back to the altar. When he rose to leave he glanced towards Mbekhi again, but this time there was a space where he had been. His footsteps echoed on the polished aisle. He crossed himself and left the way he had come in, hoping to catch up with the boy and remind him of his promise to his mother. Mbekhi, however, must have been walking quickly, for he was nowhere in sight. He didn't appear again that evening, or the next or the one after that. They had all grown used to Mbekhi's sudden disappearances and reappearances, and his whereabouts during his absences were never speculated upon, at least not out loud.

Fran was washing Jim's dishes when Henry McBride pulled up outside her gate. She heard the car and went to look through the window beside the front door. So far there had been two reporters and a neighbour shuffling their feet on the porch. And practically everybody she knew had telephoned. Davy, though, hadn't called. She imagined him cruising round the streets near the school, trying not to feel hopeless. Not many people walked the suburbs at night, and certainly no lost little white girls. The worst had been calling her parents. Her mother, hard of hearing at the best of times, had not understood what she was trying to say.

'There's a little parcel on its way up to you, dear. It should reach you before Sophie's birthday but –'

'Mom –'

'And Dad says not to forget the Churchill you promised him. Is Sophie in bed already? I'm sure she's not too sleepy to have a quick word with her granny.'

Fran found difficulty getting the words to the front of her mouth. It felt as if they were slipping back towards her throat, slimy, scrambled letters collapsing on top of one another, none of them wanting to be first out with the news. For a minute Fran even considered not telling her, not saying anything, just pretending that Sophie was safe across the hall, breathing.

'Sophie's disappeared, Mom,' she said. 'I think she may have been kidnapped.'

Was that what she thought? If it was, it was the first she knew of it.

'Oh, all right. Don't get her up then. Can I put Dad on?'

Fran began to cry. She put her hand over the mouthpiece and slid down the wall she was leaning on until she was crouched on the floor. She had seen desperate, cornered men do that in movies when they'd been shot to pieces. She imagined a smear of blood against the white paint tracking her descent. From the telephone still in her hand she could hear her father's voice, calling her name. It was a small, trapped sound. It was almost as if he were really inside there, a genie waiting for the magic words so that he could spring out, stretch to abnormal size and make everything all right again. There was a time when she thought her father could do that. Now he was just an old man with thin grey hair and a faulty valve in his heart.

'Frances?'

Fran saw Jim take the phone from her hand. At the same time he bent and lifted her by the elbow. She could smell garlic and chives on his breath. He tried to put an arm round her shoulder and pull her into his armpit, but she could not bear it, the smell of him, the doughy fleshiness. Nor could she bear the thought of hearing it all again, the blow-by-blow account of – what? Nothing. There was nothing that she could hold on to, not a shred of substance. Not a dropped shoe nor button. No trail of pebbles shining in the moonlight. She stumbled across the hall to Sophie's room where she closed the door behind her. She could still hear the murmur of Jim's voice and she blocked her ears with her fingers. When she took her hands away there was silence. She sank down on the low bed in the darkness and pulled the knitted coverlet round her knees. Sophie's slippers were lying on the carpet as if they'd just been kicked off her feet. She picked one of them up and held it to her nose. It smelt of Johnson's baby powder.

'Your father will call you in the morning.' Jim's large head was silhouetted in the light from the hall.

Fran nodded. 'Thank you,' she whispered. 'Jim –'

'Yep?'

'I don't want you to think I'm ungrateful, but would you mind going home now? I need to be by myself, I think.'

'I thought I might spend the night here,' said Jim. 'Your father –'

Fran sat holding the slipper. It was dark in the room. Everything seemed somehow to be holding its breath. A row of Sophie's bears stared straight ahead from the top of the dresser. They all looked grey in the grimy light, except for one which had a stripe of golden light from the streetlamp outside the window banded across his chest like a sash.

Fran was too tired to be horrified. 'No,' she said. 'No, Jim. Thank you. I know you want to help, but there's no need. Davy's coming back here later anyway.' It was a lie but not entirely beyond the bounds of possibility.

Jim was reluctant to abandon his role. 'Well. I'll clean up the kitchen before I go,' he said, turning away.

'Cu-ckoo!' It was Sophie's clock on the wall above her bed. Nine times the small plastic bird bounced out of the door in its plastic wooden house. They both watched it till it was finished, until it flounced inside, slamming the door with the tip of a dingy wing, and the innards whirred and grumbled into silence.

'I'll clean up,' said Fran. She stood up. 'It will give me something to do. I can't just sit here.' She put on the light and pulled the curtains closed, as if it were any other night and the household was preparing for bed. 'Please, Jim,' she said firmly when he still stood there. 'Please go now. I'll be all right.'

And Jim had gone without further protest and Fran had turned on the radio in the kitchen and scraped hard bits of yellow egg off Jim's plate. As she rinsed and stacked the dishes, Fran heard a car coming down the road. All her senses alert, she went through to the sitting room and looked through the window. It was a white *bakkie* with a canopy and she saw it slow down as it drew towards her gate. She switched off the overhead light and stood drenched in sudden darkness, watching. The *bakkie* slowed to a crawl and she could see two people inside it, but their torsos only, not their heads. Then the driver accelerated noisily and the vehicle sped off, its exhaust blasting and farting into the distance.

Fran went to the telephone and dialled Davy's number. There was no reply. She felt her arms trembling.

It was with a feeling of relief so tangible that her legs almost buckled again beneath her that she saw Henry McBride's car pull up. She had the door open before he had locked his door and was smiling at her over the roof of the Volkswagen.

'All right if I leave it here in the street?' he called.

'Should be. The street's well lit.'

He fumbled with the catch on the gate. He was a big man, and probably clumsy. He held out his hands and Fran took them with her yellow washing-up gloves and he pulled her head against his chest where the zipper of his windcheater was icy cold against her skin.

'I heard of course,' he said when they were inside and he was making coffee while Fran finished the dishes. 'And I would have come by earlier only I –'

'I know. Thabo's party,' said Fran. 'We have a present for him.' She gestured to the parcel still on the kitchen table.

'And I thought,' McBride went on, 'that perhaps there were some avenues yet to be explored and two heads may be better than one in thinking this through.' He looked around. 'Or three heads,' he said. 'I would have thought Davy ...'

'Davy was here,' said Fran, not meeting his eyes. 'He went to try and ... to drive around ... you know.' She pulled her gloves off by the tips of the fingers. They made a squelching sound. 'Davy will be coming back later,' she said.

They took their mugs into the sitting room and Fran turned on the gas heater. McBride stretched out on the carpet.

'The police think Sophie ran away from school,' said Fran. 'Although they never actually said so. But I know they think that, given her unsettled situation at home. Tamzin must have told them, I suppose.' She held her mug cupped in both hands. The heat stung the cut on her palm. 'But they're wrong. She didn't run away. I'm certain of that.'

'No,' said McBride. 'Do –'

'I have a feeling that she's not ... alive.'

'Why?' McBride asked gently. 'Why do you think that?'

'I'm her mother,' said Fran.

They fell silent for a few moments. Then, 'There's something on my mind,' said McBride. 'I don't know whether it's worth bringing up, but I'm sure it has to have been something which will have occurred to you and Davy.'

'What's that?' asked Fran, although she knew what he was going to say.

'I know you've been threatened before. There was the evidence in –'

'The commission of inquiry? I know.' Fran sighed. 'I know.'

'Is there ... do you think ... I'm sure this must be very painful for you, my dear, but –'

'It's the diary, the list, that everyone's talking about,' said Fran. 'Yes, well. I know that my name is on it again.' She pulled a face. 'And I have had a call. A crank one, I suspected at the time. A lot of us did after Boksburg, you know. But still, it seems –'

'Too below the belt?' McBride ran a hand over his face, then felt for his pipe and tobacco. 'I would have thought so too.'

'I've thought about it,' said Fran. 'But it doesn't fit into any pattern that I know of. It just doesn't feel right. If Sophie had been kidnapped to put pressure on me or Davy to ... well, wouldn't we have heard something by now?'

'Do you want me to put some feelers out?'

'I can do that. I wouldn't want you to get involved, Father.'

'It's my job. And you're my friend. I hope.' He smiled at her and took her hand.

Fran didn't look up. 'Thank you,' she said. 'I do know that.' She took her hand away and rubbed at her stinging eyelids.

'You should try to get some rest,' McBride said. 'Why don't you go to bed? I'll wait up for Davy.'

'I'm not tired,' said Fran, although her eyes were red around the rims and her shoulders were bowed with strain.

McBride didn't push her. He picked up his tobacco pouch and began to press sweet-smelling brown tobacco into the bowl of his pipe. He lit it and drew hard on the dark wooden stem and as the smoke drifted up towards the ceiling and the strong smell filled the room, Fran felt almost comforted in a small, detached way.

Tamzin, too, was a long way from sleep and when Jessica called her, she confessed to feeling ill and nauseous. She had sent Ray home, under protest, after supper and had regretted it ever since.

'You sound awful,' Jessica said with a sinking feeling and one eye on the clock.

'Have you talked to Fran?' asked Tamzin. 'Is there any news?'

'Yes, earlier on. And no, nothing yet,' said Jessica.

The line was silent. Jessica could hear Tamzin breathing.

'Tammy? Are you OK?'

There was no answer. Jessica felt drained herself, but there really was no choice. 'Would you like me to come over?' she said, not very hopefully.

Tamzin made a gasping sound. Jessica guessed she was crying again. Ray ought really to have stayed with her, she thought. 'Sit tight,' she said. 'I'll be there.'

'It's in the paper,' Tamzin told her glumly before she'd walked through the door.

'I know,' said Jessica. 'I've seen it.'

'I didn't talk to anybody.' Tamzin was defensive. 'There was a reporter. Ray tried to fend him off. He did his best.'

Jessica attempted to be soothing, although her nerves were all on edge. 'Do you mind if I sit down?' she said. 'And have a drink?'

Tamzin held out a tumbler of whisky. The ice-cubes jiggled against the glass. She fixed another drink for herself, while Jessica sank heavily into a chair.

'Oh, Tam,' she sighed. 'How on earth could this have happened?'

'After the police and all of you left,' Tamzin said, her eyes on the carpet, 'Ray and I went over the grounds again, every inch, and up and down the roads around Rosepark. We even went as far as the dam.'

'Nothing?' Jessica took a long drink. She wasn't a whisky drinker but tonight it seemed not inappropriate.

'Zilch.' Tamzin looked at her miserably. 'And that's not all.'

'Not all?' What more could there be?

Tamzin pulled open a packet of crisps and turned them unceremoniously into a wooden bowl. She gave a short, unhappy laugh. 'Congratulate me, Jess,' she said. 'I'm pregnant.'

'Never rains, huh?' Jessica's eyes flickered to Tamzin's waistline before she could stop herself. 'How far?'

'About six weeks.'

'Are you sure? When did you find out?'

'Yesterday. And there's no mistake. No such luck,' Tamzin said moodily.

'I gather you've been to your doctor?'

'God, no. Not Luke. I couldn't possibly. I went to the Family Health in town. Gave a false name.'

'Oh, Tamzin, you twit.'

Tamzin looked defiant.

'Does Ray know yet?' Jessica asked, more gently.

'That's the best part,' said Tamzin. 'It's not his.'

Three

It was a small dam, with reeds and murky water. At weekends people tried to picnic there, squeezed on to the rough damp grass at the water's edge. Now and again the city council had attempted to lay out gardens and had once even experimented with rustic wooden benches spaced out at intervals round the dam. Their energy and inventiveness had finally run out. The beds were continually vandalised and the benches had been ripped up for firewood almost immediately.

A little way up the hill there was an exotic herb garden. This was quite well known in the country for its rare specimens, although whether anyone ever got to see them was debatable. The herbs were protected by a thick bay hedge on two sides and by a wall with razor wire on top on the other two. The wall was covered with graffiti. The garden was seldom open to the public any more. Today, however, the steel door was thrown wide and the garden was being used by a ladies' sketching class. Gardeners turned the earth nearby with sharp brown spades.

Suddenly a brown-overalled man with a pair of shears in one hand stepped out from a clump of lavender bushes and stood, his mouth working but no sound coming from it. Then he shouted to one of his fellow workers and a torrent of Tswana burst from his lips. His eyes were wide with terror. The two men started to run down the hill, shears and spade dropped on the grass. The women stared after them. Not one of them understood the men's language. They began to speak, but stopped again when the men came running back, this time with a supervisor at a trot beside them. He wore a brown peaked cap and a thick leather belt. The gardeners gesticulated, pointing, pointing, and the three men walked through the bushes, stepping nervously, as if they were expecting something wild and dangerous to leap out at them. In single file they proceeded, silently, cautiously.

The women had deserted their easels. They inched forward in a bunch like a clutch of guinea-fowl, eager for diversion. The supervisor put his head round a bush and held up a warning hand. The group stopped, middle-aged women playing statues.

'My men have found the body of a little girl in here,' he told them bluntly. 'I would appreciate it if you wouldn't come any closer.' He gestured at their equipment. 'If you don't mind –' Still they stood as if transfixed. At last the silence was broken by a plump woman in beige ankle socks. 'Oh dear,' she said to the others as the man disappeared, 'I only hope it's not a white child.'

Nobody responded. They hovered, as if waiting for a signal, but dared not venture any further. The gardeners were hanging about, smoking cigarettes and talking in undertones. Slowly, one by one, the women turned away. They began to attend to their belongings.

'I wonder if it's the child reported missing in the paper a couple of days ago,' someone said. It was a woman in sensible panama hat with built-in sun visor. The light which filtered through it gave her a seasick, luminous look.

'Goodness, I suppose it might be,' said another, straightening up and turning to study the bushes anew.

'There are some dreadful types about these days, what with all the Communists allowed out now.'

'And all the unemployment. So many blacks out of work, nothing to do but live by their wits, stealing and so forth. Nobody's safe these days.'

'It's usually the elderly folk they go for though,' said a grey-haired woman with surgical stockings and stout walking shoes.

'Yes, but there the motive is money, isn't it? An easy snatch from someone who's helpless to defend herself. But a *child* ... '

'A *white* child, remember. It makes my blood run cold.'

'You're presuming, of course, that whoever killed her – if indeed she was killed – was black. Isn't that rather jumping to conclusions?' a voice said mildly. They turned in a body to its source. It was the newcomer to the group, Virginia Stephens, the gynaecologist's wife.

'Well,' began the grey-haired woman doubtfully. 'It usually is.' She cast around for support. 'Isn't it?'

Just then the supervisor emerged and hurried away down the hill. The sketching class passed him on his way up again, this time accompanied by two policemen in uniform and an older man in a baggy suit. The gardeners got to their feet uneasily at their approach. They shifted about in an uncomfortable little knot. After a couple of words with them, the supervisor sent them about their duties and they moved away sluggishly, looking back at the scene like disappointed extras sent off a movie set. The man who had stumbled upon the child stayed behind and, when asked, indicated a narrow path leading into the thicket of bushes. One of the policemen and the man in the suit stepped gingerly on to the soil, ducking their heads to avoid overhanging branches. The remaining policeman drew the gardener to one side. He took a notebook from his pocket and a pen from behind his ear. There was a great deal of head nodding and shaking from the man, who was clearly still upset by his discovery. The pencil moved unsteadily over the page.

The child fitted the description of the one who'd gone missing from Rosepark playschool. Hardened policemen weren't supposed to be affected by the grim realities of their job, but the man who gently rolled the little girl over on to her back, softly brushing the dirt from her cheeks, had a daughter of his own. He rested a big hand for a moment on the clotted auburn hair. At first glance he guessed the cause of death was strangulation. The belt from her sundress had been wound tightly round her neck. The colour was vivid against the pale skin. Her hair was matted and caked with soil, and around her mouth and nose were smears of dried blood and mucus. A pair of child's panties, yellow polka-dotted, had caught on a lavender bush beside the lifeless body. They hung there limply, accusingly, a flag at half-mast in a children's game. Her feet pointed upwards, slightly apart. The toes of her Jack and Jill shoes were scuffed.

The man brusquely pushed his way out into the clearing, scratching his face painfully on a bush as he went. Down below on the dam he could see two young boys trying to right a sailboard in the shallow water of the reeds. The sound of their voices reached him quite clearly.

This was not the first such victim he had seen but somehow the pallor of this child's thin thighs, the grazed hands with their torn nails flung out on the stony ground, wrenched at his stomach. He heard the siren and watched as an ambulance sped across the bridge spanning the dam and turned into the car-park. Straightening his shoulders, he cleared his throat and called out to the young sergeant who appeared to have finished taking down statements and was carefully replacing the pencil behind his ear. 'Wynand!'

'Sir?'

'Not a pleasant job, I know, but I would appreciate it if you would inform the parents right away. They will need to identify the body.'

He watched the blue uniforms of his men recede down the path and out of sight. The sailboard was up now and scudding confidently across the thick water, its jaunty sail proud and taut. It was a gay streak of colour against the sky. He picked his way out of the flowerbed, ignoring the supervisor's pained expression at the green shoots flattened beneath his boots. He dusted his hands off and waited for the paramedics with their stretcher.

When Fran saw the young policeman in uniform standing outside her front door she knew immediately that Sophie was dead. As she pressed her eye to the spyhole set into the wood of the door she watched his face, huge and distorted, swim in and out of focus. It looked as if he were leering at her. A gloating face. A 'just deserts' face. Hippie Communist parents didn't deserve to have children.

But when she managed to prise the chain on the door out of its groove and wrench the yale lock open, all she saw was a kid of about nineteen, blushing with embarrassment and pity.

'You've been sent to tell me that my daughter has been found,' she said, and the boy nodded, a jerking duck of the head that could probably have been interpreted either way.

Fran had no doubts, however. She could think of only one question to ask. Not, is she alive or has she been injured, but 'Where? Where did they find her?' Why it was so pressing to know this she didn't know. Perhaps because she, Fran, had failed to find her in time. How far out had they been? Had they walked right past her, calling her name? Had Davy's headlights scanned across her waving in the dark?

'At the dam, Mrs Phillips. Down the road from the school.' He cleared his throat. 'Is your husband in?' It would be easier talking to a man.

'No,' said Fran faintly. 'I ... ' She felt herself falling and saw the boy in uniform reach forward and take her by the arm. His grip was strong and she allowed herself to lean against him for a moment and be guided to the chair beside the telephone table in the hall.

'Is it possible to locate him?' he asked.

'Who?' said Fran, confused.

'Your husband, Mam. Can we reach him somewhere? I'm afraid it will be necessary for the both of you to come down to the ... er ... We need identification. It's regulations.'

'Regulations,' she repeated flatly.

'Yes, Mam.' He paused. 'I'm sorry.'

Fran lifted her head and looked at him. She knew that she did not want him in her house. It wasn't that he wasn't being kind, or doing his job to the best of his youthful ability, but this was a private thing, a family matter. She did not know him, nor he her.

'I wonder,' she said, quite calmly, 'if you wouldn't mind waiting outside for a few minutes? There's a bench on the stoep.'

Fran closed the door behind him and stood leaning against it for a second or two. So, she thought, this was it. This was what it felt like to lose a child. She noticed in a detached way that her cheeks were wet and she looked in the mirror hanging in the hallway and saw the tears coming down from her eyes. It was strange. She didn't feel as if she were crying. There was no pain in her chest, no prickling in her nose. Just the tears coursing down her face like water. When Sophie had been about three she'd had what the doctor had called a 'weepy eye', when a tear duct had become infected and her left eye had wept, all by itself, for a few days. She had been quite unaffected by it and Fran would find her peacefully colouring in a colouring book, smiling up at her and weeping.

The telephone rang. It was Davy. Fran told him, wondering at the calmness of her voice, that they had found Sophie, that she was dead, that the police needed them to identify her body. 'I'm sorry,' she said, 'I can't do this on my own.'

'Christ,' said Davy. 'Oh, fucking Christ.' He gave a moan, a keening sound which sounded remote, as if he were holding the telephone away from his ear, as if he didn't want to hear any more.

'Davy.'

All Fran could hear were muffled sounds, crying probably. She felt her composure beginning to disintegrate, as if pieces of her body were starting to become detached from one another. She felt as if only her clothes were holding her together, that if she took off her jeans her legs would come away and crumble into powder. Like those heavy, ornate garments from centuries gone by, preserved behind glass, which fall to dust the minute someone puts out a hand to marvel at their texture, her sturdiness was an illusion, her being alive a fraud.

'Davy, please.'

'I'm sorry, Franny. I can be there in ten minutes. Will you wait for me?'

'I'm not going anywhere without you,' said Fran. 'I don't think there's any rush.'

While she waited Fran got herself moving. She checked the latches and locks on all the doors and windows in the house, as if she was going on holiday somewhere. She even watered the plants. Then she wondered whether she ought to change into something more suitable. What did one wear to go and identify one's dead child at the police morgue? Should she cover her head? In the end she put on a jacket over her jeans and T-shirt and brushed her hair with hard, painful strokes until it bristled with static and glued itself in spiderweb strands across her cheeks and mouth. She twisted it into a ponytail, then left it loose, then plaited it over one shoulder. She could hear the scuff of the policeman's boots on the stoep and smell the smoke from his cigarette.

When Davy arrived they left immediately. They travelled in the back seat of the police car. The young policeman who had come to break the news hadn't looked much reassured at the sight of the tear-stained father in grubby sweater and an ear-ring in his ear. Davy had not shaved for a few days either and his cheeks were swarthy and rough to Fran's touch. His hair stood up on his head in matted curls.

At the morgue it was quite a lot like she'd seen in movies, except that the fluorescent light was harsher and it hurt her eyes as she and Davy followed their guide down in a lift. There were two nuns in the lift with them. One of them held her rosary beads in her hand and her lips moved slightly. Fran looked back at her as she and Davy stepped out of the silver doors. 'Say a prayer for my child, Sister,' she whispered and the nun looked up at her, startled, before the doors slid together.

The room they were shown into was cold. Fran had been to a morgue before, though not this one, with Agnes Radebe in '76 after her son had disappeared. It had been harrowing enough second-hand.

'Can we get this over with?' said Davy desperately.

There was a stretcher on wheels to one side of the room. In the centre of it was a shape, a small shape which filled only the middle portion of its white length. There was no toe sticking out with a tag on it, Fran saw with relief. A black man, expressionless, pulled back the green cloth at one end and nodded to them to come forward. He looked bored. He probably did this all the time.

Sophie's eyes were closed and her lips slightly parted. She looked asleep, like some other child asleep. Sophie had never been a peaceful sleeper. She had frowned and muttered and ground her teeth. She had never lain on her back like this, serene and unfathomable. Her lips had a purple tinge like a swimmer who's stayed too long in the water and the skin beneath her eyes looked puffy and bruised. Fran bent over and kissed her on the forehead. She shook her head and smiled a little. 'Where did you get to, Sophie?' she murmured. 'Where did you go?'

Cassandra and Mike Symons were not short of a buck or two, not by any stretch of the imagination, thought Jessica, as she stopped her car before the imposing wrought-iron gates. As she wondered whether she ought to hoot discreetly, or whether that was a contradiction in terms, they swung silently open. She drove up to the house, passing the swimming pool, the tennis court, the squash court and sauna.

'Out.' She opened the doors for her children, and released Edwina from the belt of her car-seat. She was dressed for tennis, white shorts and Reeboks. Although no one had ever stipulated that they wear white on their Friday afternoon tennis sessions, it seemed as if it was expected of them. Cassandra was immaculate as usual in her designer tennis gear right down to sweatband and sunglasses. Jessica always found her intimidating.

'Cassandra,' she said. 'Hi. I had to bring the whole brood with me today, I'm afraid. I usually try to leave Edwina with Anna, my ... domestic, but she had to go off to the clinic today to see about her varicose veins. Very close veins, Glenda calls them. She –' She stopped abruptly. Whenever she was with Cassandra she found herself talking too much and too fast. Fran had pointed that out to her once and she'd been conscious of it ever since.

Cassandra's lips curved in a smile. She waited patiently for Jessica to finish. Then she took a lace-edged handkerchief from her sleeve and held it out to her. 'I think Edwina's been sick down your arm,' she said.

Up on the patio there was lemonade on a silver tray.

'I don't suppose Fran will be playing today,' Cassandra said.

'Oh no, I doubt it,' Jessica said. 'This thing with Sophie has hit her hard. I saw her yesterday and she was looking really grey. There's still no sign of Sophie. It's as if she simply disappeared.'

'You're good friends, aren't you?' Cassandra said, almost wistfully, Jessica thought, with surprise.

'We were at university together in Cape Town, oh God, way back. I met Fran when we were in the same residence.'

'Her break-up with Davy was very sudden, wasn't it?'

Jessica nodded. Privately, she didn't feel she needed to share any details with Cassandra right now.

Just then Selena appeared from inside the house and called Cassandra to the telephone. When she came back out she smiled wryly. 'Mike,' she said. 'Working late – again.'

Jessica looked at her closely. Good heavens, she thought, could this be a chink, a hair-line crack in the impenetrable composure? Was all not well in paradise after all? She couldn't see Cassandra's eyes behind the dark glasses, but something about the set of her mouth seemed to suggest a tension she'd not picked up before.

'Here comes Tamzin,' said Cassandra.

'It doesn't look like she's planning to play tennis today, either,' said Jessica.

Tamzin walked across the grass and when she reached the patio she stopped for a minute. Her face was pale. Jessica could make out a cinnamon dusting of freckles against the skin.

Jessica took a step forward, then stopped. 'They've found her, haven't they, Tammy?' she whispered. 'Haven't they?'

Tamzin nodded, an almost imperceptible movement. She cleared her throat. When she spoke her voice was flat and toneless. 'In some bushes at the dam near the school. Some municipal workmen found her there this morning. A policeman came to the school an hour ago.'

'Oh, no,' breathed Cassandra. Goosebumps stood out on her arms.

'Dead?' Jessica couldn't prevent the word sliding past her lips. It hung obscenely before them in the air.

Tamzin nodded shortly. She turned her head away. The children's raised voices reached them from the bottom of the garden where some sort of argument was in full swing. Jessica could discern Andrew's loud bossy voice and Rosalie's inimitable whine. In a minute there would be tears. The women stood in the shade of the patio, motionless as statues, each caught up in herself, each a mother for that moment. Somewhere in the street outside a car's anti-theft device erupted suddenly, rudely startling them into motion. They all began talking at once.

'Does Fran –'

'Do they know –'

'She'd been –'

Cassandra and Jessica both turned their eyes to Tamzin, their questions dying on their lips.

'Well,' said Tamzin. 'It seems likely she'd been raped, or at least molested or whatever they call it. And then strangled. With the belt from her dress, the policeman said. She'd been dead about forty-eight hours.'

Cassandra turned abruptly and walked into the dim sitting room which opened off the patio. They could hear her calling out as she went further into the house. 'Selena! Could you bring us some tea, please? On to the patio. Oh, and the brandy decanter from the drinks cabinet. And some glasses.'

Jessica looked at Tamzin and thought suddenly how vulnerable she looked, and how very young. She was younger than most of the mothers who entrusted their children to her care. When all was said and done, and no matter how this ghastly tragedy had come about, Tamzin had been responsible for Sophie Phillips that morning. She would carry that knowledge with her wherever she went for the rest of her life.

Tamzin sat down on a chair and put her face in her hands. 'I'll never be able to face Fran again,' she said softly.

Jessica wasn't very good in these situations. Platitudes did not come easily to her. She went and knelt awkwardly beside her and patted her arm. She didn't know what to say.

Suddenly a dented panel van came backfiring up the long driveway, music blaring from its open windows. Startled, the two women looked up and watched as a young man slammed open the door and moved to the back doors of the vehicle. A couple of black workmen in overalls got out. They exchanged vociferous greetings with the gardener, then squatted on the low wall alongside the drive. The driver stared up towards the patio where Tamzin and Jessica were sitting. He shaded his eyes. Jessica got up to go and look for Cassandra when she reappeared, followed by Selena in crisp peach-coloured uniform and matching *doek*, with a tray of tea things and a brandy decanter. She stopped. 'Oh, Lord, the painter. I'd completely forgotten. Excuse me a minute.' Composure restored, she stepped smartly across the lawn, smiling, hand extended. Tamzin and Jessica looked at each other in astonishment. Tamzin gave a tremulous smile.

'You know what I think,' said Jessica slowly, standing up and taking the brandy thoughtfully in her hands. 'I think Cassandra's a Stepford wife.'

And suddenly they were in each other's arms, laughing, laughing fit to burst. They laughed until the tears came, great splashes and snorts of laughter rising up from the gut. They laughed until their chests ached and their noses streamed. When Cassandra came back she stood taking in the scene with an expression of such bafflement that their laughter threatened to erupt afresh. They were saved from explanations, however, by the diversion which hits all mothers sooner or later. The four children came straggling up the lawn, bored with tennis balls and hungry and thirsty. Edwina's nappy, hanging down almost to her knees, was as sobering a sight as any. Jessica picked her up and held her warm body tightly in her arms, squeezing her too fiercely against her cheek until Edwina wriggled and squirmed and bit her on the shoulder.

'Tea, brandy, or both?' Cassandra's voice, brittle and excluded, interrupted. 'If nobody feels like tennis, and I gather we don't?' She raised her eyebrows, looking from one to the other.

They had tea, and Jessica persuaded Tamzin to drink a small glass of brandy. None of them really wanted to be there now, Jessica especially. She wanted to go to Fran. Perhaps it was politeness, perhaps shock that kept them there on the patio, talking uneasily.

'Why aren't you playing tennis?' Andrew asked.

Jessica believed, wrongly probably, that children should not be shielded from reality. She felt that if unpleasant or complex issues could be explained to them in a sensitive way and at a level they could understand, they ought to be kept informed. Fran felt that way too.

'We don't really feel like playing today,' she said. 'You see –' Cassandra passed her a brandy and she took it, without really noticing. 'You see, the policemen have found Sophie. They found Sophie dead.'

'Like the cat in the road on Sunday?' asked Glenda with some interest.

'Well, no, not really ... ' Jessica looked at Tamzin and Cassandra who were clearly quite keen to leave this issue entirely to her. 'Somebody ... somebody horrid, has hurt Sophie. And she died.' Pathetic attempt. Truly.

'Oh,' said Andrew. 'Is she in heaven then?'

This was something else Jessica didn't mean to shirk and hadn't really got round to deciding how to tackle yet. 'That depends on –'

'Yes,' Tamzin broke in. 'Sophie's with God now, Andrew. She's in heaven. And she's very happy there, with the angels and everyone. We don't need to worry about Sophie now.' She looked at Jessica firmly.

'*I* wasn't worried,' said Jason, swinging his racket. 'Can we play on the tennis court if you don't wanna?'

They ran off, racing each other, quite unaffected it seemed. Then Glenda stopped, turned and came back to stand in front of her mother.

'Mom,' she said, wheedling. 'Who's going to have Sophie's toys?'

Jessica decided it was time to leave. She looked at Tamzin, who nodded and began to pile cups and saucers on the tray.

'Selena can do that,' said Cassandra.

'I was just –'

'It's what she's paid to do,' said Cassandra smoothly.

In a minute, thought Jessica, they would all be sniping at each other. She could feel her own shoulders stiff with tension, and Tamzin looked ill. She picked up the nappy bag and her tennis racket. Tamzin handed her her sweater. 'I think we're on our way,' she said to Cassandra. 'We're all upset. And I must go and see how Fran's doing.'

'Of course.' Cassandra stood up. She walked with them to their cars. Jessica put an arm round Tamzin's shoulder and, after a moment's hesitation, another round Cassandra's, gripping them tightly. Then Cassandra broke away and went into the house to activate the release device on the security gates.

When Tamzin and Jessica were gone, Cassandra went in search of the painter. She found him at the servants' quarters. He straightened up as she walked over to him, squinting against the brightness of the setting sun. He had very dark eyes, almost black, and straight black lashes, unusual for someone with such barley-coloured hair. The hairs on his brown forearms caught the light. Cassandra felt uncomfortable noticing them. He had square hands with flat, wide fingers, schoolboy hands, and a phone number printed in red ink on one of his palms. He looked at her expectantly, waiting for her to speak first. When she hesitated, he grinned and said, 'We're on our way now, Mrs Symons. But we do like to start early in the morning, if that suits you. Around seven?' His voice was deep and resonant. 'Mam?'

'Yes,' said Cassandra. 'Yes, of course. If you need anything and I'm not around, talk to the maid or gardener. I'll have a word with them.'

'Thank you.' His eyes crinkled in the corners when he smiled. He walked round to close the back doors of the van, patched canvas jeans hugging his small backside. Without needing to turn round, Cassandra could feel him watching her go and she felt confused. He was just a child, a boy.

It was cool on the patio. Cassandra lit a cigarette and inhaled deeply. She released the smoke through her nostrils and looked at it hang before her for a moment, a wispy grey veil against the evening sky. The garden was deep in shadow now. The tea-tray was still on the table and she leant forward to pour herself a finger of brandy. She felt inexpressibly sad.

Out of the corner of her eye she saw a sudden movement from a sandy patch in the lawn just off the edge of the paving. As she watched, it moved again and some grains of earth rolled in slow motion down the side of the small heap pushing up through the grass. Then the movement became more urgent, more rhythmic. She watched and waited, but the mole (for that is what it was) must have decided to carry on underground for, apart from those few seconds' eager thrusting, a last skitter of soil was the only testament to its activity. Cassandra leaned back, feeling disappointed.

Jason and Rosalie came on to the patio, both bathed and in their pyjamas. Cassandra felt affection for her two small children then, for their small compact bodies, their soapy smell. Selena came out behind them. 'I've given them supper. They bathed too, Mam,' she said. She piled the empty tea things and glasses back on to the tray. She hesitated over the decanter, then left it to one side. 'Will there be anything else?'

'No, thank you, Selena,' said Cassandra. 'The master is working late tonight. You can go off.'

'Can't we have a story first?' Rosalie cried. 'Just one, please, Mummy?' She came up close to her mother. She put urgent arms around her neck. Cassandra could smell cough mixture on her breath.

'Well, just a quick one then,' Cassandra said. Selena was a natural storyteller, and Cassandra had on occasion caught herself feeling almost jealous when she'd found her two children curled up together in an old armchair in the servants' quarters, listening to Selena's stories, while their own collection of books stood in neat untouched rows on their bookcases.

'I'll be in in a moment to tuck you in,' she said.

'Selena can tuck us in,' Rosalie called back over her shoulder.

Cassandra felt depressed.

Inevitably her thoughts turned to Fran Phillips and her dead child. It was ridiculous, but for a few moments this afternoon, when Tamzin had arrived to tell them the news, she'd felt something akin to a sense of well-being, standing close to the two women, almost as if they were all three of them friends, sharing their sense of shock. She'd felt accepted, 'one of the girls'. It had lasted only a few moments, though, until she'd sensed the barrier standing like a concrete block between the two of them and herself, the intruder in their grief.

What was it that set her apart? Was it as crude as money? All her life she'd never lacked for any material thing. Her father was a mining man, from an old Johannesburg family, and she'd grown up in the city in as much of a privileged position as her own children were doing today. Mike had been regarded as the heir apparent in her father's company from quite early on. Educated at the right schools and university, Rhodes scholar, Oxford, competent all-round sportsman – he was good-looking too, in a bland sort of way. Everyone had said they made the perfect couple when his engagement to the boss's daughter was announced.

Cassandra was not conventionally beautiful. Her mouth was too wide and her nose rather flat, but her air of serenity and poise, and her exquisite grooming, made up for it. The glossy, raven-black hair would turn heads for many years to come. And yet people kept their distance, and she felt helpless to lessen the gap. Trite though it sounded now, she thought marriage to Mike would change all that. When it didn't she thought they could at least be happy together and they had actually been content in those first years. When had things started to go sour?

Cassandra stood up and walked to the edge of the patio. It was quite dark now and the lights from the house behind her threw huge golden squares on to the lawn. She brushed a toe lightly across the mole heap, flattening its small, conical shape slowly, by degrees, until it was no more than a patch of brown sand.

A memory of Alfred, her parents' garden boy, came to her suddenly from the past, and the rusty old moletraps he used to set on the croquet lawn. Clumsy brown things driven through the grass, with a pointed metal spike poised to stab any unsuspecting rodent who triggered it off in its private tunnel. She'd seen many a limp, soft body prised from this primitive instrument, had watched from a safe distance as Alfred dug a hole near the back fence, tossed it carelessly down. When he'd gone she would make crosses with poplar twigs and hold a funeral and sing 'Oh God Our Help in Ages Past'.

When she was older and more concerned with creatures' rights, she learned that a swift kick with a tackie to the relevant part of the moletrap mechanism when no one was looking would set it off prematurely and leave the underground passages free. Alfred caught no more moles after that and her parents' croquet guests on Sunday afternoons had to flatten with their wooden mallets the annoying little heaps. After that summer Alfred had been stricken with rheumatism and had gone home to wherever it was he'd come from – Transkei, Zululand – nobody knew exactly. Her mother, too, had left that summer, with a visiting Argentinian polo player.

As Cassandra locked the patio door and turned on the driveway light for Mike, the painter slipped into her head like a shadow. For heaven's sake, she told herself impatiently – you're old enough to be his mother.

Jessica had left her children in the car. Fran could see them indistinctly in the evening gloom – two white shapes pressed to the glass and Edwina's feet and hands waving wildly in her car-seat.

'You don't have to do that, you know,' she said from the stoep.

'Do what?' Jessica stopped a few feet away.

'Hide your children from me just because I haven't got one of my own any more.'

Jessica burst into tears. Fran was resolute on the doormat. She held a coffee mug in her right hand. Her own eyes were raw, the lids swollen and tender. 'Go and fetch them in, Jess,' she said gently. 'It's not a good idea to leave them like that.' Jessica tried to wipe her eyes. 'Besides, they might drive off with the car.' Fran smiled wryly.

'Fran – I'm so sorry.'

'I know. Thank you.'

'Is Davy here?'

Fran shook her head. 'Davy's not taking this too well,' she said. 'I sent him ... home. To bed. He'll handle things better when he's rested.'

She waited in the doorway while Jessica went back down the path to her car. She saw her talking earnestly to her children, probably telling them to behave themselves and not ask questions about Sophie. It didn't matter. She was surprised that Jessica would think it mattered. She was quite used to the candour of children. Once Sophie had gone up to a one-legged beggar outside the OK Bazaars and asked him what would happen if she took his crutch away. He'd sworn at her and she'd backed off, alarmed. 'Tamzin says we should ask questions if we want to know things,' she'd said indignantly, loudly. 'She says that's how people LEARN!'

The children came into the house quietly, except for Edwina who barrelled along the passage, saying 'Where Pophe? Where Pophe?' in her high-pitched voice. Andrew rushed along and grabbed her roughly by the arm.

'It's all right, Andrew,' Fran called after him. 'Why don't you guys go and play in Sophie's room? She'd like you to. Really. It's OK.'

Fran and Jessica went into the kitchen. Fran poured coffee for her and another mug for herself.

'How did you hear?' she asked heavily.

Jessica hesitated. Then, 'Tamzin,' she said. 'We were at Cassandra's. The police told her earlier today.'

'Ah,' said Fran. 'Tamzin.' She felt her face flush. It felt like a small betrayal, Jessica consorting with the enemy. She was suddenly very tired, overwhelmingly tired. The rims of her eyelids were stinging and making her blink. She could think of nothing to say. All superficial conversation had completely deserted her. She felt as if she would never have reason to talk again. But she was thankful that it was Jessica sitting across the table from her, Jessica with her long slim legs stretched out beside her own. She wasn't drinking her coffee, just sitting there looking sad and deep in thought. She didn't look uncomfortable or awkward, as if she were trying to dredge up the right phrase, the suitable sympathetic noises. She was just being Jessica, unobtrusive yet solid. Fran was glad she was there.

'Is there anything that needs to be done that you don't feel up to?' Jessica asked.

Fran shook her head. 'No,' she said. 'It's all taken care of.'

'Have you told your parents?'

Fran felt her eyes prickle and she pressed her thumbs across the lids.

'Yes,' she said. 'I've told them.'

Her mother was seventy-five. Fran was her only child too. When Sophie was born she had knitted her eighteen jerseys in twelve months, and then two a year thereafter. She liked knitting for children, she told Fran when she'd protested; the jerseys were small and the job went quickly. 'They'll be on the early flight,' she told Jessica. She imagined her mother knitting on the plane, finishing a last sleeve because she didn't know what else to do with it.

'Are they staying here, with you?'

'No. They prefer to go to a hotel, I don't really know why. I suppose it's more, you know, comfortable. And they don't want to put me to any trouble, sorting out linen and that sort of stuff.'

They fell silent again. Fran drank her coffee. Edwina came into the kitchen on Sophie's tricycle. She was wearing Sophie's woollen cap and her dark curls were pulled down flat against her cheeks. She beamed up at Fran. 'Oh Jesus,' Fran whispered, staring. 'Jessie, what am I going to do without her?'

Jessica stretched out across the table and took Fran's hand. Tears blurred her eyes and she shook her head. She had no words of comfort.

'I went to see her,' Fran said in a firmer voice. 'Me and Davy. To identify her.'

'Oh God,' said Jessica. 'That must have been hard.'

'In a way,' said Fran. 'But I don't think it's really sunk in yet. That part doesn't feel real. This is where I can't believe it.' She gestured around her. There were drawings on the kitchen walls – Sophie's rainbows, butterflies with huge staring eyes, a heart with 'I Lov Mummy' written right round the outer edge. There was a mug on the dresser with S. Phillips written on it in red nail varnish. Fran knew that Jessica's kitchen was the same, only hers would go on. There would be real school schedules with netball match dates ringed, raffle money reminders, debating club nights circled on the calendar, the Matric dance. Her own kitchen graffiti would stop right here. The pages would yellow and tear. She would take them down eventually, keep them for a while, then throw them in the dustbin. 'God, I'm so tired,' she said. She put her head down on her arms. 'You must go home.' Her voice was muffled.

'I can't leave you,' said Jessica helplessly.

'I'll be OK.' Fran looked up briefly. 'Actually, I want to go to bed.'

Jessica looked dubious.

'I've got some sleeping tablets – I went through a spell when Davy left of not being able to sleep. I'll take a couple now and crash out.'

She didn't have any sleeping tablets. They both knew it.

Andrew and Glenda came into the kitchen.

'When are we going home?'

'Can we watch TV?'

Fran sat upright and smiled at Jessica wearily. 'Go on,' she said. 'Go on, Jess. Take your children home.'

Mike Symons stepped out of the shower. 'Does the name Gail Fleming mean anything to you, Cass?' he asked. Drops of water flew from his silver-blond head as he shook it vigorously. Cassandra had the evening paper spread out on the bed. She sat cross-legged, eating a marmalade sandwich.

'Simon's mother,' she said. 'She sells houses. She comes to our Friday tennis sessions sometimes.' She licked her fingers. 'Why?'

'I met her husband. At least her ex. He's a stockbroker. Nice chap. Going places.' Mike was into corporate jargon. Perhaps he was thinking of head-hunting James. Welcome aboard, he would say.

Cassandra wasn't really reading the paper. She flipped over several pages, glancing at captions and photographs. She was really watching her husband. Mike sat down on the edge of the bed and pulled on his yacht club socks. Cassandra was in her nightdress, ready for bed. 'Where are you going?' she asked, keeping her voice casual. Mike began to lace up his shoes. He'd only been home half an hour. 'It's ten o'clock,' she added.

'Heavy day tomorrow,' he said. 'Breakfast meeting with your father. I need some papers from up at the penthouse, so I thought I might as well go through the figures there. Then I don't need to disturb you.'

It was no good telling him that she wouldn't be unduly disturbed if he worked in the study, five rooms and a flight of stairs away from the bedroom. She had tried that before and been humiliated. If he wanted to go to the penthouse that's what he would do. Cassandra felt defeated.

'James is a nice chap actually,' said Mike, as if Cassandra had denied this. He bent to kiss her and she moved fractionally out of reach.

'Gail says he's a worm,' she said, turning a page and not looking up.

'Oh – well.' Mike was already half-way out the door when he paused. 'What did you do today anyway?' he asked cheerfully. 'Lunch with les girls, was it?' He smiled at her patronisingly in the way Cassandra found insulting but endured.

'I went shopping,' she said. 'And played tennis. But –' He wasn't even pretending to listen, but still she got off the bed and walked with him to the front door. He kissed her like a departing guest, a light brush of lips to cheek. A warm gust of wind sent a pile of swept-up leaves scurrying round in a frenzied circle on the lawn. Cassandra watched her husband reverse his car into the street. Then she closed the door and locked it.

Shopping. She'd been shopping all right. She took a plastic carrier bag from the back of the linen cupboard and carried it through to her bedroom. Her manner was desultory, even diffident, and for a while she left it lying on the floor as she sat in the rattan chair at the window, smoking and looking out at the moon. A pyramid of new hardcover novels stood on the breakfast table. Their jackets were crisp and colourful. ('Book club night?' Mike was fondly indulgent. 'Just an excuse for a gossip with the girls, I know.' Sometimes he could sound just like her father. He probably did it on purpose.) Mike liked her to have a social programme like his colleagues' wives. It made him feel successful. Shopping with friends. Book club with the girls. If it wasn't so depressing it would have been funny. The truth was Cassandra didn't have a friend in the world to go shopping with. Book club, too, was pure invention.

She tipped the contents of the bag out on to the bed. First a cascade of snowy undergarments spilled softly down, then a cashmere sweater, a light designer summer suit, and an off-white silk camisole. She almost felt pleasure in the garments as she touched the material with her fingers. Then abruptly she shoved each one back into its packet and threw them all amongst her shoes at the bottom of her walk-in dressing room.

Then, as if it were an afterthought, she opened her handbag and reached inside. The colour of the emerald pendant was almost shocking as she held it up to the light. It danced and flashed on the end of its gossamer chain. It warmed the room. Cassandra held it in the palm of her hand. It was light as a butterfly. She placed it against her throat. It was cold and her flesh broke out in goosebumps. Delicately, using the ends of her long manicured nails, she worked the price tag loose. It was a small oval of cardboard, the price R3 575 pencilled lightly on to it. In the bathroom she slipped the tag carefully down the plughole in the handbasin and allowed a thin stream of water to help it on its way.

She took the pendant to her wardrobe and dropped it into a shoebox on the top shelf. It fell with a small sound amongst the other pieces there – a string of pearls, three gold bracelets, a cluster diamond brooch. None of these items had appeared on any of her credit card statements. She wondered whether Mike would even have noticed if they had.

Four

It was a cool, clear Sunday morning. The bells from Rosepark convent church rang out like they did every Sunday, signalling half an hour to first Mass. Ansie had been up since six o'clock. She was planting out seedlings at the far end of the garden before the day grew too hot. The night's dew on the grass had left matching wet patches on the toes of her canvas shoes and the knees of her gardening trousers. She sat back on her heels and pushed her hair behind her ears, listening to the pealing of the bells. Father McBride would be saying Mass for Sophie this morning. If she had been a church-goer, Ansie might have walked along to the service, but her God wasn't in the ritual and the words. Her God was out here and all around her and in the green shoots labouring up through the moist black soil.

Gardening was Ansie's passion and her therapy. From their first spring in Johannesburg she had taken on as her personal task the landscaping and sorting out of the rambling mess of a garden they had bought with the house. While Petra lay on a blanket beneath the trees, playing with her toes or struggling up on to chubby knees and elbows, Ansie had dug and cleared and planted, drinking in the heady scent of springtime blossoms – the jasmine and lemon verbena, and the huge wild rosemary bushes.

'You really are a country girl,' William would say when he came home from work to find her still on her knees with fork or trowel, her thick blonde hair wound up into an untidy plait and her cheeks ruddy with heat and effort.

'It seems such a pity not to be outside in this beautiful

weather. And anyway, I enjoy it,' she would reply. 'And I think it's good for Petra too. *And* there's nothing wrong with being a country girl, thank you. I don't know if I'll ever get used to this big, dirty city of yours, all the people and noise and smog.'

William had urged her to get some help, a gardener or at least a maid, but Ansie dismissed the idea and in the end wouldn't even discuss it. 'I don't need black hands in this house,' she said darkly. 'Breaking things and getting in the way. I can do everything ten times more quickly. And with them it's always take, take, take. You've got to feed them and clothe them, and now they want rooms with baths, too. And they're never satisfied, never grateful for what you do for them. Before you know it they're pregnant and they're sick and can't work, and then someone's uncle dies and they go home for the funeral which lasts six months. Turn your back for a minute and they steal you blind. Uh uh, *nee dankie, Willem*!' This was clearly a can of worms William hadn't been aware of before.

Ansie had been born and had lived all her life on a farm outside of Welkom in the Orange Free State. Her family were cattle farmers, going back four generations, and their farm, Soetwater, was still run by her father, with the help of a manager. Ansie's sister Nella had married a doctor and moved to Bloemfontein, and their younger brother Stephan, who stood to inherit the farm, had just completed his compulsory military service. Stephan was a *laatlammetjie* and a mystery to his father. A shy child, a dreamer, he had dark hair and dark, watchful eyes. He showed so little interest in farming matters that his father had become deeply worried. He hoped his spell in the army would straighten his head out. It hadn't. When he came home he announced that he wanted to go to university to do an arts degree and his father hadn't spoken to him for three days.

'Stephan, I think, is a little bit of a disappointment to your father,' Ansie's mother, always given to understatement, had written in a letter, 'but the old man will come round eventually. Stephan may be the quiet one in our family, but he knows his own mind. He's old enough to make his own decisions and it's time we all accepted that ... ' Her solution, in the short term, was for Stephan to spend a holiday with his sister and Ansie was looking forward to his visit.

But Stephan was not on her mind this morning. She had been unable to sleep for most of the night, not since Jessica had called to tell her that Sophie Phillips' body had been found. She'd lain awake till after midnight, tossing and turning beside William's quietly breathing bulk. He was a sound sleeper and no amount of restlessness on her part ever disturbed his eight hours. Around two, Petra had had one of her nightmares, crying out in her sleep as if in pain. When Ansie had gone through to see to her, she was fast asleep, but breathing raggedly in the back of her throat, as if someone had been choking her.

At first light Ansie had been up and into the garden. By the time Petra's light touch on her shoulder made her look up, she had bedded out three seedling boxes of mixed petunias. Petra was still in her nightdress. She was wearing her slip-slops on the wrong feet, and her toes stuck out awkwardly off the edges of the rubber soles. Her long fair hair was tangled and loose. She had what William called her 'otherworld look', which always seemed to follow one of her nightmares or sleepwalking spells. Ansie studied her carefully but last night's terror seemed to have left no mark on her.

She wondered whether to mention Sophie, but decided now wasn't a good time. In fact she had a busy morning ahead of her, as Stephan arrived on the Bloemfontein train at ten and she had much to do to prepare for him. This business with the school had quite put her off her stride. She certainly hadn't meant to get involved with gardening this morning. However, in times of crisis it was always to her garden that Ansie turned. It was almost a compulsion. Other people popped Valiums with their morning tea when they couldn't cope. Ansie Barker took up her trowel and gardening forks.

By the time William was up and showered, she'd put together a breakfast of muesli and nuts, toast and homemade marmalade, and a large steaming pot of *boeretroos*. William liked his coffee strong and very sweet ('like my women', he sometimes added, which comment Ansie had grown rather weary of) and she served breakfast on the back stoep, under the shade of the avocado tree.

'Mmm. This is what I call living!' said William, catching her round the waist as she got up to refill his cup. 'Nothing quite like a family breakfast on the stoep, with the sound of birds in the garden, and everything smelling like springtime.'

'Everything except me,' she retorted, wriggling away from his arm. 'I'm going to take a shower.'

'Excited hey, Ans? Little *boetie* will be here in –' he looked at his watch '– an hour and twenty-three minutes.'

Ansie looked at her husband and her expression softened. He was such a good man, a good provider, so uncomplicated and honest. And he loved his family. She knew how precious she and Petra were to him, how devastated he would be if anything happened to *his* daughter. But outside of his own family circle nothing really touched him. Sophie's sudden death to him warranted no more than 'Ag, that's tragic, hey, Ansie? Poor kid.' And after that the matter was forgotten. Last night, after Jessica had called in the middle of dinner, she'd been unable to eat another mouthful. William, on the other hand, after pausing for a suitable time for sympathetic noises, had consumed a steak that stretched from one side of his plate to the other, four boiled potatoes in their jackets, two helpings of salad, and a slice of bread and blackcurrant jam. Then he'd read the paper and watched *What's Up, Doc?* on TV.

William took Petra off to the station to meet Stephan's train, while Ansie tidied the house. When she'd finished she took a glass of apple juice out on to the back stoep. As she sat on the steps she caught a movement through the fence at the far end of their property and heard raised voices. Over the top of the fence she could just distinguish the roof of a truck backing slowly towards it. Moving-in day for the new tenants. Ansie still felt on edge. The bizarre and abrupt death of her child's friend must be affecting her more than she realised. Why one child and not another? Could it as easily have been Petra?

*

Zinzi Mokoena stood at the window and watched the driver of the van manoeuvre his way carefully up the driveway, his head sticking out of the window as his assistant waved him in. The twins, Freda and Jonas, were playing at bumping down the dusty wooden stairs on their bottoms. Jonas's shorts were already stained brown and Freda was only seconds away from getting splinters in her bottom.

She slipped an apron over her head and went outside. The driver jumped athletically down from the cab. He came towards her, holding a sheaf of documents.

'Morning,' he said. 'Madam in?'

Zinzi gave him a look. She took the papers from him. 'Yes,' she said. 'Madam is in all right. Are you ready to start unloading?' The driver was embarrassed, put out. He slammed open the doors. Zinzi felt the throb of a tension headache beginning.

Jonas came shooting out of the front door. He was followed by his sister, stiff pigtails flying. 'Give it back. It's mine. I saw it first!' she yelled in Xhosa. It was an old tennis racket, all broken strings and unravelling handle, an obvious discard forgotten in a cupboard somewhere. Then they were gone round the back of the house and Zinzi gave her attention to directing operations.

Later, she stood in the road as the last of the boxes were carried in. The place seemed dead. She thought she saw a lace curtain twitch in the house across from her, but decided she was probably mistaken. She was startled out of her reverie by Jonas, who came running towards her, crying noisily.

'What is it?' cried Zinzi. 'Where's Freda? Why are you crying?'

The boy gulped and shuddered. Freda came slowly round the side of the house. She looked sullen and angry and she looked back furiously in the direction of the back garden.

'There's a swimming pool in the house at the back,' she told her mother. 'And Jonas and me, we climbed over the fence to have a look. And a white woman came out of the back door and chased us away. She made Jonas cry. But I didn't cry. I'm not scared of her, stupid woman.'

Zinzi had been afraid of this. She hadn't anticipated it quite so soon however. 'What did she say, Freda?' she asked, gently rubbing Jonas's back.

Freda scuffed her toes in the sand. She looked at the ground, her bottom lip a stubborn shelf.

'Freda?'

Jonas pulled himself roughly out of his mother's arms. The light and pleasure and excitement had drained from his eyes with his tears. 'She said "Hey, kaffir kids, what do you think you're doing here? *Hamba!* Get out of here!" That's what she said.'

'I have been much criticised in the past – and not a little even in the present climate – by my friends, by complete strangers, in the columns of the press, even by my parishioners for, as they say, "bringing politics into religion". As a man of the cloth I have been urged to consider my position of some small influence, to weigh up my allegiances and my responsibilities. I have been the recipient of an interesting variety of labels, too. I've been called a troublemaker, a meddler, a fool, a Communist lackey, an agitator, a disgrace to my calling, a pain in the neck, and a thorn in the side of the Nationalist Government. A crusader and a traitor.

'I have been told that I have Too Much to Say, that I talk too much, and this last is probably true as I am a convivial man and, with my advancing years, an often garrulous one, I suspect. I toyed, in my youth, with a career on the stage as I have always liked an audience, especially a captive one like yourselves. I enjoy so much the art of discourse that when, for fifteen years, I was prevented from participating in debates of any kind, or from addressing any audience of more than one person at a time, I will confess I felt the deprivation keenly.

'Deprivation. A word, my dear friends, which, in the basic material sense, is as foreign a concept to most of you as it is familiar to the majority of your countrymen. And yet you, too, are deprived. In a country which, as no less a personage than a former state president assured the nation at a National Party congress in the middle of the 1987 unrest and state of emergency, a country which has, and I quote, "no political prisoners", there are parents in this city whose children had, at the time he made that outrageous claim, not slept in their own beds for 290 days. Why? Because they had been detained, without charge, without trial, without access to legal representation, without access to their own mothers and fathers. They were in prison, having dared, perhaps, to question, to defy, to speak out in protest against an unjust and immoral social order. But you and I were never allowed to know this. We were deprived of information because, in terms of the state of emergency in South Africa, then in its second year, the media was not allowed to investigate it, nor report on it. You may say, Yes, but things have changed now. This is our brave new world, our new South Africa. Now we have no political prisoners any more, with previously banned organisations allowed to operate freely. And yet – what has really changed in our hearts and minds?

'I believe the Church has a social responsibility and a vital role to play in our society. Wherever people are deprived, the Church has a job to do. Whether that deprivation takes the form of food and drink, spiritual need or human rights, the Church, and I as its servant, have a job to do. And the dismantling of apartheid, whether legislation is off the statute books or not, still has a long way to go. I believe that the Church has a moral responsibility to speak out and act against injustice and it is my bounden duty as a man of God to contribute in whatever insignificant way I can to opening people's eyes and minds to those injustices still predominating in our country.

'Many of you are parents. I am appealing especially to you for your support. I am asking that you turn your minds for just a moment to those young men, returned exiles, who had a day's outing at Boksburg lake last month, and the seven young men who were cut down where they stood by that faction who continue to close their ears to the changing song. When our youth, after years of exile, in refugee camps outside our borders and elsewhere, are given free passage back to the land of their birth – what do we do? Welcome them home, help them as Christian people to find their families and their feet? No – we gun them down like dogs at a picnic on the lily-white shores of Boksburg lake for the audacity of their thinking they can expect to be treated like human beings. Do we assist them with employment, food, accommodation? No – we lock our doors, we fill columns in our press complaining about the soaring crime rate. We sit back and say, "See – what did you expect?"

'Well, I can sense your restlessness and I'll not keep you from your Sunday golf much longer. My appeal to you, this time, does not involve money. I am asking only for your time and your prayers – and a small amount of effort.'

Kelly Stephens stared out of the window. Old Father Whatsit didn't half go on. She stifled a yawn, ignoring a look from her mother at her side. Virginia was leaning slightly forward, her soft, sweet face wearing its most trying do-gooder expression. Kelly picked at her thumbnail with the edge of the hymn sheet. Drone, drone, would the old fart get a move-on! She played with a strand of silky blonde hair that had escaped from its bulldog clip, twirling it round and round her index finger, then back again the other way. Why don't you have a Crunch Perm, her friend and aspirant hairdresser Denise had suggested. It would look really wild. The really wild part about it, Kelly knew, would be her father, but still she was giving the idea some serious thought.

Finally, amidst a general shuffling and coughing, the organ launched into 'The Day Thou Gavest' and Kelly shifted from one foot to the other while the congregation ploughed faithfully through four slow verses. Her mother's rich contralto grated on her ears. Why did she always have to sing so loudly?

'I want a quick word with Father McBride,' Virginia whispered to Kelly as they moved into the aisle. 'It won't take a moment, dear, do you mind?'

Kelly sighed exaggeratedly and rolled her eyes.

'I'll wait in the car,' she muttered.

McBride stood at the bottom of the steps as his flock came out. He could sense Virginia hovering. 'Ah, Mrs Stephens,' he said. 'I see your ravishing daughter is with you this morning, but the good doctor – no?'

'No, Father. Luke had an emergency at the hospital. He had to go off early.' Luke had been an immobile mound beneath the duvet when she and Kelly had left.

'I suppose babies don't wait for anyone, do they? How're the painting classes coming along?'

Virginia blushed coyly, an unattractive mottling of her neck. 'I find them relaxing, Father, but probably irrelevant, I know. A small luxury of mine.' Virginia smiled nervously. Something was obviously on her mind. McBride wished he could tell her to spit it out. He was getting hot. He looked across to the car-park where the last few cars were manoeuvring to get into the queue for the street. A small posse of regulars, old-fashioned lace mantillas fixed to their heads with those wrinkly hairgrips he could even remember *his* mother wearing, were conferring beside the wisteria. They kept glancing his way and huddling again, pulling their cardies round their shoulders. They hadn't approved of his sermon. One of them had hair almost exactly the colour of the wisteria blooms. When she stood at a certain angle, he noticed with some fascination, she seemed to be descending from the tree like some aberrant offshoot. He wrenched his attention once more to Virginia, who appeared to be coming to grips with whatever it was she'd been struggling with.

'Father – I just wanted to assure you that I, at least, will be at the service next week. And if there's anything I can do – transport, anything. Well, I want you to know you can depend on me.' She licked her lips. Somebody hooted impatiently from the car-park and Virginia looked anxiously over her shoulder.

McBride had to smile. So that was it. 'Mrs Stephens,' he said. 'Thank you. I shall bear your kind offer in mind.' He began to move away.

'Oh, and Father –'

McBride turned back, suppressing the uncharitable thought.

'About the child ... '

McBride had started off the Mass by asking the congregation to pray for Sophie Phillips' soul.

'I was there.' She stood with eyes downcast.

'I beg your pardon?'

'I was there. My painting class. We were at the dam when they found her poor little body. I ... I don't know the parents well, but Luke was her mother's doctor at one time. He delivered her, you know. The little girl, that is.'

'Oh. I didn't know.' McBride tried to move off again. 'A tragic thing,' he murmured. He didn't want to linger another moment.

'Father, I just ... well, if there's anything I, we can do ... '

Virginia's plain face shone with such open-hearted eagerness that McBride winced. Here, he recognised, was one of those 'good' people who rolled up their sleeves and set to work to redress whatever injustice presented itself at any given time. Putting it less kindly, she was also, he could see, a soft touch. She probably gave generously to whoever knocked at her door with a plastic-covered collectors' sheet, without even asking the nature of the cause or the destination of the funds. She would be the willing neighbour upon whose doorstep countless kids would be dumped when their mothers had other things to do. She was the one who would pull over in the street for a drunk in the gutter or a flattened dog. Never asking for reward, she would take it upon herself to 'get involved'. No wonder the poor woman looked pinched and exhausted. Had the meek ever inherited the earth?

'Mrs Stephens. Virginia,' he said. 'That's kind. I think Fran and Davy have a strong support system of friends and family round them right now.' Virginia looked deflated. 'But if you want to pay your respects I shall be conducting a memorial service tomorrow. I'm sure they would appreciate your sympathy if you want to come along.'

The hooter sounded again and he swung round. 'Who –' he began.

'Oh, I'm afraid it's Kelly,' Virginia said apologetically. 'I'd better be getting along. I'll try to make it tomorrow, Father. Thank you. I'll talk to Luke.'

In the car Kelly was fuming, her mouth set in an unpleasant, childlike pout. Slumped down in her seat, she ignored Virginia's nervous request to strap up her seat-belt. She put her bare feet up on the dashboard. Tight denim skirt rucked up round her thighs, she refused to remove her legs even when they pulled up beside a busful of people at a set of traffic lights. Virginia was distracted, her attention only half on her beautiful fifteen-year-old daughter scowling fixedly at a point somewhere between her knees. It registered with some surprise, therefore, that the bang and the thud that broke into her thoughts seemed to have come from the region of her front bumper, and it took her a good few seconds to see that the driver of the car in front of theirs was striding purposefully towards her door wearing an expression that was less than friendly.

'Jee-sus, Mother.' Kelly slid even lower in her seat, covering her face with her hands.

Virginia was winding down her window. 'I'm so sorry,' she said with what she hoped was a winning smile, 'I thought you'd gone.'

By the time they got home it was almost lunch-time. Kelly faced her mother across the roof of the car. 'I think you should know,' she said, 'that you have just ruined a perfectly good day for me. I had plans for this morning which, thanks to you, are now Ballsed Up.'

Virginia was contrite. Teenagers were so difficult. 'I'm sorry dear,' she said. 'It was quite unforeseen. I'd offer to drive you –'

'Hah!' Kelly poured all the scorn she could muster into the word. Without make-up and with her hair tied back she looked younger than fifteen and Virginia couldn't help but regard her with tender confusion, this angry urchin child with glaring green eyes. She'd been petulant and wilful all her young life, really. And she and Luke had been too indulgent, she knew. Luke led a stressful doctor's life and while Kelly was a toddler Virginia had taught in a Coloured school to supplement their income. Kelly was their only child. She had been born prematurely and hadn't stopped doing things her way since then. She was head-strong and demanding, and Virginia was often left bewildered at the determined, stubborn creature she had given birth to. She had at times seriously entertained the notion that someone had switched babies at the nursing home because Kelly showed nothing of either her or Luke's placid natures. She knew that a mother-to-daughter talk was well overdue but if the truth be told she was a little afraid of Kelly. She seemed to be living a life apart from them already. She shared nothing of herself with them. She was the lodger in the upstairs room with the closed door and loud music.

'Leave her.' Luke looked up from his journal as Kelly strode past him and up the stairs. They were all used to these scenes. He put out a hand. Virginia took it and he pulled her down on the sofa beside him.

Upstairs the telephone rang and they heard Kelly's door open as she went to answer it. Ten minutes later she bounced back down the stairs and paused briefly in the doorway. She still wore the denim skirt, but with it a black off-the-shoulder T-shirt and black tackies. Her thick blonde hair was swept to one side and tied up with a piece of Virginia's tapestry wool. She looked fragile and defiant.

'Where are you going, Kelly?' Luke asked.

'Denise's.'

'Let me give you a lift.' Virginia was getting to her feet, anxious to make amends.

'That's OK. I'll get there quicker if I walk.'

Luke frowned. 'It's lunch-time,' he said. 'Have Denise's parents invited you for lunch?'

'Yes. No. I don't know. Look, why the third degree? I'm just going over to listen to music and stuff. I don't need lunch. I'll get you guys later.'

Virginia and Luke looked at the space in the doorway. Luke was the first to speak. 'Was that really an AK-47 hanging from her ear?' he said.

Five

Tamzin did not attend the memorial service for Sophie, and Jessica told Fran that Rosepark was closed for the day and that no one had seen or heard from her the whole weekend. Fran had not really meant to ask, but Ray was there and she had allowed his embrace, mainly for Davy's sake. Davy and Ray were intermittent friends and, when their often conflicting timetables allowed, enjoyed a night out playing pool together at the Radium Beer Hall. Davy looked drawn and very out of place in his wedding suit. It was shiny at the knees and elbows and had flared bottoms to the trousers.

Fran seemed preoccupied with clothes at the moment. Probably for the first time in her life she kept noticing what people were wearing and spending long periods standing thoughtfully staring into her own wardrobe. Pausing in front of the full-length mirror in her bedroom before leaving for the church, she thought she looked like a Quaker schoolmistress in her pale grey cotton dress which accentuated her natural pallor. She had pulled her long auburn hair into a French plait and her neck was as white and as rigid as a statue's.

'I look like Mary Queen of Scots,' she said to Davy in the car. 'Don't I?' Davy had not answered and she had sat beside him, head high, dry-eyed, pale and calm in her despair.

Television had sent along a camera crew to record what had become a medium-sized media event. A shot of Sophie, taken about a year ago at a Christmas party, wearing a paper hat over one eye and grinning through a mouthfull of marshmallow fish, had dominated TV screens for the past few evenings, and another picture, a family one of the three of them at a People's Concert, with Sophie on Davy's shoulders and Fran looking distracted, had been on the front pages of the Sunday papers all over the country. The other aspect that the press had seized on, of course, was the death squad connection. Fran was a known activist and rumoured to have been a member of MK, the ANC's military wing, and she had been quite prominently named in the investigations into the activities of the shadowy Civil Co-operation Bureau, or CCB, when that organisation's link with the death squads had been exposed. There was renewed speculation as to whether she featured on the list in the diary which nobody appeared to have actually seen but every journalist wrote about with confidence. Both Fran and Davy had declined to comment on the possibility of a connection with Sophie's murder.

The service had attracted the public too, curious passers-by who slowed their steps, lingering, whispering in small groups, even pointing her and Davy out. Jessica had left her children at home and she and Ben had come along together. Fran was not over-fond of Ben although she had known him almost as long as she'd known Jessica. He and Davy had even less in common. An engineer by profession, who liked a good tune he could hum along with, Ben and Davy were on different wavelengths completely. Davy, the sensitive musician, deep thinker, agoniser over Issues, just didn't connect with Ben's overriding preoccupations: who would win the Northerns-Western Province rugby match, the advantages of the BMW over the Merc, the challenges of scuba diving. They didn't socialise together all that often, therefore, as families. She and Jessica would see each other on their own or with their children. Occasionally they would all get together for a barbecue and sometimes Davy would bring his guitar and be persuaded to play a medley of old Beatles songs. Then Ben would hang up his 'Who's Cookin'? Goodlookin'!' apron, throw an arm round Jessica's shoulders and bore everyone to tears with stories of his student days.

Fran was touched by the number of friends and supporters who came to the service. Ansie was there with her husband William. Cassandra came and so did Gail, wearing heavy black and with a run in her stockings. Many of her comrades (her 'leftie Communist friends' Ben would call them) and a number of her African colleagues ('noo-vo South Africans' – Ben again) had come along to show solidarity, as well as lots of musician friends. Carole Abrams, looking like a slimmer, younger version of Whitney Houston, had sung 'The Greatest Love of All', accompanied only by Elias Mothopeng on his tenor sax, and Jessica, sitting near the back, had burst into tears and sobbed so wretchedly that Fran had to turn her head and look fiercely at her. She could not let Jessica's tears call up her own. As it was her mother had had to be taken out into the porch where Luke Stephens was attending to her. Fran's brittle composure was as fragile as a house of cards. At any moment she might topple.

Henry McBride kept the service brief and simple, as Fran and Davy had requested him to. He talked about forgiveness and about faith, but Fran found herself unable to concentrate. Her eyes roved over McBride's vestments and the stained glass windows behind the altar. Each window was a saint with eyes uplifted. Saint Anastasia stared up at a crack in the ceiling with a pained expression. She appeared, also, to have a deformed baby toe on her left foot. Thabo Thekiso was assisting McBride and he stared at Fran throughout the service with his soft black eyes.

Afterwards a few people came back to the cottage, where Jessica made tea for everyone and small-talk with Virginia Stephens. After a while Fran went into her bedroom and closed the door. She was startled to find Davy there already. He was standing by the window looking out into the garden.

'There you are,' she said. 'I wondered ... '

He had taken off his jacket and rolled up his sleeves. 'I wish they'd all go,' he said. 'I wish they'd all just leave. I couldn't breathe in there.'

'It's all right. Nobody expects you to be a gracious host. Jessica's taking care of things.'

In fact they could hear the front door opening and closing as people began to go home. Nobody felt comfortable about being there. Jessica opened the door quietly. 'Ben's taking your folks to their hotel,' she said. 'That doctor chap says your mother needs to rest.'

'Thanks, Jess. Are we being anti-social?' Fran looked at her vaguely. 'We just –' She made a helpless gesture with her hands. Davy couldn't, or wouldn't turn from the window. 'There goes Jim,' he said.

'Thank goodness,' said Jessica. 'He's about the last. Oh, and Carole, the singer? She wants to know if you're going to stay here or whether you want a lift back into town with her and her brother?'

Davy looked at Fran. 'Go,' she said. 'There's no need for you to stay.'

Jessica arrived home after seven that evening, red-eyed and irritable. Ben was irritable by then, too, having had to ask Anna to stay late to bathe the children and give them supper. Edwina had made such a fuss about being put to bed that they'd both given up and let her cruise round the house until she was frantic with exhaustion. When he'd finally managed to settle down with the paper Ben found there were no cold beers in the fridge, only a diet Sprite with the top half off, and not a shred of evidence to show that supper was even a possibility. Just a packet of stale wholewheat rolls with a note saying 'Ducks' on it in the breadbin.

All of this was packed into a thick silence from behind the evening paper as Jessica came slowly into the lounge. 'What kept you?' Ben asked, not looking up from the sports pages. 'Had fun?'

'Oh, Jesus, Ben, that's a really pleasant remark, even for you,' Jessica said.

Ben turned a page noisily, patting the creases out of the paper with brisk, sharp slaps. He glanced up briefly. Jessica thought about conversation but decided it wasn't worth the irritation. Instead she went down the passage and into Edwina's room. She bent over her cot. The baby was lying flat on her back, arms above her head. She lay so still Jessica could hardly see the rise and fall of her chest as she breathed, deeply asleep. She stroked her head. It was hot and damp. Then she tiptoed out of the room. Glenda was also asleep, a blanket clutched against the side of her head, one thumb half in, half out of her slack mouth. Andrew stuck his head over the side of the top bunk. 'Mummy?' he said. 'Anna gave us scrimple eggs for supper. Glenda gave hers to Martha under the table and Daddy was cross. But I didn't.'

Jessica kissed her son and went into her own bedroom. She sat on the edge of the bed. She slipped her shoes off and took off her skirt. She lay back on the pillows and closed her eyes. Her head was spinning. She and Fran had sat together long after the others had gone, drinking red wine and talking. They must have had more than a bottle between them and driving home afterwards she'd felt the effect. Jessica had been stunned by Fran's revelations. She knew, of course, of Fran's political involvement, the periods in detention, the trips to Lusaka, the endless rallies she helped organise. She knew about the death squads too, mostly from the papers, and about the connection between these clandestine teams and Fran. But surely, *surely*, they wouldn't have killed a child. In cold blood.

Fran was oddly calm. She had looked at Jessica and said, 'Why not? They've done it before.' The raids into Swaziland. The attack a year or so ago on a safe-house outside Magaliesburg in which a three-year-old had been murdered.

'Yes,' said Jessica, 'but they were –'

'Black children?' Fran raised an eyebrow, and Jessica blushed. She had felt ashamed of herself. Then Fran had told her about the diary Mary had got hold of in Botswana and how the hit-list of names in it was true, and how Fran's name was apparently about half-way down this merry catalogue.

'Is there anything you can do?' Jessica asked.

'Not yet,' said Fran non-committally. 'It will be released when the time is right.'

'And what time is that, for God's sake? When you're all dead?' Jessica could have bitten her tongue and they had both lapsed into miserable silence. Now, lying on her bed, Jessica felt that life was passing her by. She didn't know anything about anything when it came down to it. She'd had all the chances to make something of herself, of her life, and she'd let it all slip through her fingers like sand. How incredibly mundane it all was. Marriage to Ben, then the children one after the other, and then she never seemed to have time any more, for anything real. She'd not been to the toilet alone, she reckoned, for about four years.

And Ben. When she looked at him these days, she seldom saw any trace of the confident student, fit, good-looking, who had swept her off her feet all those years ago, courted her with Jacques Brel and sweet champagne. Now all she saw was a heavy-featured man, increasingly short-tempered with his children and with her, who liked his home comforts and routine. The fine, even features had fleshed out; his cheeks were covered with broken red veins. Even his nose seemed lately to be taking on a permanent sort of flush. He was drinking steadily.

Jessica heard Ben's footsteps approaching. He stood in the doorway, looking at her. 'I'm sorry, Jess,' he said. She held out a hand and he came and sat down beside her. She sensed that compromise would be less trouble. 'Sorry I was so late. Fran needed to talk.' She knew she ought to ask whether he'd eaten, but she couldn't bring herself to.

Ben was loosening his tie. He undid his shoe-laces and placed the polished brown brogues neatly side by side beside the bed. Then he stood and removed his belt and pants, laying those over the back of a chair. Jessica watched with a sinking feeling as he methodically unbuttoned his shirt. When he was naked he stood and smiled down at her fondly, with just a trace of the old lopsided grin that used to make her heart turn over. It looked somehow silly on him now. His eyes, she noticed, were bloodshot and bulbous, and his expression just short of maudlin. She felt embarrassed for him. Still, she moved up on the bed, regretting her reluctance only a little. His breath smelt and his cheeks were rough as he eased himself on top of her and started in on his love-making routine.

As usual Jessica felt cheated. She looked at the bedside clock. Four and a half minutes, give or take a grunt or two. Her body felt strung out and jumpy and her back ached. She couldn't remember her last orgasm with Ben. He had become a real 'wham bam thank you ma'am' man, she reflected resentfully. He liked his sex regular, quick and no pillow talk.

Noting the predictable change in his breathing, she eased herself, with some difficulty, out from under him. She padded quietly down the passage and out through the glass sliding door of the playroom into the back garden. There was a full moon tonight and the garden was brushed with silver. The pool looked like a sheet of blue plastic, so still was the water. Without giving herself time to think about its temperature, Jessica dived into the deep end, gasping as she surfaced and struck out for the other side. Ten lengths later she hauled herself up on to the side, clumsily scraping a knee. She lay on the cool cement, breathing hard. What on earth was the matter with her? She usually did thirty lengths every evening. She shivered suddenly as a gust of wind sent ripples skidding across the water and rustling the bougainvillaea beside her. She looked up, and saw that the sky was clouding over. In the distance a faint flash against the horizon and an answering rumble of thunder. And then, quite clearly, she heard a dull boom. It didn't sound like thunder, more like an explosion of some kind. Moments later she heard the sirens and got up quickly, unaccountably afraid. She wrapped a towel around her shivering arms.

As she passed through the kitchen, she paused at the grocery cupboard. All of a sudden she was hungry, realising that she hadn't eaten all day. She took out a tin of sardines and slit open a new packet of cream crackers. She rubbed vigorously at her wet hair. When Ben came sleepily into the kitchen yawning and scratching his stomach, he found her at the kitchen table, reading the paper.

'Place stinks of fish,' he said.

Fran sat up in bed and screamed. Her body was wet with perspiration. Her thin nightdress was stuck to her chest and armpits. She felt her heart pounding in her throat, her pulse racing. What had frightened her? She knew only that she felt an overpowering terror. Then she remembered the service, Sophie,

Davy's terrible face, and she sank back on to her pillow and put her hands over her eyes. But it wasn't just that. There was something else. She felt as if she was being watched, as if some living thing was breathing and watching her as she slept. The curtain at her open window flapped wildly in a pre-storm gust of wind. She got out of bed and crossed over to it. Out in the garden it was almost as bright as day as the full moon shone through the cloud directly into the room. Then Fran noticed something which jerked her heart right into her mouth. The heavy pot of geraniums which usually stood on the windowsill outside was lying in the flowerbed below. It hadn't broken, but she could see that the impact had jolted one of the plants out of the soil. It was a very heavy container, not easily budged. Could someone have been looking in at the window and knocked it off scrambling to get away? Or had someone deliberately pushed it off to scare her? Was she being paranoid?

She closed the window tightly. Still she felt uneasy and disturbed. Were they really coming after her this time? Although the police seemed to be treating Sophie's case as a conventional crime – if indeed it could even be called that – which had started with a huge manhunt the day of her disappearance, the possibility of it being a 'political' act was gaining credence daily, helped along, of course, by the ever-hungry press. When she had been named as a death squad target during the first commission of inquiry, she had read, in a disconnected sort of way, of how it had been planned to tamper with the brakes on her car, the trusty old Morris ('Bit Nancy Drew, wouldn't you say?' had been Jessica's dubious comment). Her route in the mornings started with a descent down a steep hill and the idea, so desperately obvious, had been brake failure and a messy heap at the bottom. Nothing of this nature had happened, but the casual way in which the unnamed and heavily disguised witness had described the plan to the commission had had Jessica, furious, on her doorstep within the hour with a 'Fix Your Own Car' manual and a set of totally rusted spanners.

Fran lay wide awake in her bed, unable to contemplate sleep, until the sky lightened in the east and the birds began to chatter in the garden, like they did on any normal day. When she woke again it was warm in the room and a glance at her watch on the bedside table told her that she had slept half the morning away. She ran a bath and put the kettle on to boil. The morning paper was on the front steps. She shook it out as she went back inside and stared at the headlines, six centimetres of bold black type:

ANC MAN KILLED IN CITY CENTRE BLAST

Below it pictures of devastation dominated the front and several inside pages. A limpet mine placed beneath a metal dustbin had exploded outside the Van Dijk Club in the city. At eight p.m. guests were arriving at the club, members of the Johannesburg press club mainly, expecting to be addressed by Robert Oliphant, the newly appointed Press Secretary of the African National Congress, a man who was one of the last to be released from Robben Island after twenty-five years' incarceration. Timing had been faultless: Oliphant's legs had been blown off and he had died on the pavement before the police or paramedics could get near the scene. The force of the blast had shattered all the windows in the club and those of most of the buildings along the street. Broken and flying glass inflicted dreadful injuries on the people going into the club and the dancing, toyi-toying supporters waiting outside. Oliphant was a hero of the struggle. Fran and he had corresponded while he was in prison. She had been to his welcome home celebration not long ago.

Nobody was claiming responsibility, but speculation was rife. It did not seem like the work of one of the splinter right-wing groups which had sprung up over the past months. And to Fran it was too targeted, too accurate.

And besides – Robert Oliphant was on the list.

Six

The next day was blustery and quite cold. Fran stood in the shadow of the wall beside the house, not moving, just breathing softly and listening. On a normal day the school would have been empty by now, but all the cars parked outside in the road told her that something unusual was going on. She could hear children's voices coming from the bottom end of the playground beyond the classrooms, and closer by, coming from almost above her head, she could hear Tamzin's voice. It sounded as if she was making a speech. She must have called a parents' meeting. Maybe she'd mislaid another child.

It was too late to turn back. Besides, if she didn't do this now, she wouldn't do it again. Just coming to the school, pulling up outside the gate, had been enough of an ordeal. Fran walked softly down the path, keeping to the side of the wall like a thief. She didn't think anyone could see her from the office, but she walked quickly, with her head down. Inside the classroom everything seemed threatening. The mobiles suspended from the ceiling swung at her with a rush in the breeze from the open door. They were all from the Wizard of Oz, grotesque, squashed cardboard Munchkins swinging this way and that. She ducked her head and picked her way across the carpet where large sheets of white paper with fresh blobs of paint on them were weighted down at the corners with shells. Fran made for the lockers, then stopped, startled, as one of the Michael Jackson wigs moved suddenly from the pile on top of them, but it was only Tamzin's black cat stretching and repositioning himself. Fran felt furtive and unsettled.

Sophie's locker was empty. Each child had a symbol above his or her locker, and over the peg in the cloakroom where they hung their face-cloths. Sophie's had been a star – she'd loved that. Someone else would be the star now, Fran thought, knowing that that was being maudlin in the extreme. She shook her head to try to clear it. It's just a locker, for Christ's sake, she told herself. Just a fucking star. She looked around and saw a cardboard box on Tamzin's table beside the door. In it was Sophie's suitcase, lunch-box, an assortment of pottery creatures, a filthy pink jersey (which wasn't Sophie's) and a wad of drawings clipped together with a small plastic clothes-peg. Taking slow, uneven breaths, Fran reached out a hand to take the box but found herself standing motionless, staring at the things and feeling an absurd image taking hold of her. A parody, in miniature, of the dismissed employee who comes into the office one morning to find his desk cleared and a box of files and personal items awaiting his collection. 'Clear out your locker, Phillips, and hand in your library bag.' Tomorrow some other child would be scratching out Sophie's name and putting in her own.

This is no good, Fran. Fran tried to hear Jessica's voice in her head. She needed to get into motion again. The top paper on the pile of drawings had a scrawled heading: MY HAND – MY FOOT – MY BIG MOUTH! S. PHILLIPS. and there they were – a perfect handprint with fingers evenly splayed, a fairly smudged footprint and a red lipstick kiss. Fran remembered all the kids coming out of school that day, hysterical with laughter, all with one blue hand, one green foot and Tamzin's Sultan's Kiss lipstick on all of their mouths. I suppose I'm going to put that beneath the glass on my dressing-table, she thought wearily to herself, and keep it there forever, frozen like a fossil. She probably would too.

Fran wondered what Tamzin had intended to do with this box of Sophie's belongings. Driven by and left them on her doorstep in the dead of night perhaps? She picked up the box and started back up the path.

Glenda looked up from the sandpit and saw her. 'Hi, Aunty

Fran,' she called. Fran waved and hurried on. She really didn't want anyone to see her. She felt ashamed. She felt guilty. And at the same time she was consumed with a wretched anger so sapping that she wanted to kick and bite and scream. She already had a tender bruise on the side of her forehead where she had hit herself repeatedly on the door frame in Sophie's room when she had gone in there this morning to open the curtains and had seen the bed unslept in and the half constructed igloo Sophie had been making for days with Lego blocks.

Outside the office window she paused to shift the box into a more comfortable position. She could just see Tamzin standing facing into the room. She did not think Tamzin could see her. If she did, she gave no sign and did not falter in her speech. Fran could see the tops of heads, all close up beside each other. All the mothers, all right. Perhaps even some fathers if this was a crisis meeting. She stood like an eavesdropper, which indeed she was, but worse, like a snooping outsider, straining her ears to listen to what no longer concerned her.

Tamzin seemed to have come to a decision. She stood with head erect and eyes clear. She seemed calm and in control. She was wearing Ray's favourite skirt – her gypsy skirt, he called it. It was black and full and slashed with scarlet and yellow stripes. She had a scarlet plastic alice band in her hair and gold loops in her ears.

The small office was indeed crammed to capacity. She thought she had everyone's undivided attention. Only Gail Fleming tapped the end of her filter tip on a gold cigarette case and took a surreptitious look at her watch.

'Rosepark school has been a dream of mine for a long time,' Tamzin said. 'Ever since I began my teacher training course and realised that it was the small children who interested me the most. I love their imaginations, their spontaneity, their guilelessness. My grandmother left me this house in her will, as most of you know, and when she died I immediately seized the opportunity of converting the outbuildings into the playschool it is today. The property is large with plenty of room for expansion, and it has been, and still is, my ambition to extend our facilities over the next couple of years, and take in more pupils, graded, eventually, into three pre-school groups.'

Tamzin's voice was quietly confident. There was no trace of the tremulous, guilt-stricken Tamzin of the past days. There was a new determination about her and a strength which surprised her audience and captured their attention.

'The events of the past few days have been a great shock to all of us. It is too late for if onlys or for apportioning blame. I am sorry that this happened at all, and I am desperately sorry that it happened during the time when Sophie was in my care. I think – I hope – you all know that as a teacher and as your friend, I try to take care of your children as if they were my own. How this tragedy happened is something we all hope and pray the police will be able to unravel for us.'

Tamzin stopped to draw breath. 'What I need from you today,' she went on, 'is an indication of your support or its withdrawal. I know I have been criticised in the press of negligence, and there may be among you some who feel your children would be better off elsewhere. If the latter is the case, and you wish to remove your child or children, I shall refund in full your term's fees immediately.' She fell silent and her eyes searched the faces in front of her. The gold ear-rings glinted and swung. Nobody spoke. Only Gail coughed and looked away. Tamzin began to look uncertain and a flush crept up her neck and throat, when Ansie, seated on the arm of a sofa, spoke up, in her deep, Afrikaans-accented voice.

'Tamzin, I for one – well, William and me – are very happy with the school. We think you have done, *are* doing, wonders for Petra. She loves you and she loves coming here, and ... well, we would like to continue at Rosepark.' As if that was the signal they'd been waiting for, everyone started talking at once. All expressed support for Tamzin and her school. Jessica almost went forward to hug her. There were tears in Tamzin's eyes. 'Thank you,' was all she said. She held up a hand. 'Just one other thing. I'd like to introduce you to Zinzi Mokoena, whose two children Jonas and Freda join us this week.'

All eyes turned to the woman in the patterned headscarf who had been sitting, unnoticed or unremarked, on a chair in the back corner of the room. She smiled, inclined her head. Tamzin served tea and everyone relaxed. Only Ansie excused herself and left. She seemed in a hurry all of a sudden, and called out impatiently to Petra as she went. Gail sipped daintily from the china cup Tamzin passed her.

Zinzi had earmarked Gail straight away as a woman to be wary of and she stiffened as she watched her approach. Gail smiled, and touched Zinzi's smooth brown forearm with the tips of her fingers.

'Zinzi,' she said. 'What a lovely name. And where do you stay – in which location?' She enunciated each word slowly and carefully, as if speaking to a child, in the manner of many a white matron obliged to converse with a black person on a social occasion. It no longer annoyed Zinzi; these days it just amused her. She knew the type, the 'some of my best friends' school. It made them feel really progressive having black pupils mixing with their own precious kids. They even invited them to their homes sometimes and would get quite chatty on parents' day. But that was where the contact ended. Not for them the bridge evening invitation. And the closest they got to the dinner party was the casual reference, thrown in between courses ('I think it's *so* marvellous that Johnny has friends at school like Sipho, *so* overdue. It's such a wonderful opportunity for the little black children, and it's so *important* that they mix at that level, don't you agree? We must all "build bridges" in this new South Africa – Dinah, will you clear?'). Just rubbing shoulders now and then, at a suitable distance, made them feel good enough, but open the public swimming pools and beaches to all races and they skipped smartly back to the laager. Well, she was used to it.

'We live in Rosepark,' she said now, as Gail leaned forward expectantly, smiling and nodding encouragement. 'Just a couple of blocks away.'

Predictably, Gail immediately misunderstood, as Zinzi had expected she would.

'Oh, I see,' she said, chasing her smoke away with her hand. 'You work nearby. Isn't it lovely that you can have your children with you?'

'No ... Gail –' Zinzi saw with some small satisfaction the quick shadow in the eyes as she made free with Gail's first name '– I'm not in domestic service. I *live* nearby. I don't have a job at the moment. I find taking care of the twins takes up all my time.'

Clearly the woman was still puzzled, but Zinzi was bored with the game. The true situation had simply not occurred to this woman: that of a black woman who could afford to send her children to a school in this suburb, not to mention *live* in the area without being subsidised or in service of some kind. Fortunately they were rescued from the deadlock by Tamzin and Cassandra who were coming over bearing plates of biscuits and fruit cake.

'Oh, darlings, not for me!' Gail whooped, glancing triumphantly at Zinzi's plump, homely figure stretching the bounds of her jersey dress. 'Not with my waistline.'

Fran felt mortified. Caught listening to Tamzin's absurd speech, she had lingered too long and before she had time to collect herself people were spilling out of the office into the garden, and the children were coming up from the playground. Quickly, perspiring with advance embarrassment, she retreated further into the bushes, crouching down against the damp black soil like a child playing hide and seek. She sat with the box clutched in her arms, holding her breath and praying that no one would see her. Legs walked past so close to her that she could have stuck out a foot and tripped them up. She saw Cassandra's expensive boots at eye level, and Jessica's jeans, and Gail's pink, hairless calves and high pink heels. Finally, all was quiet and she heard the office door close. Feeling more than ridiculous, she pushed her way out of the bushes and stood up, brushing sand from her clothes and leaves from her hair. If she hadn't been trembling so much she might almost have laughed. She stepped out on to the path again, cursing softly as the box began slipping from her grasp.

'Can I help you?'

Fran swung round, blushing. An African woman was coming up behind her with two children holding on to her dress on either side. They were identical twins and they looked at this dishevelled woman with interest.

'Oh,' said Fran. 'No, thank you. I can manage.' She felt a profound sense of relief that these were people she had never seen before. Newcomers to the school perhaps. The woman held the gate open for her. 'Do you have a child at the school too?' she asked as Fran passed beneath her arm with her plunder.

'Yes. No ... I, well ... '

'Oh. You must be – I'm so sorry.' The woman had seen the pathetic bundle in her arms and put two and two together. Her gaze was warm and direct. Fran tried to smile at her but nothing on her face would work properly all of a sudden. Humiliated, she turned rudely away and walked straight to her car.

Zinzi and the children strolled home, stopping at the corner shop for ice-creams. Freda and Jonas were excited at the prospect of their first school and having friends. They jumped around her on the pavement. Freda dropped her ice-cream in the sand. Their front gate was open, swinging on its hinges. As they entered, Zinzi stopped abruptly, flinging out her arms instinctively in a protective shield. The children stopped too and looked up at her.

'Mama?' said Freda, then, in Xhosa, 'What is it? What's wrong?'

'Nothing, nothing. Let's go inside.' Zinzi had her front door key in her hand and it was steady as she stabbed the metal into the lock. She pushed the twins inside in front of her, prodding Jonas quite roughly when he lingered. At four years old they couldn't read, not even simple signs, but there was something about the slogan 'KAFFIRS GET OUT!', jaggedly slashing the wall beneath the dining-room window, that Zinzi felt even a four-year-old might get the gist of.

'Charming,' said Ansie. She stood at the edge of the patio, hands on her hips, looking across the back garden at the fence which separated the Barkers' property from the one which backed on to it.

'What's charming?' Stephan had strolled out to join her. He was wearing black rugby shorts. His torso was bare and brown and he held a beer in one hand. Petra was hanging on to the other.

'I've discovered that our neighbours over there –' she indicated expressively with her chin, a contemptuous thrust '– are black as the ace of spades.'

'And you can't get blacker than that. What's all this about, Ansie, *skat*?'

William, just come in from the bank, stood at the patio door, loosening his tie. Petra let go of Stephan's hand and ran to her father.

'Your new neighbours,' said Stephan, 'are black people.'

William didn't appear at all taken aback, but then nothing ever seemed to faze him, much to Ansie's irritation, especially in this instance.

'*Wragtig*, really?' was all he said. 'I could do with a *biertjie* myself, Faan. Get me a can, will you, while I take this suit off.'

Ansie made one of her impatient noises. 'Is that all you can say?' she demanded.

'What do you expect me to say, Ans?' William said mildly. ' "There goes the neighbourhood" ? '

'Well, it wouldn't be far wrong,' said Ansie.

William laughed. 'Ag, don't get so upset,' he said. 'We don't need to have anything to do with them if you don't want to.'

'Easy for you to say,' Ansie retorted. 'Their wretched children are going to Rosepark school. They'll be in Petra's class!'

'I thought there was a little black boy there already.' William was puzzled.

'That's different,' said Ansie. 'He's from the convent.'

William softened when he saw Ansie was really upset. 'Times are changing, you know, Ansie,' he said.

Ansie wasn't having any. 'Not for me, they're not,' she said.

Late in the afternoon, after everyone had gone, Tamzin went down to the classrooms. She looked at the space where the box had been with all Sophie's things and recalled with vivid pain Fran's furtive scuttle down the path as she had watched from the office out of the corner of her eye. She had longed to run after her, to – what? It was no good. She had to try to put Fran out of her mind. She would go crazy if she didn't. Boris, curled up in a doll's pram, watched her roll up her sleeves, his eyes narrow stabs of green. When she'd finished clearing away the surface mess, she took down all the children's pictures which decorated the walls. Then she moved all the furniture out into the garden, the chairs and tables, the carpet too. The blackboards and the dolls' house – out everything went on to the lawn.

Then she stood, looking at the bareness of the room, her hands on her hips, breathing heavily. The cat stared at her without blinking from his wicker-work crib and began to wash his ears.

When Ray arrived the shadows in the garden were lengthening and the evening was growing cold. Finding the house locked and in darkness, he made his way round to the back garden where he saw lights blazing from the classroom. Tamzin was standing on a table, scrubbing at the walls with a large, heavy-duty scrubbing brush. Her skirt was hitched up into the elastic of her knickers, her curly hair tied up in a topknot. Her face glowed with exertion.

'For Christ's sake,' said Ray.

Tamzin looked down at him. 'What's the time?' she said. 'Are we going to be late?'

'It would appear so,' said Ray. He sighed irritably.

Dinner with the visiting celebrity from London, who was playing the lead in Ray's new play, and Tamzin had completely forgotten. Ray was very annoyed. 'What is it with you?' he said. 'Couldn't this have waited for another time?'

'The classroom was filthy,' Tamzin said stubbornly.

Having started out badly, the evening got steadily worse. The leading man was a self-opinionated bore and Tamzin had trouble staying awake as he held centre stage. It galled her to see Ray so sycophantically entranced. All that energy she had dredged up from the depths of her reserves had simply drained away and now she felt utterly worn out. Not only that, but the smell of the restaurant's rich food was making her feel ill. Fighting down waves of nausea, she wondered what it would be like to faint. Like in a silent movie, she watched mouths opening and shutting, clamping down on forkfuls of pâté and lobster. The producer's wife had lipstick on her teeth and when she laughed, throwing back her head, Tamzin could see half a spinach salad clinging to her tongue. Muttering apologies, Tamzin pushed back her chair and ran clumsily to the cloakroom.

'Rough week,' Ray said tamely, when it seemed that some comment was expected of him. 'Trouble at the school. I'd better go and see if she's all right.'

Tamzin emerged from the cloakroom, chalk-white and smelling of vomit. 'I want to go home,' she said. 'Will you ask someone to call me a taxi?'

Ray was torn. This was an important night for him. It was an opportunity to talk to one of London's leading theatrical figures, not to mention the agent he'd brought along. On the other hand, Tamzin was in distress. He hesitated just long enough for her to notice. He thought she owed him that. 'Don't be stupid,' he said brusquely. 'I'll take you home.' He made their excuses and returned minutes later with his jacket and Tamzin's diamanté cape and tatty evening bag with half the sequins falling off.

In the car she turned her face to the window, staring out miserably. A hobo was pissing on their front tyre but she didn't seem to see him.

'I'm so sorry, Ray,' she said in a small voice. 'I don't know what came over me tonight. I feel awful.'

'Tammy –'

'I know it was an important dinner for you. And I had to go and screw things up.'

'Tammy –'

'And it's not just the thing with the school. There's something else –'

'Tamzin, will you belt up for just a moment!'

She looked at him, startled into silence, and he took her hands. Gently he wiped the damp from her cheeks and kissed them each in turn. 'Let's go back to my place, put on some Mozart, whadya say?' Ray was a great mood setter.

Tamzin smiled ruefully. '*And* I've cheated you out of your dinner,' she said.

'Ah,' Ray grinned. 'But I managed to salvage something from the evening nevertheless – taraaa!' He produced from beneath his jacket a bottle of white wine, still dripping from the ice bucket. 'Some excellent Frog plonk too,' he said, starting the engine. 'Goes better with Mozart than lobster bisque, *n'est pas*?'

'Ray!' Tamzin gasped. 'Did you *steal* that?'

'Right from beneath their noses, my sweet. Clever, aren't I?'

Ray's cottage was in Mayfair, a suburb which had shed designations as a snake sheds its skin. It had started out 'Coloured', become 'grey', progressed to 'open' and now, now that the Group Areas Act had bitten the dust, it was a place where neighbours could be neighbours without labels. Or at least that was the theory. Journalists liked to highlight such areas now and again, examples of racial harmony or a suburb of crime or conflict, depending on which newspaper they worked for. The neighbours on Ray's right were a mixed couple, he white, she 'Coloured', and the neighbours on his left were Muslim. Ray liked living there. He liked the sense of community, he told people, frequently, whether they asked or not. He had also resisted putting razor wire on his garden wall, but had joined the Neighbourhood Watch scheme when the Masakelas did.

Tamzin dropped her head against his chest as he unlocked the gate to the driveway. She desperately needed to sleep. The people next door were having a party. They could hear music coming from the open windows and smell the sweet pungent aroma of Malawi Gold mixed with hot spices. There were three Mercedes cars parked on the pavement outside. Cassim was in exports and wore cream-coloured suits and thick gold jewellery. All three cars belonged to him.

Once inside Ray switched on some lamps and moved Tamzin to a comfortable chair. She leaned her head back and rocked slowly. Her stomach still felt queasy and, watching Ray pour out a glass of the French wine, she wondered whether she would manage to hold it down.

'Put some music on, Tam. It doesn't have to be Mozart. I'll get some cheese and Melba toast.'

Tamzin listened to the familiar voice as Ray sang to himself in the kitchen. She heard the knife drawer clatter and squeak. Ray stuck his head back into the living room. 'Music,' he said.

'OK. OK.' She flipped through the albums which hung, suspended, in a rack Ray had acquired on a trip to Hong Kong. She suspected it was the reason why he hadn't yet converted to compact disc. She chose Tom Waites and knelt by the speaker on the floor, waiting for his warm, late-nite throatiness to reach out to her.

'If it's Waites, Tammy, there's definitely something on your mind. Is it this whole Sophie thing?'

'Partly, I suppose.'

'What else? I'm a good listener, remember. I listened to Ben Tucker's blow-by-blow account of his car's upsetting experiences at Pat's Panelbeaters, and that wasn't easy.'

Tamzin smiled.

Ray patted his knee. 'Come and sit here,' he said.

Tamzin wondered if she ought to marry him, now, before it was too late. Jessica had advised against this, however. The trouble was, he hadn't exactly asked her anyway and she wasn't sure that she could bring herself to ask him. Ray was ambitious. He had his career path meticulously charted. It included the West End in the not-too-distant future. They had talked about going to Europe together.

'I went for a check-up the other day –' Tamzin began.

Ray brushed some crumbs from the corner of her mouth, lightly, with the tips of his fingers. 'And?' he said.

'And … well … '

'Who on earth –?'

It was the doorbell. Ray reached out an arm and pulled aside the curtain for a view of the stoep.

Tamzin looked at her watch. It was very late.

'Davy,' Ray said. 'It's Davy. At this time of night.'

Ray swung the front door open. 'Hey,' he said. 'How're you doing?' They shook hands, like male friends.

Davy came into the lounge. He was wearing a plaid lumberjack shirt and cut-off jeans. The tip of his nose was pink with cold and he blew on his hands. 'I saw the lights on,' he said.

'Have a pew,' said Ray. 'Tammy –?'

They heard the sound of bathwater, saw the closed door off the hallway. Ray shrugged. He took a clean glass for Davy and poured the last of the bottle into it. 'Tam's –'

Davy held up a hand. 'It's all right,' he said. 'I understand.'

'It's just that she ... well, she and Fran ... '

'I know. It's all right. Really.'

Ray and Davy looked curiously alike and, sitting there in the semi-dark, they could easily have been taken for brothers. Davy's normally tanned skin had the pallor of someone who hasn't been exposed to daylight for some time and he told Ray he was spending long hours in the recording studio. He had deep brown smudges beneath his eyes. Ray watched him smoke seven cigarettes in less than two hours.

Like everyone else, they talked about the attack on the club in town. Davy's flat in Hillbrow had been rocked with the force of the blast less than a kilometre away.

'Do you ever think about leaving the country?' asked Ray, who had been doing a lot of that himself lately. 'There doesn't seem to be an end to the violence and it's beginning to sicken me. Physically. I can't bear to see another picture of a panga buried in someone's skull. Frankly, I liked it better when the pictures were censored. And that's something I never thought I'd hear myself say.'

It was true, in a way. Before, it had always been the government versus the 'terrorists'. Now it was groups, both left and right, which flared sporadically, but regularly, into bloody conflict.

Davy yawned. 'I suppose it might sound glib to call it a natural cycle of events, which doesn't mean that I think this is how things should be. But it's not unexpected, you know. We're still in a war situation. People are feeling insecure, but it's still all part of the struggle. Sure, the violence has escalated and the factions swing one way and then another, but really it's been there all the time. We've just been cushioned by government propaganda for so long. And the restrictions on the media during the years of the state of emergency. Christ, the kids in the townships have known practically nothing else all their lives.'

Ray got up to put the kettle on. 'I get fucking depressed, I'll tell you that much. I don't know whether I really want to live here any more.'

Davy smiled. 'Where d'you want to go – Beirut?'

'I'm serious. I look at some of the mothers from Tamzin's school and I just don't know. How on earth are we all going to get it together? A few token black kids sprinkled throughout the white schools and they think that's all there is to it.'

'You're not going to see much change in attitude at that end of the scale, I admit,' said Davy. 'But come down on the street sometime. Apartheid doesn't exist there any more and it hasn't existed for a long time. Think about it. Go to any of the clubs in Hillbrow. Go to movies downtown – not the Mall or Sandton – but down in the city. We're all alike down there, man. Nobody feels any different. And it's such a good vibe. Haven't you felt it?'

Ray looked sceptical. 'Not lately,' he said. 'I'm back in Tsarist Russia at the moment.'

They were silent for a while. Davy asked for a glass of milk and he sat sipping it and smoking.

'So how're you doing?' said Ray softly. It had grown very quiet. The next-door revelry appeared to have stopped and there was no sound at all from Tamzin.

'OK, I guess. Well – not really.' He looked down at his hands, clasping and unclasping them in his lap.

'Do they have any idea, the police? Anything to go on?'

'No.' Davy sighed. He reached for his pack of cigarettes and shook one out into his palm. He lit it and took a long, deep pull, putting his head back and letting a stream of grey smoke push up towards the ceiling. He looked at Ray. 'Not so far anyway,' he said.

'Tamzin feels so badly about it. The kid's really devastated.' He got up to open a window. 'She loved Sophie so much.'

'I know.' Davy looked away. 'It isn't Tamzin's fault. I wanted to tell her that. I *will* tell her that. It's just difficult, I think, for Fran to take it all in and separate out the threads, you know. I don't think, in her heart, she really feels Tamzin's to blame. But Tam'll have to give her time.'

'I'm sure you're right. And the press? What about this hit squad business? Do you think there's anything in it?'

Davy stood up. It was two a.m. He stubbed his cigarette out in an ashtray. 'It's not impossible, I suppose,' he said vaguely.

Ray saw him to the door and went in search of Tamzin. He found her fast asleep, lying on her stomach with her knees tucked up to her chest.

Seven

The scent of rosemary was very strong. Bees flew about, settling and crawling all over the bushes, greedily possessive. There were some empty Coke cans lying on the grass and there were bees inside them too, their buzzing magnified by the hollow aluminium container. Fran stooped and picked them up. She tossed them into a refuse bin at the side of the path. The area around the dam was not unfamiliar to her. She had been for walks here many times. When she and Davy were first married and Sophie had been a baby, they lived in a small flat without a garden, and at weekends they would bring a picnic lunch to the dam and a packet of breadcrumbs for the ducks. Sophie had taken some of her first steps right here on this path, pushing her pram along the paving, staggering and beaming with achievement. In summer the rose garden was particularly beautiful and, as she walked through it, Fran saw that some of the early budders were already beginning to appear. There was no one else around up at this part of the gardens, just a few single men sitting reading their newspapers on the grass near the public toilets. Fran remembered with a strange feeling that this was supposed to be prime pick-up land for the gay men of the northern suburbs. She looked curiously at a pink-cheeked boy stretched out on his elbows with his face turned to the sun. He smiled at her as she passed. He looked like a cherub, with the big blue eyes and soft skin of a child.

She had reached the herb garden and found herself puffing a bit from the long walk up from the car-park. She took off her jersey and tied it round her shoulders. The iron gates were closed and padlocked. There were two workmen there painting over the graffiti in a lazy, uninterested kind of way. FREE THE HUNGRY STRIKERS could still be discerned beneath the first coat. The men paused to look at her. She supposed it was probably strange to see a solitary woman in this remote part on an ordinary weekday morning. She didn't even have a dog for an excuse. Where had these painters been when someone had dragged her child up here? And why had the gates been open then? Don't play detective, she told herself for the hundredth time. These were elementary things the police had covered more than once.

She needed to go inside the garden. She gestured to the gates. 'Who has the key to the gate?' she asked one of the men.

The both shook their heads immediately and emphatically. 'Can't go in there,' said one.

'Why not?'

'It's locked,' said the other, looking at her as if she were a half-wit.

'I know. But – where will I find someone with the key to the gate? I would like to go inside.'

They exchanged looks. Then one of the men said he would go and call the supervisor who was clearing weed from the weir at the far end of the dam. Fran sat down on the grass to wait. She leaned against the metal gates and felt their heat burn into her shoulder-blades like a branding iron. Like a dog on guard at the site of its dead master, she sat there for a full half hour. Greyfriars Franny. Eventually, she saw two men approaching. The supervisor's boots were festooned with dark green slime. He narrowed his eyes at Fran as she got to her feet. He had seen her picture in the newspapers.

'Good morning. I'm –'

'Mrs Phillips. I know.' He held out his hand. 'I am sorry for your loss.'

'Thank you. I don't mean to be a nuisance, but, if it wouldn't be too much trouble, I would like to go inside and ... '

The man had a big bunch of keys on his belt like a gaoler.

'I don't know ... ' he said doubtfully. He didn't need an hysterical woman on his hands when he had weed to clear.

Fran could see what was going through his head. She hastened to reassure him. 'I need to see for myself the place where my child died,' she said in a low, measured voice. 'That's all. I won't be any trouble, and not more than a couple of minutes.'

The man was still reluctant, but he unlocked the door and stood aside while Fran went through. She felt guilty intruding on his time and probably instructions, but guilt was an emotion that was becoming almost companionable. Inside the herb garden she stood still for a moment, breathing in the thick, sour smells. She broke a leaf off a dusty green shrub and rubbed it between her finger and thumb. It had a familiar but unplaceable smell, like something her mother used to rub on her chest when she was ill as a child. Camphor. Was it camphor? She didn't really know what she expected to find here once she was inside, or why in fact it had become such an important pilgrimage. It was quite a big garden, with roughly laid out beds and winding paths twisting this way and that in and around them. She had no way of knowing where exactly it was that they had found Sophie's body, and she could not bring herself to go out again and ask the man himself. Excuse me, but I thought there might have been a sign? This way to the murder site. There were any number of little paths seemingly leading into thickets which looked dusty and impenetrable in the morning sunshine. So Fran walked up and down the paths, drinking in the strange, conflicting scents, and felt a quietness in her. It was a tranquil place and, for the first time since Sophie's death, Fran felt that it might yet be possible for a sort of control and understanding to return to her spirit. She thought she could go on to the bookshop and do some work. She had to start sometime.

First she went by Jessica's house. Anna was polishing the front stoep with strong-smelling red polish. Edwina had an old rag tied over her nappy and she sailed back and forth on her bottom, working up a shine. Fran shook her head, smiling. 'Interesting division of labour,' she said. 'Where's Jess?'

'Gone to the doctor,' Anna replied. 'Check up.'

*

Doctors' waiting rooms were all alike: mock leather chairs with metal arms and legs, the world's most boring magazines stacked in blocks on glass-topped tables. A box of reject children's puzzles. In Luke Stephens' rooms there was also a large perspex container of wool and knitting needles, inviting patients to add a few rows to make up blankets for the needy while they waiting their turn. They'd have to be really needy, Jessica reflected, looking at the tangled mess of wool and the few token squares. She felt guilty that she couldn't knit and she wondered whether tidying up the wool would count.

The morning had started out bright with sunshine, but it was turning into a dismally overcast day. Jessica stood by the window looking out towards the city. Cloud dense as fur and the soft spitting of a relentless spring rain. It matched her mood somehow, which was nervous to the point of tearful. She could hear the murmur of a male voice from down the passage and the doctor's receptionist, a girl with a square haircut and firm jaw, smiled humourlessly at her and said, 'He won't be long, Mrs T. He's just on the phone.'

Jessica didn't know Luke Stephens apart from meeting him only briefly at the memorial service for Sophie. He was Tamzin's doctor though, and she had spoken highly of him. Her own gynaecologist, a motherly Belgian woman with thick ankles, had recently left the country, sending a brief, impersonal circular letter to all her regular patients. Jessica felt resentful now at having to bare her body to this unknown quantity. Besides, she had a terrible suspicion about her current rundown state.

'I've missed two periods,' she said baldly when at last she found herself face to face with the doctor at his desk.

'Do you think you could be pregnant?' he asked.

'Christ, I hope not. I'm thirty-three and I've got three children already.'

'Just asking.' He was writing on a pad. 'Did you bring a urine sample with you by any chance?' he asked without looking up.

Jessica was ready for this. She dug out the Robertson's herb and spice bottle (Oregano), the only near suitable receptacle she'd been able to find at short notice. It had either been that or Edwina's juice mug with the lambs on the lid. She handed it over to the nurse.

Luke Stephens stood up, motioning her to his examining room. He was smiling. 'Let's take a look first, before we panic,' he said.

Jessica began to resent him a little less. He seemed kind. And she was an inch or so taller than him in her Woolworths socks.

'I think you're a little anaemic,' he told her after he'd examined her and she was dressed and sitting across from him again. 'I'd like to prescribe a course of iron tablets, and have some blood taken. But don't worry – I don't think you're pregnant.'

Jessica's relief was tangible.

'Do you feel run down?' Luke asked her.

She nodded.

'Tired all the time?'

She nodded again. 'I've had bronchitis quite badly this winter,' she said. 'I can't seem to shake off the cough.'

Luke made some notes on his pad. 'Nauseous?' he asked.

To her embarrassment, Jessica felt the sudden sharp prick of tears behind her eyelids.

'I'm pressing all the right buttons?' He had a soft, light voice.

Jessica felt her nose start to run. 'Oh God, I'm sorry,' she said, reaching wildly for the Kleenex box on the desk. It was empty. 'I keep doing this, I don't know why. It's not a bit like me.'

Luke looked at her. He handed her his own handkerchief. It was one with his initials embroidered on it, inexpertly, by Virginia in her needlework phase. Jessica blew her nose but the tears kept coming.

'Is there something you want to talk about? Perhaps I can help?'

Jessica flapped a hand at him. 'No, oh no,' she said. 'I'm fine. Really. I'm so sorry. You don't even know me. I could be a stranger on a bus –'

Luke laughed. 'I have seen tears before, you know,' he said. 'And shed a few myself in my time.'

But Jessica was desperate to be gone. She gathered her things, snatched the form for the blood test from Luke's fingers and fled from the room. Luke sat looking after her and smiling to himself. Then he made a couple of additions to his notes, chuckling. A stranger on a bus. Jessica Tucker was a breath of fresh air.

On her way home Jessica stopped off at the shopping centre where Fran's bookshop was. She needed to get in some supplies. Ben's meals had been rather lean of late and she went through periods of trying to please him through his stomach. She also had a theory that if he ate well he didn't snore so much at night. It was a thin theory, she knew, based on sporadic culinary experiments. She even had a menu in her head today – vichyssoise with a sunflower-seed loaf from the home industries shop, followed by tandoori grilled chicken and saffron rice, with a tomato and chive salad. To finish, a lime sorbet if she could get it home without it melting.

The traffic out of Hillbrow was heavy. It was still raining steadily. Water ran in the gutters at the side of the road. Waiting at the traffic lights, Jessica idly watched a small black newspaper seller battling to cover the early edition of the *Star* with a sheet of plastic. He wore a bright yellow rain-proof poncho, miles too big for him. It reached almost to his ankles, but his feet were bare and he hopped from one foot to the other, whether to keep warm or not it was hard to tell. Ben would have marvelled. 'These people, they're all such good dancers.' Ben knew blacks. He'd worked with them on the mines. Once, at dinner with Fran and Davy at a club in town, Ben (drunk, naturally) had applauded the all-African band loud and long. 'Natural rhythm,' he said earnestly to Fran across the table, shouting so that she could hear across the hubbub. 'They've all got it. It's in-bred. I've seen it on the mines.' Jessica had been mortified, but Fran had winked at her and grinned.

Noticing her watching him, the newspaper seller skipped nimbly to Jessica's window. She shook her head at him and smiled, thinking he wanted to sell her a newspaper. 'No, thanks,' she mouthed, but when he made urgent winding motions with his hand, she opened the window a crack.

'*Tien sent,*' he said aggressively. '*Vir brood.*' Whether she would have given it to him or not, Jessica didn't have ten cents handy, and she was pretty sure it wouldn't have been for bread anyway. The traffic lights had changed. 'Oh, gosh, sorry, no.' Someone hooted behind her and she stalled the car in her confusion. Water was coming in the window.

'*Ag, vok jou,*' said the boy half-heartedly. He splashed back to the pavement, a surly yellow gnome in a pixie hood. Jessica jerked forward, unnerved by the encounter.

Once in the shopping centre she cheered herself up by buying a pair of lacy red knickers with a G-string up the bottom. Then she set off to find Fran.

'I can feel a case of the spends coming on,' she said to Fran's back. 'So why stop now, I ask myself.'

Fran looked up from sorting a box of new paperbacks. She looked tired. 'Jess,' she said. 'What are you doing here?'

'Buying you a cup of coffee? Come on, I hate to drink on my own.' They sat at a corner table in the Double Dutch. Jessica told Fran about the doctor.

'There's nothing wrong with you, I hope?'

'Just run down, anaemic. Normal white northern suburbs ailments. It's the pressure, doll. I had to have a blood test too. Does that mean anything, do you think?'

'I'm sure it's just routine. AIDS and stuff.'

'I've been back-tracking,' Jessica said, half seriously, 'and I think I'm probably clear. But I don't seem to have any energy at all these days, and fuck-all resistance to passing viruses. Everything the children bring home from Rosepark I get.'

'I thought your doctor'd gone back to wherever it was she came from?'

'She has. I went to Luke Stephens.'

'Luke. Did you like him?'

'Yes, I did actually. He was sort of laid back. Calm. I got a bit emotional and he took it in his stride.'

'He delivered Sophie, you know.'

'Yes, I did know. Fran, I –'

'He's a nice man. His wife is sweet too. Virginia. They came to the service. I think Virginia's a bit too sweet actually. Does a lot of charity work. A good causes sort. She worked in the Sash advice office for a while once.'

The waitress brought their coffee.

'Fran,' Jessica said. She put her hand over Fran's where it lay on the table. 'Are you all right?'

Fran didn't answer at first. She pulled her hand away and stirred her coffee round and round and round. Then she put in two spoons of sugar and stirred it some more. 'I went to the dam,' she said finally.

'To the dam? When?' Jessica sat back and stared at her.

'This morning. I had to go.' Fran shrugged. A nervous smile flickered.

'Oh, Fran. Why didn't you ask me to go with you?'

'I needed to go on my own really. Besides, you had Luke.'

'I could have put that off. What did you want to do there – just walk around?'

Fran smiled a tired smile. 'I guess so. Nothing more. I had to see where it ended, that's all.'

Jessica poured milk into her coffee. 'Listen,' she said. 'You know I won't make any "life goes on" speeches, I promise, but you know I'm here for you, don't you?'

'What are friends for?' said Fran lightly, but her mouth turned down at the corners and her voice came out in a whisper.

'Anything from the police yet?' Jessica asked after a pause.

'There was a message when I got into the shop this morning. Sophie wasn't raped, thank God. And her killer wasn't black as the papers all implied and everyone assumed. Scrapings from under her nails showed that whoever attacked her was the same colour as you and me.'

Jessica knew what that could mean. It made the political motivation more plausible and the significance appalled her. She tried to speak but Fran stopped her.

'I have ... friends ... doing some sleuthing, for want of a better word. And the police are not unaware, although how actively they're pursuing that line is anyone's guess. They're all brothers in arms, as it were.'

Suddenly, not for the first time or the last, Jessica's life seemed to her quite irrelevant. Her chatter, her clothes, her hairstyle, the make-up on her skin. Everything about her was meaningless. She wondered that Fran could ever need her.

While Fran and Jessica drank coffee at the Double Dutch and Luke snatched a quick cup of tea at his desk, Luke's daughter Kelly sat drinking a chocolate double thick through a straw in the basement of the Midnite Sun club, a mere block away from her father's Hillbrow rooms. In the bag at her feet was her school uniform. Her pale, heavy hair hung in straight blunt sheets, almost completely hiding her face as she drank.

Her companion watched her from beneath the brim of his hat. He chewed rhythmically on a piece of gum, moving it steadily from one side of his mouth to the other. His eyes were dark and without expression. He had very high cheekbones and his face was a sallow colour, made more so by the fluorescent strip above their heads. In daytime the club was empty, except for a uniformed cleaner who lethargically moved a mop, a bizarre dance partner, over the lino of the dance floor. Her aluminium bucket clanged as she pushed it with her foot. Kelly looked up as one of the resident band members arrived and moved on to the stage, where he began to fiddle with the wiring of an amplifier. Pedro yawned. He took out his gum and stuck it beneath the edge of the table. When he spoke his voice had a peculiar high pitch to it, as if it had never broken properly.

'Got any tom?'

Kelly looked towards the cloakroom door. Denise, her partner-in-crime, was taking a hell of a long time. 'Why?' she said round her straw, without looking at him.

'Just asking.'

'Uh uh.' She shook her head. 'Denise might. Why don't you ask her?'

The musician was playing quiet, intricate riffs on a guitar. He wore red *velskoens* and tapped one foot in time to a rhythm inside his head. Kelly saw Denise slip out of the cloakroom door and go across to him. He nodded at her but didn't stop playing. She sat on the edge of the stage, resting her chin on her knees.

Kelly came to the end of her double thick. She got up languidly and draped an arm round Pedro's neck. He pulled her down on to his lap and kissed her, on her mouth and neck. She moaned and pushed him away.

'Denise,' she called. 'Got any cash on you?' Denise met her half-way across the dance floor. She took Kelly by the shoulders and moved her round to the strand of blues now coming from the stage. Kelly giggled and allowed herself to be led, round and round, faster and faster, her hair thrown out behind her like a cape. She was a burst of colour in this dull place.

Pedro seemed to have gone to sleep. His hat was over his eyes and his boots rested casually on the table. He was the bouncer at the Midnite Sun and, although he wasn't a big man, judging by the bulge of muscle beneath his cut-away T-shirt, he was probably the right man for the job. Hillbrow could be a rough place on a Friday night, but it was his stamping ground. It was where he felt most at home. Kelly and Denise had been hanging out at the club for the past couple of months. Denise was attracted to musicians. Fights broke out quite often. Once a group of white thugs from Roodepoort had tried to force their way in when Sipho Kubeka's band had been playing there. They were all drunk and looking for trouble. Kubeka was a Soweto '76 child who had fled the country and joined Umkhonto we Sizwe. He was rumoured to have been high on the death squad's hit list at one time. Kelly couldn't imagine him with a rifle in his hand, he played so sweetly on guitar. Not that she cared, one way or another, sitting on her barstool in the draught from the street, watching the world go by through the haze of a rude cigarette. Pedro personally had no time for terrorists, but this was his club and he had seen the gang off very smartly. They weren't going to threaten his territory.

He shared a flat nearby with a girl called Jackie. She had a night job too, she had told Kelly, and Kelly, to her eternal embarrassment, had asked if she was a nurse. 'Sometimes,'

Jackie had said and then roared with laughter. She had a heavy, smoker's laugh. 'In my line you have to be prepared for anything.' Jackie was her first hooker, Kelly had confided to Denise. And actually, she was quite nice, if a little stupid. She had a small boy, Leon, who lived with them too. He had bold staring eyes and smelt of urine and peanut butter.

The first time Kelly went home with Pedro she had been drunk on vodka and she'd given up her virginity without really noticing. It soon became known that Kelly was Pedro's chick. When she thought about it, in her 'other' life, day-dreaming at her desk or lying listening to the radio in her room, Kelly couldn't say what she felt about Pedro really. Only that she felt attached to him as if she were on the end of a long, invisible cord. He had only to twitch it and she'd move, unquestioning, towards him. His right to her time and her body was undisputed.

'I've got a couple of bucks. How much do you want?' said Denise.

'I dunno. Pedro was asking.'

The girls looked at him, then giggled. Denise put her hand over her mouth. She'd only recently jettisoned her braces and was still self-conscious. Pedro really was asleep. With each snore from his open mouth, the brim of his hat lifted slightly. 'Ag shame,' said Denise.

Kelly tiptoed over to him and stood in front of him for a moment. Then she plucked off his hat and danced away with it, laughing. Pedro was on his feet in a second, lithe and crouching as a cat. His black eyes were narrow with fury. In one stride he reached for Kelly and his hand clamped over her wrist with a grip like a vice. The hat dropped from her fingers with a soft plop. She stared down at the white knuckles of his hand, then up at his face. Her green eyes were wide with surprise and shock. A smile hovered at the edges of her mouth.

'Don't fuck around, you little tart,' said Pedro. His lips barely moved as he spoke and his eyes never left hers.

Kelly gasped. 'It was only a joke, Pedro. Can't you take a –'

'No. And don't ever forget it.'

Kelly bit down hard on her bottom lip. Her eyes filled with tears. Denise stood, frozen, behind her. Then Pedro released Kelly's wrist, flinging it from him and away. Kelly let it fall to her side and stood watching as he walked towards the stage.

'I've got some money … ' she called to his back. 'Pedro –'

He turned and came back towards her. 'How much?'

Kelly looked at Denise. 'Ten rand.'

Pedro took the note grudgingly and eased it into the back pocket of his jeans. He picked up his hat, dusting it off against his thigh. Kelly hadn't moved. She stood like a statue, an angel in a pantomime. Two bright spots of pink stood out on her cheeks and her straight, thick hair shone like butter beneath the overhead light. Pedro came up close to her. He put the flat of his palm gently against her cheek, then lifted her hair back and behind her shoulders, carefully, one side at a time. He smoothed it flat. 'OK,' he said. 'OK.'

Eight

Cassandra went to the hairdresser on Friday mornings. She loved going to the salon. Her visits were an unnecessary extravagance as her short dark hair was easy to manage and in beautiful condition. She felt there was something almost sacrificial about putting her head back and fitting her neck into the smooth, round enamel of the basin and allowing strong, neutral fingers to have their way with her scalp. It was an utterly passive experience, but one which she found strangely sensual.

On her way home she stopped on impulse and bought a packet of lemon-grass tea from the health shop. Selena was hanging out the washing when she drove in, chatting to the painters who were sitting in the yard in their overalls. They held mugs of tea and door-stopper sandwiches. In the kitchen, Cassandra switched on the kettle.

'Selena!' she called out. 'Where do you keep the teapot?'

'You don't know where the *teapot's* kept?' a voice said incredulously from behind her.

'I beg your pardon?' Cassandra turned slowly and looked coolly at the man leaning over the bottom half of the kitchen door.

'Sorry, I just ... Do you mind if I come in and wash my hands? Mam?'

Cassandra felt an inexplicable squashed feeling in her chest as Joel Cunningham, Painter and Handyman, stepped into the room. He was wearing tight blue jeans today. His arms were very brown. She felt ridiculous and caught out, in her designer suit, holding a box of pretentious tea, looking helpless in her own kitchen. The painter ran the tap noisily in the sink and grinned up at her.

Cassandra felt conversation was called for. 'You're very young,' she began, 'to be running a business. Shouldn't you be in school or something?'

'Well, I guess I am still in school, Mam.' He was unfazed by her tone, and his smile was boyish, friendly. 'In a way, that is.'

Selena came into the kitchen and silently went about laying a tea-tray. She passed him a drying up cloth for his hands and he said something to her in Zulu that made her giggle. She put two cups on the tray, misinterpreting the situation. She took a milk jug and a teapot from a cupboard above the sink. Cassandra allowed the box to be taken from her hands.

'On the patio, thank you, Selena,' she said, and to Joel – 'What do you mean exactly?'

'This business is, I hope, only a temporary one. You see, I'm trying to scrape enough together to put myself through medical school. I inherited the truck and equipment – and staff – from my father. He passed away some months back. It was his business. He was Joel too.'

'Oh. I'm sorry. Look – I didn't mean to pry. Can I ... would you like a cup of tea?'

They sat on the patio. Cassandra found her eyes drawn relentlessly to the hand which was wrapped round the bone china cup. She noticed the blue veins that stood up in ridges on the back of it. She wondered that the cup didn't burn his palm. His forearms were flecked with white paint.

'You must get fairly messy, doing a job like this, Mr Cunningham?' she said lamely when she saw he'd noticed her looking at him.

'Please,' he said, 'call me Joel. I'm not a very formal person.' The smile again. It made her drop her eyes.

'Joel – then. How is the business going? Are you going to get to medical school?'

'I think so. I hope to start in the new year. I've been accepted, so that's one hurdle over with. I also have a couple of bursary options I'm exploring.'

'Will you go to Wits, here in Johannesburg?' Cassandra asked, not that the answer mattered. She was just making conversation, and heavy weather of it too.

'That's right.' He stood up, smoothing down his jeans. 'Well, thanks for the tea, Mrs Symons. Interesting flavour. I'll get back to work now.'

His eyes held hers for a moment and Cassandra felt a physical jolt in her stomach. For the rest of the day she went about feeling unsettled and irritable. She was relieved when she watched the panel van make its noisy way to the gate.

It was Friday afternoon and tennis, and Cassandra was still busy changing into her skirt when she saw Tamzin's car pull up. Ansie was making a fourth today and she, Cassandra, Tamzin and Jessica were just knocking up when they heard the Morris buzz up the drive.

They stood and watched as Fran got out. She had her tennis racket with her.

'Fran. We didn't –' Cassandra went off the court to meet her.

'Expect me? I'm sorry. I should have called. I felt I needed some exercise and some company.' Jessica and Ansie walked over to the fence. Tamzin was hitting balls against the practice wall with strong backhand strokes.

Fran had tied her bright hair into a ponytail and she wore a sun visor with a miniature ANC flag on it. 'I also wanted to come in person to say thank you for all the support you've all given to Davy and me. We really appreciate it. And people tell me I need to get on with my life and do normal things – so,' she smiled bleakly, 'tennis seems like a good enough start. But carry on with your set. I'll be linesperson.'

Jessica, Ansie and Cassandra stood looking at her uncertainly. Fran was very pale and she seemed unsteady on her feet. 'Go on,' she said. 'Stop staring at me as if I were a ghost. I'm all right, you know. Tell them, Jessie.'

They turned reluctantly back to their game and Fran sat on a chair in the sunshine, fondling the ears of the little white dog at her feet. When the set was over she stood up as the four women came off the court. 'You're a little off form today,' she said to Jessica.

'I played like an asshole actually,' said Jessica. 'You don't have to be polite. Feet of clay and a hole in the racket. Sometimes I don't know why I bother.'

Tamzin slipped out of the gate and past the group. She headed up to the house. 'I'll sit this one out,' she called as she went.

Fran played a strong game of tennis and once she got her concentration she began to play well. She had a natural eye for the ball and was light and quick on her feet. The four were evenly matched and, despite Jessica's grumbling, it was a close match. When they had finished Cassandra went ahead up to the house to organise drinks. Ansie looked round. 'Where's Tamzin gone?' she said. 'Her car's not there.'

'Perhaps she parked round the back,' said Jessica.

'I think she left,' Fran said. 'I'm afraid it's me. I shouldn't have come.'

'Oh, rubbish.' Jessica put an arm round Fran's shoulder. 'But, Fran – don't you think ... I mean, are you and Tamzin never going to speak to each other again? I know you're feeling pretty rough right now, but to tell you the truth I think Tam's hurting badly too. You know.' She shrugged.

Fran's face was stony. 'You mean, we shouldn't let a little thing like the death of my daughter come between us?' she said.

Ansie looked embarrassed. She moved off up to the house.

'Oh, Fran –' Jessica took a step forward, but Fran held up her racket like a weapon. 'Of course I didn't mean it like that. It's just ... '

'That you like to pour oil on troubled waters. I know. The old olive branch routine. Thanks, Jess, but don't preach to me, please. You ought to know better than that.'

'All right,' said Jessica. 'All right.'

She frowned as Fran turned and walked away from her. Fran had never talked to her like that before. Suddenly she felt dizzy and her head seemed full of bright light and black, swimming spots. 'Jesus,' she said, reaching out to hold on to the fence. 'What the fuck –'

She was dimly aware of fuzzy faces and voices, spinning, circling, fainter then clearer. She struggled to sit upright, but someone was pushing her back, gently but rather firmly. 'Lie still,' said a voice. Unfamiliar, male. She closed her eyes.

'Jessica? Can you hear me? Are you OK? Say you're OK.'

Jessica opened her eyes and tried to focus on the faces leaning over her.

'Jesus God,' she muttered. 'Did I faint? I've never done that before. Probably the effect of Fran winning her service for once.'

There was relieved laughter. 'You gave us such a fright,' said Ansie. 'You just conked over.'

'If it hadn't been for – you'd probably still be lying with your face in the marigolds. You're heavy, you know,' said Fran.

'Thank you – Joel.' Cassandra stood up from where she'd been kneeling beside Jessica on the *chaise longue* and faced him. She walked with him across the lawn. 'You gave me a surprise appearing like that out of nowhere. That's the second time today. I thought you'd left?'

'I had to come back to fetch my workmen. They're just packing up. Glad I could be of help.'

He was standing so close to her, Cassandra could see a small pulse beating in his neck. 'Well,' she said. 'Thank you again.'

As she turned away to return to the patio, where Jessica was now sitting up and drinking from a cup, she heard him call.

'Mrs Symons. She ought to check in with her doctor, you know. Will you see that she does?'

'I'll try. And, Joel –'

He came back a step or two and stood, arms by his sides.

'It's Cassandra. I'm not really a formal person either.'

'Who *was* that guy?' Fran asked when Cassandra was within earshot.

'Oh, just the painter. We're having the house redone.'

Jessica looked over the rim of her cup. 'Nice bum,' she said.

As Fran drove towards home she felt almost relaxed. Maybe it was true what they said about exercise. She'd never put it to the test before. But certainly hitting a tennis ball was clearly more beneficial than hitting her head against a door frame, and more enjoyable in retrospect, although at the time she'd taken a perverse and miserable pleasure in the sharp, rhythmical pain. She was glad she had made the effort to go to Cassandra's.

She found Jim Walton sitting on a canvas chair on her front stoep. He was wearing red satin running shorts and new-looking running shoes. His fat thighs spilled over the sides of the chair and his legs were very white. His T-shirt was stained dark with sweat.

'Hello,' said Fran. 'What's all this?'

'Been for a jog,' Jim replied. 'Excuse me if I don't get up. I don't know if I can.'

'If I had to think of the world's unlikeliest jogger, I'm afraid it would have to be you, Jim,' Fran said. She unlocked the front door, as usual now with a small feeling of trepidation.

'Went for a check-up the other day,' Jim panted. 'The doc says I have to cut down on smoking, get some regular exercise. This is my first run. Can I have some water?'

One thing about Jim Walton: once he made himself at home, it wasn't easy to dislodge him. He seemed to have appointed himself Fran's personal bodyguard since Sophie's murder, and his hovering, ever-anxious face seemed to float about her even in her dreams. In a way he was useful to have around. He filled in gaps ('*more* than filled,' was Jessica's caustic comment; she couldn't stand Jim), Fran explained. The house could feel unbearably empty. Although she'd had no more threatening calls, and seen no evidence of her movements being watched, Fran's nerves were taut and finely tuned all the time. Having Jim bumbling about the house lent her life a semblance of normality.

But Jim was there nearly every day and it was getting a bit wearying. Jessica said bluntly that he was obviously in love with her and didn't she see where it was all leading? Admittedly, the thought had crossed her mind once or twice but she shrugged it off; Jim was being a good friend, that was all. She and Davy spoke daily on the telephone, but with no apparent progress in Sophie's case, their conversations were edgy and defensive. After Davy's desertion their only reason for keeping in touch had been Sophie. Now that she was gone it was only guilt and duty that tied them. Or so Fran felt. Most of her friends had families and commitments of their own and now she found she hated to impose. Whereas before she would have thought nothing of dropping in unexpectedly on Jessica and bumming a meal, or of calling up Tamzin at the last minute and suggesting a movie, now she felt simply unworthy. People felt uncomfortable around her – it had been obvious at tennis today. They also made her feel guilty. Guilty for what had happened to Sophie. Guilty because she was given to fits of unseemly weeping in public places. Guilty for feeling guilty. If they didn't treat her with kid gloves (and even Jessica tended to do that, as had happened when she had treated Jessica abominably rudely at Cassandra's), they avoided her eyes in conversation and tried never to mention children, their own or anybody else's, when she was in the room.

Only Jim acted normally around her ('And how normal is *that*?' Jessica would probably have said), and for that alone she was grateful. And Jim brought up the subject of Sophie quite naturally, perhaps a little too readily, almost as if she were still around. Fran sometimes thought he'd forgotten what had happened. She didn't like to talk about Sophie to Jim; Sophie had never really taken to him, and it was like betraying a trust to discuss her behind her back. Fran was an intensely private person. She usually shied away from confidences, even with her closest friends.

'Any news?' Jim asked, coming out of the kitchen. He held a beer-mug filled with iced water in his hand.

'You'll get stomach cramps if you drink all that.'

Jim ignored her. 'Any news, I asked, about Sophe's killer?'

Fran winced. Her face went white, then red. Then, 'I wish you wouldn't call her that,' she said quietly. 'She hates it. Hated it.'

'Sorry.' Jim drained the mug and left it on the sideboard, where it made a wet ring. 'Sorry, Fran. Tactless. But – is there?'

'No. Well, no real leads, that is. Davy talked to Lieutenant Els this morning. They've had a couple of false leads, which they've had to follow up as a matter of routine, but have come to nothing. They did find out two things, though.'

'Oh?'

Fran looked at Jim. He was still sweating profusely. There was a drop of moisture on the end of his nose. She wished he would wipe it off.

'She wasn't raped, as they thought at first. And whoever killed her was white, not black.'

'How could they tell?'

'Her nails. They analysed skin samples from ... from under her nails.'

Fran looked up but Jim was back in the kitchen again. She could hear him at the biscuit tin.

'Amazing what they can do, hey, Franny?' he called. 'Anything else?'

'No, not so far,' she whispered. 'But they're keeping on it. Round the clock, as they say in the murder mysteries.' Fran didn't want to discuss the other nagging possibility. She didn't altogether trust Jim, and Jessica had flatly advised against it.

Later, when he had been persuaded to go home, Fran picked up the phone and dialled Jessica's number.

'I was a rat today. I'm sorry.'

'Forget it. I understand. I was out of line, but you know me – can't keep my nose out of other people's business. But it's only because you're my friend and I love you.'

'Yuck, but thanks.'

'Listen – are we still on for tonight?'

'That's the other reason I called. Do you feel up to it after what happened today? Did you call Luke?'

'Oh, I'm fine. Really. You don't need to worry about me. I'm anaemic, remember?'

'I still think you should get it checked out. What does Ben say?'

'I haven't told him. He's out on the piss.'

'Again? Do you think it's a problem?'

'I'm not sure. I guess it could turn into one. Look – I'll be waiting by the gate. *Edwina – no! Don't do that!* I'm going to have to go, Fran. Ed's into vomit. Anyone's.'

Apart from the bookshop and her ANC work, Fran was involved in a number of other activities, all of which she had let slide since Sophie's death and she knew this was a dangerous situation. She sometimes helped out in the advice office of the Black Sash and she acted as a liaison person between that organisation and the End Conscription Campaign. Ever since her student days, when she and Jessica had been in res together, she had been politically active. It was time to get back to work. She'd asked Jessica to come with her to an ECC meeting tonight so that she wouldn't have to face it alone. She needed someone to prod her in the back.

Jessica was waiting for her in the road. Fran steered the Morris through the back streets to an address in Yeoville, land of graffiti on walls and drug pushers on street corners. There were cars parked in the street outside the house where the meeting was to be held. It was easily recognised by its own graffiti, persistently spray-painted on the wall outside: COMMIES. THE ANC SUCKS. KAFFIR BOETIES.

The meeting was already in progress when they slipped in at the back. They squeezed up beside an Indian boy with a long, beaky nose. His name was Ahmed and he was supposed to be a poet of some note. Fran looked around the room to see who else was there. Agnes Radebe caught her eye and smiled, lifting her knitting from her lap in greeting. Her grandchild was asleep squashed up beside her. He wore a yellow knitted cap with ear flaps, Agnes's handiwork no doubt. She turned her attention to the centre of the room where the committee members faced out from an oval table. Her heart sank when she saw it was Marsha chairing the meeting tonight. That meant that whatever was under discussion would remain under discussion until midnight, without coming close to being resolved. Always a few steps behind, Marsha was in her militant phase. She was wearing heavy combat boots and a sort of tartan horse-blanket. Her mouse-brown hair was tucked up behind her ears and she chewed seriously on the end of a pencil.

Marsha was a type Fran had come to recognise and put up with over her years of involvement on the political fringe. She and Jessica used to play at picking them out from the freshmen. A Marsha had popped up on every committee she'd ever served on, and although her guise changed every now and then according to affiliations and functions, she saw herself as an integral part of the Movement. Perhaps that was part of the trouble, Fran sometimes thought in unguarded moments, with the inefficient way things were so often run. She had found herself growing increasingly weary of going through the motions, the discussions, the drafting of letters of protest or support. Its relevance was often in serious doubt, she thought. You couldn't really knock Marsha though; she meant well and she did work hard. But when it came down to it, wasn't she just playing games? Just as Sophie and her friends had played school-school, weren't the Marshas of the world just playing activist-activist? Not that she didn't take it seriously, after a fashion, but she didn't really *live* it. She thought she did; she thought she communicated and empathised. She believed the struggle for a non-racial, democratic South Africa was her struggle too. So she served on committees, did the legwork and the paperwork and raised her banner or her fist when required. She even served time in gaol and surrendered her passport and experienced a bit of the discomfort which goes with protest politics. But ultimately, Fran wondered, what was she doing it *for*? Fran herself teetered on the brink of boredom now and again. Politics was politics, after all.

A Marsha was there in embryo on campus in first year at university, taking on a bit of charity work – building houses in the homelands, supervising day-care centres in the townships – before this was viewed as a cop-out and pandering to the system. Fran remembered accompanying a Marsha on a mortifying door-to-door tour of a bleak 'Coloured' housing estate after they'd razed District Six, getting signatures for some petition or other. As early as that she'd been aware of a growing uncomfortable feeling, a feeling of going about things the wrong way. Marsha, though, had picked up no such vibes. This young white girl, fresh from her private school, so sure of a welcome in every home, had thrust her piece of paper beneath the nose of one suspicious householder after another. One bony woman, holding a baby whose head was alive with microscopic white things, had simpered and said, 'Bless you, madam, for helping us in our struggle,' and Marsha had felt fulfilled all the way back to campus.

In second year she became more intense. Minis were out and clogs and African print dresses down to the ankle became the uniform, with hair worn long and loose. Then it was house meetings and police raids and very select parties in unfashionable suburbs with the obligatory cheap red wine that made your tongue black in the morning. By third year Marsha wasn't attending too many lectures but she was on the platform of every protest meeting and travelling the country for solidarity encounter groups with sister organisations. She stopped drinking red wine and drank black coffee from styrofoam cups and wore her hair cut short and parted in the middle.

After university there was a period of wavering, but she soon found her home in small research institutions, legal aid clinics, alternative education and literacy programmes and various advice offices.

This was the stage when the men got sorted from the boys, as it were. Jessica maintained this was the point at which Marsha married a dentist, had a baby and managed a token job at an advice office, answering the phone in the morning and doing lift-club in the afternoon. She wore tracksuits a lot and had her short hair permed or styled. Alternatively, she became increasingly dedicated, stepped up the number of functions she carried on and regional sub-committees she served on and let everything that was irrelevant to the Cause go by the board. She dressed with studied carelessness, wore men's socks and carried a heavy shoulder bag.

Fran's eyes flickered to the floor beside Marsha's seat and there it was, a beige bag bulging with files and notepads. Jessica was staring at it too. Her eyes slid across to Fran and Fran had to look away and breathe deeply for a few seconds.

Fran tried to concentrate on the matter being discussed. A statement was being drafted in support of one Samuel Levy, who was electing to go to gaol rather than do his military service. Nobody could agree on the wording, it seemed, and everyone was entitled to a say. Eddy, whose house this was, sent out cups of coffee from a tiny kitchen off the lounge. A plastic spoon, heavily encrusted with sugar, was passed along. These meetings were held regularly here as it was fairly central and the living area could accommodate quite a few people, given the sparseness of the furnishings. Eddy was an ANC comrade (*pre*-unbanning era, he always managed to mention casually), and he took himself very seriously.

When the meeting finally broke up at eleven thirty, and Fran and Jessica were rinsing out their mugs at the sink, Agnes Radebe came up behind Fran and put an arm round her shoulders.

'I heard the bad news,' she said. 'As a mother I grieve with you.' Agnes's daughter, Faith, had spent 156 days in detention the year before and her son had disappeared after '76 and had never been heard of since. Fran felt the now familiar solid lump squeeze its way into her throat again and stick there like a piece of indigestible food. She and Jessica drove home in silence. They parted silently too and Fran watched Jessica walk up the driveway to her house with shoulders hunched. On the way to her own house Fran suddenly had to pull off the road when the tears came. They rolled effortlessly from her eyes and the more she wiped them away, the faster they came. This was a phenomenon she couldn't get used to. The other morning she had woken up amazed to find her face and pillow wet with weeping.

Eventually she made her slow way home, listening to Sophie's tape of nursery rhymes. 'How *much* is that do-ggy in the window,' she sang along weakly. 'The one with the waggerly tail ...'

Sunshine streamed into the window and on to the bed. Fran heard the doorbell, but a heavy lethargy prevented her from getting up. She turned on to her side and pulled her pillow into her chest. Perhaps whoever it was would realise she wasn't at home and would go away.

'Fran?'

Then she recognised Jessica's voice and knew Jessica would get the fire brigade and break in before she went away.

'Coming,' she mumbled. A passing glance in the bedroom mirror made her wince. She ran her hands through the tangled mass of hair and on her way to the door bit her lips and pinched her cheeks to try to give herself some colour. She didn't feel eccentric about doing this. It was a trick she'd practised for years from feeling self-conscious at school about her pale skin. At dances she would spend a couple of minutes every half hour or so going through her pinching-biting ritual behind a cloakroom door. Why she hadn't gone for make-up with lipstick was a question she couldn't answer. It was like cheating somehow.

She opened the door. 'You're as white as a ghost,' said Jessica. 'Are you all right?' She walked past her into the hall.

'I'm fine,' said Fran. 'I've just woken up.'

'I can see that.' Jessica's shrewd look was not lost on her. 'Can I make some tea?'

'For yourself. I don't want any.' Jessica looked at her sharply. 'I had a cup earlier. Really.'

Fran had woken up before it was light to the realisation that nothing was working. Getting back to playing tennis. Going through the motions at the bookshop. Attending a political meeting. All these activities were just activities, nothing more. They held no meaning for her whatsoever and it was probably this realisation that had stopped her from getting out of bed. There didn't seem any point to it. She would just have to make the bed after all, put on clothes and dirty cups and plates in the kitchen. All of which were unnecessary actions when you thought about it logically. Far easier to stay in bed where she was going to end up anyway just a few hours later. So she had stayed where she was, drifting and dozing and waiting for the time to pass.

'Why don't you get dressed?' Jessica said. 'I'll clear up here and make a pot. You might feel like a cup once you've spruced a bit.'

There was no point in arguing with Jessica when it came down to it, Fran knew. If she did what she suggested perhaps she would go away sooner so that she could curl up under the duvet and have a rest. She knew what Jessica was up to. She wasn't a fool. Chivvy the bereaved friend out of her gloom with a bit of bright talk and encouragement. Well, she could play along.

By the time she had pulled on yesterday's jeans and sweater, all the curtains and windows in the house were open and a curl of steam was coming from the spout of the teapot on the table in the kitchen.

'That's better,' said Jessica when Fran came into the room in her slippers, still with hair uncombed. 'I bet you feel better now too.'

'I feel like shit,' said Fran. 'Jessie, promise me something: don't patronise me. Don't try to pretend everything's going to be OK and that I can snap out of this with a cup of tea and a change of clothes. If *we* can't be honest with each other, I ... Just let me wallow for a bit, will you?'

Jessica's smile slid from her mouth. 'You're right,' she said. 'I can't believe I'm doing this. I'm sorry, Franny. I won't try to jolly you. Permission to be depressed granted. But if it gets to be too long and you find yourself wallowing when you don't want to any more and you can't get out, promise me you'll let me throw you a rope or something?'

'OK,' said Fran. 'Just pour me some tea.'

It was a grey, overcast day again, with rain threatening. Jessica looked sceptically at the sky through the kitchen window, then at her watch. She rinsed their cups at the sink.

'Where are you off to?' asked Fran. 'Shopping?'

Jessica leaned against the sink and folded her arms. 'I'm going to see Tamzin,' she said steadily. 'You could come with me if you like.'

It was the wrong move. 'So that's it,' Fran said slowly. 'Nice try, Jess. Thanks, but no, thanks.' She picked Jessica's jacket off the back of a chair and held it out to her by the shoulders. 'You'd better be getting along then.'

Jessica turned to Fran in the hallway. 'Fran –' she began. Then they heard footsteps running heavily up the path and Fran froze. Her fingers clutched at each other instinctively and she stared at the door in fright as the doorbell pealed.

'Fran?'

'Oh, for fuck's sake,' said Jessica. 'Not him.'

But Fran had the door open already and Jim was inside, dripping and panting from his gallop in from the street. 'Morning all,' he said. 'Am I in time for tea?'

Jessica scowled, but Fran smiled up at Jim and said, 'Sure you are. Jess is just leaving.'

*

'Tamzin? Can we talk?'

Tamzin opened her front door to find Jessica standing on the porch. She was holding a small bunch of snowdrops wrapped in silver foil. 'I don't know how these things forced their way into our garden,' she said. 'I sure as hell didn't plant 'em.'

They sat at a kitchen table covered in thick pages of newspaper. Tamzin was busy painting foot-high plaster gnomes with poster paint. There were at least fifteen of them and they stood one behind the other like a queue of ghostly dwarves, waiting for the magic of the paintbrush to breathe life into them. It was raining softly outside and the slide in the playschool garden was slick with rain, the path across the grass a muddy stream.

'You disappeared yesterday,' said Jessica. 'From tennis.'

'I'm OK,' said Tamzin.

'Have you decided yet what you're going to do? About the baby?'

'I'm trying not to think about it.'

'OK.' Jessica waited a moment. 'I hate to break this to you,' she said, 'but it's not going to go away by itself. Like some psychosomatic pain.'

Tamzin looked at her mildly. She completed a sleeve with red paint. 'This is Dopey,' she said, as if introducing a friend Jessica had been lax about acknowledging. She smiled a pleased smile. 'They're supposed to be the seven dwarves, but we have a few extras on account of the numbers. So we've got three Sleepies, four Docs –'

'Tamzin.'

Tamzin put down her paintbrush. 'OK,' she said. 'I know you're trying to help. I'm just – confused, that's all. I told you it wasn't Ray's baby, didn't I? But if I told you whose baby it is –'

'You don't have to. I wasn't asking. But ... does the father know? Couldn't you work this out together somehow?'

'Tricky.' Tamzin sighed. She took a grey cloth and rubbed at a fleck of red on Dopey's cheek. Jessica could smell the turps on her fingers. 'I guess I do have to tell him but ... it's complicated.' She started on the gnome's pointed cap. Jessica watched her without concentration. 'Oh, you might as well know,' said

Tamzin finally. She wrote a name in red paint on the newspaper. Jessica stared at it.

'Oh, fuck,' she said. 'That *is* complicated.'

Tamzin started to paint careful blue and green stripes down Dopey's legs. Her mouth was open and she breathed carefully, like a child. 'It's not what you think, though,' she said. 'We're not involved or anything, not in that way anyway. This was ... an accident.'

'Some accident,' said Jessica.

Tamzin had a stripe of green paint across the bridge of her nose. 'Ray's new play opens next week,' she said. 'One of these Dopeys is his good luck present.'

Jessica wondered what was happening to everything. Not long ago she'd been chugging along with her uneventful life. And now she felt as if she was teetering on the edge of a patch of quicksand, watching helplessly as her dearest friends slipped out of sight, like the kid in *Lawrence of Arabia*.

'Shall I tell you what happened then?' said Tamzin.

'Only if you want to,' said Jessica feebly. Tamzin was going to anyway.

Tamzin began to talk and Jessica listened. Coffee grew cold in front of them and the sound of Boris's purring was the only other sound in the room. Finally, Tamzin stopped. She stroked the cat's fur. It was dry and crackled with static. Jessica was having a problem digesting the story. She took the practical route. 'Where was Ray when this happened?' she asked.

'On a modelling assignment in Mauritius. That Martini commercial? Then he went on to Hong Kong. There's no way it could be his baby, if that's what you're thinking. And Ray's too sharp not to work it out.'

'I can see that,' said Jessica. 'And I can also see why you're reluctant to tell the world about it.'

'Quite,' said Tamzin.

'So what *are* you going to do, Tam? Have an abortion?'

Tamzin shrugged. 'I don't know,' she said. She took the next dwarf firmly by the elbows and set him down inches from her nose. 'What do you think, Sneezy?' she said.

Nine

By Sunday morning the rain had stopped. The sky was a solid, flat blue and the sun would dry the moisture from the grass before noon.

Jessica was on the phone early. She wasn't about to give up on Fran, that was clear, and Fran was secretly relieved. She knew she had not behaved very well.

'Ben's invited some of his awful work friends for brunch. Could you bear to come over and help dilute them?'

'It's the march today. Laurike's commemorative do. And the service for the Boksburg boys,' said Fran. 'I thought I told you.' She had got out of bed quite easily today. Today had a purpose to it, a structure.

'Oh. Yes, you did.' Jessica sounded disappointed nevertheless. 'And it's Sophie's birthday. I am thoughtless, aren't I?'

'No. It's all right.'

'Fran?'

'What?'

'Are you ... well – are you sure you shouldn't be keeping more of a low profile right now?'

'I shouldn't think it would make much difference, to be honest. When your number's up – you know.'

Jessica wasn't sure that Fran in flippant mode wasn't more dangerous than Fran in morbid mode, and she said so. But she knew better now than to try to change her course. 'Well,' she conceded, 'just be careful.'

'I will.' Fran paused. 'You could come along if you could get away for an hour or two.'

Jessica hesitated. 'Naah. Better keep the peace around here,' she said.

Fran had planned to go to the service at the cathedral with Henry McBride and the usual convent contingent. At the last moment Jim had asked if he could tag along and Fran hadn't had a ready excuse. They had arranged to meet at the convent and leave their cars there. McBride would drive them into town in his old Austin Princess. They drove towards town in the early morning sunshine, the fistful of tall buildings that was the central business district a sharp contrast to the trees and parks of the suburbs. A light breeze ruffled the petals in Mbekhi's bunch of flowers as he sat beside the open window in the back of the car, squashed up beside Jim and Fran.

McBride hummed a snatch of Ravel's *Bolero*. He lifted both hands off the wheel the better to conduct. The backs of his hands were mottled as leaves. Sister Joseph glanced at him. She smiled nervously and felt for her rosary beads.

'Marvellous. Quite marvellous!'

'What's that, Father?'

'Those two youngsters. The ice-skaters we watched on the television last night – Torvill and Bean. Didn't you think so, Sister?'

'Oh. Oh, yes, indeed, Father. Mind the bicycle. Very graceful.'

'You should have seen them, Mbekhi,' McBride said enthusiastically. He turned right round to face the back where his passengers sat looking anxiously at the oncoming traffic. McBride's contempt for the laws of the road was well documented. Legend had it that in his younger, more bellicose days, he'd punched a traffic officer. He'd apparently stopped at the side of the road, so the story went, to open his door and release a trapped seat-belt. While he was bending down to wrestle with the belt, the officer, who had come up quietly behind him, had made the mistake of tapping him on the shoulder. McBride, who stood six foot in his socks and was hefty even then, had swung from the floor and knocked the man right out of his shoes. 'CLERIC KO'S COP' the papers read. He'd had to do some fast talking to get out of that one, and the Bishop had sent a stern reprimand.

'Ah, here we are,' he said now, swerving across two lanes and jolting them into the cathedral parking lot. 'Good and early.' There were a few cars there already, and the two hired buses, although they wouldn't be needed before ten. Their drivers were leaning against one of the vehicles in the sun, talking and eating white bread sandwiches. They tipped their caps to the priest as he strode past in his black cassock.

'It's going to get hot,' Sister Joseph said thoughtfully. 'Mbekhi, come with me. Let's see if we can find some buckets of water for people to put their flowers in. They'll wilt otherwise, during the service – the flowers, that is.'

Mbekhi, Fran and Jim followed her inside. Fran saw that Mbekhi had dressed carefully this morning in neatly pressed white jeans and shirt. Thabo had told her he'd helped clean Mbekhi's tackies, which he wore on bare feet. Mbekhi had seemed quiet and nervous in the car. The flowers were a bright, incongruous splash in the strong black hands which looked too heavy for his delicate wrists. He'd tied their stems with string. Sister Joseph had brought daffodils and they nestled beside McBride's freesias, tucked into her belt.

Fran stood in the sunshine, leaning against the door of the porch. Some more cars were arriving now. Gwen Sutherland from the Black Sash was in one of them. Resplendent in a busy floral print, she hurried into the side door of the cathedral with a brief wave of the hand to no one readily apparent. The bus drivers were studying a copy of the week's racing guide at Turffontein.

Soon the parking area was full and as cars began to line the streets outside, the cathedral bells rang out. It was a solemn, thrilling sound, rich with portent. Fran left Mbekhi sitting near the back of the church where he was keeping a space for his mother and Thabo beside him. They were coming in the convent's minibus, picking up other people on the way. People were streaming in. She recognised a number of faces, some who came regularly to meetings, some who were often in the news.

Many people still held their flowers, but others had made use of Sister Joseph's plastic buckets inside the porch. It was cool inside. The organ was playing now. Very slow, very dignified. Funereal, thought Fran grimly. She thought of Laurike, lying bleeding on her cell floor. She thought, inevitably, of Sophie, red faced and hiccuping, plucked from the warmth and safety of her womb five years ago today. She prodded Jim, extra fat today in his golfing trousers and sporting a bow tie, in front of her and they joined Laurike's parents up near the front. Oom Bram took her hand and held it to his cheek for a long moment.

By the time the service got underway, there was standing room only. With the first hymn, sung with fervour by almost a thousand voices, Mbekhi felt his arms prickle with gooseflesh. Thabo slipped a small hand into his. He smiled down at his brother, standing proudly beside him in a new pair of Grasshopper Loafers, and he felt a stab of affection go through him like a knife in his heart. He could hear his mother's voice, sweet and low, but her face was obscured by her wide-brimmed church hat.

The service was a subdued one. Even the bishop's sermon was devoid today of the emotional outbursts he was known for. When Patience Mkhize spoke everyone rose to their feet by silent accord, and when the names of the seven assassinated young activists were read out a woman near the front began to cry. Her sobs continued throughout the reading, like a desperate punctuation. Mbekhi shifted uncomfortably and strained to see who it was, but she was too far in front. He felt his own throat constrict.

There were a lot of press people there, foreign and local, and cameras flashing. And of course there were more than a few security police dotted among the congregation. They were never difficult to spot. Mbekhi identified one of them at the side entrance. He had an ECC pamphlet sticking from his jacket pocket and a floppy hat in camouflage colours. His eyes raked ceaselessly across the pews. There were other faces too, single men, whose presence jarred. Mbekhi looked hard at a swarthy man with hollow cheeks who was unobtrusively pushing his way towards the front. He looked familiar – probably a cop too. The notorious security police had officially been disbanded as a division some time ago, but nobody had felt this was cause for celebration. They had disbanded the CCB, too, hadn't they, Fran had said not long ago, and shortly thereafter three former Askaris had been shot in the neck just this side of the Swaziland border.

Mbekhi felt immensely proud of Father McBride, proud that he knew him, that he could call him a friend. He knew he was a man very much respected in older left-wing, liberal circles, although he was getting old now and preferred to stay out of the limelight. There was a time before his banning when he had travelled throughout the country and had appeared on countless platforms in support of the struggle. He had been in hospital with nervous exhaustion more than once as a result, and he suffered from high blood pressure. Mbekhi watched as the priests filed from the altar, McBride bringing up the rear. In profile his large stomach lifted the hem of his cassock, revealing open-toed brown sandals and mauve socks. Miriam saw them too and he caught her quick smile under the brim of her hat.

Outside in the morning sun, the parking lot was congested. People milled about, waiting for someone to direct them. The bus drivers were seated in their own cabs now, waiting. Their engines hummed. Bees buzzed about the buckets in the church porch as hands plucked out bunches of flowers. Water dripped on to the cool flagstones and the usually musty incense smell of the church was overpowered by the scent of spring.

'We could have hired another bus,' McBride remarked to Sister Joseph. 'Gwen Sutherland says we're a couple of hundred strong. Apparently there's a large welcome committee waiting for us at the township entrance.' He smiled wryly. 'Do you know – I don't see a single member of our parish here, Sister. Isn't that discouraging?'

'Good morning, Father,' a breathy voice said at his elbow.

Henry McBride turned. Virginia Stephens smiled toothily at him. She was dressed in an unbecoming dark green suit, too warm for the morning. The wisps of hair on her forehead were damp.

'Well, one member at least.' He smiled. 'Hello, Mrs Stephens. Good to see you.'

Mbekhi, Miriam and Thabo secured their seats in the second of the buses. There seemed to be some purposeful movement now and Mbekhi soon saw why. Mrs Sutherland, wearing a black sash over her dress, was shooing people in the direction of the buses. She swept them before her in wide arcs. She had them squashed three-up in the buses before excuses could reach their lips.

An urchin with a runny nose was selling posies at the entrance to the parking lot. Sister Joseph and Mbekhi watched him through the window. Sister Joseph observed how cunningly he had made each bunch from the plastic buckets into three smaller bunches in such a short space of time. 'Fifty cents a bunch!' he sang out. 'Fifty cents for the struggle!'

Finally they were off, lurching through the quiet downtown Johannesburg streets. On this Sunday morning there was little traffic. Even the terminus was quiet today and the usual fruit vendors and hawkers on the pavements were absent. As they neared their destination, the passengers fell silent and an atmosphere of apprehension prevailed. Although unremarked on, no one had failed to notice the procession of police vehicles which had passed them on the highway and had taken the turn-off up ahead. These days, though, it was the unmarked cars which were the more suspect at rallies such as this. The buses had thick wire grilles over their windows and the drivers' windscreens. They'd been into the townships before when things were hot. The driver of Mbekhi's bus looked unconcerned, however. He was whistling to himself, inaudibly above the noise of the engine. His cheeks puffed out and in again, out and in.

The road to the township, once off the highway, was badly tarred and barren of any vegetation. The sidewalks bore the imprint of the countless feet which daily walked to and from Alexandra. They were dust paths, strewn with stones and litter. Rusting cans and chip packets were everywhere. The streets were empty of people. It was like entering a ghost town. The only signs of life were the few nondescript dogs scrounging for scraps in the litter, their ribs sticking out like hoops. On each corner the buses passed stood an army vehicle, two wheels up on the pavement, two on the road. On an open patch of land they saw three yellow police vans, standing hood-to-hood. A group of policemen watched them silently as they passed. Mbekhi turned his head and saw one of them lift a two-way radio to his lips. Nobody in the bus spoke.

Finally they pulled on to a soccer field. It was bare earth, with a couple of crooked goalpost at either end. Here the ANC had erected a banner with the pictures and names of the dead activists written on it in large black letters. It was pulled taut on its string. On the other goalposts was a rather faded blown-up poster of Laurike Malan and an SACC flag. In contrast to the deserted streets around, a crowd of about a thousand people was gathered here on this open patch of ground, where a makeshift platform had been put up in the dust. The bishop was already there, standing on a platform in a group which, Mbekhi saw, included Father McBride.

Mbekhi also saw the hollow-cheeked man again, moving about, edging through the crowd. He felt an icy premonition break over him, like sweat down the back of his neck. He couldn't place the man, but he knew he was dangerous. Then he lost sight of him again, as his view was obscured by the throng. Mbekhi realised that he was holding too tightly on to his flowers. Their stems were hot in his hand. His eyes moved about nervously as the crowd swelled. The back of his neck prickled with sweat. There was a mood here that was as tangible as a smell. Although there were no police or army vehicles right here, there was a tense feeling of apprehension. No one had forgotten why they were here. There was a rumour that permission to hold this meeting had never been granted. Suddenly Mbekhi grew aware of the sound of engines revving. He looked behind him, in the direction they had come. Others were doing the same. The noise grew louder and somebody on the edge of the crowd gave a shout. Then a line of army vehicles rounded the corner and wheeled to a halt at the township entrance, effectively cutting the crowd on the field off from access to the streets beyond. The crowd murmured. Thabo pulled on Mbekhi's hand, craning to see, and Miriam moved closer to him. They seemed to be right in the middle and Mbekhi found it difficult to see over the heads and shoulders blocking his view. It was a mistake, he thought uneasily, for his mother to be here, and Thabo, although there were other children around. A small girl with no front teeth and a half-peeled orange was playing a peeping game with Thabo from behind her mother's skirt. The smell of the orange was sweet in the dusty air.

The assembly on the platform had thinned out now and Mbekhi could see the bishop, Patience Mkhize and Father McBride sitting on yellow plastic chairs facing out over the crowd. The bishop stood up and moved to the front of the platform. The microphone before him crackled and whined. 'One, two,' said the bishop. 'Testing, one, two,' and the crowd roared and clapped. Then he raised his arms and began the Lord's Prayer. 'Our Father, Who art in Heaven,' piped Thabo's clear voice down below Mbekhi's shoulder. The last 'Amen' had barely died away when a man with a loudhailer stepped down from one of the Casspirs and walked towards the platform. He climbed on to it with one step. He wore heavy brown boots and carried a rifle in one hand. The crowd shifted restlessly. It seemed to have swelled in numbers. Thabo tugged at Mbekhi's sleeve. 'What's going on?' he asked urgently.

'Ssh,' said Mbekhi. 'I can't see properly. Keep still.'

'THIS IS AN ILLEGAL GATHERING. I REPEAT, THIS IS AN ILLEGAL GATHERING. PERMISSION FOR THIS RALLY HAS BEEN WITHDRAWN.' The loudhailer crackled with static. A pair of hadedas flew overhead, calling out raucously. 'FOR YOUR OWN SAFETY I ASK YOU TO LEAVE THIS PLACE. YOU HAVE FIVE MINUTES TO DISPERSE AND RETURN TO YOUR HOMES. I REPEAT, PLEASE DISPERSE AND RETURN TO YOUR HOMES.'

The crowd rippled and swayed like a field of corn in a sudden wind. Father McBride got heavily up off his chair and spoke to the man with the loudhailer. His gestures were difficult to interpret, but the man seemed not to be listening to him. He continued to look out over the crowd, the loudhailer still raised. McBride was joined by the bishop and a white man Mbekhi did not recognise. There had been an escalation of violence in the township in the past few weeks in spite of a stringent curfew, and this was the third rally in as many weeks that had ended in disarray. The mood was very tense.

The man prepared to talk into the loudhailer once more, when a stone from the back of the crowd struck the metal with a loud ping. Thabo, who had found an empty milk crate somewhere and was standing on it, now level with Mbekhi's shoulder, giggled, but Mbekhi snatched him roughly off the crate into his arms and, pushing his mother in front of him, started moving to the edge of the crowd. 'There's going to be trouble, Ma,' he said, and before the words were even out of his mouth, stones began to rain down on the vehicles and the man and his loudhailer. There was clearly going to be no conciliation today. Mbekhi was squashed and buffeted in every direction as the solid mass of people began to surge forward. In every hand around him he suddenly saw a weapon – sticks, stones, broken bottles, pangas had appeared out of nowhere. He saw a man with a knife neatly slice through the strap of a woman's handbag and melt into the crowd.

Then he saw the man again. And he seemed to be moving directly to where he knew the Malans and Fran Phillips to be standing. They were quite close to him. Mbekhi gave a shout, saw the man turn to stare at him – and then the acrid smell of tear-gas was in the air and the crowd disintegrated.

Everyone was running and gasping, scrambling to get out of its choking reach. He heard the crackle of birdshot fire and heard cries and shouts of pain. Someone pushed between him and Miriam. 'Mbekhi!' He heard her frightened call. Her church hat had fallen to the ground and when he looked again, he couldn't see her. Thabo was crying into his shoulder, clinging like a monkey.

Just then he was aware of a swish of white skirts and a pair of strong, white hands with reddened knuckles plucking the boy from his arms. Sister Joseph cut a swathe through the sea of black faces like the parting of the waves. 'Excuse me. Excuse me,' he heard her say politely, like a patron at a cinema who had decided to leave before the end of the show. And then she, too, was gone, bearing his brother with her. The noise was deafening as the crowd split open and began to run in all directions. Mbekhi went stumbling this way and that, falling on the uneven ground. He lost any sense of direction. He ran over a banner and many discarded bunches of flowers. Then he felt a sharp, hot pain in his right shoulder and another on the back of his leg and he went somersaulting over and over. He lay where he had fallen, his cheek bleeding from the stones beneath his face. He was breathing hard, his heart pounding painfully in his chest. He felt a warm trickle of urine run down his leg.

'This one's shat himself,' he heard a voice say, and then someone was pulling him roughly to his feet. Mbekhi was conscious only of the burning pain in his shoulder and his leg, and of a feeling that he was going to vomit. He felt himself pulled along by his shirt collar on one side and prodded from behind at the same time. He turned his head once and looked into the eyes of the national serviceman whose shepherd's crook was a rifle butt. He was all of about seventeen years of age. He was sweating profusely and in his eyes was fear, such naked, painful fear that Mbekhi forgot for a moment his own terror and almost put out a hand to him. Then the boy kicked the back of his knee and Mbekhi's legs buckled. He felt himself lifted up and bundled into the back of a police van like a sack of potatoes. He struggled to his knees, collapsed and vomited into his cupped hands.

Fran held a scarf over her mouth. She was coughing and retching. Her chest was on fire. Her eyes itched and tears coursed down her face. The air was hazy with dust and brown uniforms as the last of the crowd disappeared. The platform had been overturned in an attempt to use it as a barricade and the plastic chairs were lying upside down on the stony ground. The microphone was a twisted piece of shiny metal, trampled quite flat. She could see the man who had given orders into the loudhailer standing smoking a cigarette beside one of the Casspirs. He had a gash above his eyebrow from a sharp stone or piece of broken bottle. Fran felt a helpless, futile rage flow through her like a wave. It rose and fell, leaving her empty of energy and emotion. She saw Henry McBride standing beside the bus, one foot on the bottom step. He caught her eye and lifted his shoulders in a gesture of comic despair. Then he beckoned her over and she went slowly to him, tripping over the rocks and rubble on the ground. She was surprised at how shaky her legs felt. One by one the vans drove off, kicking up more dust from their wheels. Black faces stared out as they passed. The army vehicles started their engines.

Only one bus remained and into it was packed a large portion of the crowd from the cathedral. The other driver had taken fright at the first sign of trouble and had left, his empty bus rattling almost unnoticed back the way it had come. The Malans had gone off with the bishop in his official car. Patience Mkhize was one of those arrested.

McBride helped Fran up the steps into the bus. Suddenly she put a hand to her mouth. 'Oh, Lord,' she said. 'Jim.' She climbed back down the steps and looked wildly about her. 'Jim!' she called. The driver started the engine and the bus shuddered and juddered into life. The patch of ground was all but empty now, strewn only with broken flowers and pamphlets. Someone had retrieved the banner and folded it up neatly. It was tucked into the luggage compartment of the bus next to the driver's Tupperware sandwich box. Fran felt exasperated and exhausted. She stepped back into the bus and her eyes searched the seats. Faces stared back at her impassively. Everyone appeared to be in a state of shock.

'Over here,' said a small voice suddenly from the rear of the bus. A hundred heads turned in slow motion. 'I think I'm stuck. Oh dear,' said the voice and a hundred pairs of eyes moved downwards. From the furthest corner of the bus, right at the back, an enormous bottom in flamboyant trousers protruded like a beach ball half buried in sand. A pair of legs scrabbled and scuffed and then, with an almost audible pop, out came Jim

Walton, ashen faced and dishevelled, his bow tie askew beneath one ear. It was the catalyst they needed and in a moment the bus was rocking with hysterical, derisive laughter as arms reached out, some rough, some more good-natured, to pull him to his feet. Fran, standing white-faced in the centre aisle, turned on her heel.

The bus swung its way bumpily off the clearing and back on to the road. Within minutes they were on the highway heading south and the passengers had fallen silent once more. McBride looked pensive sitting beside Fran. Of Sister Joseph, Miriam, Thabo and Mbekhi there was no sign. The bus driver began to whistle. He pushed his peak cap back on his head and his cheeks puffed in and out, out and in.

Back at the cathedral Fran and Jim waited beside McBride's car. Fran was furious. 'Well, frankly, Jim, I'm embarrassed,' she said. 'I'm embarrassed to know you. I'm embarrassed at the way you behaved today, and I'm embarrassed at your attitude to the whole fiasco. You treated it like a Sunday school outing and you don't give a damn about what's really going on in this country. People were hurt out there this morning. People got arrested. And you treat it as a joke.' She glanced sharply at his profile. His hang-dog demeanour seemed to irritate her further. 'Can't you look at me when I'm talking to you?' He said nothing but when he slowly turned and their eyes met, she felt a chill run up her spine. This time she had gone too far. Jim had dark brown eyes and what she saw in them at that moment was an expression so blank, so dead that it changed his face into the face of a stranger. Then he put out a podgy hand and patted her arm, leaving his fingers on her skin for just a second longer than felt comfortable.

'You're shaken up,' he said. 'I'm sorry. I did take it seriously. I was there, wasn't I? I just didn't expect violence. I'm not very good at violence.'

'So we noticed.' Why was she turning into such a bitch?

'I couldn't help it. It was the shock. My legs just had to get away.' He tried to smile and elicit a response from her, but Fran wasn't ready to be accommodating.

'You know what bugs me, Jim?' she said. 'You know what really gets to me?'

'What?' He looked sullenly at his feet, and then past her into the street.

'You're not *concerned*. It just doesn't touch you. You're just like the rest of them. When it comes down to it, you really couldn't care less. As whites, we have so many choices, so many opportunities. We always have had. Those people out there today –' She frowned, struggling for words. She looked both puzzled and angry. Her pale cheeks were flushed. Then she saw McBride approaching. 'Oh, forget it,' she said.

Jim heaved himself into the back seat of McBride's old car. 'Next time –' he began.

'No.' Fran shook her head vehemently, moving up next to the window. 'No next time, Jim,' she whispered fiercely. 'We don't need you.'

By nightfall there was still no sign of the Thekisos. Sister Joseph, too, was not back. McBride paced the floor in his apartment. He and Fran, who wouldn't go home till they got some news, made half a dozen phone calls, but they had been unsuccessful in tracing them. Gwen Sutherland had not been available either. They watched the news on TV but there was no more than a brief mention that an illegal gathering had been dispersed outside Alexandra township and a few arrests had been made. Three people had been slightly injured. Virginia Stephens' face swam briefly in and out of focus, holding a handkerchief to her head. 'Isn't that –?' said Fran. 'Yes,' said McBride. The rest of the news was unexceptional. Somebody had broken the record for the Woodstock beach to Robben Island swim. The Animal Welfare Society had rounded up a total of thirty-seven emaciated horses and donkeys in Soweto over the weekend and seventeen people had been butchered in ANC–Inkatha violence in Natal.

Fran brought McBride a mug of soup at nine o'clock and they sat together in his room, trying not to watch the clock or listen for the phone.

'It's Sunday night,' Fran said. 'It's difficult to get anything out of anybody on a Sunday night.'

'Yes, I know,' McBride sighed. He was pacing again, his pipe clamped between his teeth. Fran would never have put him down as a pacer.

'I suspect Sister Joseph can look after herself quite well actually.'

'I know. She's very capable.'

'The last I saw of her she had Thabo in her arms, Father.' Which was what was really bothering him.

McBride pulled the curtain aside and peered out. 'But where *are* they?' he said. 'I can't help it. I'm plain worried.'

'It's Mbekhi I'm more concerned about.' Fran looked speculative. 'I only hope he managed to get away and into the township. He'd be safe there.'

'I'll get on to old Sutherland first thing. The Sash are good at tracking people down. If he's been detained, they'll let us know.'

Fran knew immediately that someone had been – was in? – her house. There was no obvious sign at first, but as she stood in the hallway taking off her jacket she suddenly felt the hairs rise inexplicably on the back of her neck. She stood stock still with fear, one arm half in half out of a sleeve. She stood rigid on the carpet beneath the soft circle of light in the hall. The rest of the house was in total darkness. Her first coherent thought was to leave again, to run back out to her car and drive away as fast as she could. But she was too afraid to go either backwards or forwards. She looked for the telephone. It was gone.

Davy had once suggested that she carry a gun. She was often out late at night at meetings or other functions. She spent a lot of time in dubious neighbourhoods. 'Just in case,' he'd said, but it was a meaningless suggestion really. He had known she wouldn't have heard of it. 'What if Sophie got hold of it?' she'd said, and that had been that.

Oddly enough, as she stood straining her ears to any sounds in the dark house, she never thought she might actually have to defend herself from bodily assault. The threat which was so tangible was not a physical threat. It was a taut and menacing atmosphere, a presence with no substance.

She could hear nothing at all. Slowly she began to move, her shoes making no sound. She walked stealthily to the living-room door and turned on the light, sliding her finger round the door-frame and stabbing quickly at the switch. She was surprised to feel a moment's blinding anger, anger directed unerringly at Davy for allowing her to have to face this kind of situation alone. She looked around. The curtains were half drawn. She had not left them that way this morning. She certainly hadn't expected to be home after dark so there would have been no need. One of the curtains moved, billowing into the room with the night wind. She walked over to it and pulled it aside. The window was wide open. Point of entry, she thought matter-of-factly. She was sure now that whoever it was had gone. The house had not been ransacked in traditional fashion, but the signs were unmistakable nevertheless. There were no overturned tables and smashed pictures, no drawers emptied in heaps on the floor. But all the drawers in the desk were open and the cupboard doors in the wall unit were open too, just left standing carelessly ajar. Some books had been pulled from the bookcase, though, and they lay on the floor where they had fallen. Sophie's plastic container of felt-tip coloured pens was lying on the coffee table and it was these which had been used to write, quite neatly, the message on the white living-room wall. *Waar's die dagboek? Ons gaan die dagboek kry.* Where's the diary? We're going to get the diary.

'Oh, honestly,' Fran said aloud. She didn't even have the bloody diary. And if she did have it, she wouldn't be so damn stupid as to keep it in her desk. All the same she was shivering. She wished someone would hurry up and tell her what to do. She stooped to pick up a book and smooth back a bent cover. Then she went through the house, putting on lights. The other rooms had been disturbed too. Her wardrobe was open; so was Sophie's toy cupboard – although they would have tried to shut that again pretty quickly once they saw the threatening avalanche of soft toys that lived up there. Jumped by a zoo of stuffed giraffes – it wouldn't look good on their report.

The kitchen was the worst hit. The fridge was open. A bottle of milk had tipped over and run out all over the floor. All the fruit in the fruit bowl was gone, as was all the meat in her deep freeze. Opportunistic seekers of stolen property. As she made for the scullery and a bucket and mop, Fran was brought up short by a sharp, unpleasant smell. Looking down she saw the scullery floor was smeared with shit. She took a step back. Human faeces on the tiles and, by the looks of it, spread along the scullery walls. She stumbled, gagging, to the bathroom and began to rip off her clothes. There was shit on her shoes. She turned on the hot water in the shower. She felt filthy, contaminated. Bundling up her skirt and sweater she picked up the lid of the laundry basket, recoiling suddenly at an unfamiliar black object crouched at the bottom. It was the telephone.

With hair still dripping and shivering in a tracksuit and three jerseys, she dialled the number of the convent. The phone was snatched up right away as she knew it would be.

'Father? It's Fran.'

'What's wrong, child?'

'Father – something ... someone ... Can I come back to the convent? I can't stay here ... I can't –' She began to sob, rocking back and forth on her haunches. She clutched the telephone tightly.

'Are you able to drive, child?'

Fran stared at herself in the hall mirror and the sight of her blank, strange face jolted her into some sort of control. 'Yes,' she whispered. 'I think I can drive.'

'Then come,' said McBride. 'Then come right away.'

The priest had a mug of Horlicks and a sleeping tablet ready as soon as she arrived. He had prepared a bed for her in the small guest room alongside his own. He asked no questions, only held her in his arms. Explanations could wait for the morning. It was late and Fran could only mutter incoherently as her teeth chattered against the ceramic mug. She took the tablet without protest and fell, exhausted, into immediate sleep.

Next morning McBride was awoken by the sound of a car revving noisily outside the convent gates. He had not slept particularly well and he was up and at the window in a matter of moments. Breathing a prayer of thanks while his fingers fumbled with the straps of his sandals, he hurried to get down the stairs to open the door. He held out his arms and Thabo threw himself into them. McBride held him out at arm's length and considered his crumpled clothes and scratched knees. The child's eyes were bright and excited. He was bursting with importance. Over his head he could see Miriam standing by the door. She was wearing a borrowed coat and looked a little strained. Sister Joseph took McBride's hands in hers. Her palms were cool as paper. She looked refreshed and rosy cheeked, like someone just returned from a fortnight's holiday at the coast.

'Well,' McBride said gruffly. 'We are most grateful to see you home, safe and sound. But where did you spend the night? Wherever it was it seems to have agreed with you, Sister.'

Sister Joseph lowered her eyes demurely. 'In a shebeen, Father,' she said. 'They were most hospitable.'

'The rally was a fiasco,' said Fran.

Jessica cupped a hand under a teabag and carried it to the sink.

'What happened exactly? It turned nasty, I heard. You didn't get hurt, did you? And the Malans? They must have been disappointed. It was their day, in a way, wasn't it?'

'Yes, well. But we were all fine. It could have been worse actually, but it wasn't a particularly big crowd, and the trouble came from outside not in. The stupid thing was, it was disorganised as usual. It seems nobody had confirmed whether permission had been granted or not. It appeared not.'

'So what happened?'

'We hadn't even got under way properly before the army appeared and took over. We didn't even get close to the Centre. A real pathetic effort.'

'And how did the human blimp take to his first exposure to protest politics?'

'Oh, God,' said Fran. 'Jim dived for cover under a seat at the back of the bus as soon as the army pitched. He stayed there, like Winnie the Pooh stuck in Rabbit's doorway throughout –'

Jessica was convulsed. 'Why, oh *why* do you put up with him?' she gasped.

Fran smiled reluctantly. 'Oh, habit, I suppose,' she said. 'You know – he's just there. He's always there.'

'The guy's not *all* there, if you ask me,' said Jessica. 'Seriously, Fran. I can't put my finger on it, but there's something odd about him. Not just the way he moons over you. Something else. Something sinister. Maybe he's CCB?'

'No.' Fran dismissed the idea. Privately she didn't think Jim was bright enough for subterfuge of that sort. She changed the subject.

'I'm going to be out of town for a few days. I'm going up to Gabs to see Mary.' She looked forlornly at Jessica and gestured at the kitchen. 'I have to get away from here.'

Jessica nodded. 'It will do you good,' she said.

They had spent the best part of the day cleaning up the house. Fran had woken at the convent feeling 'bloodied and bowed', she told McBride and Sister Joseph over breakfast. On his insistence she had called Jessica who had come over at once with the boot of her car full of a motley variety of cleaning utensils and an extra pair of rubber gloves. It had taken the horror out of going back inside the house, Jessica saying without a trace of irony – 'Look, I'm good at shit. I've had years of practice.' She had taken on the kitchen single-handed, not allowing Fran inside the door until it was finished.

All Fran was allowed was to listen to the running commentary as she cleared up the rest of the house.

'Jesus Christ, Franny. Great house guests! Couldn't you tell them where the bathroom was?' And 'Where's the Kleen Green anyway? No one who lives with obscene graffiti on their walls should ever be without it.'

Fran was smiling by the time they sat down to their tea. She wondered how she would ever get through anything significant in her life without Jessica. Not once so far had Jessica pressed her for her theory of what exactly was going on. Her only muttered comment had been 'And my mother always told me keeping a diary was a sensible thing to do.'

As she was gathering her things she turned to Fran and said, 'Where is it anyway? In a flowerpot?'

'It's not here,' Fran replied, exasperated. 'I've never laid eyes on the fucking diary.'

'Oh,' said Jessica. 'But the diary does exist?'

Fran sighed. 'Yes, it exists,' she said. 'I'm going to fetch it.'

Jessica frowned. 'I know every time I make a suggestion I see as important, you throw it out of court,' she said. 'But I think you should reconsider reporting this –' she waved her arms at the kitchen walls '– to the police.'

Fran shook her head. 'No,' she said. 'It wouldn't be any use, Jess.'

'You've been *threatened*, Fran, for Christ's sake. They could protect you. It's their *duty* to protect you.'

'The diary belongs to a cop,' Fran pointed out patiently.

Fran walked Jessica to the front door. They hesitated, then hugged each other closely, something thcy had never been prone to in the past, such displays of affection. Today they both felt better for it.

Ten

Jessica had a lot on her mind. There was Fran, especially, who needed her more than she was prepared to show. And there was Tamzin, into whose confidence she had reluctantly allowed herself to be taken and of whose secret she was now the uncomfortable custodian. Jessica had learnt over the years the importance of her friends, her network of support that never failed her. Once, when she was about sixteen, her mother, in a moment of unasked for advice, had said to her: never neglect your friends or exclude them; you will need them when you are married. Jessica knew, of course, that that was precisely when you no longer needed them and her mother, as usual, had got it all cocked up. She was into a hot romance at the time with an Older Man. Ashley was nineteen and had a car and a job (assistant pastry chef at a four-star hotel). Jessica had found true love and nothing else mattered. For a whole summer they were inseparable and she had hardly seen her friends at all. Then Ashley had got his call-up papers for the army and had gone off to bake chocolate éclairs in the Angolan bush, where the army canteen took a direct hit the day before Christmas. That was when Jessica had begun to understand about friends, but it wasn't until she was married to Ben that her mother's advice had sunk in.

Today she felt heavily burdened with Tamzin's problems. She also felt weak and faintly dizzy. Stress. Too much stress was getting to her. After breakfast she got Luke Stephens' receptionist on the telephone.

'Oh yes, Mrs Tucker,' she said. 'Doctor wants a word with you.'

'Oh?' said Jessica cagily. 'What about?'

The woman wasn't someone who would divulge confidential information under any circumstances. 'Perhaps you would like to ask him yourself,' she said.

When Luke came on the line Jessica thought she'd better get in first. 'I feel rotten,' she said. 'And I think I fainted on Friday.'

'And I thought you were just calling for your blood test results,' said Luke.

'I was only out for a couple of minutes,' said Jessica. 'And there was the weekend in between. And I've been busy,' she added. 'Fran's had some problems.' She thought she could hear him scribbling on a pad.

'Can you come in today?' Luke asked.

Jessica hesitated. 'I guess so,' she said reluctantly. 'Right now?'

'If it's convenient. We need to have another chat.'

'That bad, huh?' Jessica laughed, a little shakily. She really didn't feel well and Luke's serious tone was making her nervous. 'All right. I'll come in.'

Although the waiting room was full when she got there, Jessica was shown straight through by Luke's receptionist, who clearly didn't approve of queue jumping. Jessica closed the door behind her and looked at Luke. He was sitting where she'd last left him, as if he hadn't moved in the interim. His fingers were steepled beneath his chin and he looked at her, almost through her, for a second or two, without speaking. She waited, nervous again.

'I brought your handkerchief back,' she said finally. 'At least, it's not the original. Yours got used as a bandage for a doll with gangrene, I'm afraid. I hope you don't mind.' She stopped, out of breath, as if she'd just run up a flight of stairs. Luke laughed. It deepened the lines at the corners of his eyes.

When she thought about it afterwards, that was probably the moment – if there ever really is A Moment – that Jessica knew for certain. This man, she thought, as she stood leaning against the closed door, was going to be important in her life. It was a feeling so strong, so sure, that it was as if they had decided upon it together, right there and then, as if the words had been spoken out loud.

Luke broke the spell by gesturing to the empty chair. Jessica sat down. She put the folded square of handkerchief on his desk, lining it up with a pair of plastic Fallopian tubes doubling as a paperweight. There was a framed photo on his desk, half turned towards her, of a child with long, blonde hair. She was staring straight at the camera, her mouth set in a hard, ungiving line.

'I want to examine you again, if I may,' Luke began. 'I'm afraid you may even be pregnant after all.'

'Oh God,' said Jessica.

'But first I'd like to run some more tests – not here. At the William Ford.'

Jessica looked confused. 'Pregnancy tests? I thought – why the Ford?' She pulled her jacket across her chest. 'Is ... is there something wrong with me?'

Luke hesitated just long enough to make Jessica's eyes widen.

'Possibly,' he said.

'Oh,' said Jessica. She looked scared.

'How are you placed this week?' Luke asked.

Jessica shrugged. It was a brave, helpless gesture. 'I'm easy, I suppose. What do you want me to do?'

'I'd like to check you into the Ford for a couple of days. In fact, I took the liberty of reserving a bed for you tomorrow evening – ?'

'Now you're frightening me,' said Jessica. 'And you might as well know I don't like hospitals.'

Under the fluorescent light her skin had turned sallow and the violet eyes were huge and almost black. Luke thought about a reassuring, professional smile but changed his mind. He sensed in Jessica someone who wouldn't be patronised or fooled.

'So tell me,' she said.

'Shall I be frank?' he asked.

'Brutally,' said Jessica.

*

'I'm sorry ... Cassandra. I hope it's all right. You weren't here, so I asked Selena if I could make a call ... '

'Of course. No problem.' Cassandra stood in the doorway to the study. She held her keys in her hand. The children were in the kitchen, demanding juice. She came further into the room. Joel, standing by the telephone with his hand still on the receiver, seemed to fill the small room by his sheer physical presence. His body from the waist up was bare and brown and gleaming with sweat. A red and white sweatband was tied round his head, bandanna style. Cassandra fancied she could smell him from where she stood. She tried to put disapproval in her voice. 'Use the phone any time,' she said coolly. 'It's quite all right.'

Joel made no move to leave. Instead, he lowered his eyes and said, 'It's my mother actually. She's not been terribly well. I like to check on her when I can.'

Immediately Cassandra felt sorry and unkind. 'Mummy, will you do puzzles with us?' Rosalie came into the study, carrying a glass of orange juice in an unsteady hand. Some of the liquid slopped on to the Persian rug. She glanced at Joel, then ignored him. She was a South African child, used to the presence of servants and workmen. She picked up nothing of the atmosphere, nothing outwardly at least, but she moved closer to her mother, and plucked at her sleeve.

'Don't,' said Cassandra, disengaging her fingers. Then she said, her eyes on the painter, who had not moved away from the desk, 'You can't do puzzles now. Ansie's picking you up in twenty minutes for ballet. And Jason's got karate.'

Joel looked steadily back at Cassandra. 'Go and get ready, Rosalie,' she said.

Not taking his eyes off her face, Joel walked across to where Cassandra stood. He stopped an arm's length away. He raised a hand to her face and she flinched. 'Eyelash on your cheek,' he said softly. 'There. It's gone now.'

When Cassandra saw the children off on their various pursuits Joel was nowhere to be seen. She slipped on a bathing costume and dived into the pool, then lay sunning herself like a lizard on the hot paving slabs until she felt dizzy with heat and had to go inside.

She didn't hear Joel come into the room. He might have been standing in the doorway for some time for all she knew. His discreet tapping against the door frame made her turn from the window where she had been looking out towards the purple Magaliesberg mountains in the distance, letting the breeze cool her off. Joel didn't speak. He just stood there, looking across at her with a curious expression in his dark eyes. Cassandra wished she had put a shirt over her costume, or at least a towel around her waist.

'Joel,' she said. 'How can I help you? Do you need to use the telephone again?'

'No,' he said. 'Thank you.'

'Well,' said Cassandra. She knew she had asked for this, but suddenly she wasn't at all sure she could go through with it. Joel walked over to the window. 'What are you looking at?' he asked.

'Oh, nothing really.' Cassandra felt disconcerted. 'Just the mountains. I love the view from up here. We're right on the ridge, you know.' Joel took her hands, in a perfectly natural gesture, and he held them lightly, casually. Cassandra stared into his eyes in fright. Was this actually what she wanted? Up close, Joel's eyes were very black.

'Mrs Symons,' he said. He put both unresisting hands to his lips, brushing lightly across the knuckles with his teeth. Cassandra felt weak, like a Danielle Steele heroine in her seventeenth reincarnation. In a moment he was going to say Run away with me forever. Cassandra wasn't the sole member of her book club for nothing.

'You know I'm attracted to you,' said Joel. His eyes were mischievous. 'And I know you're attracted to me.' He bit softly on her knuckles.

Cassandra felt she might faint. Or swoon. Georgette Heyer, rather. 'So where does that leave us?' she said weakly.

Innocent eyes. Innocent face of a boy. Joel grinned. 'So let's fuck,' he said.

Cassandra half wanted to laugh. At the same time her body was doing the strangest things. It was responding to this schoolboy's touch as it had never done to anyone else's, Mike's included. Mike, she discovered, was the last thing on her mind. Alarmed and exhilarated, Cassandra watched herself being led to the bed like a lamb to the slaughter.

They had showered together afterwards, and made love again right there, with the warm water sliding down their faces, making them choke and gasp. It was only when Joel used Mike's monogrammed towel and pulled a face at his Soap on a Rope that Cassandra had felt a small pang of remorse, but all in all she was surprised at how little guilt she felt. What she did feel was lighter, younger, and quite drunk on sex, as she had never felt before in her life.

Jessica felt the car go. It swung violently to one side, almost pulling the wheel out of her hands. She swerved and felt the thud and jerk of the kerbside hitting her front wheel. Her temple connected painfully with the glass of the window. 'Jesus God,' she said. 'What was *that*?'

She was on her way to fetch the children from Tamzin's, where they'd spent the afternoon. Perhaps fortunately today, she'd taken a short cut through the back roads and she now found herself half-way up the pavement outside the Rosepark Catholic Church. Closer inspection revealed a messily burst front tyre. Bits of hot rubber flapped on the tarmac.

Jessica cursed again. How to change a tyre was something she'd always meant to learn but had never got round to doing. She even had a book somewhere. She wasn't even sure that she had a spare, or whether it was a good one or not. She was in a quiet residential road. There was no one in sight except a uniformed domestic catching the last of the afternoon sun on the pavement opposite. She stared at Jessica impassively.

Jessica looked about her in exasperation. Then she opened the boot and lifted the cover off the spare wheel compartment. At least it was there. As she made to lift it out a wave of nausea made her close her eyes and rock back on her heels. She put out a hand to steady the swimming road. She felt perspiration break out on her forehead.

'You make a habit of this sort of thing?'

Jessica looked up. She recognised the painter with the dark eyes.

'I didn't hear you pull up,' she said. 'But I think I'm glad you did.'

Joel put his head on one side, taking in the ruined tyre, the car only centimetres from a telephone pole. He whistled through his teeth. 'Looks like it's your lucky day,' he said.

'Oh, yeah,' said Jessica. 'Tell me about it.'

'I'll give you a hand with that tyre. Petrus, the lady needs our help.' He parked the van in front of her, then came back and jerked the spare out of its nest. 'Tools?' He looked at her. 'Hey, are you all right? You're not, are you? Come and sit over here. Put your head between your knees.'

'I suppose it's shock,' said Jessica. 'I feel terribly feeble. You must think –'

'You do the thinking. I'll change the wheel.' His grin was certainly charming, infectious, and Jessica couldn't help smiling back at him as the dizziness faded.

'So,' said Joel conversationally, 'been playing any tennis lately?'

'No, I … I think I've got cancer actually.' Jessica was apologetic.

'And the fainting spells? They're a symptom?'

'Apparently. And the nausea and –'

'You really shouldn't be driving a car, should you? If you're liable to black out, I mean? Are you having treatment? Chemo?'

Jessica stared at his back as he tightened the bolts with his spanner. He had a strong, muscular build, if a little on the stocky side. Cocky, but undoubtedly an attractive kid, even if the smile was a touch too winning, too practised.

'I don't mean to be rude,' she said, 'but would a housepainter be as medically clued up as you appear to be?'

The smile again. And a cosy crinkling of the eyes. 'Make that "temporary housepainter",' he said. 'I'm aiming to put myself through med school on the proceeds.' The wheel was done. Joel took a handkerchief from his pocket and wiped his hands. He helped Jessica to her feet. Now his eyes were all concern. 'I'm sorry,' he said. 'I hope … I hope … '

'That I don't croak?' Jessica helped him out. 'Me too. Thanks for the help. I do appreciate it.'

After the van had disappeared round the corner, Jessica sat for a moment in the driver's seat, massaging the bump on the side of her head. Then, on impulse, she got out of the car again and walked up the path to the church door. Inside filtered sunlight through stained glass brought a soft glow to the light oak of the pews. A few candles in a heavily ornate wrought-iron stand before a small side altar flickered brightly. Jessica walked up the aisle and paused awkwardly at the front pew. She hadn't been a regular church-goer really, since her father'd died, and she felt an impostor now, seeking solace only when she was in trouble.

She cleared her throat and looked round nervously at the sound, as if it had come from someone else.

'Hey, listen … er … Lord,' she began out loud, then quickly lowered her voice. 'Between you and me, I have to say I think this is a lousy hand someone's dealt me. Nothing personal and I'm not pointing any fingers, but – hell. Dying isn't something I'd planned on just yet.'

Henry McBride had heard some pretty strange things in the confessional in his time, but sitting in the shadow of a pillar opposite to where Jessica Tucker was now standing, he found himself an unwilling but fascinated eavesdropper to the oddest whispered conversation. At first he thought there might be two people out there, meeting clandestinely, but a discreet peep revealed only Jessica, standing dead centre in the aisle like a soldier at attention. Her gaze was fixed about midway between the altar rail and Christ on the Cross. Her whole posture was rigid with tension. Her hands were clenched tight. He hesitated, wondering whether to reveal himself, she was so clearly in trouble. Then the voice ceased abruptly and when he allowed himself another peep, he saw Jessica at the candle stand. He watched as she pushed a ten-rand note into the St Vincent de Paul slot. A new box of small white candles was balanced on the altar rail against the wall. There were thirty-five to a box, he knew; he'd put that one out just this morning. He watched, intrigued, as Jessica took up one candle after another and lit it. She fixed each one on to its little iron spike, until the four-tier stand was ablaze with light. He could feel the heat from where he sat. Her face was orange from the glow. Then she smiled and he thought it was the saddest smile he'd ever seen.

McBride half expected Jessica to blow the candles out from the deep breaths he saw her taking. She seemed to be battling for control. Instead she said 'Cheers' very gruffly in the general direction of the altar and padded down the aisle on the balls of her feet.

Eleven

Jessica and Ben sat facing each other in the sitting room. Ben's tie was askew and his hair rumpled, as if he'd run exasperated hands through it until it stood up every which way on his head. His eyes were bloodshot.

'I'm not drunk,' he said. Opening round.

'I didn't say –'

'Well. In case you were going to. I'm not. Just had a couple of ales on the way to the hospital. Sorry I was late.'

'It doesn't matter.'

'So.' Ben stood up, a little too quickly. He had to regain his balance by holding on to the back of the chair. 'I've got a thirst on me. One quick Castle before bed. Can I get you anything?'

'Coffee,' said Jessica, although she didn't really want any. But it was something Ben could make, quite easily too.

Ben went into the kitchen and came back with a can of beer. He held it in his right hand and pulled back the ring with his forefinger. White foam shot out and he put his lips over it, swearing. 'So,' he said again, sitting in his chair with matching footstool. ('For gout,' had been Jessica's answer to Fran's pointed look when she'd bought it for his birthday. 'Believe me, he's working on it.') 'How d'you feel?'

'Bleak.' She did too.

Ben leaned forward. 'Listen, old thing,' he said 'you're going to be all right. I know it. Everything's going to be fine.'

Jessica looked away. Her suitcase was still standing in the hallway. She could see a cloud of midges hanging over the fruit bowl on the dining-room table, and she caught the soft reek of rotting apples.

'Tamzin's been calling,' Ben said.

'Did you tell her?' Jessica knew he hadn't.

'Tell her what?'

'What do you think, Ben? That I've got cancer.'

Ben shifted uneasily. He couldn't meet her eyes. 'We ... we don't know that for sure yet,' he said. 'No point going round upsetting people.'

'So you didn't say anything?'

'Just that you were having some tests done.'

Jessica felt something like anger begin to shoot in quick spurts along her veins. 'It's nothing to be ashamed of, Ben,' she said. 'Lots of people have cancer. It's not a dirty word. Try saying it. Cancer. See? I can do it.'

'Jessica –' Ben looked crumpled.

'Oh, I'm sorry.' Jessica suddenly felt very tired. 'I'm going to bed. Forget the coffee.' She got slowly to her feet and went to pick up her bag. On her way down the passage she heard Ben get up and go into the kitchen again. She heard him open the fridge and heard the pop of another can opening. Then the muffled music of the television. Jessica went into the children's rooms. She looked down at the sleeping bodies as if seeing them for the first time. She tried to imagine her children growing up without her. It was unthinkable.

She lay in the bath looking at her body beneath the water. She thought of the cancer cells, parasitic, growing and feeding on her, spreading while she slept, like the fungus on a tree, sapping the life from her. As she dried her thick, dark hair she examined her face in the mirror, looking hard for any signs of change. In the gentle light of the lamp her skin looked golden and unlined. It was a young, vulnerable face, but Jessica was not fooled. She turned the lamp directly on to her skin and noticed, for the first time, the quite definitely demarcated lines along the corners of her mouth. And bad crows' feet beneath the eyes. Carrion crow.

In her dressing gown, she went down the passage again. Ben was watching a boxing match, sitting forward on the edge of his chair. One of the boxers had blood trickling down his chin.

'Ben,' she said. 'Dr Stephens has asked that we meet him in his rooms tomorrow. He wants to see you. To talk about my treatment.' She paused. 'He waited for you this evening.'

'I'm sorry. I said I was sorry. It could be tricky for me tomorrow, Jess. I've got a meeting at the office.'

'It's Saturday tomorrow.' Jessica tried to keep control of her voice.

'I know that. But we're having some contractual problems with the Vereeniging plant and there's an urgent meeting tomorrow with the lawyers.' Ben's eyes flicked back to the screen. A boxer was down.

'Jesus God, Ben,' said Jessica. 'I've got *cancer*.'

'Jessica, I –'

'Don't you think I need a little support right now? From my *husband*?'

'Mummy?' said a voice from behind her. 'What's cancer?'

'Oh, Glenda,' Jessica breathed. 'What are you doing out of bed?'

Glenda came uncertainly into the room and Jessica went down on one knee and took her into her arms. 'Go back to bed now, sweetheart. I'll tell you in the morning. I'll tell you all about the hospital, I promise.'

When she'd gone, Ben got clumsily to his feet and came and put his arms round Jessica. She allowed him to pat her back, to kiss her ear. For once she didn't recoil from his breath, almost finding comfort in the strong smell of alcohol. 'I'm sorry,' he said. 'I'm sorry. I'll be there, Jessie, don't worry. We'll get through this thing together, you'll see. You'll be right as rain in no time.'

Jessica allowed Ben to take her to bed, to tuck her in and smooth the hair from her forehead. Soon she pretended to be asleep. As she lay in the darkness she thought of Luke, who had sat patiently with her in the clinic lobby, waiting for Ben to come and pick her up. They'd sat very close, like old lovers, without talking. Her eyes had moved restlessly to the clock as first five o'clock and then six came and went. Finally, Luke couldn't wait any longer. He'd taken her hand in both of his. It was a natural, supportive gesture, full of warmth. It was what had got her through the next half hour that she waited until Ben had pushed through the swing doors with the harrowed look of a man under pressure.

Jessica woke up with a headache and gritty eyeballs. She desperately needed to talk to Fran. She dialled her number but got no reply. Then she remembered Fran was in Botswana, visiting Mary. She could smell toast burning. Ben was giving the children breakfast in the kitchen.

And then suddenly Tamzin was there, hidden behind armfuls of flowers. She swept into the room with dogs and children in tow, just as Jessica was pulling on her jeans.

'You're up.' She looked crestfallen. 'How can I play the ministering angel when you won't lie down and look poorly?'

'Are those for me?' said Jessica. 'They're dripping all down your skirt.'

The children took the flowers to the kitchen. When they were gone, Jessica pulled Tamzin down beside her on the bed. 'It's good to see you,' she said. 'Thanks for the flowers.'

'Jess.' Tamzin lowered her voice. She was given to the dramatic. 'Are you ill? I mean, really ill?'

Jessica lowered hers. 'You mean – as in terminal?' she said.

'Stop taking the piss. I'm serious. Ben wouldn't tell me anything.'

'Oh, Ben. Well. Since you ask, yes, it would appear that I have a fairly rare form of cancer.'

'Oh, Jess,' said Tamzin. 'Are they sure?'

'Pretty well. But, Tammy, there's worse.' She looked towards the door, but all was quiet. It was Jessica's turn now.

'Worse? You mean there's more?' Tamzin was shocked.

Jessica glanced at the door again. She smiled nervously. 'I know this sounds ridiculous,' she said, 'but please don't laugh. I'm in love with Luke Stephens. Desperately.'

At ten o'clock Jessica and Ben were in Luke's consulting rooms. He'd got there before them and was waiting in his office. He was dressed casually, in sweatshirt and jeans. He gestured to the chairs and they sat down. Ben reached over for Jessica's hand. She felt embarrassed. Ben smiled broadly, settling back into his chair. He was ready for a talk, man to man. Jessica thought he would have been more comfortable if she hadn't been there at all; they could have cleared this messy business up between them in no time.

'So,' said Ben. 'Let's have it, Doc.'

Jessica winced. Luke looked at her, then steepled his fingers beneath his chin, a gesture with which she was becoming familiar.

'What we are dealing with,' said Luke, looking directly at Ben, 'is a disease known as GTD – gestational trophoblastic disease. GTD covers a whole spectrum of variations, but what we have to treat Jessica for is a fairly rare type of carcinoma, called choriocarcinoma, and –'

'Whoa.' Ben held up his hand. 'You're losing me, Doc. Can we dispense with the technical terms and explain in words of one syllable?'

'I'm sorry,' said Luke. 'I'll do my best.'

Jessica took her hand away from Ben's clammy hold. She felt sorry for him. He was not taking this very well. He was battling to keep the conversation on a jokey level.

'There are a couple of theories,' Luke continued. 'Early symptoms of the condition are often typical of those of early pregnancy: nausea, missed periods, sometimes a small amount of vaginal bleeding. Jessica has also felt faint, actually blacked out –' Ben turned his head and stared at her – 'together with a persistent chest cold and painful cough. These are all tell-tale signs.'

'Do you mind if I –' Ben took a packet of cigarettes from his pocket and lit up before Luke could respond. He reached behind him to the window-sill and passed Ben a coffin-shaped ashtray. Ben didn't seem to notice the death's head design but Luke and Jessica exchanged a smile. 'Sorry, Doc,' said Ben. 'Go on.'

'Well, one of the causes that has been suggested is that of a defective or blighted ovum. Early on in a pregnancy, where this is the case, the embryo aborts or becomes blighted. What can happen in GTD is, after fertilisation, the placenta develops into what is known as a hydatiform mole and – as has happened in Jessica's case – it may become invasive and perforate or penetrate the uterus. Choriocarcinoma is the malignant form of GTD and, as I said, it is still quite rare. But, I'm afraid, it is also serious and must be treated swiftly and sometimes drastically.'

Jessica had had this conversation with Luke the day before. He'd sat on the foot of her bed and taken her through it step by painful step. Downstairs someone was mowing the lawn and the drone of the mower and the sweet smell of freshly cut grass came through the window as if it were a day like any other.

Ben mashed his cigarette out in the coffin. He was pale, less on top of things. 'The treatment,' he asked. 'Can it be treated effectively, this type of ... of ...'

'Cancer,' said Jessica.

Luke looked at her. 'We're very hopeful,' he said. 'Fortunately, we've diagnosed it early. But the first step, I'm afraid, is surgery. The disease has become invasive and a full hysterectomy is recommended.'

Jessica felt her chest constrict again at the words. She'd seen two women who'd had hysterectomies when she'd been in the nursing home having Edwina. They walked around bent double, with grey, defeated faces.

'If arrangements can be made as quickly as possible,' Luke said, 'I'd like to operate next week.'

Ben reached over for Jessica's hand again; he appeared to need her support. 'And after that?' he asked.

'We'll need to do regular tests for some time – blood, urine, chest and so on. And a course of chemotherapy.'

Jessica felt superfluous. She'd sat passively throughout Luke's patient explanation, conscious only of Ben's discomfort. Whenever Luke's eyes flickered over to hers, she imagined there was something there which probably wasn't. She felt stupid: everyone fell in love with their gynaecologists, didn't they? Tamzin said she'd been in love with Luke for years. She'd laughed with relief at Jessica's sombre confession. Luke Stephens was a marvellous, compassionate, attractive man. Naturally Jessica thought she was in love with him. Everyone did.

No, thought Jessica now, as they stood up to leave and Luke shook Ben by the hand. This was different.

She and Ben sat in the car together for a few minutes without speaking. Ben looked stricken, as if it were he who'd just been given the death sentence. Jessica knew she ought to have some words of comfort for him. She leaned over and kissed him on the cheek. 'Cheer up,' she said. 'I'm getting used to it already. I plan to be around for a bit still, you know.'

'Don't joke.' Ben's voice was husky.

Jessica had never seen Ben cry, not even when Transvaal had lost the Currie Cup, and the prospect alarmed her. 'Sorry.' She felt reprimanded, like a child making fun of a disabled person. 'It's OK, Ben. We'll cope with it somehow. Don't look so down. Listen: let's go to a movie tonight. I'll ask Anna to stay with the kids.'

'A movie?' Ben looked at her with disbelief. 'How can we go to a movie, for God's sake, when you're –'

'Dying?' she said lightly.

Ben made an impatient noise and started the engine. They drove home in silence, as if they'd had a fight.

The midday sun in Gaborone sent most sensible people indoors for a siesta. It burned relentlessly on the hard-baked earth from a sky that had not seen a cloud for some time. A small group of cattle stood in the shade of a low-spreading thorntree. They looked like clay figures, very thin, with pinched flanks and their heads drooping. Now and then a tail flicked at the ever-present flies, tight black bunches worrying fiercely at eyes and nostrils.

On the other side of the fence in which the cows were enclosed stood a low-roofed, whitewashed farmhouse. It, too, seemed defeated by the sun. The glare off the white walls might once have hurt the eyes, but dust and flaking paint had softened it. There was no sign at first of human life other than three small boys sitting close together on a bank of tufty grass near the fence. They hugged their knees to their chests and talked in shrill voices. One of them had a long, pointed stick with which he was drawing patterns in the sand. At the side of the house was a large shade tree and beneath it stood a swing-bench that had seen better days. It had cheap plastic cushions and the supports were black with rust.

Fran lay on the bench on her back, too limp with heat to

swing, looking out along the dirt road. A closed book and empty drinking glass were beside her on the ground.

A woman with a baby on her hip and a toddler holding on to her hand appeared in the doorway of the house. She called to Fran, 'Look who's on time for a change,' and gestured in the direction of the dirt road, where a spiral of dust could be seen in the distance. 'Here comes Sam.'

Fran sat up. 'Wonders never cease,' she said, shading her eyes. The dust spiral was moving rapidly. It hung against the deep blue of the sky like a smoke signal. 'I hope he remembered to bring beers,' she added. She got off the swing-seat. Her shirt was pasted to her back. 'Hey, little Charity.' She smiled softly, lifting the baby unprotesting from its mother. 'Hey, little girl.' Pale blue eyes danced and twinkled in coffee-coloured skin as Fran swung her gently round. The baby laughed and clapped her hands.

'Daddy's home,' said the toddler as a much-travelled Datsun groaned to a halt in front of the house. It was weighed down at the back. The exhaust pipe was only centimetres from the gravel. The child let go of his mother's hand and ran to the car. A tall black man got out and lifted him up. He opened the boot and began to offload a number of boxes. Then he waved aloft a carry-pack of Castles and the watching women grinned. 'Bet you thought I'd forget,' he said.

'You did last time,' Mary pointed out.

'Help me work up a thirst, anyway,' he said. He pointed to the boot. 'You know how us black folks like to see our women work.'

The boxes were heavy and they all worked up a sweat and a very definite thirst. 'Who else is coming tonight?' Fran asked as she rested, panting, on the cool cement of the veranda.

'Oh – Digby, Rose, Annawe. And Mothobe, if he can.'

'We'll have a fish braai, hey, what do you think?' said Mary. 'That deep freeze is on the blink anyway. I don't want to leave stuff in there for too long.'

'Cool,' said the man. 'Suits me.'

'Suits me,' said the little boy and they all laughed.

Later that evening, the sky awash with thick clusters of stars, stars like you never saw in the city, Fran stood apart from the group. She wandered away towards the fence, her boots crunching on the brown, spiky grass. The air smelt of dust and smoke from the fire. She could faintly hear Phil Collins playing from a battery-run tape recorder Digby had brought along and hooked up in a branch of the tree near the braai. From somewhere far away a dog was howling. Maybe at the moon, she thought, looking at its round, yellow fullness as it rose from the horizon. Jessica said she'd known a girl at school once who'd howled at the moon.

Standing alone for a few moments, Fran took comfort in the lazy murmur of the voices of her friends just out of earshot. If she called out they would turn to her, Mary would hurry over. They would be able to pull her back. There was something very attractive, suddenly, about removing herself from her life back home, about taking refuge in a softer, wilder community. It wouldn't be dropping out. One didn't drop out any more. But it would be a breathing space and a slowing down of the heartbeat. And would it really matter where she did her thinking? She seemed to have lost her centre somewhere back there and it wasn't just Sophie, or just Davy – it was something else, a drifting, an imperceptible drifting away. She had tried to describe the feeling to Jessica: how a cohesive, organised, fulfilled life had all of a sudden disintegrated, with different particles spinning away into space. There were bits and pieces of her soul scattered all over the place. 'Sort of like a black homeland,' Jessica had suggested helpfully.

Fran wondered who was prowling through her house at this moment. Would she go back to find more slogans on the walls? Did she need that any more? Would it matter, ultimately, if she simply didn't go back at all?

It would have been trite to say she felt close to God out here, with the warm Botswana night wrapped around her skin. But she did feel somehow cocooned, protected and safe. Perhaps it was the beer and the tiredness, but she wanted to hold on to that feeling forever. Fran hadn't said a real prayer for years, not even when Sophie was killed, or not properly, not formally. Now, without articulating the words, she looked up at the silvery night sky and she prayed for Sophie, for Davy, and said a wry few words for Africa. And she drank from the brown bottle of beer in her hand and listened to the sounds of the night.

'Mbekhi.'

Mbekhi scrambled hurriedly to his feet and stood nervously, not meeting Fran's questioning gaze. His clothes were stained with sweat and dirt. He looked as if he'd been wearing the same jeans and shirt for a long time.

'We've been worried about you. Are you all right?'

'I'm all right.' He seemed uncomfortable and ill at ease.

Fran was puzzled. 'Are you ... have you ... '

'Please –' Mbekhi threw her an agonised look and moved awkwardly towards the door. Before Fran could say anything more the screen flapped open and slammed and Mbekhi was gone. She walked disconsolately through to the kitchen. Bacon, unattended, spat in a small black frying pan on the stove. She turned it over with a fork. The smell made her stomach rumble. She'd drunk too much beer last night and slept very heavily. She yawned and stretched, then positioned herself on the step leading out into a concrete yard. It was eight a.m. and hot already.

'*Padkos*. Bacon and banana sandwiches all right?' It was Mary. 'Food for the journey,' she prompted.

'Mm. Smells delicious.'

'I see you bumped into Mbekhi.'

'Is he OK? He disappeared after the march last week. Nobody's seen or heard from him.'

Mary took the bacon from the pan and laid it out on some kitchen paper to drain. 'Oh, they took him in,' she said, glancing at Fran. 'Nothing's changed you know. They gave him a hard time.'

'Old habits. When did he arrive here?'

'Last night. After you'd gone to bed. He's very uptight at the moment. Don't be upset if he's uncommunicative. He'll come out of it.'

'Everybody's spooked,' said Fran. 'Including me.' She brushed languidly at the flies buzzing round her head. She took out the small diary she'd put in the pocket of her skirt and flicked through it. It was one of those plastic-covered diaries, the sort you got sent from the chemist with your end of year account. There was an ad for bunion plasters on the back. And tucked into the plastic flap of the cover were the receipts, the bank statements, and the incriminating signatures: J van Rensburg, Cabinet Minister, clear as day on one, and another name, indecipherable, on another. It was Van Rensburg, though, that was the trump card. Lies, lies, lies. Where would it end?

'Mbekhi will be driving home with you,' said Mary.

The curly-headed baby crawled over to where Fran was sitting and pulled herself on to her lap. She grabbed at the beads round Fran's neck. Fran slipped the string over her head and dangled them in front of her face.

'Want to give me a hand here?' said Mary. She looked out into the yard. 'You should be off soon. Before it gets too hot.'

They stood side by side at the counter. Fran cut slices of freshly-baked brown bread. The bread was moist to the touch. It had sesame seeds in it, and raisins. She tore off a crust and gave it to the baby. Fran glanced at Mary. There was a sternness about her profile and the set of her mouth. 'We haven't talked about Sophie,' she said to her.

Mary washed her hands and dried them on her skirt. 'I know,' she said. She bent and picked up the baby and looked at Fran over the top of her head. 'I have been trying to find the right words.' She looked away.

'*A lutta continua*?' Fran murmured.

'That's not fair,' said Mary. She put the baby down and took Fran by the shoulders. 'That's not fair ... Do you know how I've gone over it and over it ... Fran, Sophie was ... Christ, you know ... She was part of our family. She was –'

Fran took some kitchen towel and blew her nose. She felt her eyes fill as she saw Mary bend her head and turn away. 'Here.' She tore off a strip of the paper and thrust it at her. They stood together looking out of the kitchen window.

'You know,' said Mary. 'That time when we looked after her? And she broke her arm when she fell out of the treehouse?'

Fran nodded.

'Well, I went through agonies not knowing what you would say. How angry you would be with me for not taking care of her properly. She could have broken her neck and I couldn't even get a message to you. I keep thinking about that. I don't know why.'

Fran had been in detention at the time and she hadn't even known about the arm until Davy brought Sophie home when she was released and Sophie had proudly carried in the plaster cast with a dried flower arrangement in it, her arm all healed. A friend of Mary's had drawn a village scene on it in charcoal and they'd kept it for ages in a corner of the lounge.

'Sophie loved it here,' said Fran. 'At home she was a city child. I can't believe she's gone. I don't think I'll ever come to terms with it. I keep looking out of windows – like this one – and expecting to see her run past.'

Mary handed her a glass of orange juice. 'I wish you would stay a little longer,' she said softly. 'It would do you good.'

'I can't,' said Fran. 'What about you? Have you made any decisions yet – about coming home?'

'Nothing's been decided. Not for a while, anyway,' said Mary. She laughed ruefully. 'We're still too well-known for comfort. And there's Tom and Charity to think of.'

'What about this?' Fran patted her pocket.

'Someone'll make a decision on it soon.'

'How soon? People are getting killed out there, you know,' Fran said, half apologetically, as if it were Mary's fault.

'I know.' Mary sighed. 'But there's not much I can suggest. You'll have to hang on to it for the time being.' She looked hard at Fran. 'Unless you'd rather not,' she said. 'You don't have to, you know.'

'I know,' said Fran.

Later, as they were stepping into the car, Mary came hurrying across the sandy driveway. 'Your beads,' she called. 'You forgot your beads.'

Fran smiled and shook her head. 'Let Charity have them,'

she said. 'They're not special. Just wooden beads.'

'Well, thanks. Go well.'

Hands raised in farewell and then dust. Clouds of soft, brown dust thrown up by the wheels, hanging about the car like a hot, dry mist.

It was already dark when Fran got home. A week away and the cottage smelt dank and musty. Mbekhi came inside with her and together they walked cautiously from room to room. With everything in order and all the lights blazing, she let him go. Jessica had been there. In the kitchen there was a note on the fridge: 'There's fresh bread, milk and cheese in here. And apples in the bowl. *Eet smaaklik* – enjoy. J.'

She'd barely put her bag down when the phone rang.

'Fran? Oh, good. You're back. I missed you. Can I come over?'

Fran's heart slipped a notch. 'I'm really tired, Jim,' she said. 'I've only just got in. It's a long drive and I'm hot and sweaty and I need a shower. Can we skip it tonight?'

He sounded disappointed, but she refused to care this time. Jim wasn't her responsibility. She had to get tough about things, she'd decided in the car, and Jim was as good a place to start as any. Besides, she had a lot on her mind tonight. She couldn't believe it when, an hour later, just as she was combing out her hair after her shower, the doorbell rang. She recognised the large frame filling the glass of the front door. Before she could protest, Jim was in the hallway, grinning sheepishly.

'I had a surprise for you,' he said. 'It couldn't wait.' From behind his back he pulled a plastic covered dish. 'I made a fresh chicken pie for your supper. I knew you'd get back late and wouldn't have any provisions in the house, so ... '

Fran wasn't hungry at all and she said so, rather ungraciously. They'd stopped on the way home for a hamburger and *slap* chips at five o'clock. The pie was just an excuse, anyway, and Jim himself was eyeing it greedily. The smell of it was making her feel queasy. 'Come in anyway,' she said. 'I'll have a small piece if you'll help me.'

She could have saved her breath. Jim had already made himself at home in the lounge. He seemed a little on edge, Fran thought, but that was probably her own state of mind. Jim kept getting up and going to the kitchen for something to drink, or getting up and walking round the room. Moving seats.

Suddenly Fran found him sitting beside her on the couch. The buttons on his shirt were beginning to strain. She could see his large, white stomach bulging through the gaps, soft folds of skin with a bristling of fine dark hairs. He was sweating and his eyes were very bright, as if he had a fever.

I don't believe this, Fran thought. She shifted away from his smell.

'Franny –' Jim slid an arm along the back of the couch. She felt a soft plucking at the material of her shirt. His fingers were damp and clammy. When he began to stroke her shoulder Fran felt close to panic. Jim was breathing heavily. She could see him trembling. She ought to have seen this situation brewing; Davy had warned her long ago. So had Jess. Now she wasn't sure she was going to be able to handle it.

'Jim – I don't think –'

He was strong and very heavy. She wasn't prepared for the bulk of the man. His fleshy face burrowed into her neck like a slug. She felt lips on her neck, sucking and nibbling. She struggled to free herself but she was smothered tight against the soft cushion of his fat chest.

'Fran, oh Fran,' he panted. She felt a big, hot hand clamped on her breast, felt the nipple being squeezed hard and painfully. Foreplay was clearly not his strong point. Then Fran pushed again with all her strength and sprang to her feet. Her face was scarlet. Jim stared up at her. His breath came in gasps. She could see he had an erection.

'Please leave,' she said. 'Now. And don't come back.'

Jim continued to look up at her, still panting. His eyes were absolutely blank. Then he smirked. There was a bubble of spit at the corner of his mouth. He got up from the couch in a surprisingly agile movement for such a fat man. Fran backed away as he advanced towards her.

'Jim,' she said. 'Don't do anything you'll regret. I'm warning you.'

He laughed then, and put both hands up in a parody of a suave, peace-keeping gesture. 'All right. All right,' he said. 'Don't get so upset. I apologise. I came on too strong. Too sudden. You need time, I can see that now.'

'Let's get this straight, Jim,' said Fran, breathing a little more easily, but keeping her distance. 'I don't think I've ever given you any reason to believe that ... that ... well, as far as I'm concerned, we're friends. I thought good friends. But further than that – I'm sorry. I'm not available for any relationship with you other than a platonic one. Or with any other man, for that matter. I'm sorry.' Why was she apologising, for God's sake?

She watched tensely as Jim took his car keys and went towards the door. On the way past the table he picked up a chunk of chicken pie and squashed it into his mouth. Fran shuddered. Flakes of pastry floated to the floor. 'Goodbye,' she said. She couldn't help herself. She was still trying to appease.

Jim didn't answer. His back stiff with hurt dignity, he walked on to the stoep and up the garden path. Fran closed the door and locked it. She leaned against it, feeling limp with fright. And then there it was again: guilt. Like a grubby security blanket, it trailed along after her, pitiful and faithful as a stray dog. Had she in some way led him on, encouraged him without realising what she was doing? Had she been so wrapped up in her own misery as to have been unaware of what was going on around her? She hoped she wasn't as careless of others' feelings as she'd so obviously been with Jim's.

In the morning she lay in bed, listening to the silence in the cottage. How many times had she yelled at Sophie to turn down the radio, stop bouncing a ball, to try closing a cupboard door instead of slamming it? Now it was the silence that was too loud. Soon she would start talking to herself like a lunatic. It took an effort to get herself moving but she made a cup of tea and drank it on the front stoep. Then, for something to do, she connected the garden hose and walked around the garden with it, giving the plants a desultory watering. This had been Davy's job to start with and then Sophie had taken it over when he'd left, but she'd get bored too quickly and everything looked parched and neglected. The bird-bath had a scummy film on it and it took a strong jet of water to dislodge the leaves and mud. After a while Fran felt more relaxed and oddly restored by the smell of wet soil, and then absurdly touched by the sight of a Cape robin perched nervously on the rim of the bird-bath, his soft head twisting this way and that.

She went inside to call Lieutenant Els for news on Sophie's case. Still nothing. No progress at all. Then she called Davy, but he was in the middle of a session and had to cut their conversation short. Finally she called Jessica.

'I'm back,' she said. 'How about meeting me for a salad at lunch-time?'

'Can't today,' said Jessica.

'I'll tell you about how Jim Walton groped me.'

'You'd expect me to eat?'

'Seriously – what are you doing that's so diverting?'

'How does having a hysterectomy sound? You can bring me grapes if you like.'

'Come on – what are you talking about?'

'You see what happens when you go off into the bush and don't take me. Things fall apart. Time doesn't stand still just for you, you know. You've missed out on an awful lot, Frances.'

'Tell me.'

'Short and sweet? I've got cancer.'

'Cancer?' Fran said blankly. 'You can't have cancer. We played tennis last week. You're anaemic. You told me.'

'I lied. They did some more tests while you were away and found a whole bunch of nasty little malignant chaps galloping around my uterus.'

'Don't move,' said Fran. 'I'm coming over.'

She found Jessica in the bedroom, with a suitcase open on the bed. Fran stood watching her. 'D'you feel grim?' she said. 'You know I'll do anything. You just have to say the word ... '

'I know. I know.' Jessica patted her shoulder absent-mindedly, affectionately. 'You could witness my will, if you like.'

'All in good time,' said Fran. 'I haven't checked over your stuff yet.'

She sat on the bed. Edwina came crawling down the passage, her face split open in a smile. She'd been eating something sugary and had white crystals on her cheeks and in her eyebrows. Fran picked her up. She was wearing nothing but a nappy. Her bones, small as a bird's, moved beneath her fingers. Jessica looked at her over the thick, chestnut hair. There were tears in her eyes. 'I don't think I want to die,' she said, 'just yet. My life is devoid of any achievement. There's so much I want to do, that I've been putting off until ... you know, the right moment. You know what I mean? All the clichés. I haven't got time for this.'

'Tell me what the doctors say,' said Fran.

While Jessica packed clean nightdresses and toiletries into her suitcase, Fran sat with Edwina on her lap, listening while she talked. Then Anna made them tea and they took their cups out into the garden. Jessica looked a little less distraught. 'You know, it really does help,' she said. 'Talking to you about things. I think I'm getting out of my pathetic, self-pitying, why me mode. Thanks.' She smiled and Fran smiled back. 'I think I can even say the words now, without freaking out. Hysterectomy. Hospital. See?'

'Chemotherapy,' said Fran. 'Vomit.'

'Cancer. Death. Needles.'

'Suppurate. Tumour.'

They began to laugh and they laughed until Fran had to wipe her eyes on the hem of her skirt. Edwina chortled too, waving the lid of a shoebox happily at them from the sandpit.

'Oh Christ!' Jessica leapt to her feet. 'She's got Andrew's silkworms.'

They were all dead, buried beneath a mound of fine white sand. Jessica grabbed Edwina up and out of the sandpit, while Fran picked gingerly with a fingernail among the fat, grey corpses.

Twelve

'Good Lord.' Gail took a thin slice of lemon between finger and thumb and slid it into a cup of milkless tea.

'Don't tell me another bomb,' Ansie said. 'I'm bored of bombs.'

She put a string of gingerbread men on to greaseproof paper to cool. She licked her fingers and went across to look at the newspaper over Gail's shoulder. Gail pointed to a photograph of a small girl, plump and bashful, in a ballet tutu. 'Another child murdered. Found at the dam again. Police are linking it with Sophie's killing.'

'*My magtag*,' Ansie murmured. Instinctively her eyes went to the window where she could see two blonde heads, Petra's and Simon's, at the garden fence, behind the swimming pool. She frowned. Two small black heads were bobbing over the fence from the other side. An animated discussion appeared to be taking place.

'Not another child from Rosepark?' she said, turning back to Gail.

'That's not the link,' said Gail slowly.

The child, according to the report, was the grandchild of one Ellen Frampton, an activist from the 1950s, one of the first white women to be a card-carrying member of the ANC. Ellen had been dead for some years, and her own offspring did not appear to have any strong links with the organisation. Nevertheless, the paper speculated, it was too coincidental not somehow to be connected with the brutal slaying of Fran Phillips' daughter, Sophie. There was a small inset of Sophie, too, a detail taken from one of the larger photographs the papers had been using. The paper quoted the Human Rights Commission calling for a major investigation and deploring the lack of progress in the Phillips case.

'I think Fran's more involved in this monkey business than she lets on,' Ansie said darkly, but without clarification. 'Do you think it's true what the papers have been saying?'

'About the death squad thing?'

Ansie nodded. 'Think about it,' she said. 'We don't really know what exactly Fran does with all this left-wing stuff. I don't think even Jessica knows.'

It was getting late. The children came into the kitchen and Ansie wrapped some gingerbread men in paper for Simon to take home. She gave him another to eat in the car. Simon looked at it calculatingly, then bit its head off. Ansie and Petra went out with the Flemings to wave goodbye. No sooner were they back in the house than Petra started up with her usual theme: 'I wish they could come and play, Mama. I *wish*.'

Ansie pretended she hadn't heard. She washed the dishes in the sink, running the hot water noisily and lathering up the liquid at the same time. Disconsolately, Petra wandered off to her room and Ansie tried, unsuccessfully, to put the issue from her mind. Those wretched black kids. Why did Petra have to decide on them for her friends, she'd complained to William. The mother was irresponsible too. They'd already had an upsetting run-in last weekend. Ansie recalled how she had stood on the back stoep, a thick, blue child's jersey in her hands, fingers holding the neck open ready for a head, looking for Petra. It had been raining and it was cold. The garden looked sodden and everywhere the sound of dripping and gurgling was in the air. The pungent scent of the lemon verbena caught in her nostrils and thrushes picked their way delicately among the damp wads of leaves on the ground.

Ansie wasn't really anxious. Petra was a resourceful child. She was used to her own company and to entertaining herself. She'd probably gone out to play in the garden when the rain had stopped. But in the garden all was still, front and back. Ansie looked at the sky.

It was thick with cloud. The rain would start again soon. Typical capricious spring weather. She began to get worried, thinking all of a sudden of Sophie again. Her mind raced. A child-napper (was that the right word?) stalking the streets? Her voice rose and took on a sharper tone. 'Petra-a-a-!'

Just then a head appeared through a gap in the back fence. 'She's here!'

Ansie's eyes narrowed as she tried to locate the source of the voice.

'I'm sorry – I thought you knew she was here.'

Ansie swore beneath her breath. This she didn't need. She strode down the steps and through the wet herb garden, her brown skirt swishing through the long grass. She crunched across the peppermint lawn, releasing its sharp, fresh smell into the cold air. Her honey-coloured hair was loose and fuzzy from the damp weather. It streamed out from her face behind her like a head-dress. She looked like a Viking warrior maiden wading into battle through a green sea. Her blue eyes flashed with anger. She seemed not to notice the wide white smile in the brown face peeping through the fence.

'No, I didn't know,' she said brusquely, stopping a comfortable distance away. 'Will you get her, please. I want her home.'

'Oh.' Zinzi's smile vanished. Her face fell. 'They're having such a good time. I made them –'

'I want her home. Now. Kindly go and fetch her.'

'Yes, Madam. Right away, Madam.'

'There's no need to be facetious.'

'What's the matter? You don't like cheeky kaffirs, is that it? Are we getting too white for you these days? Moving into the neighbourhood when you thought the northern suburbs were safely out of our price range?' Zinzi's face was wooden.

'Don't be ridiculous. I don't like my child going off to strange houses without my permission,' said Ansie. 'I don't like not knowing where she is.'

'I have apologised. I was not aware you didn't know where she was.'

'All I want is Petra home – now.'

'All right then. I hear you. But … could I not offer you a cup of tea at least?'

'No. No, thank you.'

The two women looked at each other.

'I will call your daughter,' said Zinzi.

Zinzi's face disappeared and minutes later three children erupted from the kitchen door and came running over to the fence. There they skidded to a stop. Two identical round brown faces, two identical mouths frozen into identical holes as they saw Ansie standing, arms folded, on the other side. They had met Petra's mother before and had not forgotten their reception. Not a muscle moved. Petra, one ribbon gone from her swinging plait, stood grinning at her mother, cheeks pink and a smile from ear to ear.

'These are my friends, Mama,' she said. 'They go to my school. Can I come and play again?'

The dish-washing water was growing cold. Ansie turned her thoughts back to the present and finished up, stacking and drying quickly. Later that evening, after supper, the news on television carried the story of the new child murder. William and Stephan, playing chess on the coffee-table, shook their heads. William pulled Petra to him and smoothed her fair hair with his big hands. She burrowed in to him. Her eyes were on the screen but she seemed not really to be listening or concentrating on what was being said. Her expression was dreamy, almost sleepy. It was after the sports and weather reports that she turned to her mother and said, in an odd, sing-song voice, '*Dis dieselfde man, Mama. Dieselfde man*.'

'*Hmm, wat, liefie*?' Ansie looked up from the word puzzle she was doing to improve her English. Stephan turned the television off.

'The same man. It's the same *man*.' Petra repeated. She looked impatiently from one parent to the other. They exchanged puzzled glances.

'What man?' asked William.

'The *same* one,' Petra repeated. Tears of exasperation started to her eyes.

'Petra?' Ansie got up and took her in her arms. 'What is it? What's the matter? I don't understand. What man?'

But Petra burst into loud sobs and would not be comforted. She stayed rigid inside her mother's embrace. Finally Stephan took her to bed and read her a story. She lay very still with her eyes open and on the ceiling. When he'd finished she turned over and fell instantly asleep.

'I've got a proposition for you, *boet*,' said William when Stephan came back into the lounge. He waited while Stephan moved his knight, concentrating on lighting his pipe. 'We – the bank, that is – are sponsoring a Miss Hillbrow beauty pageant this year. Actually we do it every year in November.'

'I don't think Stephan is pretty enough,' Ansie interrupted.

'Ag, I don't know ... ' Stephan blew his sister a kiss.

'When you two have finished –' William went back to the board and made his move. 'What I was going to suggest is that you might like to co-ordinate the pageant for us this year. Our PR dollybird who usually handles it has slipped a disk or something, and we need to set up the committee right away. Well, what do you think?'

Stephan grinned. 'Miss Hillbrow?' he said. 'How could I refuse?'

'Good. Then it's settled,' said William. 'I'll set up a meeting tomorrow or the day after and you can come in and meet the team. It's quite a show actually, ask Ansie. We were there last year. Music. Dancers. The costumes are very flashy and of course the birds aren't bad.' He winked. 'You might even pick up a date.'

'Checkmate,' said Stephan.

'I want you to meet a friend of mine,' said Pedro.

Kelly looked up. A fat man in a black shirt stood filling the doorway.

'Greg – meet Kelly.'

'Howzit,' said Kelly. She looked across at Pedro. He was cleaning his ear with a cottonwool bud. He inspected the tip closely, gave it one more gentle turn, then lifted the toilet seat he was sitting on and threw it in. The bathroom in the flat was very small and, with the visitor standing awkwardly half in and half out, it was crowded to capacity.

'I'm getting cold,' said Kelly pointedly. 'I want to get out.' She was in the bath, up to her chin in cheap bubbles. A candle standing in an empty peanut butter jar was the room's only source of light, though not on account of the ambience. A couple of rusty wires protruded from the discoloured ceiling where a light bulb should have been and perhaps once was.

'I'll wait in the other room,' said Greg. He looked embarrassed.

'Whatsa matter? You don't like my chick?' Pedro's eyes were pencil thin slits.

'Pedro –' said Kelly. Her hair was tied on top of her head and in the soft light she looked very beautiful. Her skin was the colour of the candlewax which dripped on to the chipped enamel of the bath beside her.

Greg was uncomfortable.

'Pass us that towel,' said Pedro. 'Here, kiddo, I'll dry you. Come to Daddy.'

'I'll wait outside. No problem.' Greg had gone a dark shade of red.

'No,' said Pedro. He held out the towel. Kelly looked sulkily at him for a moment. Then she rose up like a water nymph, white bubbles sliding from her flat stomach like foam. Greg's adam's apple bobbed in his throat. Her body was soft and supple, a child's body, with rose-tipped nipples standing out from her small, firm breasts. Pedro held the towel steadily. His eyes did not move from the fat man's face. As Kelly reached for the towel he flicked it deftly beyond her reach. 'Here,' he said. 'Dry the kid, Greg. It's cold in here. Isn't it, Kelly?'

Greg clumsily wrapped the worn bath towel round Kelly's shoulders. Her hair trickled from its clips and he scooped it up, scratching her neck in his anxiety. Kelly stood without moving. He began to dry her back. Once she tried to take the towel from him but a glance from the man on the toilet seat stopped her in mid-movement. 'He's doing fine, kiddo,' Pedro said. His voice was just a murmur. 'He's doing just fine.'

'Will you get my clothes?' said Kelly. 'I have to be home soon.'

'Whatsa hurry?' said Pedro. 'The night is young.' He got up and took her breast in his hand. It was a proprietary gesture, casual in its intent. Greg was beginning to relax. He permitted himself a tiny smirk.

'Greg here has come all the way from the northern suburbs to take us to a party,' said Pedro. 'And you want to desert us so soon. Come on, Kelly, be nice. Be nice to my friend, too.' He pulled her head back and kissed her neck. She turned into his arms. She was trembling. 'Pedro,' she said. 'I don't ... '

'Sure you do,' he said. 'We'll have a good time.'

'Ever been to Thatcher's?' said James Fleming. 'It's a kind of supper club. And it's on your way home.'

Mike and James had been playing squash, and Mike had told Cassandra not to hold dinner. Once inside the club it hadn't taken Mike more than a few minutes to realise what sort of a place it was, and it wasn't long before James vanished, never to be seen again. He sat alone, cradling a whisky in a corner booth, feeling decidedly out of place. He marvelled at the existence of this place, though, deep in the northern suburbs. Actually he'd driven past it many a time and never given it a second glance. There were some pretty girls serving drinks, but when they got up close he could see that most of them would never see thirty again. Except one, he noticed. There was a young girl serving behind the bar with Greg, the proprietor's pock-marked son. She had long blonde hair and was heavily made up, with black outlines to her green eyes. She couldn't have been more than sixteen, thought Mike. Like him, she didn't belong here, it stuck out a mile. He wondered what she was doing working in a place like this. Perhaps she was a runaway, like those kids you sometimes read about in the Sunday papers, accompanied by mournful pictures of mothers and fathers holding a favourite teddy bear.

The girl came across to him to clear away his empty glass. Before he could stop himself Mike said, 'What's your name?'

The girl looked at him briefly, disinterestedly. 'Kerrin,' she said.

'Won't you sit down for a minute?' There were other girls sitting at tables around him.

Kerrin wiped the table with a suspect-looking cloth. Her hands were long and slim. 'No,' she said shortly. 'No, thank you.'

Depressed, Mike sat back, fumbling for money in his pocket to pay for his drink. There was no sign of James, of course. He stood up to go and caught the girl watching him warily from her position behind the bar. Mike thought she was captivatingly beautiful, and he hesitated. Then he saw his own reflection in the mirror behind the bar. In between the whisky bottles and rows of glasses he saw a pathetic, middle-aged man scrabbling fruitlessly after his youth. Humbert Humbert. He left quickly, allowing the heavy front door to bang resonantly behind him. Greg's heavy-jowelled mother, standing beside her son, pulling at a cigarette in a long white lighter, chuckled and murmured, 'We've got ourselves a new regular. Young Kerrin's caught his eye all right.'

Mike drove home angrily. He turned on the news to try to distract his thoughts from the Thatcher's child. The lead story was of another child found strangled at the same dam where the Rosepark kid had been discovered. And the posters outside the café where he stopped to buy cigarettes screamed the headline: HIT SQUAD CHILDREN? The world was going crazy all of a sudden. When he got home Cassandra was on the telephone and he kissed the side of her head, feeling guilty, and went upstairs to change and shower.

'I've been talking to Fran,' Cassandra said when he came downstairs again. 'She's in a very bad way.'

'Who's Fran?' said Mike.

Cassandra had probably told Mike five times about Fran and about Sophie, and about Fran's political connections. She told him again, patiently, but his attention seemed elsewhere. 'Heavy day?' she asked him instead, but Mike was noncommittal and distracted. Cassandra had been unsettled by the news.

The papers were all calling out for something to be done about the seemingly wanton killing of children in the name of politics. They all appeared to assume that this new murder was political and that it somehow proved that Sophie Phillips had been a hit squad target too. Fran was very agitated and spoke incoherently. She had told Cassandra to leave her alone and Cassandra was trying not to take it personally.

'You could take the phone off the hook,' McBride pointed out. He was pacing again.

'No,' said Fran miserably. 'Davy might call. He *will* call, as soon as he's seen the paper.'

The telephone rang again. It hadn't stopped all day. The doorbell rang too, almost simultaneously. More reporters, more newspapers.

'Oh, no,' Fran moaned. 'Oh, God, no. I can't stand it.' She folded her head in her arms and pulled at her hair. Her knuckles were white knots of anger. Then she ran over to the shrilling telephone and yanked the receiver. 'There's no connection!' she shouted. 'And I have no comment!' Then she pulled the plug out of the wall and shouted, 'Now fuck off!' She looked momentarily stricken. 'Sorry, Father,' she said, and burst into tears.

But McBride was at the door and might not have heard her. Through a kind of rushing noise in her ears she heard him say, 'I'm sorry, but Mrs Phillips is not available for comment. In fact, she won't be available for comment, not now, not tomorrow, nor the next day. Please, leave her in peace, for the love of God.'

Sitting curled up on the floor out of sight of the window, out of the eye of the probing lenses, Fran felt her body begin to shake. She had never felt so confused in her life. It was all jumbled up in her head – Sophie, Davy, this other poor child, the family she'd never even met, the threatening callers who claimed to have done it, her parents. Everyone wanted a piece of her and all she wanted was Davy. When Sophie was born by Caesarian section, Fran had had an epidural anaesthetic and she had watched, entranced, her baby being born without feeling a thing. But later, when she was left alone to try to sleep and Davy had gone home, she had begun to shake and shiver. She lost any control over her limbs as she lay in the hospital bed with the curtains drawn round her. For two hours she lay there, excited and shaking. Luke had told her next morning that it was a normal side effect of the anaesthetic. Lots of women shook like that, he'd smiled. Nothing to worry about. But here she was doing it again, shaking uncontrollably. She had a pain in her chest too, and her heart was beating so loudly that it was the only sound in the room she could hear. She could feel tears running down her face and they were cold as snow. She tried to get up, to tell Father McBride, but she couldn't. He was bending over her, saying something with a worried look, but she couldn't hear him above the noise of her heart. She wondered that he could hear himself speak against the din. *Why didn't Davy come?*

McBride was at the telephone again. She hadn't heard it ring, but that didn't surprise her. She saw him talking into it, looking over his shoulder at her. Then he put down the receiver and waded slowly across the room to her, holding out his hands. He was smiling. Fran tried to smile back but her vision kept blurring and she couldn't see him properly through the mist and spray sent up by her tears.

'There's a friend of yours on the fourth floor,' said Luke.

Jessica was still groggy. She struggled to focus on his face. 'Who?' she whispered.

'Fran – but she's all right,' Luke said hastily as Jessica's eyes widened in fear. 'She's fine. Really. She's just exhausted, suffering from stress, that's all. What she needs is a couple of days complete rest – like you do – and she'll be all right. She wouldn't want you to worry, so please don't.' He smiled and took her hand. 'Your husband's here,' he said.

Later Ben travelled down in the lift with Luke. They stood in silence, watching the flicking floor numbers on the panel above the door. 'Well, Doc,' said Ben, when the doors opened, 'I must thank you for what you're doing for Jess. She thinks a lot of you, I know she does.'

'She's a plucky lady,' said Luke. He smiled reassuringly. Husbands like Ben liked to hear that their wives could cope. Ben's florid face had turned oatmeal beige under the fluorescent light. Luke actually felt a twinge of something like pity. He could see he was eager to be off and into the night, and into the nearest pub.

Luke wasn't wrong. Ben turned the BMW south, heading into town. He pulled into the parking area of the Dome. He was hungry and the thought of a Double Whizz-Burger and chips made his stomach rumble. He elbowed his way into the noisy room and found a table against the wall. The table-top was wet with someone's spilled drink and the ashtray was overflowing. The pub was heavy with smoke and the crowd at the bar was about four deep. Ben hadn't been into the Dome more than a half dozen times, and only with clients. He wasn't over-fond of crowded places and the live music on offer was not really to his taste. But tonight he needed the buzz, the anonymity, and a drink. Intent only on getting a cold glass into his hand, he made his way to the bar and carried two double Scotches back to his table. He downed the first very quickly, feeling it burn straight down to his stomach. The second he drank more slowly, waiting for his hamburger. When it came it seemed to him unappealing and he ordered another drink instead and pushed the plate aside, untouched. The whisky was like a blanket. He crept beneath its warmth and lay still.

Jessica. He tried to think straight but all he could see was his wife in a white hospital bed, her eyes groggy with pain and her lips cracked and dry. It wasn't fair.

The band was tuning up on a small platform at his end of the pub. They were called the Cool Boys. Ben regretted his position so close to the bank of speakers. He looked about for an empty table further back, but the pub was packed now, standing room only, and he turned back to his glass, prepared to stick it out. He wasn't ready to leave. Surprisingly, they were not as loud as the barrier of speakers implied, and they played a quick, rhythmic township jazz that he found pleasantly soothing. He even found his fingers tapping on the table-top as he settled back into his chair and lit a cigarette. The Coloured boy on the piano had a light, sure touch. He was bending over the keyboard, his black beret hiding his eyes. They played a set which must have consisted of about ten numbers; Ben lost track, as his eyes closed and he allowed himself to be lulled into near sleep. While they took a break, he ordered two more whiskies. He was drunk but he felt good, in a comfortable, relaxed sort of way.

The band members were sitting together at a table right across from him. He looked more closely and recognised Davy Phillips' profile. He was with a very pretty Coloured girl whose face was familiar. The piano player was leaning towards them, talking earnestly. Then Ben remembered where he'd seen them: it was at the memorial service for Fran's and Davy's kid. She'd sung that song which had got Jessie so choked up. Part of him needed company and he almost got up and went across to Davy, but another part craved solitude and in the end, morosely, he stayed where he was. When the Cool Boys went back on stage, the girl went up with them to a murmur of approval from the crowd. She was really very pretty – slight and sexy. But her voice was strong and uplifting and there wasn't a sound while she sang. Ben clapped loudly when she sat down, clapping long after everyone else had stopped, oblivious of the half-amused, half-annoyed looks that were thrown his way.

It was past midnight when the pub began to empty and the Cool Boys packed up their gear. Ben stayed in his seat until asked to move by the barman. He didn't feel so very drunk when he was out in the crisp air, but he did feel extremely tired, so that his legs were leaden, and he walked slowly to his car like an old man.

Walking in front of him he recognised Davy again, with the keyboard player and the singer. They were walking in perfect step, the singer in the middle, with the two men's arms around her shoulders.

Luke was in his rooms early. He took off his leather jacket and hung it behind the door. He put on his white coat. When most working people's day was just beginning, Luke had already done his hospital rounds. He had checked on two new mothers in the Gen. He'd also checked in on Fran and had found her still sleeping, with Davy sprawled fully clothed in the chair beside her bed, also fast asleep. Thank goodness Father McBride had managed to find him. He must have spent all night on the telephone.

Luke had also been in to see Jessica Tucker.

As he stood looking down at the street below, hands in pockets, Luke tried to put a finger on what it was that was making him feel so disturbed. He treated hundreds of patients, all women – young, old, some with mid-life crises and nothing physically wrong with them, many with more serious illnesses. He saw lots of very attractive women too. He had never, to this day, considered any of them in anything other than a clinical, dispassionate light. He cared about them, certainly, and some perhaps more than others, and he took a serious interest in their well-being, both mental and physical. What was it, then, about this patient that was different?

Jessica was seriously ill. The prognosis was not encouraging. But there was a spirit there, a spark, that burned out of her smoky-blue eyes beneath the fear that he found irresistible. He felt curiously drawn to it. He felt protective of it. But there was something else too, so elusive that it teased at him and he couldn't give a name to it. An hour before she was due to go into the theatre for surgery he had put his head round the door of her room and been startled to find her bed empty. A hasty search had discovered her in the bathroom down the hall where he and a contrite nurse had come upon her sitting on the edge of the bath with a guilty expression on her face and a razor in her hand.

'Mrs Tucker!' said the nurse.

'Jessica!' said Luke at the same time.

'Forgot to shave my legs,' said Jessica. 'I won't be a sec.'

It was that. It was that thing about her. What was that called?

Luke's receptionist put a hot cup of tea on the corner of his desk. She gave him a sharp look as if she could read his thoughts. 'Your better half's on the phone,' she said. 'Shall I put her through?'

Virginia came directly to the point. 'Luke,' she said, her voice pitched high and taut. 'Kelly hasn't been at school all week. Her class teacher just called.'

Luke's last patient of the day was Tamzin. He hadn't seen her for a long time, and not since the tragedy of Fran's daughter. She wasn't very regular in her visits anyway, but it gave him a much needed lift today when she flew into his office and put her elbows on his desk. She had at least fifty bracelets on her arms.

'Those look heavy,' he said.

'Not really,' she replied. 'Just noisy.'

He smiled at her. 'You're looking good,' he said. 'What can I do for you?'

'Well.' Tamzin crossed her legs and everything jangled. She had bracelets on her ankles too. 'I'm pregnant. And ... I don't want to be.'

Luke looked at her thoughtfully. 'You're pregnant and you don't want to be,' he repeated slowly.

'That's right. Luke –' Tamzin leaned forward again '– can you help me?' Luke sighed. 'Can I check you out first?' he said. 'Slide in there and change. Everything off. Then step on the scale and let's weigh up the evidence.'

Tamzin opened her mouth to protest, but he pointed sternly to the other room and she went meekly off to change.

'How do you know you're pregnant?' Luke called after her.

'Never mind,' she called back. 'I'm about eight weeks. Take my word for it.'

Afterwards Luke confirmed her suspicions. 'I can see you're in trouble,' he said. 'But what do you want me to do – other than see you through to term?'

It soon became clear what Tamzin had in mind, but when he studied her, her body language, her voice, everything he saw in front of him jarred.

'I think you need to give this some more thought,' he said. 'You're less than lucid.'

'I've thought about nothing else for weeks,' Tamzin said stubbornly.

'Believe me. You'll regret it. And resent me.'

Tamzin stood up.

'Tammy –' Luke called after her, but she was gone, leaving the door wide open.

As days went, this had not been the best he could remember. Luke called home as he put on his jacket. Virginia was there but Kelly had not yet appeared.

'Will you come straight home?' Virginia sounded anxious.

'Shortly,' said Luke. 'I have to check on a patient.'

Thirteen

The papers were full of it: HORROR BOMB BLAST IN KRUGERSDORP HOTEL. Attacks like this were becoming more and more frequent but they still warranted the thick black headlines and pages full of photographs. This seemed to be a particularly vicious incident, however. Lunch hour in Krugersdorp in the section of a shopping centre which included a busy banking mall and a small hotel. At this time of the day it buzzed with people all through the week. The Russian-made limpet mines, three of them, went off at staggered intervals of twenty minutes each.

The first one, in the hotel lobby, shattered glass windows for three blocks and sent pieces of jagged metal from the cars parked outside the hotel entrance spiralling into the sky. Dead and injured lay everywhere and people ran about in panic. No sooner were the police and special bomb units on the scene, trying to control the mayhem, than the second blast rocked the area and shortly after that the third.

When order was finally partially restored, the death toll was twenty-four and the injured amounted to over a hundred people. Most suffered lost limbs and cuts and lacerations from broken glass and metal from the ruined cars and buildings. Seventeen parked cars had been totally destroyed, and a truck belonging to a district farmer, loaded with livestock for the abattoir, had added to the devastation.

Later, a man who lived in a block of flats on the other side of the street made a report to the police.

He confirmed seeing a white woman and a black man running

out of the hotel side entrance only seconds before the first explosion, with their hands over their ears. They had run round the nearest corner and disappeared from his view.

It appeared that the hotel was the target. It was owned by 'Pote' ('Paws') van Schalkwyk, a former member of the Murder and Robbery Squad and alleged commander of a CCB cell. It was claimed that he was the mastermind behind several assassination raids over the years, the last a raid on an ANC house in Swaziland in which five ANC members and three children had been mercilessly gunned down. It was also rumoured that his hotel was a front for his particular cell, whose activities had not been curtailed despite the ongoing investigations into them and the official disbandment of the CCB by the Defence Force. A letter, purported to be in Van Schalkwyk's hand, anonymously leaked to the press, revealed a programme of violence aimed at disrupting the fragile negotiation process over the months ahead. The police dismissed the letter as a forgery. The Defence Force immediately stressed that there was not now nor ever had been a hit list.

Ansie picked up the newspaper from the grass and held it out at arm's length while she sipped lemonade. Her tennis racket lay beside her outstretched legs. Her cheeks were red from two hard sets on Cassandra's court.

'Ai, this is rough,' she said over her shoulder to Fran, who was lying on her back with her sun visor over her eyes. 'If you don't mind me saying so, *die donnerse* kaffirs are getting badly out of hand with this stuff. Now that their organisations are free to move about, they think they can get away with this kind of thing, but they can't. They'll get what's coming to them, that's for sure.' She glanced carefully at Fran, who lay unmoving and might just as well have been asleep for all the reaction she showed. 'Fran?' said Ansie, prodding her with a foot. 'What do you think, hey?'

Fran tipped the visor up and her eyes slithered over the front page which Ansie held out indignantly before her. 'What do I think?' she said softly. 'I think *die donnerse* kaffirs are retaliating.

If you read a bit further you'll probably find a connection with the last right-wing atrocity. There's usually a logical strand to these things, believe it or not.' She put the visor back down again and Ansie saw that she was flushed and her hand trembled. Fran had only been out of the clinic a few days. They said she had suffered a nervous collapse. Ansie personally didn't hold much with nervous collapses; it showed a weakness of character. And anyway, they'd only heard about it once she was out – no one had actually *seen* Fran in the clinic. Who knew where she'd really been? She hadn't been at home because Ansie had gone round with some fruit and a dateloaf and everything had been locked up. Jessica said Fran was staying at the convent with Father McBride, but he was one of them too, wasn't he? And Jessica didn't really know either. She was still in hospital. It was all very disturbing, and Ansie hated secrets. She stared at Fran with her mouth open. 'Do you mean to say you approve of these tactics?' she said incredulously.

'What tactics?' Gail had come off the court and flopped down beside them. She shook out her highlighted curls.

'It's this bombing thing, the one in Krugersdorp,' said Ansie, pushing the paper over to her. 'I think enough is enough. I think the ANC or whoever they are these days should give up this violence number, and Fran here approves, if you don't mind, *approves* of it.'

Cassandra, chewing on the sweet, pale end of a grass stalk, frowned at Ansie who ignored her. Somebody had to say something.

'I didn't say that.' Fran rolled over and sat up. She seemed agitated. 'All I'm saying is that you're looking at it from a very narrow, simplistic point of view. You're just seeing pictures in the paper, you're seeing bodies flying through the air. What you're not seeing, or are refusing to acknowledge, is the train of events that has led up to this situation.'

'I must say I'm with Ansie on this one,' said Gail apologetically, before Ansie could comment. She was applying pink lipstick, using a small hand mirror. 'I simply can't condone violence in any shape or form. I think they should blast those guys off the face of the earth. They're all cowardly scum who should be hunted down and roasted.' She squashed an ant which was crawling up her thigh, blotted her lips on a tissue and got up to pour herself a glass of lemonade.

'You're missing the point, too,' said Fran tightly. She pushed her hair back from her forehead and fanned herself rapidly with the sun visor. 'But then most white South Africans have been missing the point all their lives. Do you think violence and "acts of terror", as the SABC still insists on calling them, were ever the ANC's first choice? Do you think they didn't try every other possible avenue just to get a little justice in this country? Do you honestly believe there is some sort of twisted pleasure in blowing people up –' She lay down again and the three other women looked at each other blankly. 'And anyway – what makes you so sure it's the ANC in the first place?' Fran went on suddenly. 'And what about the hit squads? What about right-wing attacks, like the one at the Van Dijk Club? Don't they count as violence? Don't *they* get you het up, Ansie?'

'You know a lot about it,' Ansie persisted stubbornly, avoiding the question. 'But don't throw that one at me. The ANC started it – just watch the news on TV sometime. There was a documentary –'

'Just a second,' Gail interrupted. 'Correct me if I'm wrong, but I was under the impression that while negotiations are in progress, the violence – at least the orchestrated violence – would stop. Or am I missing the point again?'

Fran sighed with exasperation. She was close to tears. Cassandra cast about desperately for some distraction. 'Oh God,' said Fran. 'Do you think just because the Nationalist Party has allowed organisations like the ANC and the SACP to operate legally within the country and the word negotiation has everyone mellowed out, especially the whites, that everyone will automatically come out smiling with their hands up? If you were an MK soldier and had spent nine years in the bush swatting mosquitoes, how would you feel about a cease-fire for no apparent reason? They've been gunned down once too often to make that mistake. And for heaven's sake, even if it is the ANC we're talking about, the ANC is by no means one big happy family. What political organisation is? There are any number of members, especially among the youth, who aren't actually grateful for the crumbs from the negotiating table. You don't raise people's expectations and not deliver. This country is in the most precarious position it's been in since Sharpeville.'

'Sharpeville?' said Gail.

Fran groaned and flopped down on her stomach again.

'Oh, let's not talk politics,' Cassandra said feebly. 'It's too hot.' She looked towards the house. 'Excuse me for a moment ... ' and she walked off to where the house-painter was standing, apparently waiting for a moment to catch her attention. He stood smiling, with his hands on his hips.

Gail looked at them with interest. 'Girls,' she murmured. 'Take a look, will you? I may be way out of line here, but ... '

Ansie and Fran looked distractedly in the direction of her voice. It wasn't anything Gail could have put her finger on, and neither Ansie nor Fran made any useful comment at all, but Gail could have sworn that there was something about the way Cassandra was standing close to thc young man, something about the intensity of what he was saying to her, the angle of his head perhaps, which told her without anyone needing to articulate it, that they were not discussing PVC or rising damp. Gail smiled, a slow curling of the pink lips. 'Ooh la la,' she murmured.

The four women played another set and then Selena brought tea on a tray on to the patio. 'You'll make tea for the workmen, please, Selena?' said Cassandra. 'And for the boss too?'

'Wouldn't the boss like to join us?' Gail asked, cosy as a vulture, her eyes slip-sliding along to Ansie, who looked away impatiently.

Cassandra looked at Gail levelly. 'I think not,' she said.

Fran had lapsed into moody silence. She was very pale. Cassandra, as hostess, felt responsible. She passed her a cup of tea. Fran's hand was trembling as she took it and Cassandra touched her gently on the arm.

'We've all seen what they've been saying in the papers,' she said. 'About the other child and – Sophie. Is there ... any, well, development yet?'

'No,' was all Fran would say. They all looked, and felt, embarrassed.

'Listen – Fran,' said Ansie. 'I ... I'm sorry. It was insensitive of me to bring all this ... I didn't mean to upset you just now.'

'I know,' said Fran. 'It's OK. I'm just a bit uptight today. Take no notice of me.' While they had been having tea, Gail noticed, Fran had completely unravelled the towelling round the handle of her tennis racket.

Just then the children came out on to the patio. Rosalie looked tearful but defiant. 'It was Jason,' she said immediately. The women turned to them and they all gasped. Jason, Rosalie, Simon and Petra were covered in blood. On closer inspection they saw it was red paint from Jason's poster paint set. Streaks and stripes in their hair, down their legs, across their mouths. They stopped, then all took a step backwards and blinked uncertainly at their mothers.

'What on earth –' Gail demanded. She advanced on them menacingly, followed by Ansie and Cassandra. Simon hazarded a small smile, which his mother switched off with a glance.

'We were playing death squads,' he said.

'Death squads,' said Jessica. 'Jesus God.'

'If it wasn't so depressing, it might have been funny,' said Fran. 'This country's a fuck up,' she added. 'How're you doing? At least you're all in one piece.'

'Well, not exactly, if you want to be pedantic about it.' Jessica was very weak and still heavily sedated. Her words slurred as if she were slightly drunk. She smiled at Fran. Her lips were cracked and dry.

'Oh fuck,' said Fran. 'I'm sorry.'

Jessica laughed, then winced. 'God, I hate hospitals,' she said. 'It's the smell. All that disinfectant. And it's so bloody noisy. Bells ringing, buckets clanging, lights going on and off at weird hours. That woman across there –' she pointed with her chin across the ward '– was woken up at eleven o'clock last night to have her sleeping tablets, for Christ's sake.'

'Weird,' said Fran. She picked at the cover on the bed.

'So how're you going?' Jessica asked. She felt for Fran's hand and held it. 'Luke told me a bit, but I haven't been reading the papers much.'

Fran took a while to answer. 'I keep wanting to run away somewhere,' she said finally. 'But then I can't think of anywhere to go.'

'I'm not sure whether you mean that literally or figuratively,' said Jessica, 'but could you stick around a while longer until I'm fit enough to come with you?'

Fran smiled. 'How long are they going to keep you here?' she asked.

'Luke says I can go home on Sunday.'

'Isn't that a bit soon?'

'He doesn't seem to think so. Obviously, I can't do anything too strenuous or anything.'

'And then? What comes next?'

'I start my treatment. First they'll do some more tests, and then begin with a course of chemotherapy.'

'Are you scared?'

Jessica pulled a face. 'What do you think?'

'Oh, Jess.' Fran put her hand to her mouth.

'My hair's going to fall out,' said Jessica. They looked at each other. 'I had planned to cut it short for summer, but I don't know how good I'll look as an egg.'

Fran bit her lip. Her eyes were swimming. 'Everything into a joke, hey, Jess,' she said.

'Will you do something for me?'

'Anything.'

'Come with me when I buy my wig. I want something outrageous. Punk maybe.'

'Punk's out. How about –'

The door opened and Ben put his head through. He carried a bunch of chrysanthemums. They were stiff and yellow and very bright. Fran got up to leave. 'Don't go,' said Ben, 'on my account.'

'I must. I have a meeting to go to.' Fran smiled at Jessica. 'Maybe Tina Turner,' she said. She kissed Ben on the cheek. 'Are you OK?' She looked at him critically.

'Oh, bearing up,' said Ben.

When Fran had gone Ben took the chair at the side of the bed and pulled it closer to Jessica's side. He wasn't any better at hospitals than she was and he showed his discomfort by shifting about, talking in whispers and glancing about him repeatedly. Jessica was in a small, semi-private ward, with four other beds, only two of which were occupied now.

There were lines alongside Jessica's mouth which Ben hadn't noticed before. He fancied they were pain lines, that they had only just appeared, like hairline cracks in a wall after an earth tremor. He bent awkwardly towards her. Involuntarily, she drew back. 'God, Ben,' she said. 'Is your breath ever free of the smell of whisky these days?' Ben sat back in the chair and said nothing. He looked like a reprimanded child. Jessica put out a placatory hand. 'Luke says I can go home on Sunday,' she said.

'Good. That's good,' said Ben. 'We'll soon have you fighting fit again.'

'Ben,' said Jessica wearily. 'I do wish you wouldn't keep trying to jolly me along. I'm not going to be "fighting fit" or "right as rain" or even "get my sea-legs back" for quite some time, you know. This operation is just the start of a lot of delicate and none too hopeful treatment, don't you see? I think it would be more helpful to me if you and I could try to come to terms with that, rather than pretend to each other that this is about as serious as chickenpox. I have cancer. I may die. We have to look at that possibility, head on, and make plans and provision for any number of eventualities. Please help me on this one, Ben. I need your support.' Jessica had half sat up on her elbows and now she collapsed back on to the pillow, her face tense with strain.

Ben didn't speak. He looked at the floor. He played with his hands, cracking the knuckles softly. 'OK, Jess,' he said finally, not looking up at her. 'But it's not easy for me. I hate to see you like this. I don't know what to do without you.' His nose was running and he wiped it with the back of his hand. Jessica looked at him, this poor slack-faced man who was her husband. She did not have the energy, nor the desire, to comfort him. She wished he would leave.

Wearing his white coat, Luke Stephens walked into the ward. A glance at the clock over the doorway told Jessica that visiting hour was over. Ben never stayed over the limit and he stood up now, smoothing down his trousers. When Luke reached the bed he looked at him like a dog hoping for a crust to be tossed his way, but Luke offered no more than a smile and a handshake. When Ben was gone he drew the curtains round Jessica's bed and sat down. A young trainee nurse had helped wash and brush her hair that morning and it lay heavily on her pillow, smooth and thick. Her colour was pale but not the chalk-white of the past few days. She'd thought about putting on lipstick for visiting hour, but rejected the idea. She wondered whether Luke could tell by looking at her face, devoid as it was of make-up or guile, how she felt about him. She had all the classic symptoms: heart beating faster at his approach, nervous perspiration of the armpits, shyness (by no means a characteristic of hers). Lying here in bed between his visits, she'd had many mental conversations with herself. I'm just attracted to him, anyone would be, and women always fall in love with their doctors, like men fall for their nurses. He's married. I'm married. He's not available for an affair, and I'm ... well, we'll come back to that one. He's a Catholic, it's against his religion. He's a lot older than me. I'm vulnerable and sensitive right now. It's the shock of my illness. I'm delirious. I'm fantasising. It's natural to fantasise, an important part of one's sexual awareness. As long as I recognise that that's what it is, I'll be all right. I'll get over it without him even knowing about it. He doesn't act any differently with me than with his other patients (you don't know his other patients).

None of it helped. Jessica looked into Luke's eyes, then looked away. There was no getting away from it. She felt lust written all over her face. It was disgusting.

'I ... I didn't know you were coming back this evening,' she said lightly when Luke said nothing. 'I thought I'd had my treat at lunch-time.'

He took her wrist in his hand and Jessica's stomach lurched. He was taking her pulse.

'How's the pain?' he asked. 'Did you try getting up today?'

Jessica grimaced. 'I tried,' she said. 'Fran told me that's what Caesar patients feel like. All I can say is I'm glad my three popped out the way they did. I'd choose piles over a Caesar any day.'

Luke smiled and stood up. 'Don't overdo it, Mrs Tucker,' he said.

He was leaving. Jessica couldn't believe he was leaving. She wanted to grab on to his white coat and hang there, like a rider caught in a horse's stirrup, carelessly dragging. Instead she lay back and closed her eyes. In another ward somebody turned on a television.

Luke had intended to drive straight home. Instead he found himself taking the long route round the back of town, driving automatically, without concentration. He felt bewildered and anxious. He knew what was waiting for him at home. Virginia. Dear, sweet, loyal Virginia, and his difficult, petulant daughter. And another family confrontation. He and Virginia had tried to have a heart-to-heart talk with Kelly once this week which had gone horribly awry. She had been stubborn and defiant and the evening had ended with him raising his voice in exasperation and Kelly, blinking back tears, running up to her room and locking them out.

They had dropped the issue for a day or so, but this morning he and Virginia had agreed that they couldn't let it go. They would have to try and talk to her again. They would keep the conversation light and reasonable, firm but fair. Luke was not a confrontationist at heart and he was dreading it.

He had found himself talking to Jessica about Kelly, about her truancy, her attitude to school and her constant late nights out, who knew where. In fact he found himself telling Jessica lots of things. To take her mind off her illness. She always listened carefully and responded with sensitivity and intelligence. She also told him when he was talking crap.

As he peered at the names of streets in the gathering darkness, realising that he was somewhat off course, Luke wished he didn't have to go home tonight, just this once. He wanted to go back to the hospital and sit beside Jessica and watch her sleep. Instead he turned into the driveway of his home and saw his wife whisk back the curtain in the sitting room and wave and smile before she opened the front door and pulled him inside.

Virginia had cooked a meatloaf. It was a little burned on top (that was his fault for being late), but Luke accepted the second helping she pressed on him. The baby carrots were saturated in honey and he pushed them stickily around his plate. Kelly had hardly touched her food. She was very subdued. Virginia looked hard at Luke and he sighed. He wiped his mouth on the embroidered table napkin.

'How was your day, Kell?' he began.

Kelly's eyes flickered up to his, then back to her plate.

'Hmm?' Luke felt like a genial old uncle.

'It was OK,' she said.

'Just OK?' Virginia said brightly. 'What did you do today? Anything special or interesting?'

'No, nothing special or interesting, Mother,' said Kelly. 'Just school, you know. Boring, deadly, pissy old school. What is this anyway? Why are we suddenly playing happy families?' She looked blankly at Luke, then at her mother.

'Your father and I ... ' Virginia started to say and Kelly rolled her eyes and tapped with bored fingers on the ethnic print table-cloth, one of a set Virginia had bought recently at a Save the Whales fête.

'Kelly,' Luke tried. 'Look at me, please. And I'll tell you what we're trying to do.'

Kelly dragged her eyes over to his and Luke thought he detected misery behind the irritation. He persevered. 'We're all at fault here. Mom and I for not realising that you're growing up and for not being there when you probably needed us most. And you, too, for taking your interests and your life outside of the family. For looking elsewhere for fun and pleasure. Now that's natural, especially for a girl your age, but we're also part of your life, you know. We care about you, about your friends, your interests, what you think about, what you want to do with your life when you finish school. All those things.' Luke took a sip from his wineglass. 'What I'm saying is, All right, we haven't been very good parents to you so far, perhaps, but we would like to make amends, to try to bring this family closer again. We need your help. We need to know that you'll try too.' He sat back, satisfied, waiting for a reaction. Virginia smiled at him.

Kelly looked at the clock on the sideboard. 'Oops,' she said. 'Gotta go.'

Virginia and Luke stared at her. 'Haven't you heard anything I've said?' Luke said quietly. He felt his temper rising.

'Sure,' said Kelly. 'I get the picture. You want to play happy families. Well, I'll give it some thought, but right now there's somewhere I need to be.'

There were bright tears in Virginia's eyes and her chin was trembling. She had a piece of carrot stuck to the corner of her mouth. 'Oh, Luke,' she said helplessly. 'This can't go on. What are we going to do with her?'

'Where is she going anyway?' asked Luke. He was thoroughly irritable now, having failed to retrieve a situation he'd imagined was well within his grasp. 'Did you say she could go out tonight?'

Virginia felt for a tissue up her sleeve. 'Didn't I tell you? She's got a part-time evening job, waitressing at a steakhouse. For extra pocket money.' She sniffed damply. 'It's all above board, darling. I thought it would teach her some responsibility, the value of money and work and all that ... ' Her voice trailed away. 'Oh, Luke,' she whispered. 'We've lost her.'

'Oh, for God's sake,' said Luke. He flicked at the carrot on her mouth with his napkin, rather more briskly than he'd intended. 'She'll come round.'

Fourteen

Mbekhi had not been to the convent since his return from Botswana. They were all accustomed to his absences, true enough, but it was not like him to avoid making any contact at all. Still, McBride was sure he had his reasons and Fran, who had spent a few days staying at the convent recuperating, had been reassuring. She and Mbekhi had apparently been in touch and she didn't appear concerned.

The convent garden was filled with birdsong and sunshine. Thabo was swinging on the garden hammock, but gave it up when he saw McBride bearing down on him with the Sunday papers. However benign the priest's smile, there was no question about whose claim to the hammock was the stronger. He ran off, barefoot like a street urchin, kicking a soccer ball and whistling through his teeth.

The papers were still carrying accounts of the Krugersdorp bomb blast. Two policemen, who had been seriously wounded by the second blast when they had arrived on the scene, had since died in hospital of their injuries. There were photographs of both young men in their uniforms, one at his passing-out parade, and the other receiving an award for bravery from the State President. They had both been twenty-five years old. How very cheap life was, thought McBride. How little we value it. Someone else had caught sight of the suspected bombers as they fled the vicinity and had given a more detailed description to the police. Police artists had drawn pen sketches of them and enlarged versions of these formed a sizeable part of the report. The African was thin-faced and wore a dark coloured cap, township street fashion at the moment, pulled down low over his forehead. The cheekbones were high, the chin rather pointed, but other than these he had no real distinguishing marks or features. The white woman, too, wore a similar cap, with tendrils of long hair falling round her face in wisps. The artist had given her large, startled eyes. She looked like a comic strip character. Modesty Blaise. McBride mused for a moment on this unusual but not unheard of partnership, and he sat looking contemplative, staring out towards the road. His reverie was disturbed by the arrival outside the convent gates of a minibus taxi, packed full with bodies. The luggage rack on the roof held a heavy load of cases and boxes. A number of passengers got out here, exchanging strident farewells. He recognised one woman as a friend of Miriam's.

Just before the minibus pulled off, a slim, familiar figure, walking lightly as a cat, put a hand on the bricks of the low wall and vaulted it. He couldn't be sure whether he had emerged from the taxi or whether he had been obscured by it as it stopped at the kerb. In any event there was no mistaking him and McBride got to his feet and jogged heavily across the lawn, his face beaming and his grey hair flopping across his forehead.

'My boy!' He embraced Mbekhi, who smiled sheepishly at him. Then his eyes moved off the priest's face and he drew hard on the cigarette he held between thumb and forefinger.

'Good to see you, Father,' he said.

'And you, Mbekhi.' McBride had never seen Mbekhi with a cigarette before. 'I need not tell you we've been worried about you. What's that you have there?'

'Soccer boots for Thabo. I promised him a pair and these come from his cousin in Soweto who's grown out of them. They look a little worse for wear, but they'll do, I think.'

Thabo came skidding through the garden at that moment and he yelled with pleasure when he saw his brother, even more so when he saw the boots which Mbekhi held aloft by their laces.

'Go in and see your mother,' instructed the priest. 'And then come outside and talk to me.' Mbekhi started for the side door. 'And, Mbekhi, I don't know if you've seen the newspapers but

I'd put that cap away somewhere, if I were you. It makes you look suspicious.'

Ansie had spent the past week inviting children over to play with Petra, trying to extend her daughter's social circle. Petra had been co-operative, as she usually was, but unenthusiastic. On Sunday night she begged again that the twins be allowed to come over and play. Ansie, aware of her irrational feelings towards the children, struggled with herself, while Petra waited, unblinking, for an answer. Ansie would have preferred not to call herself a racist and indeed she didn't really believe that that was what she was. She believed in live and let live ('as long as it's not next door to you,' William had teased) but mixing on a social level with black people was something that made her uncomfortable. She didn't want her child to grow up prejudiced, or that her own doubts and misgivings should be transferred to Petra. And yet she wished, and she was not ashamed of it, that Petra would make friends in her own, white group. It would be less complicated in the long run.

She was silent, aware of Petra's face looking at her from the pillow. '*Ag, liefie,*' she began, and Petra began to pout. 'All right. I'll speak to their mother at school tomorrow. I'll see what she says.'

Ansie usually drove Petra to school and then went off shopping or on errands straight afterwards. Sometimes they passed the Mokoenas walking down the road and Petra always waved and shouted, but it never occurred to Ansie to slow down and give them a lift. She kept her eyes firmly on the road ahead, yet sometimes she felt ashamed.

On Monday morning, when Petra yelled, 'There's Jonas and Freda! Mama, you promised you'd ask, you promised!' Ansie slowed down and stopped the car a little ahead of them. The twins ran to catch up with them. Petra already had the door open and they bundled in beside her, quite sure that this was the intention, although they looked up at Ansie with some apprehension. Zinzi caught up with the car and came round to the driver's side. Ansie wound down her window.

'Were you stopping for us, Mam?' said Zinzi. There was humour in her eyes.

'So it would seem,' Ansie said coldly. 'Actually ... Petra wanted to ask if your children would like to come over –? Would that ... um ... would you ... ?'

'Let them?' said Zinzi. 'I think the question here is, would *you*?' The smile had gone from her eyes. Zinzi wasn't going to make it easy for her and Ansie felt a gust of annoyance sweep through her like a warm, unpleasant wind.

'I could collect them at twelve o'clock,' she persevered. 'I'll give them lunch and you could come round and fetch them again later this afternoon. Would that be all right?'

Zinzi hesitated. She looked at the bright, eager faces in the back seat. She spoke in rapid Xhosa to Jonas and Freda, putting her head round Ansie's stiffening shoulder to do so. The faces grinned back and they both chattered away to her at the same time. She withdrew her head and smiled graciously at Ansie, who felt rather like a chauffeur waiting for permission to get into gear.

'Thank you,' said Zinzi. 'That will be fine.'

As they drove off, Ansie gritted her teeth in irritation at the stout figure waving behind them on the pavement.

At lunch-time she went to fetch the children from school. They were ready and waiting for her.

'Petra and the twins have hit it off so well,' said Tamzin.

'Yes, I know,' said Ansie drily.

Once home, she hardly saw the children. Petra took them to her room and her toys and Ansie gave them some fruit and sandwiches and left them to it. A short while later she heard soft footsteps enter the kitchen where she was preparing supper. She turned. It was Jonas. He held out three empty plates, neatly stacked one on top of another. 'Thank you for the lunch,' he said politely. 'May we have some juice now?' He was shy and wary of her. Ansie wondered whether she ought to say something about the day she had shouted at him, but thought better of it. She took the plates and handed Jonas a cardboard carton of orange juice. 'Walk carefully,' she called after him. 'Two hands please!' He gave her a dazzling smile over his shoulder, as the carton wobbled dangerously. 'Easy peasy,' he said.

Next it was Freda. She wanted the toilet and Ansie showed her where the bathroom was. In spite of herself, she could not suppress the swift feeling of uncertainty. They're only children, she said to herself. What would I rather do – send her out to the garden to crouch behind a bush? A black four-year-old bottom or a white four-year-old bottom on the toilet seat – was this really an issue? Her mother would not have allowed it, she knew that. But then, her mother would never have permitted the interaction in the first place. Still, she could not prevent herself from checking the bathroom when Freda had finished, and was immediately ashamed of herself. What am I looking for, she wondered. A pool on the floor? The loo paper stolen?

Ansie liked life to be clearly defined and simple. She hated any grey areas or uncertainties that she didn't know how to cope with. But this issue of the Mokoenas preyed on her mind. She honestly didn't know how to handle it. Maybe she needed some lessons from Fran.

Zinzi arrived shortly after four. Ansie kept going to the window to peer out into the road – 'No sense of time, these people,' she muttered rattily, not caring if the children heard her. Zinzi had walked round the long way and rang the front doorbell. In her hands was a platter with a white cloth. Ansie had been prepared for her for half an hour and had already seen to it that the twins were ready and waiting, with their school cases put beside the front door, so that she wouldn't have to invite their mother inside. Now she was thrown by the conciliatory smile on Zinzi's face and the delicious smell coming from beneath the cloth.

'Do you eat mealie-bread?' Zinzi asked.

To tell the truth, Ansie hadn't tasted mealie-bread since she was about twelve years old, and the smell transported her back to the farm, back to the huge, flagstoned kitchen and the kitchen staff baking bread, mixing sauces, bottling fruit. She didn't need to close her eyes to see again their colourful headscarves, their black faces glistening with sweat from the heat of the Aga cooker, their strong forearms with sleeves rolled up to the elbows. Or to re-live again the feeling of busy activity, of warm bodies jostling one another, the hot smells of the Sunday joint.

Ansie usually entertained her friends in the kitchen. It was after all her favourite room. Now she hesitated, beset by doubts. If she invited this woman into the kitchen, perhaps she would feel insulted. Perhaps she would think Ansie did not think her good enough to take her into the living room. Where would Fran entertain her black friends, she wondered anxiously. Zinzi had followed her and saved Ansie from her dilemma by setting the platter down on the kitchen table and pulling out a chair. She settled herself comfortably. She rested her elbows on the top of the kitchen table and looked around. 'What a nice big kitchen,' she said. 'Did you fix it up like this yourself? It must have taken a lot of work.'

Before she realised it, Ansie found herself talking to Zinzi, quite easily in fact, and she began to feel less awkward. She had worried for a private moment over which cups to use, the best china ones or the usual mugs she used for the family. When she had opted for the latter and sat down, Zinzi unveiled the hot mealie-bread. Ansie took a knife from a drawer and Zinzi pushed the blade through the steaming loaf. It glistened with moist golden crumbs.

Concession was called for. 'Delicious,' said Ansie, as graciously as could be allowed. She found herself having a second slice, cutting a third. She poured tea. When the children came in Zinzi cut slices for them too, and sent them out into the garden. Ansie saw her put out a hand to Petra as she went past and watched how she pulled her close, and how Petra responded with a quick, shy smile. Finally, Zinzi got up to leave. Despite everything, Ansie was relieved.

'Thank you,' she said at the door, 'for the mealie-bread.' They seemed to have left something behind in the kitchen. Ansie didn't know what it was – warmth, perhaps.

William was amused when he heard that his wife had entertained their African neighbour to tea.

'So she was human,' said Stephan. 'You'd better watch out, *sus*. Next thing you know you'll have Sambo there inviting Petra to the school dance.'

'His name's Jonas,' said Petra quietly.

Stephan had been in to the bank for the day to begin preparations for the Miss Hillbrow pageant. He met with the committee and, William told Ansie later, had offered some useful suggestions. Ansie was proud of him. She hoped he would meet a nice girl through this function and get out a bit. He was good-looking, charming. On holiday, he had allowed his army haircut to grow out. It curled softly into the nape of his neck.

'I'm meeting with the producer and the artistes involved with the show,' he told her. 'At eight o'clock. At the theatre.'

'Well,' said Ansie. 'You'd better get a move on. Take my car, if you like.'

Stephan had been counting on that. 'Thanks,' he said. 'Don't wait up, Ma.'

He got lost in the maze of small streets surrounding the theatre in the middle of Hillbrow. By the time he arrived, out of breath from running five blocks, the rehearsal was already in full swing. He slipped into a row of seats near the back to recover his breath and his composure. The house lights were down and only the stage was bright with light and movement. Dancers in jerseys and legwarmers were on the stage. On the night there would be a full orchestra, but for the moment taped backing tracks were being used. Stephan had rather hoped that the finalists might have been going through their paces but their rehearsal, he learnt, was scheduled for the following day.

During the first break he introduced himself to the producer, who in turn introduced him to members of the cast, the lighting men and the sound engineer. This last was a placid man called Davy, who bummed cigarettes from him and asked him about the Free State and the drought. When the rehearsal broke up Davy invited him to come along to a pub called the Dome for a drink. Stanley, the show's keyboard player, did a late-night session there, with a band called the Cool Boys. Davy and Stan shared a flat in Hillbrow.

Stephan got quite drunk on beer and euphoria. He hadn't had such a good time since the night he'd come out of the army. He wasn't even shocked at the fact that Davy was white and Stanley Coloured. This was Jo'burg after all. Joeys. And didn't his sister have a black neighbour? He waited for the moment when he could throw that in, casually, but there didn't seem to be one so he let it slide.

At one point, around midnight, he had a sudden mental vision of his father's AWB uniform, starched and pressed by Lena Meintjies, the Coloured washerwoman at Soetwater, and for a moment he felt disorientated.

Fifteen

Jessica was utterly exhausted and she looked it: deathly pale and eyes huge and dark, like holes burned in her white face. After a morning of tests followed by a chemo session, she felt dizzy and very ill. She was waiting now for Ben to come and take her home. She was the only patient today in the recovery room and, but for Fran in a chair over by the window, she was alone. A nurse had drawn down the blind and the room was grey and dull to her eyes. She tried to think about Luke, but even he was hazy today. She had no strength with which to fantasise.

She heard a door open. A doctor in a white coat came across to her and checked the chart at the foot of the bed. She looked at her and smiled. It was a tight, professional smile. Jessica was getting used to those, that and the way the doctors talked to each other in code, as if she were invisible. She had been shunted endlessly round the hospital, parked in queues in her wheelchair, left waiting in passages with draughts whistling round her ankles. And in each room had been another doctor and new sisters. They all smiled at her like this one did, and they were all busy and preoccupied and evasive. You'd think their patients were incidental to all the heavy, real work they had in hand.

All except Luke. Only he was slow and sure in his movements. Only he came close to her and treated her like something more than dogmeat. She knew it was his support alone that had enabled her to get through this morning's ordeal. She had asked Ben not to stay, making the excuse that as Fran wasn't working at the moment, she had the time, unlike busy Ben, to sit around and hold her hand. Actually, Ben made her nervous. And he had been relieved really, hadn't even made a show of reluctance at her suggestion that he go into the office and come back to fetch her when it was over. Fran never intruded anyway and it was easier without Ben, easier to focus on that point inside her where the fear nestled, where she could dig for it, like a needle picking at a splinter, until it lay at last exposed and less terrifying. It was something she had to do with full attention and she couldn't concentrate with Ben there. She could do most things better these days if Ben was not there.

The strange doctor smiled at her and left the room. She left the door ajar and, as Jessica watched her back disappearing, Luke came in. He closed the door softly, as if he thought she might be asleep. When he saw she was watching him, he said, 'How do you feel? Are you ready to go home?'

'Is my husband here?'

Fran strolled over from the window and Luke looked at her enquiringly. 'Hello, Fran,' he said. 'Are you feeling better?'

'Stronger,' said Fran. 'I'm getting there, I think.'

'Where's Ben?' asked Jessica.

Luke turned back to her. 'He's been held up,' he said. 'I'm taking you myself.'

Jessica felt too weak to protest or to wonder why.

'Are you sure –?' said Fran, looking from one to the other. 'I can take Jess.'

'You go on home now,' Luke said. 'You've done enough for one day.'

Fran looked at Jessica who smiled bleakly and said, 'I'll call you.'

'Sure.' Fran touched her hand. 'We'll do lunch.'

Luke helped Jessica into his car, but instead of turning north in the direction of her home, he got on to the highway and drove west. Jessica didn't notice at first, but when she did she didn't ask where they were going. He was hardly going to drive her into the veld and rape her at knife-point. She allowed herself to relax deep into her seat. She closed her eyes to try to stop the surges of nausea. Luke drove in silence. Once he leaned forward to turn on the radio. Finally, slowing down to take a sharp corner, he pulled the car into the parking area of a park laid out beside a lake. It was deserted. The only movement came from the Egyptian geese and coots out on the water. Luke turned off the radio. He wound down his window and looked at Jessica.

'This is nice,' she said inanely, when a comment seemed appropriate. 'This is a good idea. I don't feel very well and I need to get myself together before I go home to the children.'

'I thought you would,' said Luke.

'You're a very sensitive person,' she said. 'You should have been a woman.'

Luke laughed. 'I'll take that as a compliment,' he said.

'Haven't you got somewhere you ought to be?'

'Yes.'

'Then I do appreciate this. I feel a bit stunned –' Jessica made a helpless gesture with her hands. 'Am I going to die?' she asked. 'Would you tell me if I was?'

'Would you want me to?'

'I think it would be easier to cope with if I knew. It's the uncertainty, the *not* knowing. I can't sleep any more. I've never had a problem with sleeping, not ever. Now I close my eyes and I'm choosing headstones in a funeral parlour. I'm not used to feeling helpless. I've always been in control of my life. If something goes wrong in it, I handle it. Now I can't do anything. It's as if some alien force has taken over my body and is doing things to it that I don't even know about, much less have any control over. You haven't answered my question.'

'I couldn't get a word in,' said Luke. He smiled at her. 'Listen,' he said, 'cancer is one of those diseases, when all is said and done, that we know precious little about. I don't know if you're going to die. You have a very serious form of the disease, that's true. It's a form into which there's a lot of research funding being put at present. It is also a form that we don't come across too often. Treatment has met with a measure of success, and we are hoping to isolate the disease to some extent. With the chemotherapy, hopefully, we may even arrest it. But I cannot give you any guarantees, Jessica. At this stage it's too early to make any predictions anyway. That is as honest as I can be.'

Jessica said nothing at first. 'Well,' she said eventually. 'I asked for it.'

They looked out over the lake. A phalanx of large white geese was tramping steadily up the bank to where a small boy and his nanny were approaching across the grass. The child began to look apprehensive at this solid reception party and hid his half loaf of bread behind his back. The nanny was knitting, a ball of wool squashed in her armpit. She looked bored. The geese stretched out their long necks and the bolder of them reached round the child and tugged at the bread. He screamed in fright and tried to move it out of their reach, which only made them advance more determinedly now that the prize was in full view. Competition was fierce. The nanny kicked out with her foot and shouted at them in Zulu. She dropped her wool and the geese trampled all over it, dirtying it in the mud and goose turds. She shouted some more. Then she grabbed the loaf and threw it into the water, where it bobbed away like a small, soggy boat. The geese turned in a body and flapped back to the water's edge, while the child sat down on the grass and cried bitterly.

'Oh dear,' Jessica said. 'I've been there. Those bloody geese. They're so pushy, they can be very frightening. Andrew, my son, got zapped on a finger once doing just that. He wouldn't go back to that park for ages. Luke –'

'What?' Luke was still looking at the geese on the water, where a dozen white necks stabbed and pulled at the bread ball.

'I think I'm going to be sick. Will you excuse me for a moment.'

It was after lunch when Luke got back to his rooms and a crowded waiting room thick with disapproval. A pile of files was on his desk. He went through the routine, working on automatic, until finally, at five thirty, he was done. He took off his white coat and hung it on the hook behind his door. He straightened the papers on his desk and was about to pick up his bag and leave when he heard a light tapping behind him. It was Tamzin. She filled the doorway with colour, vivid in scarlet skirt and ear-rings. A velvet alice band held back her hair, taking the curls back and off her forehead. It gave her face an open, child-like look that was appealing and innocent.

'I came to apologise,' she said.

'That's all right. You were upset.'

'May I sit down for a moment?'

'Of course.'

Luke was glad to see her. He wasn't quite ready to go home to Virginia and Kelly. And he had been worrying about Tamzin.

'Also to thank you, actually,' she said. 'I was in quite a state when I came to see you. I wasn't thinking rationally and you picked that up. Abortion seemed the only thing to do at that stage. Now I've sobered up and –'

'And?'

'I've decided to go ahead and have the baby.'

Luke wasn't sure this wasn't as irrational as the first idea.

'Have you discussed it with the baby's father?' he asked. 'Are you still involved with the actor? I didn't have time to ask you last time.'

'I'm sorry.' Tamzin fiddled with an ear-ring. 'Yes,' she said. 'I am still involved with the actor. But ... he's not the father of this baby.'

'Are you sure?'

Tamzin nodded.

'I see,' said. Luke. He always said 'I see' when he didn't. 'Are we talking problems here? Does the father know?'

'Not yet,' Tamzin said carefully.

Luke sat with his fingers steepled beneath his chin. 'Tamzin,' he said. 'Listen. I am your doctor and your old friend. We've been through many things together. What you say to me within these four walls, or anywhere else for that matter, is between the two of us. You can trust me. Anything you want to tell me will be treated in strictest confidence. If I can help you or advise you, or just listen to you, you know I do it with an open heart and mind. You need to talk, don't you? Don't try to fight it. Talk to me.'

Tamzin's eyes filled. She sat with her hands in her lap while the tears brimmed over and spilled down her cheeks. She wiped them away with the edge of her skirt. Luke listened in silence to the whole story. She did not feel that he was sitting in judgement on her. Nor did he interrupt. When she had finished, he waited while she composed herself.

'What can I do?' said Tamzin at last, smiling fearfully at him across his desk.

'Look,' said Luke. 'My main concern is for you. You, after all, are my patient and your health is my concern. Now you have a baby to think about, you're doubly my responsibility. Our priority is to see to it that you have a good pregnancy and a healthy, unstressed baby.'

'And a stressed mother makes a stressed foetus. I read the magazines in your waiting room.'

'Something like that,' said Luke. 'But let's take this situation one step at a time.'

Tamzin looked at him expectantly.

'From what I can make of it,' said Luke, 'I suspect the baby's father is not going to want to take responsibility for it, at least not now. And I think, if you can, you need to absolve him of that responsibility, both for your own peace of mind and because he needs to know about it. And to absolve you too.'

'I have to tell him, don't I?' said Tamzin. 'That's what you're saying.'

'Don't you think he has a right to know?' said Luke. 'Yes, I think you should, not just for his sake but for yours. Whether the two of you decide that it's to be your secret, well, you will work that out. It's an unfortunate situation and, if I say it myself, rotten bad luck. But there it is – there's another child on its way into the world, and perhaps that child deserves a shot at life, just as you do.'

'What about Ray? What should I do about him?'

'I don't think I can answer that one. I don't know anything about him other than what you've told me. How serious is your relationship? Do you have long-term plans that include each other?'

'We don't talk about it much,' said Tamzin. 'I care about him, and I know he cares about me. But he's so ... involved in his career. He's so ambitious to make it as an actor. I don't know

– marriage plans and a family and all that – well, it just hasn't come up, really.'

'Until now.'

'Until now.'

'Let's be practical,' said Luke. 'Short of hiding yourself away for the next seven months or so, and then giving up the baby for adoption, which we've agreed is not the route you want to go –' he smiled '– Ray's not going to fall for the immaculate conception line, is he? It's not original anyway.'

'Right so far,' said Tamzin.

'I've never been one to advocate keeping lifelong secrets,' said Luke, the irony not escaping him. 'They tend to get heavier with each passing year. I think you are going to have to take a chance on this one. I think you are going to have to talk openly to Ray, tell him exactly what you've told me. We all make mistakes, God knows. We're all human. Perhaps your relationship is strong enough to weather this storm.'

'Perhaps it isn't,' said Tamzin grimly.

'You don't have much choice, do you?'

'I guess not.' Tamzin stood up. She looked gloomy as Luke walked her to the lift.

'Hey,' he said, 'we'll get you through this. I'll help.'

'You already have,' said Tamzin. She leaned forward impulsively and kissed him on the cheek.

I'm the one who needs help, Luke thought wryly as he locked up the office. His feelings for Jessica defied all logic. He should find a vapid young nurse to flirt with, if that was what it was all about. Wasn't that what men his age did, men who had recently celebrated their nineteenth wedding anniversary with a Julio Iglesias concert? And yet, watching Jessica Tucker crouched behind a hydrangea bush and walking shakily back to his car, looking cross and embarrassed at the same time, it had taken all his willpower to resist putting his arms round her. She had given him a sideways look as if to forestall any pitying gesture. 'Bloody hospital lunches,' was all she said.

*

Mike was out of town for a few days. He'd taken a charter flight to Phalaborwa in the northern Transvaal. He called Cassandra from his hotel in the afternoon. 'We've got a few problems here,' he said. 'I won't make it home before Friday. I might even stay over till Saturday morning.'

'All right,' said Cassandra. 'Take care.'

Cassandra felt a strong surge of power coursing through her veins like the injection of some powerful drug. There was no doubt in her mind what she would do with this unexpected gift. No doubt at all. She found Joel on the north side of the house, on top of a ladder. She watched him for a couple of minutes, standing in the shade of the wall. She looked at the strong tanned legs in their heavy boots. He worked, as usual, without a shirt, his rough yellow hair tied with the red bandanna. Just watching him made her weak. She took a step forward, then stood back again, suddenly anxious. She still wasn't used to this. When Joel made love to her all her doubts disappeared. The way he looked at her, the things he said, the sheer lust – mutual lust – was affirmation of her attractiveness. She felt no guilt, no shame. Thinking about Joel and plotting their next time alone together occupied all Cassandra's waking thoughts, as well as a good many of those in her sleep. But each time he left her, with a casual kiss or a pat on the bottom, she felt an unease, as if each encounter was the last. Then she would retreat into her reserve again and take her cue from him. Up to now she had not been the one to initiate their lovemaking.

Softly Cassandra called his name and Joel turned and looked down at her. 'Yup?' he said. He jumped the last five rungs and came over to her.

'You look so beautiful,' he said. 'I wish I could –'

'You can,' said Cassandra, startled at her boldness. She touched the sweat on his chest with her hands, resting them lightly on his skin. They were out of sight here. She told him quickly about Mike.

'You mean –' he said, and she nodded. 'Here?'

'I have a better idea,' said Cassandra, temptress, adulteress, whore.

The penthouse in Berea comprised the top floor of a forty-floor high-rise. It looked out north and south over the city, which at night was a mass of lights as far as the eye could see. Intended as a place for visiting company guests, it was seldom used and it had become understood to be at the sole disposal of Mike Symons who, after all, owned the building. He did not use it often either, but when he did Cassandra guessed, rightly, that he entertained women of dubious reputation. He kept confidential figures and documents in the safe in the wall.

Cassandra arrived early. She took out an ice-bucket, filled it with crushed ice and put in the bottle of Moêt she had brought with her. She set out glasses on the table in the window. There was fresh linen on the bed. Cassandra reflected as she shook the sheets out that it was probably twenty years since she had made a bed herself. She had dressed carefully in clothes she thought would please Joel: white lambswool sweater with simple diamanté design. Tight black ski pants. Her fine hair, black as coal, hung softly to her jaw. She looked, and felt, vulnerable.

When the hands on her watch moved to eight o'clock she began to panic. She paced. She brushed her hair. She put on fresh lipstick, then wiped it off again.

And then Joel was there, coming up behind her like an intruder. 'You scared me,' she said.

'Who did you think it was?' he said. He held out a single red rose. Cassandra tried to overlook the fact that the stem was wrapped in some fairly old-looking silver foil.

Later, sipping champagne, they looked out over the magical city together and talked, and he told her about his childhood, his mother's angina, his ambitions to be a doctor, a healer. In turn she told him about her own life, her loneliness, and the great joy he had brought to her. Gone tonight was the reserve and shyness. Cassandra lay in her boy-lover's arms and felt completely at peace.

Since her visit to Luke, Tamzin had determined to tell Ray about the baby as soon as possible, to get it over and done with. But there never seemed to be quite the right moment. Their meetings were less frequent as Ray was tied up every day and most evenings with some aspect of rehearsals. And when they did get together he was ebullient one moment, drenched in doom the next, as he always was before the opening of a play. Tamzin couldn't bring herself to do it. She had rehearsed what she would say often enough, but it never felt right. Apart from Luke and Jessica, she had confided in no one else. Countless times she had picked up the phone to the baby's father, only to put it down when she heard his voice, sometimes even before the call was answered.

And then there was Fran. Every time she thought of Fran, and she did so often, she felt a pain of distress so sharp, so direct, in her gut, that she would shut it away again, as swiftly and securely as possible. It always came back though, leaking and seeping through from the place where she stored unpleasant things. It would swirl round her, ebb and flow, receding sometimes to a tiny, manageable spot, and at other times come splashing against her legs until she feared she would drown in it. She had never guessed that pain could be such a tangible thing, when it was not actual physical injury. She would never have believed how much it could hurt.

When another day had gone past and her secret remained just that, Tamzin was surprised by a ring at the door. She flung it open. Fran stood there on the doormat. Fran seldom carried anything with her, no bag for comb or lipstick, no jacket over the shoulder. Only her car keys with the Snoopy keyring Sophie had given her one Mother's Day. She held these now, clenched in one white hand by her side. Her auburn hair hung loose on her shoulders. On her upper arm she wore a black armband. 'Tamzin,' she said. 'May I come in?'

It was Jessica really, who was the key. Not because she had been urging Fran to talk to Tamzin, which she had stopped doing after Fran's violent refusal to entertain the idea. Rather it was Jessica's cancer that had done it for her. The hours she had spent with Jessica in the clinic, watching her try, sometimes well enough, sometimes with much pain and bitterness, to come to terms with the fact of her own mortality, had taken their toll. We get one shot at life, she had thought, lying awake in the early hours, if we're lucky enough. Those precious days ought not to be squandered on resentment and hatred. Those were emotions which ate away at the core of you, like malignant cells, growing and poisoning.

A bottle of wine helped them get over their awkwardness – Tamzin drinking rather less than Fran, pleading an upset stomach – and they talked long into the night, almost like they used to do, as if it were still possible. When Fran stood up to go it was one in the morning. At the door Tamzin said, 'Fran … I … '

'I know,' said Fran. 'It's over now.'

They stood on the porch, with moths flopping round the lamp above their heads. Tamzin felt heady with relief. It was going to be OK. It was almost OK already.

'The armband,' she said. 'Is that for –'

Fran smiled. 'For Sophie?' she said. 'No. A friend who was killed at the weekend in Sebokeng. Shot in the back.' She walked backwards down the steps. 'No one you'd know,' she said to Tamzin's shocked face. She had crossed Jacob off the list herself.

Tamzin fell asleep with a feeling of renewal. She thought she might be getting her life back on track, with this stage with Fran being phase one. Tomorrow, she determined, she would maintain the momentum. She would start by telling Ray the truth.

She didn't, of course. It was Friday and school in the morning and tennis in the afternoon at Cassandra's. For a change they were quite a crowd. Ansie was there, and Gail. Fran, too, who brought Jessica and all of Jessica's noisy children. Jessica herself looked pale but cheerful. She walked slowly, leaning on Fran's shoulder. They all crowded round her, Ansie straightening a cushion on a chair, Gail moving a skateboard out of her path.

'Jesus God,' said Jessica. 'What is this – support your local invalid day? Next you'll be bringing me chicken soup and a bath chair.'

'All right then,' said Tamzin. 'Where's your racket? Let's see you on the court.'

Jessica, Tamzin and Fran laughed, while the others looked on uncertainly. They were not to know that Tamzin and Fran had spent the previous evening making up, but they gathered as much as the afternoon wore on. With six women there, Jessica was never left alone as they took turns to play. Fran sat the first set out with her. Glenda was having trouble taking off her dress. The other children were already all in the pool and she yanked impatiently at the buttons, stamping her foot in frustration.

'Gently, Glenda,' said Jessica mildly. She gingerly settled a cushion in the small of her back. She was out of breath from the walk from the car.

'Let me help you,' said Fran, getting up. 'It looks like you've got your hair tangled round a button.'

Glenda moved out of Fran's reach. 'Mommy can do it,' she said petulantly.

Fran glanced back at Jessica who didn't seem to have heard and was leaning back with her eyes closed. 'Don't be silly, Glenda,' she said. 'Let me help you. You can't see behind you. You're like a puppy chasing its tail.' She put out her arms. 'Come here.'

'No!' Glenda shouted, tears starting to her eyes. 'I want Mommy to do it. It's a mother's job!'

Fran stopped short at the absurdly adult phrase from this small, angry child. She felt her heart beating in her ears and an impotent rage rushing up and colouring her face.

'Oh, Glenda,' Jessica said wearily from behind her. 'Come here then.' She struggled to a sitting position. 'Fran – where are you going?'

Fran didn't answer. She set off up the lawn at a stumbling trot and went into the house, blinking at the cool darkness after the bright sunshine outside. It was quiet and smelt of pot-pourri and furniture polish. She could hear the tennis balls clearly like a pendulum in her head, and a girlish shriek from Gail. She went into the bathroom and locked the door. She sat on the floor, leaning up against the shower doors. The tiles caused her thighs to break out in goosebumps and she rubbed her arms and legs and hugged her knees close to her chest. The noise in her head had subsided and she felt chilled and forlorn and empty. Cassandra's bathroom was tiled in black from floor to ceiling and Fran could see her reflection, dim and pink, in the squares. She felt an enormous untapped well of self-pity gurgling somewhere round her stomach.

'Fran?' It was Jessica tapping on the door. She heard her try the handle. 'Are you all right?'

No, she was not all right. She would never be all right again. Why couldn't anyone see that? She flushed the toilet and turned on the taps in the basin. She looked at her blotched face in the mirror and splashed cold water on her eyes. 'I'm fine,' she called through the door. 'Just dandy,' she muttered to herself as she turned the key.

Jessica was standing outside, leaning against the wall. She looked at Fran steadily.

'Don't say anything,' said Fran. 'Just don't say anything.'

Fran took her racket out of its case and waited at the side of the court as the others finished the last game of their set. Ansie called her on and flung herself down in the chair beside Jessica. She puffed out her cheeks and wiped her face with a towel.

'So how are you feeling?' she asked Jessica. She offered her a glass of iced water. Jessica shook her head. She was watching Fran.

'A little strange, to tell the truth,' she replied after a minute. 'But I think it's more because of the way people keep treating me, rather than because I'm ill. As if I'm going to whip a bucket on to my head as soon as anyone says the word cancer.' Ansie's face was blank. 'Monty Python,' Jessica explained. 'Oh, never mind.' Obviously the Flying Circus had never penetrated the Orange Free State. 'It's as if,' Jessica went on, 'as if I have some dreadful social disease, something disgraceful and catching.'

Ansie took up the challenge. She answered Jessica thoughtfully, keeping her eye on the game. 'Most people who have cancer die, sooner rather than later,' she said. 'My grandmother had cancer of the throat. Of course she was old, and she did die, quite quickly after it was diagnosed. I think most people are afraid to confront death, especially their own, and when someone close to them is possibly facing death – I think you want me to speak frankly – they tend to shy away from it, as if by facing it, it could somehow rub off on them.'

Jessica sighed. 'I hear what you're saying,' she said. 'But still –'

'Also,' Ansie went on, 'people are trying to be sensitive to *your* feelings, remember. Maybe you don't want to discuss it. Maybe you don't want us to ask questions. We don't know how you want us to handle it. Don't be too hard on your friends.'

'I'm sorry,' said Jessica. 'I suppose I'm asking the impossible. I just want everything to go on as before, but suddenly I feel as if I've got a label stuck in the middle of my forehead saying "Caution. Cancer victim. Contagious".'

'*Ag, nee wat*. It's not easy for any of us to accept. It came so suddenly to you, *so uit die bloute*, so to speak, quite out of the blue. We'll all handle it better when we get more used to it.'

Selena brought the lemonade out to the patio in a big glass jug clinking with ice-cubes. Fran's normally pale face was flushed pink after her set. 'You've been working on your backhand in secret, Cassandra,' she said. 'Don't deny it. Either that or someone's been coaching you. You were devastating today.'

Gail Fleming looked around maliciously, casting for support, but finding none. She went ahead anyway. 'Perhaps it's the dashing young Joel Cunningham, if I'm reading his name correctly from the quaint little panel van parked down there.'

'The rather delectable chap who came to my rescue, not once but twice?' said Jessica, sitting upright. 'I wouldn't mind being coached by him, and not in tennis.' She grinned round at everybody, ignoring – or missing – the tension of the moment. 'Well, I wouldn't blame you. Admit it, he's bloody attractive.'

'A little common for my taste.' Gail was determined to salvage the game. 'Appealing, perhaps, but a bit – how should I say it – wrong side of the tracks for me.'

Fran had to admire Cassandra's poise. Acting as if she had not heard the remark, she said, looking just to the right of Gail's head, 'Talking of coarse, Gail, I really would rather Simon urinated in the toilet, or at least in the garden, but not in my Grecian urn. I think the scented geranium might not thrive on the acidity.'

Cassandra sat the next set out and she and Jessica moved their chairs into the sun and watched, chatting inconsequentially. Jessica couldn't help feeling that there was something different about Cassandra today. She couldn't fathom it out, but decided that perhaps it was she who was different and everything else was coloured accordingly. The moment with Luke at the lake had been unsettling. She had come close to telling him how she felt about him. It made her feel uncomfortable, embarrassed to think of it now. She had tried to examine her feelings about him in a logical way, but they made no sense.

Back home, when he was sober, Ben was caring and affectionate and she had moments of real self-disgust. With her children clustering round her, hugging her in their rough embraces, Edwina curled up on her lap with her thumb in her mouth – they made her feel disreputable. Perhaps that was why she hadn't told Fran about Luke. Perhaps she felt ashamed.

'Would you ever consider having an affair?' Jessica turned to Cassandra suddenly as she asked the question. She was startled by the look on her face. It was one of pure fright. 'That wasn't a proposition, by the way.'

Composure restored, Cassandra's sudden high colour faded. 'An affair?' she said. 'I … I don't really know. Why do you ask?'

'Oh, you know. I suppose it's having a brush with death, as it were. Time running out and that. I was just wondering what it would be like.' She smiled. She felt more comfortable with Cassandra these days. She wondered why that was. 'Ben had an affair once,' she said.

'How do you know? Did he confess?'

'Oh, no. But he wasn't very discreet and he left clues all over the place. Actually, I suspect it was a very half-hearted business – it was a filing clerk in his office. She got married soon afterwards. We went to the wedding. I gave her a fish slice I bought at Clicks on a Special.'

Cassandra laughed. 'What sort of clues?' she asked.

'Notes in his pockets. Predictable, isn't it? She couldn't spell, that girl. *And* she called him Bennie. Actually, I think it was all rather innocent. Probably good for him at the time. I'd just had Edwina and I'd gone off men.'

'Did you ever bring it up? Make a fuss or anything like that? Or did you wait for it to blow over?'

'I was still making up my mind whether it would be worth bringing it out into the open when it seemed it was all over. So we never discussed it. Oh, shot, Frances!'

'I suppose with the right circumstances it might be exciting,' Cassandra said lightly. 'As long as no one was going to get hurt.'

'Ah, but there's never any guarantee, is there?' said Jessica. 'These things have a tendency to get out of hand. Or so the magazines tell us.'

'And I suppose when there are children to consider ...'

'Kids are more resilient, I think, than we give them credit for.'

'Perhaps. Still, it would be risky.'

Jessica laughed, then winced. She was still in pain. 'Listen to us,' she said. 'Having a serious discussion about the pros and cons of affairs, and neither of us has said "I wouldn't dream of having an affair because I'm in love with my husband".' She looked at Cassandra. 'That was uncalled for,' she said. 'Sorry – I must have been speaking for myself.'

Cassandra and Joel met up again that evening at the penthouse. He arrived with a take-away pizza in a flat white box and a bottle of red wine in his jacket pocket. They shared it sitting up in bed after they had made love.

'You should get a TV in here,' Joel said. 'There's good boxing on tonight. I can get you one, if you like.'

Cassandra rubbed his cheek affectionately. 'And how would I explain that?' she said.

Joel shrugged. He lit a cigarette and pushed open the glass sliding door on to the balcony. Cassandra joined him. She was wearing his shirt. They stood together on the balcony, their bodies touching very slightly. Strains of the new Sky CD, bought that morning, drifted out to them. Joel tapped his ash out into the darkness. 'Don't take offence,' he said, turning to Cassandra with his slow smile, and blowing smoke out of the corner of his mouth, 'but I hate this kind of music. You wouldn't have any George Michael, would you?'

Sixteen

The night Stephan came home after a day and night of rehearsals reeking of dagga and with a metal stud in the lobe of his left ear, Ansie began to give William significant looks across the dinner table. They were deeply involved in a wildlife jigsaw puzzle. Stephan smiled benignly at them both, plucked a dark blue wedge from the centre of the spread-out pieces and fitted it gently, almost lovingly, into the buttocks of the rhinoceros in the bottom right-hand corner.

He smiled and drifted down the passage to his room before they could say a word.

'Dear Ma,' said Ansie after a pregnant pause. 'William has given Stephan a holiday job with the bank. He's working hard and learning a lot about the banking world. He's made some good friends – Rooineks – and met some interesting local people.' She gave William a tart look over the top of her glasses. When William didn't respond, she put both elbows on the table and said, 'William.'

William looked up. 'What you got?' he said, his eyes turning keenly to the pieces on the table.

'Sometimes living with you is a tiresome business,' Ansie said impatiently. 'Don't tell me you haven't noticed?'

'Noticed what, *skat*?'

'Stephan.'

'Stephan?'

'Don't be dense, William. Ever since you put him on to this contest thing, he's not been home before midnight and now he's got an ear-ring in his ear like a queer and smells like he's been three days at a rock concert in Gaborone.'

'He's having a good time. Is there supposed to be something wrong with that? Oh, look, there's the acacia branch I've been looking for.'

'It's the people he's started to hang out with, William. You know what these musician types are like. I don't think Pa would be too pleased with us if we sent the son and heir back to the farm a drug addict.'

'That's extreme, Ans.' William sat back in his chair and smiled fondly at her, in a way she found unappealing. 'Extreme. Didn't you ever experiment a little ... no, I suppose not. Well. Most kids of his age do, you know. And he's not hiding anything from us. And, well, ear-rings are a fashion, aren't they? Like floral ties or something. *I* noticed. Don't think I don't see what's going on in front of my nose. I just don't think it's anything to worry about, that's all. It's normal.'

'I don't think it's normal.'

'Well, whatever you think, there's no cause for alarm and I certainly don't think we should interfere. He's having fun. He's meeting people he obviously has something in common with. Everyone down there likes him – I'm getting very positive feedback. So lighten up a little, Ans, OK?'

Ansie bit her lip. 'It's just that I feel we're responsible for him. After all, he's only –'

'– almost a fully grown adult, responsible for his own life and actions. Take it easy, Ansie. It's his life, and you're not his mother.'

Stephan lay on top of his bed with his hands behind his head. He felt good. He'd never thought of himself as conservative, but hanging out with Davy Phillips and Stanley and the Cool Boys had altered his perspective on life. This was living. This was what it was all about. He liked the big city, oh yes. And tonight something else had happened, something that he hadn't had time to adjust to yet, or even work out in his head. He'd met Carole, Stanley Abrams' sister.

'This is my sister, Carole,' Stan had said, holding her by the hand and leading her up to Stephan like a prize. 'She's the missing link in the show. She opens the billing then teams up with whatsisname – the country singer?'

'Oh, right.' Stephan shook hands. 'Good to meet you. You've been away on a gig, right?' He was into the terminology now.

'Swaziland,' she said. 'Sorry I'm late for rehearsals.'

'No problemo. We've been expecting you, of course. But I didn't realise you and Stanley ... '

'Flesh and blood,' said Davy, coming up and putting a kiss on her cheek. 'She's our third flatmate. Look, it's getting late. Are we ready to roll?'

Carole had a powerful, raunchy voice but a body that was slim as a reed. She had a great bush of dark hair and cool, steady brown eyes. She was sophisticated and professional on stage, but somehow gauche and very young when off it. Stephan, city slicker, took pains to put her at her ease and wished his English were better. Later they went on to the Dome and then back to Davy's flat. Stephan hadn't been invited up there before and they sat up talking until late. The more stoned he got, the funnier he found the situation: here he was, a farm boy from the Free State, sharing a joint with two arty types, a white and a Coloured, and falling head over heels in love with a Coloured torch singer.

Hold on, he told himself, swinging his legs off the side of the bed and stretching for a packet of cigarettes. Perhaps falling in love was putting it too strongly. He was attracted to her, yes, that he would admit, and he felt almost sure the feeling was mutual. He knew in his heart, though, that there was also that element of forbidden fruit that he couldn't deny was present.

He and Carole had talked until the early hours, drinking coffee, standing elbow to elbow on the balcony with the traffic sounds of Hillbrow drifting up to them. When Carole had started to shiver he'd offered her his denim jacket and had held it in place round her shoulders as if it were the natural thing to do. Without even thinking twice.

He thought suddenly of his parents, and of his father in particular, and an incident popped into his mind from way back in his childhood. His father had been employing some casual labour to help build the new stables. A group of unemployed locals had gathered round the kitchen door before daybreak, waiting. When his father came out in his khaki shorts and shirt, he stood looking at them for a moment. When he spoke, his deep voice was smooth as pebbles. 'There are two kinds of your people, I hear,' he said. 'I hear that we have blacks and we have kaffirs. Now, which of you are kaffirs?'

Two men, older than the others, murmured, '*Ja, baas. Ek, baas*,' their eyes flickering up to the farmer's face, then down again.

'*Goed. Staan julle op hierdie kant*.' The two men shuffled over to his side.

'And which of you are blacks?'

After some hesitation and some looks exchanged under the sharp-eyed brows of his father, the rest of the group affirmed that that was indeed what they were. They looked puzzled, some slyly pleased, as if they were sure they had given the right answer.

'*Goed*,' said his father again. '*Hierdie kant*.' He glanced round at the boy who was sitting on the low wall of the stoep, swinging his legs. 'Now. You blacks can take yourselves off. Your services won't be required on this farm.'

Muttering, looking to one another for guidance, three of the men finally shuffled off, with backward looks and when out of range, as it were, a shouted phrase. But the rest, their eyes wide with fright, then fixed on the flat, hot concrete of the yard, moved as one body over to the right-hand side. As one man they admitted their folly. '*Nee, baas, ons was verkeerd*,' they all said, two of them grinning desperately. '*Ons is kaffirs, baas. Vir seker ja*.' They were kaffirs; of course they were kaffirs.

'*Goed*,' said his father, pleased with himself. 'Then let's get to work.'

As the group turned to go, his father turned back. One man, who had stood slightly apart from the rest, remained in the yard. '*Jy! Hotnot*!' he called. 'Do you need a special invitation?' He was chuckling, paternal. He extended a hand to include the fortunate man in his group of labourers. The man regarded him steadily. He had very pale eyes and a cigarette which hung from the corner of his mouth. He lifted a hand to it, drew hard on the end that remained and dropped it at his feet on the concrete. Without taking his eyes of Stephan's father's face, he lifted a bare brown foot and ground the butt beneath his heel. Then he turned around and strolled out of the yard gate and down the path to the road.

The word was that his father was a fair man in the district; he worked you hard, but he paid well, and he seldom resorted to the sjambok as other farmers in the area did.

Stephan couldn't decide whether he missed the farm or not. It was a life light years away. Things were different there.

On Monday there was a late afternoon rehearsal. A friend of Ansie's, Fran, a nervous woman with long red hair, had dropped in for a cup of coffee. She offered to give Stephan a lift into Hillbrow. 'I want to catch up on some work at the End Conscription offices,' she told Ansie. 'I prefer to go in after everyone's gone home. I can get more done then, when it's quiet.'

Consequently, Stephan was at the theatre early. He looked for Carole. She was at the piano, leaning over Stanley's shoulder, slim legs in very tight, very white stretch pants. Baggy green sweater and green sweatband. Curly black hair obscuring her face. She smiled and beckoned him over.

'Stan's been working on this number for months and it's finally coming together,' she told him. 'We'd like to include it in the show.'

Standing so close to her, Stephan found himself lost for words. Stanley's sardonic expression as he played softly on the keys was not lost on him, however. It suddenly struck him how stupid he must look to this group: *Jaap van die plaas*, the kid fresh off the farm, with his clumsy manners, his broken English. And now he had eyes for the Coloured chick. How predictable it must all seem. He turned abruptly away. 'If you want,' he said. He was wearing khaki too.

Carole looked after him and shrugged. 'Must of got outta the wrong side of bed today,' she said.

*

'Lucy, it's me – Fran.' Fran let the door slam behind her and started up the stairs. The night cleaner in her uniform, with the robot-like vacuum cleaner tagging obediently along behind her down the passage, paused and smiled. 'Are you better, Mrs Phillips?' she called.

'Better. I'll be upstairs, all right?'

Fran had five different drafts of the statement on Samuel Levy's refusal to serve in the army. She had accepted the onerous task of combining them into one, succinct document. It wasn't difficult but it was the first piece of work she'd taken on since Sophie's death and she felt strangely apprehensive. It was as if she wasn't sure she could do anything right any more, as if she was going to have to learn to do things all over again, like someone with mild brain damage. She sat in front of the computer feeling inertia spreading through her. Sometimes Sophie had come into the office with her when she worked in the evenings, particularly after Davy had absconded. She'd bring her sleeping bag and pillow and doss down on the carpet in the corner, and would lie there singing nursery rhymes to herself while Fran worked. They'd left the sleeping bag in the office after a while and Fran kept it rolled up in the bottom drawer of a filing cabinet. She wondered whether to give it to Lucy. Or maybe one of Jessica's children would like it. Sophie used to draw pictures for Lucy on the back of old computer paper and she would trail up and down the passages with her, unhooking the cord of the vacuum cleaner when it got stuck on corners. Fran had begun to realise that there wasn't a single thing about her life that didn't include some piece of Sophie. In time she would probably be grateful about this and it would be a source of comfort to her, Henry McBride told her, but for now it simply hurt too much.

She turned back to the computer, realising that almost half an hour had passed with her sitting with her hands in her lap. She forced her attention back to her task and tried to remember that it was important. The fact that she didn't care much about Samuel Levy and his conscience didn't particularly matter somehow. She was doing this for herself, not for him.

The ECC offices were housed in an old Hillbrow building, in the old part starting down towards the city. It was a mugger's paradise round here as the streets were badly lit, all the neon and glitz saved for the two long main roads where most of Hillbrow's shops and restaurants were situated. Fran was always amazed to find her car outside whenever she left here, day or night. They reckoned there was a car a minute stolen in this neighbourhood. She took a can of Coke out of the small fridge in the corner of the office and sat herself down at the PC on her desk. As she switched it on she thought she heard a noise. She refused to be jumpy.

'Lucy?' she called.

There was no answer. No, Fran, she told herself. Don't. Just don't. She went back to the screen. Again she fancied she heard a sound, like a cupboard door being closed very quietly, or a window. Sighing, she got up and went into the passage. She put her head round the door of the next office, but there was no one there, as she knew there wouldn't be. Then she saw Lucy at the far end, toiling up the bend of the stairs with her plastic bucket. There was comfort in that. Lucy was humming 'The Lord is My Shepherd' in a rather nice, but quavery, voice.

It's all in your head, idiot, she told herself. She went back to her desk and heard no more unaccounted for noises.

After the rehearsal Stephan didn't linger. Digging his hands, farm boy's hands, deep into his pockets, he walked the streets of Hillbrow, alone and morose. Without being conscious of it, his striding of pavements took on a pattern – along one street, down a block, along another the way he had come. A zigzagging Afrikaans boy, deep in thought, making his way into downtown Johannesburg. Were it not for his size, and possibly the expression on his face, he might well have been a mugging statistic, but he made it, untouched and unscathed, to a park bench, close to the city centre. It was dark and cool there and he was quite alone, but for a squalid group of hobos and meths drinkers sitting round a small fire which glowed in a blackened petrol drum. They took no notice of Stephan. Up above him the lights in flatland Hillbrow began to come on. The noise of the traffic was a constant background sound. Sirens – police, ambulance? – blared and receded, going to and from the big hospital on the Brow. There seemed to be some sort of disturbance just along the road running adjacent to the park, but it was too far off for Stephan to see exactly what was going on. He was aware of blue revolving lights on the tops of cars which seemed to be blocking the road and some people gathered in groups on the street outside. They were all looking up the road towards the cars. Then he saw four young white men in brown army greatcoats walk purposefully through the park gates just ahead of him. They paused and looked around. Conferred. His bench was in darkness, half hidden beneath a bushy tree in full spring leaf. Stephan stiffened but did not move. The men walked over to the group round the brazier and talked to them, gesturing back to the road outside.

Stephan, fugitive, luster after Coloured girls, held his breath. His palms were wet with sweat and he felt his hands slip along the back of the green municipal bench. The men gave what appeared to be a cursory look around the park swathed in black and, not talking, walked back in the direction from which they had come.

Stephan stayed where he was for a full hour, and then, aching and cold, slunk through the gates and away, up the side alleys, back into Hillbrow. People. Beggars. Double-parked cars. The neon harshness of a fast-food place. He was hungry. He ate a Spuddy-Buddy standing at a counter, where a sharp-faced girl in an apron spooned pale sauce over it with her eyes never leaving the TV screen over his head. He drank two cups of scalding coffee. Then he looked round for a taxi to take him home.

'I work here,' said Fran. Her face went chalk white, then blue, then white again under the twirling light on the top of the squad car. She was shaking uncontrollably and the young policeman held her by the elbow to steady her. There was a gaping hole at the side of the steps going into the End Conscription Campaign building, a chunk out of the pavement and three twisted parking meters lying in the gutter across the street, plucked up by their metal roots, leaving holes in the pavement. A baby-faced conscript, rifle slung over his shoulder, had a big brown boot firmly positioned over a spillage of silver coins no one had yet noticed. More army personnel were busy cordoning off the street at the corner with rolls of tape.

Fran and Lucy, it appeared, were the only people in the building when the explosion just about burst their ear-drums. In fact, Fran still had an unreal ringing in her ears and a heartbeat that thumped painfully beneath her T-shirt. She had been preparing to lock up for the evening, having satisfied herself that Samuel Levy would get the best statement possible. She read over her copy, turned off the computer and threw her empty Coke can into the bin. She couldn't hear Lucy's singing any more – she must have moved on to another floor. Turning the corner of the last short flight of stairs, she paused to wonder for a moment whether to lock the street door, or whether Lucy would prefer it left open. As she half turned back to go in search of her, she found her bunch of keys wrenched flying from her hand, and felt the old building rock beneath her feet, sending her crashing against the wrought-iron doors of the lift. And then there was the noise, an almighty bang, and the sound of glass breaking. Somehow she must have stumbled down to the ground-floor landing and into the street, but the next thing she knew was the sound of sirens and squealing tyres, and people running in all directions.

The policemen questioning her had had to repeat themselves over and over again. At first she couldn't hear them at all, and then she started shaking so violently that she had to be helped to an ambulance. Lucy was sitting on the kerbside, with the apron of her uniform thrown over her head. She was rocking and moaning but she didn't appear to be hurt. Somehow Fran managed to point a shaking finger at her.

'Don't forget her,' she said to the ambulance driver, who had come round to help her inside. 'She was also in the building. She's one of the night staff. I think she's in shock.'

The driver cleared his throat. He glanced towards the huddled figure. 'They've radioed for an ambulance for her, lady,' he said. 'It'll be along in a minute, don't worry.'

In her befuddled state, Fran was confused. 'But there's plenty of room here,' she said. 'We don't need another ambulance. No one else was hurt –' she looked around '– were they?'

The driver decided to give it to her straight. 'We go up to the Gen, lady,' he said. 'The other patient goes to Baragwanath.' Having made sure she was comfortable, and with a nod to the serviceman sitting stiffly opposite her, he started to close the doors. Then he stuck his head back in again. 'In Sowetoo,' he explained kindly.

Fran stared at the closed doors as the ambulance started to move. Nothing had changed. Nothing.

In the park two men stood in the deep shadow of a low-spreading tree and watched as the ambulance made a slow, three-point turn, turned on its siren and sped away up the Brow. They clasped hands briefly, and walked away from each other, one through the south exit, the other to the north. The swarthy man with hollow cheeks spat on to the pavement as he went and turned up his collar to keep out the night's sudden chill.

Seventeen

'I'll be finishing up this week,' said Joel.

Cassandra stooped to throw a tennis ball for the small white dog that was making rushes at their feet. The ball had silver rings of saliva round it. She wiped her hands on a tissue.

'I'll be doing some renovation work in De Deur from next week.' Cassandra lifted the ball with her toe. It looped neatly down the slope of the lawn, with the dog chasing after it. She couldn't speak or look at Joel.

'That's down south, on the Vereeniging road.'

They were sitting on the patio in the shade. It was lunch-time. A tuna salad lay untouched on Cassandra's plate. It had hardened into stiff brown spikes. Joel's plate was scraped clean. He took a long drink from his glass of soda water. Ice jostled roughly with bubbles. He wiped his mouth with the back of his hand. Cassandra stole a glance at him, then leant for the ball once more. This time he was quicker than she. Smooth brown fingers took hold. A yelp, a scamper, confusion. The ball soared beyond the tennis court and out into the road. The game was over.

'Will you leave the fucking ball.' His voice was low, his face suddenly too close to hers. Cassandra gave an involuntary glance over her shoulder, then decided not to care whether anyone was watching or not. She felt reckless with misery.

'Let's go upstairs,' she said, in a voice she hardly recognised as her own. Joel smiled his approving smile and, without saying anything, pulled her to her feet.

They had never talked about afterwards, when the work on the house was finished. She knew she had avoided the subject and she wondered, watching him pull on his jeans and buckle the strong leather belt, if he was waiting for her to make the first move. Then, assailed by a sudden lack of confidence, she wondered whether perhaps this was the natural order of things for him – he, the virile gigolo, preyer on affection-starved women. It was entirely possible, probable even. She pulled on a silk dressing gown and reached for the hairbrush beside the bed. In times of self-doubt it helped not to be naked and dishevelled. The heavy silver-backed brush was part of a set, a wedding present from her spinster aunt. There was a mirror, too, which made your wrist ache just from holding it. An intricate silver-worked design showed the huntress Diana in coy flight. Joel sat on the bed and put on his socks. His feet were long and aristocratic-looking, and very pale. His second toe was longer than the first. Cassandra remembered girls at school saying that that was the sign of a sexy man. They weren't wrong.

Cassandra felt she must say something, not small talk, but something of moment, to stop him in his tracks, make him realise – what? Joel appeared preoccupied. In a panic she saw him slipping away, like a dying man already half in the hereafter, with a lifetime of things between them still unsaid.

'Joel –' She leant her head back against the headboard. He was bending to look in her dressing-table mirror, combing his hair with his fingers in serious concentration. Then he turned and came to the bed, looking deep into her eyes. She felt for his hand and his fingers were icy cold. 'Cold hands warm heart,' he said as she flinched. His eyes crinkled in the corners when he smiled. She loved that.

'I must get down to the guys,' he said. 'But I'm gonna call you,' he said, 'real soon.'

The Americanism jarred disconcertingly, but before Cassandra could respond, he was out of the door, after a final check in the mirror, and taking the stairs two at a time. She took a shower and walked out to her car in the late afternoon sunshine. The panel van was still there, but she could neither see nor hear Joel and his workmen. She resisted the temptation of one last word. After all, she and Mike would inspect the house with him before the weekend. Pay him off, for services rendered. But it wasn't the last she'd see of him. It couldn't be. Cassandra had invested too much in this. She wasn't about to let it go.

It was curious, but she had settled into adultery surprisingly easily. She managed the affair the way she managed the rest of her life, with efficiency and clarity. Compartmentalised. Joel was a part of her life which didn't impinge on any of the other parts. It was something secure and private and special. When he was gone she closed that door and opened another and she felt no guilt in handling it this way. That she might have been putting her marriage in jeopardy simply never occurred to her.

When Fran was released, first from the hospital, and then from John Vorster Square, her first call was to Jessica, who came and fetched her and took her to her car which, miraculously, was still where she had parked it, with all its wheels and hub-caps. Jessica was very shaken. She didn't make a single joke.

'What are you going to do now?' she asked. 'You ought not to be alone.' Fran had thought of that. 'I'll go to the Malans – you know, Laurike's folks,' she said. 'I need to make a few calls and it's easy enough to do it there.'

Jessica looked away from her. 'I suppose you know what you're doing,' she said in a low voice. 'I sure as hell don't.'

Fran watched her get back into her own car, stiffly and painfully. Then she noticed, with a shock, a small, bald patch on the crown of Jessica's dark head and she felt bitterly ashamed. Jessica was in no state to cope with her stress. She was certainly not supposed to be driving, for one thing. She should have thought before she got her involved. She should never have confided in her; it wasn't fair. And yet, as Jessica waved and smiled through the open window before pulling off, Fran fancied she saw something there from long ago, something which, in the end, made it OK to call on her. Which made it right.

'Your friend Jim has been trying to find you.' Laurike's mother's face gave nothing away. 'I don't know how he got on to us, but he's been calling almost on the hour. Did he know you'd come here?'

Fran gulped tea, holding the hot mug in both palms. She shook her head but said nothing. She couldn't even think about Jim, much less talk about him. But it wasn't necessary to talk here, not if you had nothing to say.

'What shall I tell him?'

'Whatever you like. Just don't let him near me.' Fran smiled sheepishly.

'All right. I've made up the spare bed. Rest, and I'll wake you for supper.'

Gratefully, Fran pulled the soft, faded eiderdown over her head and fell asleep, aware only dimly of the steady ticking of the grandfather clock in the hallway outside her door, standing sentinel, she imagined, like an old friend.

Jessica looked for a report of the explosion in the paper, and she didn't have to look hard. The police had an official theory, which did not match the paper's indignant editorial. According to a senior police spokesman, it was believed that explosives concealed in the basement of the ECC building had detonated mysteriously. Police had not been unaware of the secret cache, he claimed, and certain activists well known to the authorities were being questioned. Asked about a possible connection with the recent attack on the Krugersdorp hotel, a retaliatory action perhaps, he replied that all avenues were being investigated. A spokesperson from the ECC was also quoted. He denied that any explosive material had ever been stored, to their knowledge, in the building, and he vehemently rejected the insinuations. He claimed that the blast was nothing less than an assassination attempt on the life of Fran Phillips, a volunteer worker at the offices, and a known target for the CCB death squads as revealed by the recent commissions of enquiry. The accompanying editorial deplored the lack of progress in the investigation of the vicious murder of the Phillips child and urged that an effort be made to curtail the activities of the bands of rogue 'hit squads' which still appeared to be operating unchecked.

Jessica wondered for the first time just how deeply involved Fran really was. She hadn't told her all that much the night of

Sophie's service, apart from the diary and the list, and the threatening calls. And then, of course, there was the vandalising of Fran's cottage which had shocked her. She had tried never to connect Fran with actual violence. She had always been content to imagine her on the fringe of things, putting the literature together and organising cultural events at the Market Theatre. But suddenly she realised that perhaps she didn't really know anything about anything. After this shock, when they both knew that if Fran had been coming down those front steps, if she hadn't turned back to look for Lucy, she could very easily have been killed, or maimed, Jessica realised this wasn't playing games. It did not seem too far-fetched, after all the speculation in the papers – even *without* the diary as a factor – to believe that whoever had tried to blow up the building had known that Fran would be there at that time. It gave immediate credence to the whole appalling truth: that the diary, and the damning list of targeted people, had been traced and followed with cold and frightening accuracy. She knew that Fran knew it too, but yesterday Jessica had been suddenly too afraid to bring it up, as if by articulating it she would have shown Fran that she had no solution to offer her.

She looked at Edwina, fast asleep in a patch of sunshine on the double bed. Flat on her back, relaxed as a rag doll. She picked up her hairbrush again and turned reluctantly back to the mirror. There were bare patches all over her head now. The bristles of the brush came away full of dark hair. She picked it off with care and dropped it with the rest into the waste-paper basket along with the children's Snacker Bar wrappers.

When they met the next day Fran seemed calmer. She had a painful graze from her shoulder to her elbow where she had fallen on the pavement, and small cuts on the backs of her legs which she hadn't shown Jessica yesterday. She shrugged off Jessica's concern and raised an eyebrow at Jessica's scarf and sunglasses. 'Is it time?' she said sepulchrally.

Jessica linked her arm in hers. 'Absolutely, doll,' she said.

Fragile as glass, they felt safer clowning.

'Do you remember when we were students, how we used to

drag each other along whenever we needed to fit new glasses' frames?' Fran studied the effect of a mass of blonde curls in the mirror with a grave expression. 'And how you stopped me buying the metal granny ones I liked so much and made me buy those droopy pear-shaped things?'

'They suited you better. Listen, who's the baldie here, me or you? That makes you look frivolous anyway. Dolly Parton without the tits. How about this?'

'Mm mm. Not red, please. You haven't got the skin for it. Try the Tina Turner again.'

Saleswomen exchanged bored glances. The counters overflowed with open boxes, hair all over the place. One of them advanced with a large-toothed comb and ostentatiously began combing a silver fringed wig with solid, deliberate strokes.

'I think I'm having an identity crisis,' said Jessica suddenly. She sat down on a chair. She looked exhausted, with all colour gone from her face. 'I don't think I'm as outrageous as I hoped I was.'

'OK,' said Fran, feeling a sharp jolt in her stomach as she saw Jessica's drawn face. She turned quickly to the saleswoman. 'We'll have the dark one, the shoulder length.' She held out her hand and Jessica passed over her bag.

'In my purse,' she said. 'Credit card.' She waved the hovering women away. 'I'm all right,' she whispered.

In the car Jessica leaned back against the head rest and closed her eyes. Fran headed for Jessica's home. 'You've already got the sympathy,' she said. 'Now I'll make you tea.'

Jessica smiled faintly. She was getting some colour back in her cheeks and Fran slowed down a bit. 'Do you want me to call Ben?' she asked.

'No,' said Jessica. 'He's coming to pick me up just now anyway, to take me to my chemo session. I'll be fine, don't worry.'

They drove in silence for a while and then Jessica slid her eyes across to Fran and opened them just a fraction. 'Have you noticed Cassandra lately?'

Fran marvelled at Jessica's ability to deal with things.

'What do you mean?'

'She's different. Not so uptight. You know what I think?'

'What?'

'I think she's having an affair.'

'What? Cassandra?' Fran braked suddenly, making Jessica grab at the dashboard. 'You really think so?'

'I don't know.' Jessica smiled and closed her eyes again. 'We were talking the other day, at tennis, and something she said, a sort of furtive look in her eyes, got me thinking.'

'But who?' Fran was still incredulous. The perfect Cassandra, the model executive wife and mother – surely not.

'I have a theory ... '

'Well? I can't bear it when you're inscrutable.'

'The house painter ... ?'

Fran remembered Gail. Tennis at Cassandra's when Jessica was in hospital.

'Think about it.'

They drove in silence for a while. Then Fran said doubtfully, 'He's very young.'

'Well, isn't she lucky? He's also extremely attractive, if a little fond of himself.'

'Yes, but ... '

'But what? He's not her class? That didn't stop Lady Chatterley, did it?'

Fran laughed. 'It's a wild theory, Jess. Could there be just an element of wishful thinking there?'

'No, wrong tree, Frances. There's something shifty about him. He's not my type. I wouldn't be that surprised if he's just taking advantage of her. She's rich, bored, beautiful ... '

'Yes, but *available*? I don't know.' Fran wasn't convinced.

They were home. Anna came to open the gate with Edwina on her back tied in a blanket. Edwina had a doll strapped to her back in the same fashion with a small pink knitted blanket, and her doll had a Smurf strapped to its back with one of Andrew's socks.

'You look like a set of those Russian dolls,' said Jessica kissing the top of Edwina's head.

'Yes,' said Fran. 'In reverse. How're you, Anna?'

Anna had taken down two telephone messages. One was from Ben – to say he was going to be late home. The other was from Luke Stephens. Fran watched Jessica holding the piece of paper with the numbers and wondered why Jessica hadn't told her about Luke. She wandered into the lounge, conscious of being in earshot while Jessica returned the calls. Still, she couldn't help half-listening.

'In a meeting?' she heard Jessica say. It was probably Ben's secretary, the one with the Woolworths blouses she buttoned right up to the neck.

'Not before three,' Jessica said thoughtfully. She had lowered her voice and turned her back to the open lounge door. 'He's supposed to be picking me up at lunch-time. You don't think he's forgotten, do you?' The secretary was not the sympathetic sort, obviously. 'Perhaps it's not significant that he didn't say anything to *you*,' Jessica said tightly. 'And I don't care that they've just had pizza sent through to the boardroom – could you call him out, please?' Fran thought she had actually met the woman once at an office function Jessica had dragged her along to. She had small, deep-set eyes and Jessica told her she kept Ben's dry-cleaning slips on a spike on her desk. Fran had a sudden vision of Ben's red-veined face, with bits of Pizza Margherita stuck between his teeth. 'Oh, never mind,' Jessica said abruptly. 'If instructions were to take messages, then take this one. Just tell him I'm at the hospital. Someone'll notify him if I die or something.'

'"Will do, Mrs Tucker".' Jessica stood in the doorway. 'I can't believe the gall of that woman. '"Will do".'

'Will do' was one of her most loathed expressions, Fran knew. It ranked right up there with 'Long Time No See' and her own worst, 'How's Trix'. She also knew how much Jessica hated to rely on other people. Ill or not, she would rather die than remind Ben to diarise that he was supposed to take her to the hospital, that it was her chemo day. If he could manage to put it out of his mind, then fine. She didn't need him.

'I'll take you,' said Fran.

Jessica was taking the wig out of its box. She didn't look at Fran. 'Thanks,' she said quietly. 'I'd better not drive.' She threw the wig across to Fran. 'Here,' she said. 'Brush my hair while I call Luke.'

'What did he want?' asked Fran when they were in the car again.

'He was just checking up on me,' said Jessica. 'To see if I was all right for this afternoon. For transport. Hasn't taken him long to realise how reliable my husband is.' Jessica was grumpy and irritable. Fran glanced across at her. There were small beads of perspiration across her cheekbones and when they got to the hospital she confessed to feeling weak and nauseous and soaked with dread.

They found Luke already there, talking to a colleague. He looked at them thoughtfully before making his way over. Jessica stood mutely, breathless and dishevelled.

'Ben drop you guys off?' Luke asked.

There was no point lying. 'He couldn't make it,' Jessica said. 'So Fran drove me.' Luke tried to say something, but she interrupted. 'It's all right,' she said. 'I'm all right. Really.'

Fran caught sight of their reflection in an opposite mirror and she could see at once why Luke looked so concerned. They looked like a pair of frightened children. Both of them were pale as sand and out of breath from hurrying along the labyrinthine passages from the underground parking. If a strange doctor were asked which one of them was the patient and which the strong supportive friend, he or she would have been hard pressed to make an accurate judgement. They both looked out of it.

For a moment Luke said nothing. He seemed almost lost for words. 'I'll have to have a word with Ben,' he said.

Jessica put a hand impulsively on the sleeve of his white coat and looked nervously towards Fran. 'Don't,' she said. 'Please don't. I'll talk to him. I'll make sure he comes next time.'

A nurse came along just then and hovered for a minute, apologised and then led Jessica off along the corridor. Luke walked over to Fran, where she was sitting on the linoleum in the absence of anything like a seat. He looked down at her. 'Jessica's sick,' he said quietly. 'She needs –'

Fran scrambled to her feet. 'I'll stay with her,' she said. 'Ben –'

'I think I get the picture,' said Luke. 'But it's all right. There's no need for you to stay. I'll stick around for a while.'

Fran didn't argue. She suddenly felt leaden with tiredness.

'From what I hear you should be home in bed yourself,' Luke said. 'Take yourself off. I'll take care of Jessica.'

Later Jessica lay in the recovery room with her eyes tightly shut. Nurses came in and out soundlessly, checking on this and that, but she kept them closed, hoping that no one would notice or remark on the tears which crept maddeningly out from beneath her lashes. She must have leaking tear ducts or something. A cancer side-effect.

And then Luke was there again, this time taking her hand, not saying a word, just sitting there beside her. She wished the tears away but they wouldn't go. Her nose was running too and she sniffed wetly. Still she did not open her eyes, only clung on to Luke's hand for all she was worth.

Eighteen

Kelly hitched a ride into Hillbrow. She jogged the two blocks to Pedro's high-rise flat and ran up the stairs. The front door was ajar. Pedro and a couple of his friends were playing cards and drinking beer in the lounge. He didn't look all that pleased to see her. They went out on to the grimy balcony.

'I never see you any more,' Kelly said.

'Yes, you do. You're seeing me now.'

'You know what I mean. It's not like it used to be. I don't like that place.'

'Hey. What's this? You're doing so well there. Gregoire brings me good reports about you. I hear you have influential friends.' Pedro pulled her slim body towards him and lifted her shirt. He stroked her back with his strong hands and looked down at her from beneath his cap. He had two days' stubble on his chin and he smelt of chewing gum and cigarettes. Kelly did not pull away. She put her arms up and around his neck. As her body moulded itself to his, she was only half aware of the smiles his mates threw out to them through the glass of the balcony window. Pedro jammed his thigh between her legs.

'Pedro,' Kelly murmured. 'Not out here ... '

Pedro rolled his eyes at the window. 'Why not?' he said. He wet his lips with a thin, pink tongue. He pushed harder against her. Then, taking her hand, he led her through the lounge to his bedroom. Heads followed them idly and one short, fat boy with braces and a bow tie said in a desultory tone, 'C'n I come too?' to lewd laughter and the slap of cards on the table.

They fucked with the door open despite Kelly's protests, but no one took any notice, except for when the phone rang and the fat boy came and delivered a message in the doorway. He winked at Kelly and she turned her head away.

Later, Pedro took Kelly to Thatcher's in a borrowed car. He sat at the gate with the engine running.

'Pedro,' Kelly said. 'Please don't make me do this. I don't care about the money.'

'Yes, but I do,' he replied.

It was dusk and the sky was overcast. The smell of rain was in the air, mixing with the cloying scent of jasmine from the hedge in the parking area. Thatcher's was an imposing old home, once the official residence of the Belgian ambassador, and years before that the home of an old mining magnate. The car-park had once been a croquet lawn. A very tall, very old cherry tree stood in the middle of the driveway and the remains of a child's swing, long pieces of frayed brown rope, still dangled from a stout, smooth branch. Standing alone on the gravel, Kelly wondered what had happened to the child in her. She couldn't remember ever swinging on a swing, being pushed by strong paternal hands, higher and higher. She supposed Luke might have taken her to a park when she was little, but she had no memory of such occasions. She only ever remembered him working late and coming home tired. She picked a sprig of jasmine and crushed it in her fingers. Her mother loved jasmine. They had some beside their front door. Virginia always closed her eyes and pulled back her head, saying, 'Just take a whiff of that,' and letting out a breath with a deeply satisfied sigh. It irritated Kelly beyond anything.

Suddenly she was caught in the bright lights of a car pulling into the driveway. She stood shielding her eyes, tensing. Then the lights were off her as the car pulled into the deep shadow beside the hedge. Kelly waited. She knew who it was. She dropped the jasmine on to the gravel and ground the small petals beneath her foot. 'Call me Mike,' he'd said last time. He looked like a rugby player, big chested, with lots of gingery chest hair. He always folded his suits with care and hung them over the dumb valet with which each room was provided. He had an expensive watch and Italian leather shoes. Kelly wondered if he was one of her influential friends.

It was hot in Hillbrow. Not the same sort of heat as the nights in Botswana, though. More like hot bodies, machinery, car engines, fluorescent lights, pizza ovens. It was a man-made heat, an energy that slapped you in the face or sucked you in and carried you along the square, concrete pavements.

Fran knew where Davy's flat was but she'd never been there before. It felt ridiculous as she stood waiting for the lift, that she should feel she needed an excuse to visit him. She hadn't been able to think of one anyway, and she stood now, nervously pacing, watching the lights above the lift doors. What if he wasn't in? What if he had someone with him? What if he wasn't pleased to see her? She felt like an intruder, a spy. She held a paper packet in her hand, with one of Davy's old sweaters inside it. It was a favourite of his he'd left behind in the house and she'd been wearing it a lot. She didn't really want to give it back, but to come here empty-handed, unannounced, was unacceptable. As she stepped out of the lift doors she looked uncertainly left and right, looking for a number on a door to point her in the right direction. Hesitating, she heard voices and stepped quickly on to the fire-escape stairway beside the lifts. It was Davy, and he was with a woman. They were laughing. Fran could hear keys jangling. Cautiously, she peered round the corner and there they were. Davy and Carole Abrams, she who had sung so heartbreakingly at Sophie's service. They were obviously going out. Davy was locking the door to the flat. Carole had a sweatband round her head and orange tights and flat black lace-up sneakers. She had gold chains round her neck. Fran saw Davy laugh again at something she said and put an arm affectionately round her shoulder. Fran drew back hastily as they came towards the lift. She held her breath. She felt a choking pain at the place where her collarbone met at her throat and prayed they weren't planning to take the stairs. The packet crackled against her thighs. A black cat appeared out of nowhere and rubbed up against her legs, purring loudly. It jumped up on to the top step.

'There's that damn cat again,' she heard Davy say, so close to her she could have reached out and touched him. 'It came in through the bedroom window again last night. Sprayed all over our bedroom while we were out.'

Our bedroom. Fran felt weak. She leaned against the wall for support. Our bedroom. *Our bedroom*? Then the lift doors opened and they were gone. She stayed where she was for a full ten minutes, as if glued to the wall. And all she could think about was Sophie. Sophie and Davy chasing each other with the garden hose, sopping wet and laughing and making muddy footprints all through the house. Sophie and Davy sharing a waffle at the Milky Lane, dripping cream and syrup on to the table and their chins. Davy's face as he touched a finger to Sophie's cheek just after she was born, and his face as he looked down at her, dead, on the mortuary stretcher. And now? What was she supposed to do now? Had Sophie been the only reason they had stayed together?

Feeling unbearably depressed and despondent, Fran trudged slowly down the stairs, four floors, and out into the hot glare of the street.

There was a square of paper beneath one of the windscreen wipers of the Morris. Fran slid it out with her nails.

'*Dagboek*,' it said. That was all.

The diary. Fran felt transparent, her clothes as see-through as insect wings. The square shape of the small book stuck to her skin like sweat. She looked around her. Hillbrow was bright as day. Four black youths and a white boy were sitting on the pavement behind her car. They watched her without expression. The diary. Always the fucking diary. She wished she had never laid eyes on it. The diary was actually losing its significance by the way things were going. Robert Oliphant was dead. Jacob in Sebokeng. They'd certainly had a go at her. Sophie was the odd one out though. What would they have hoped to achieve by killing her? If it was the diary they wanted so badly, surely they would not think she would give it up once her child was dead? Threatening to kill Sophie would have made more sense; that at least would have put serious pressure on her. Fran did not know all the people whose names were on the list and she didn't know how to contact the ones she did know. Gladys Ntsonga was one she had tried in vain to get in touch with. Hers was the last name there. Fran wasn't even sure that giving the information in to her superiors had done any good. There had been no attempt to protect the potential victims that she could see. Nobody had tried to protect her. She had thought, many times, about going to the press anyway, risking censure, but Mary had advised against this. Wait for clearance, she urged. Someone will contact you when the time is right. Until then there was nothing she could do. Like an albatross, the diary dragged along with her, weighing her down with its stench.

As she drove home Fran's route took her past the small fringe theatre near the university just as the theatre-goers spilled out on to the pavement at the interval. She noticed the billboards at the same time as she saw Tamzin standing in the road, holding a plastic cup of coffee, with her back to the brisk wind. Fran pulled up beside her and wound her window down. It was the opening night of Ray's play and she had completely forgotten. Tamzin looked taken aback to see her.

'Fran!' she said. 'What are you doing here?' The wind whipped at her hair and wrapped her wide, cotton skirt round her legs like a maypole.

'I meant to call Ray before tonight,' Fran said. 'I'm sorry – will you tell him? How's it going?'

'So far so good,' said Tamzin non-committally. Fran looked unhappy. Her eyes were red and she seemed angry. She thought for a fleeting moment that Jessica might have told Fran about the baby and she wasn't ready for that. Fran would be too judgemental. 'What are you doing here?' she asked again.

Fran pulled the Morris in closer to the kerb to give a taxi enough room to pass her. 'I ... I've been at the hospital with Jess,' she said.

'Oh,' said Tamzin. 'How's Jess doing?'

'OK,' said Fran. 'She's weak but she's OK. Is this critics' night?' she asked.

Relieved at the change of subject, Tamzin pointed a couple

out to her. 'They haven't walked out yet,' she said. 'I'm not sure whether that's a good sign or not.'

'I'm sure it is.' Fran had read the play, a provocative work from a young Broederstroom playwright. The bell rang to signal the second half and Tamzin was anxious to go back inside. Fran watched her go, looking thoughtful.

Tamzin threw her polystyrene cup in the bin on the corner, noticing uncomfortably three down-and-outs shuffling towards it hopefully. She went back into the theatre. She had an empty seat next to her and it had occurred to her to ask Fran to come in and see the second half. But Fran in that glittery mood made her nervous. Their friendship had not yet got back on to that easy footing and she was beginning to realise that it could never be the same with Fran. She must have been naive to think they could pick up where they left off. Sophie would always be there like a black shadow between them.

Sitting in the darkness, in the expectant hush before the curtain went up, she thought she felt the baby move inside her for the first time. Instinctively, she put a warm hand over her belly and held it there. She wasn't sure at first, but then it moved again and she smiled. And then Ray was on stage, a pensive, brooding figure, full of charm and menace.

Everyone agreed that the play was a success, if still a little rough around the edges, and wine flowed and spirits were high at the party late that night. Congratulations were showered on all the players. Ray was ebullient. All the tension and moodiness of the pre-show weeks fell away and he sparkled and shone like the star he hoped to be. Tamzin felt proud. Quite desperately proud. She liked the theatre crowd. She drank five glasses of warmish wine in less than an hour. She was so happy and relaxed that when a little after one in the morning, Ray sank down beside her on a couch and pulled her close, she looked at him solemnly and a whole string of words raced from between her teeth before she knew they were there.

Ray looked stunned, but only for a moment. Then his broad, handsome face creased into a smile of wonder and bewilderment. 'Pregnant,' he said, while Tamzin smiled woozily at him and sipped modestly from her glass.

'Well,' she said after a minute, frowning momentarily. 'It's a bit complicated, but –'

'Tammy, this is the happiest night of my life. I feel like a million bucks. Let's get married in the morning. Hell, it *is* morning! What are we waiting for? Can I tell everyone? Can we go find a roof-top to shout from?'

In a moment of lucidity, Tamzin put a restraining hand on his arm. 'No,' she said. 'No, no. I can't marry you, Ray. I mean, not this morning. Not until we talk this thing over. This baby is ... well ... we need to discuss some of the finer points ...'

Ray looked puzzled. Then, noticing Tamzin was very pale and looking at him with one eye half closed like a cartoon bag lady, he decided that now perhaps wasn't the right moment to pursue the matter. Tamzin needed to be horizontal. He prised the glass from her fingers and helped her to her feet. 'Tam's had it,' he called cheerily as he manoeuvred her to the door. 'Got to get the old bat home.'

Tamzin woke up the next morning with a bad headache and a queasy stomach. She looked in the mirror and winced. She had absolutely no recollection of how she had got home or who had undressed her and put her to bed. When she shuffled through to the kitchen to put the kettle on for tea she found a note propped up on the table. 'Call you later, Mum!' it said. Tamzin looked at the piece of paper dubiously. Giving it a wide berth, she filled the kettle with water. It took a couple of seconds before the mists around her mind began to clear. Frantically she tried to remember what she'd said, what exactly she'd told Ray. What a stupid time to choose! What a complete idiot she must have made of herself. Try as she might, she simply couldn't remember whether she'd told him the whole story, but judging from the message, she gathered that she had probably left out one or two salient points.

Fortunately, Ray had an afternoon rehearsal before the Saturday night show. She could at least avoid him for one day, to give herself enough time to collect her thoughts. She went through to the study and turned on the answerphone.

*

The house was finished. Joel Cunningham, painter and handyman, had done a good job. Mike was pleased. He and Joel walked all over the property, heads together. They inspected each wall. Mike was glad they had chosen the cooler, pale salmon shade, and Joel gravely agreed it was a good choice. Especially in summer, when the glare off plain white walls in their position could be very bad. Mike gave the painter a cheque and they shook hands.

Cassandra watched them from the patio. She saw Joel fold the piece of paper and put it into the back pocket of his jeans. She saw Selena standing talking to the workmen beside the van. It was her afternoon off and she was on her way to town in a beige linen suit and high, red heels.

Joel looked up towards the patio, just the way he had done when she'd first seen him. He shaded his eyes. He said something to Mike, who looked her way too and waved. He was on his way to play golf at the country club. He got into his car and backed down the driveway. Joel came across the lawn with long strides. He stood in front of her.

'Well,' he said and smiled, his head on one side.

'You're off then,' said Cassandra.

'Don't sound so sad.' Joel grinned. 'I'll be in touch.'

Cassandra tried to smile. She felt as if she were shrinking, like Alice. She felt as if something was trapped inside her chest and struggling to get out. She was sure she would suffocate. Jason and Rosalie came out of the patio doors and stared at Joel. They had never taken to him. Cassandra wondered if they knew why. 'Is the painter going now, Mummy?' said Rosalie.

'Yes,' Joel answered for her. 'See you around, kids.' The black eyes met hers briefly and then he turned and walked off across the grass. He looked back once to blow her a kiss.

'What'd he do that for?' asked Jason.

'Oh – nothing,' said Cassandra. She lit a cigarette, watching her fingers shake as she held the lighter.

'Daddy says smoking is bad for you,' said Jason. 'He says smoking can give you the big C.'

'What's the big C?' Cassandra asked, smiling distractedly.

'I dunno,' said Jason, 'but I think it hurts.'

Mbekhi was asleep. He lay on a couch beneath a blanket in the front room of his uncle's house. The rest of the family was asleep too, his cousins in the room behind this one and his uncle and the old lady in the next. There was a smell of paraffin throughout the house.

A dog in the yard next door began to bark and then their own mongrel, sleeping on the floor beside Mbekhi's couch, was up on its feet, sniffing at the crack beneath the front door and growling deep in its throat. Mbekhi struggled to the surface of sleep. He heard a noise he couldn't immediately identify. Then suddenly a bright light shone on his face through the pane of glass above his head and he was up in a moment, shielding his face with his arms. At the same time a terrific banging on the front door and the dogs barking wildly all around. He sat frozen. Then his uncle was in the doorway, blinking and pulling on his pants. He looked wordlessly at the boy on the couch and gestured to him without making a sound. The banging and shouting increased and one by one the rest of the family crept into the living room, their eyes round with fear, pulling blankets round shoulders. One never knew, these days, what to expect from nocturnal visitations in the townships.

Soft as a snake, Mbekhi slid from the couch, ducking his head through the neck of his jersey. Like a shadow he slid through the bodies in the doorway. When the door flew in and the room was filled with boots and lights and sticks, Mbekhi was gone and a sleepy boy cousin was climbing off the couch, rubbing his eyes and yawning.

'It's not him,' a man in a blue-ribbed jersey said, taking the light off his face and pushing through to the rooms beyond.

'Where's the boy?' said another. 'Thekiso. Mbekhi Thekiso?' He was opening cupboards, pulling blankets aside with the point of his rifle. The dog cowered beneath the table, whimpering.

'He has not been here. We have not seen Mbekhi for a long time.' His uncle knew the fruitlessness of pleading complete ignorance. They had come for Mbekhi before now. The last time had meant a split lip for him, and a bruised cheek. The old man stood still, waiting for whatever would happen next. Whether they believed him or not wouldn't matter. But tonight they were agitated, in a hurry. Their search was rough but not thorough. He tried not to let himself think even of Mbekhi, in case his thoughts were somehow picked out of the air and interpreted.

Outside the township was in darkness. All was quiet. But it was a breathing, listening quiet, not the deep peace of souls asleep. Mbekhi trotted along the dusty road at an even pace. Still his breath came raggedly from his lips and his eyes were alert as a doe's. His bare feet hit the earth with soft slaps. He did not have a plan. If they had come to his uncle's house so suddenly, he was not going to risk any of the safe houses he knew. The chances were that they would have got there before him. He jogged on, moving instinctively towards the highway and the city.

Too late he saw the road-block, the vans on the side of the road, the barrels and the torches. He skidded to a stop, turned to flee, tripped and fell in the sand.

'Father?'

'Yes, Miriam? Is anything wrong?'

'It's Mbekhi. They say he's been detained again.'

'Come in. Sit down.' McBride took Miriam by the arm and led her to a chair. She looked drawn and desolate. 'What have you heard?' he asked her.

'I received a call,' she replied. 'From his uncle in the township. He phoned me from his work this morning. He says they were raided last night. They were looking for Mbekhi, they said.' Her eyes were on the carpet and she fiddled restlessly with her fingers, pushing back the cuticles of her nails.

'And he was there? They took him away?' McBride prompted. He reached for his pipe.

'No. When he heard them banging on the door, he slipped out through the back yard.'

'Well then. Perhaps he is all right after all. If he managed to get away, he will call you, I'm sure, in due course. To let us know that he is all right.'

Miriam looked worried. 'No, Father, I don't think so. There were road-blocks last night. All over the township. It was a big thing. Hundreds of people were picked up. I think Mbekhi is one of them this time. His uncle thinks so also.'

McBride sighed. 'That boy,' he said heavily. 'I'll see what I can find out, Miriam. I will make some phonecalls straight away. Don't worry now. We'll find out where he is.'

When Miriam had gone away downstairs, McBride stood for a few moments looking out of the window and drawing stiffly on his pipe. There were some people, he thought, who could handle the things they were called upon to do. There were others who were simply not cut out for it. Mbekhi, he suspected, was one of the latter.

Gwen Sutherland was not in the Black Sash office when he phoned, but she came back to him after lunch. There had been a placard demo outside the university medical school and someone from a passing car had driven past them several times, squirting them with water pistols. It had been unpleasant and the black koki on the placards had run, making the lettering illegible. Someone from the other side of the street had taken photographs of them with a zoom lens. She sounded quite exhilarated. Shc knew about the road-blocks in the township. The office had been inundated with calls all morning. It had been another major crack-down, a new show of strength, appeasing the right this time. All this placatory action must be making the government dizzy. Several youths had been detained but many had already been released. She promised to do what she could to track down Mbekhi again.

It was evening by the time she called. She had been unable to trace him. She would try again in the morning.

Miriam was expressionless when McBride told her. She sat with Thabo on her lap in her room. She sat in darkness. On the carpet at her feet lay a magazine and a pair of scissors where Thabo had been cutting out pictures of Princess Diana. Thabo had a thing about the British royals. But his face was solemn too and he barely smiled as the old priest got down on his haunches and stroked his head with his hard, old man's hands.

Nineteen

Ben took Jessica to the hospital for her next chemo treatment. He stayed with her stoically and paced about the recovery room afterwards like a bear in a cage. Then he stood gazing out of the window with his back to her. He was impatient to get back to the office. She could tell by the way he drummed his fingers on the sill.

When Luke looked in through the door she was getting off the bed and putting on her shoes. Ben turned from the window and the two men looked at each other. The candour of that moment's glance told Jessica, without a shadow of doubt, that Luke was not indifferent to her after all. The recognition sent a stab to her stomach and she felt her cheeks flush crimson. She wondered if the emotion she was feeling was elation or guilt. Neither man noticed her as they seemed to circle each other, warily, as male animals do before they clash.

This was a moment when Luke, too, realised what should have been obvious to him all along. Jessica was not just another patient and never had been. For better or for worse she was in his head, in his skin, in the marrow of his bones. And the thickset man with the bloodshot eyes could not possibly understand what he had in Jessica. Nobody spoke. Ben and Luke continued to hold each other's gaze. Then, finally, Ben cleared his throat. He passed a hand over his mouth.

'Ready, Jess?' he said slowly. He pulled her gently to her feet and put an arm round her shoulder. He was a tall man and when they stood close together like this, similar in colouring, they looked like brother and sister.

'All right?' Luke turned to Jessica.

She lowered her eyes. Her heart appeared to have slid to her gullet, where it made swallowing difficult.

They left then, Ben walking solidly down the polished grey corridor. He punched the button on the lift with his fist and manoeuvred Jessica through its doors with his hand like a gun in the small of her back. They didn't speak on the way down, nor out to the car. Jessica felt as if she had a secret she was concealing from her husband. It was a heavy secret, and unwieldy, and she wondered briefly where she ought to put it when they got home.

When Fran saw Jim's car parked outside her gate when she came home at lunch-time from the bookshop, her heart sank. Her first thought was how to get rid of him quickly and with the least embarrassment to both of them. A contrite, fat man fawning at her made her feel ill in anticipation. Still, there was clearly no escape as she drew up behind the car and saw him watch her in his rear-view mirror. She breathed in, took her basket of proofs out of the passenger seat and waited for him to emerge. She watched as first a foot appeared, and then the rest of his bulk came squeezing past the steering wheel. She stood without moving as he came towards her. He held out his arms.

'Franny – what can I say?'

Fran looked at him, astonished. She wasn't sure at all what the gesture meant.

'I've been trying for over a week to reach you. Since I read about the explosion at End Conscrip.' He looked reproachful. Then Fran realised with sudden shock that The Incident had completely gone from his mind. He was acting as if it had never happened, as if they had never grappled together on a couch. She decided for the moment to play it his way, wondering guiltily if she had actually imagined the whole thing.

'I've been pretty busy,' she said warily. 'Meetings and stuff. Do you want to come in?' Stupid question. Why else would he be sitting outside her house? They had tea. He'd brought a packet of biscuits from the home industries shop. Fran eyed them reluctantly. The last time he'd brought over something to eat, he'd thought it fair exchange for a grope.

They made small-talk but she was uneasy and restless. Jim, on the other hand, seemed quite at home, stretched out comfortably on the couch. His trousers, a sort of shiny grey material with a strange design worked in, were stretched like snakeskin across his thighs. He wore a tie-dye mauve vest beneath his jacket and his hair was greasy. He looked like a fifties duck-tail.

'I've got some reading to do,' said Fran at last.

Jim was never one to take a hint and for once Fran felt almost afraid of cheerfully turfing him out as she used to do. There was something proprietary about him tonight, as if he felt he belonged in her living room. Or had somehow earned the right to be there. She felt strangely powerless. She wondered whether in fact it was he who was persecuting her, but dismissed the thought, maintaining again that he wasn't intelligent enough. Jim had never been very strong on the grey matter, not even as a schoolboy. He had struggled all through school. He wasn't the stuff that cops were made of, not that kind at any rate. But signs that her life was being monitored were carelessly everywhere. It was not easy to remain in control. Jessica had urged her to move in with her and Ben for a while, but Fran was vehemently opposed to involving her. She had regretted many times talking to Jessica at all about the threats.

She needed to get Jim out of the house. 'I've got a late meeting,' she tried, although she could see at once that they both knew this was a lie. 'Do you mind if –'

'Tell you what,' said Jim.

He smiled at her and not for the first time Fran felt she was looking into the face of a stranger. Jim's eyes were as blank as a sheet of paper, the smile on his face just a thin movement of bloodless lips. 'Tell you what,' he repeated. 'I'll go out and get us a couple of take-away hamburgers and the newspaper. Then we'll have a picnic supper right here and a bottle of wine. Good idea?'

Fran felt the powerlessness wash over her again, like a dragging tide. She stared at Jim. Her arms felt heavy, almost numb by her sides. Helplessly, she whispered, 'Whatever. If you like.'

While Jim was gone Fran thought of getting in her car and going over to Jessica's after all. She could leave a note on the door, saying she'd had an emergency call or something. But she didn't. This feeling of inertia held her in its grip, as if the man had put a spell on her or something. Fran was not usually easily spooked. She'd lived too long on the edge. But everything was different now. She had no ground beneath her feet. Jim had been a solid in her life, a friend of such long standing that the turn their relationship seemed to have taken so suddenly had put in question everything else that she'd thought sure and firm.

And so she didn't call Jessica or anyone else. She waited at home for Jim to return with hamburgers and chips. She even set the table in the dining room.

No one could ever have called Fran meek. She had a stubborn will and a steadfastness that belied the husky, polite voice and the slight, pale arms. Anyone who had run up against Fran's determination of conviction would have had an inkling of the pure steel that held her fragile frame together. And yet with Jim Walton, planted like a tree in her living room, she felt like a captive in a bizarre drama.

They sat in silence, she with her novel and Jim with the newspaper. Fran had spread the pages of her manuscript out on the couch as a precautionary measure. She thought of her friends. How would Jessica or Tamzin have got rid of him? Tamzin, she decided, would have simply exhausted him. Tamzin tended to rope one in. She would have had him help her with nursery school projects: she saw Jim sitting at the kitchen table with a bag over his head while Tam circled solemn eye-holes with a black felt-tip. Or she would have had him glueing conical paper tusks together for a Save the African Elephant theme.

And Jessica? Jessica would have told Jim to fuck off.

But she, Fran, sat like a dummy, unable to concentrate, every now and then peeking cautiously over at her gaoler. He turned the pages of his newspaper with large gestures, never looking her way. Even at midnight he showed no sign of moving, when the paper lay untidily on the carpet and Fran felt her eyes wanting to close. There was no longer any pretence. They were kidnapper and hostage and the absence of weapons was irrelevant. They did not talk. In fact nothing had been said to make this situation what it apparently was, apparent to Fran anyway. She played out the macabre scene in her head. She would get up to go to the kitchen for some coffee. He would make a rough gesture telling her to stay where she was.

Jim sat staring moodily in front of him. He passed a plump hand over his face, squeezed his eyes shut, then opened them very wide, like an owl.

Fran could bear the tension no longer. 'I'm going to bed now, Jim,' she said in a low voice. 'Time for you to go home.'

He looked across at her and she held her breath. Unexpectedly, he smiled, a tired, almost tender smile. He said nothing.

'You look tired,' she said lamely. She set about tidying her manuscript, smoothing the pages across the top edges.

'I don't like you being alone here,' Jim said suddenly.

'I'm all right. I'm getting used to it.'

'Still. You're a woman alone. You need protection.'

'From whom? I have neighbours close by. I have friends. A telephone. I'm perfectly OK.' Did Jim know about the death threats? Fran had thought it prudent not to make anything of it, and she was glad of it now.

'Call me tomorrow?' Jim stood up and Fran felt the tension's hold slip just a little.

'Sure,' she said. 'If you like.' She stood up. Jim stretched, smoothed his creased pants. She preceded him to the door, reached for the handle. And then his hands were on her shoulders, two hot paws, whirling her round and pulling her to his chest. Before she could begin to struggle out of his grip, her stomach in a sweat of panic, he withdrew. He took her chin in his thumb and forefinger and tilted her head to the light. His grip hurt but Fran tried to look him in the eye, making her face blank. Again the thin smile. Then, 'Call me,' he said and was gone.

This time Fran felt oddly calm. It was as if Jim had confirmed something she should already have known. Everyone was right about him. He wasn't quite balanced. He'd developed an abnormal crush on her because she was kind to him and paid him attention. He'd just presumed, now that she was alone and Davy was supposedly out of her life, that he would step into the gap. He had had little experience with women and didn't know how to go about courting her, so the caveman approach seemed the obvious way to go. So Fran rationalised as she put the chain on the door and checked the windows in each room of the cottage. Mechanically she did these things, once, and then once again.

Jim sat in his car outside her gate until two in the morning. When he finally drove away Fran found herself dialling Davy's number, not caring about the time. All she wanted was to hear his voice.

The phone rang for some time. Then she heard it being picked up clumsily, like someone having to feel for it in the dark. She waited. It was a breathless voice, a woman's voice, that whispered hello into her ear. Fran put the receiver down, softly, and lay staring up at the ceiling. Then she got up and padded down the passage to Sophie's room. She climbed into her bed – she had never taken off the sheets and bedcothes – and pulled the blankets over her head.

Twenty

The townships were once more in turmoil. Added to the Inkatha–ANC clashes which left seventeen dead in one hostel complex after a bloody weekend, a new taxi war had arisen too, with a number of people waiting patiently at a taxi rank in downtown Johannesburg being gunned down at random from a vehicle with smoked glass windows. It was as if someone had declared open season on human beings.

On the political violence side, the police were alternately accused of complicity, then of standing by and doing nothing as battle lines were drawn and men prepared for slaughter.

The attitude of many white people in the country was one of a smug 'told you so'. AND THEY WANT TO RUN OUR COUNTRY! was the headline in one right-wing publication, whose leader, drawing on the Bible for inspiration, was quoted as saying enigmatically: 'What can you expect when you offer the people a fish and then hand them a snake?'

Fran, Jessica and Tamzin sat talking surface politics one evening over fish fingers in tomato sauce at Tamzin's. Jessica was finding more and more the fascination in developments in the country that had Fran so enmeshed. She found it helped to take her mind off her own situation, her illness and her disintegrating marriage. Besides, if she was to watch Fran's back, she knew she had to become more attuned to what was going on.

Tamzin, on the other hand, had her inner eye directed elsewhere. She was preoccupied with the reality that she was going to start showing soon, that she couldn't hide behind big shirts forever. They weren't really her style to begin with and that alone was going to make people suspicious. She had told Jessica about her drunken blurt on Ray's opening night and his ecstatic reaction.

'Oh, shit,' said Jessica. 'What have you told him since?'

Tamzin had tried to avoid him ever since, actually, but without success. Ray was prepared to take to parenthood with enthusiasm, she told Jessica dolefully. Unable to help herself, Tamzin had allowed the lie to continue but said they should put off making plans until after the play's run. Ray shouldn't be distracted. And she herself had to get used to the idea. She hadn't told anyone else, she told him, and besides she wasn't a hundred per cent sure she was pregnant anyway. She could tell he was puzzled by her attitude, but fortunately the play was keeping him occupied.

'Jesus, Tammy,' Jessica had said. 'You're really digging yourself in, aren't you? I don't honestly know how you can keep this all in. I'm having a problem with it myself.'

'I'll be a social outcast soon enough,' Tamzin replied. 'Just bear with me a little longer.'

Tonight Fran seemed very down. She made patterns in her tomato sauce with a wedge of potato. She was always pale, with that translucent texture to her skin, but there were noticeable rings beneath her eyes and a message of strain in her gestures tonight. She played constantly with small objects. She rolled pellets of bread on her side plate She twisted a lock of hair round her fingers. Coming here to Rosepark school affected her more than she thought it would. From her position at the kitchen table she could see down into the garden to where the classrooms were. Tamzin had a powerful spotlight trained on the playground and there was the jungle-gym, its smooth bars newly painted, and the sandpit and the mini road system with stop signs and traffic lights.

And still wrapped in its plastic shrink-wrap stood the pile of next year's Rosepark school calendars, waiting for distribution. The top packet had been opened and Fran had picked one out as she waited for Tamzin to finish showering and for Jessica to arrive. Tamzin did a calendar every year for the parents. She got a professional photographer in to take pictures of the children doing all the engaging things pre-schoolers did throughout the year. Then she selected the best twelve pictures, one for each day of the month, to use for the following year's calendar. Sophie featured in two of them – solo in July, sitting on the classroom steps holding a grass snake by the tail and looking at once thrilled and scared, and then in September's group shot at the top of the slide with Thabo and Simon, laughing with her head back and her hands over her ears.

When she heard Tamzin coming into the kitchen, Fran had quickly turned the calendar over and put it back on the pile. She could not bring herself to allow Tamzin to know she had seen it. Nor could she bring herself to ask for one. No doubt she was off the mailing list by now.

She wrested her attention back to the present.

'I'm sick to death of politics actually,' Tamzin was saying. She began to clear the plates away. 'And politicians in particular. Of all shades – of opinion or otherwise.' She looked at Fran darkly. 'I've even decided to stop reading the papers. It's all too depressing. There's a guy in Ray's theatre group who's from Natal, and what he says about the violence down there is desperate. Just look at Alexandra last weekend. The ANC and Inkatha will never get it together no matter how often the Chief weeps his crocodile tears in public.'

'And no end to it in sight,' said Jessica.

'You know,' Tamzin went on, 'this guy lives in Pietermaritzburg, right in the middle of town? A couple of weeks ago they were having a braai in his garden, about five o'clock in the evening. They hear shots round the corner, shouting, sirens, the works. Shouldn't we go and help, do something, says one of his guests, someone from out of town. And do you know what this guy's reply was?' She pointed a fish finger at Jessica on the end of her fork. ' "How do you like your meat?" '

Fran glanced up from her plate and gave a bleak smile. 'So what you're saying,' she said, 'is that you're opting for the head-in-the-sand route?'

'Is that such a crime?' said Tamzin. 'I can't see the point in getting involved, I'm afraid.' She looked from one to the other.

'Sorry,' she said to Fran. 'I know you think everyone should be.'

Fran's eyes were tired. She seemed reluctant to be drawn further into discussion. 'Not true,' she said. 'We see things differently, that's all. For me – well, I find I can't be neutral. I feel a responsibility. It's the way I am.'

'That's because you're a Libran, aren't you?' said Tamzin. 'Can't bear to stand by and see injustice being done. Tell me my pet astrologist isn't wasting my time?' Tamzin lived by her stars in the daily paper.

Fran smiled. 'I hate to disappoint you,' she said, 'but I'm a Virgo. And Virgoans hate to see people fucking up.'

Fran half expected to see Jim's car outside her house again and she turned the corner to her street with trepidation. She knew that friendship with Jim was now no longer possible. Jim had not only broken the rules, but he had threatened her in a way she knew she would never be able to come to terms with or forgive. Now she saw him for what he was: a fat, pink-cheeked man with cruel, cold eyes and bad body odour. And she had finally admitted to herself, and herself only, that she was desperately afraid of him. She didn't need to be afraid of childhood friends at this time in her life.

It wasn't Jim's car parked outside this time, but a familiar face from the old days of the Special Branch. Van Huyssteen, his name was, and he and Fran had become acquainted over the years. He seemed to have been assigned to her on a regular kind of basis. He had a flat, stubby nose and a rather adventurous moustache that was red and bristly as a fox's coat. He was wearing beige flannels and a sports jacket and he stood on the pavement beneath the streetlamp, smoking.

'*Naand*,' he greeted Fran as she locked her car door. He liked to address her in Afrikaans. It was almost midnight. Van Huyssteen was smooth in his movements and unhurried. He looked as if he had all night to stand there in the moonlight blowing smoke rings at the sky. Fran felt her sinews tense despite herself, although this man had never in the past physically threatened her in any way. But she didn't know, any more, who was who.

The rules had changed completely. Fran waited for him to speak again. He smiled, almost ruefully, and said what he always said to her.

'Just a few questions. If you don't mind.'

Tamzin put the dishes away in the kitchen cupboards. Her back felt sore and she was looking forward to going to bed. Then the doorbell rang and she knew it was Ray.

'All right,' he said, striding into the kitchen in his Russian leather boots and sitting down. 'What's the story? The *real* story?'

'It's late,' said Tamzin. 'How was tonight's performance?'

'Don't make conversation,' he said. 'It doesn't suit you.'

Tamzin laughed nervously. 'Do you want some coffee?' she stalled.

'Tamzin,' said Ray. 'Forgive me if I'm being a bit obtuse here, but the other night you told me I was going to be a father and ever since then you've avoided the subject whenever possible. One minute you're pregnant, the next you're not sure? What the hell is going on? I think I have a right to know.'

'No, I didn't,' said Tamzin. 'Actually.'

'What?'

'Tell you you were going to be a father.'

For a moment Ray was thrown. 'You said you were pregnant,' he said.

'Yes, well.' Tamzin hung the damp dish towel over the rack above the sink. She poured coffee into a mug and pushed it across the table to Ray. He made no move to take it, but stared at her aggressively. His long, black hair and beard made him look a bit like Charles Manson. Tamzin sighed.

'Look,' she said. 'Look –'

'I'm looking,' said Ray.

'There's no easy way to say this, Ray. Yes, I'm pregnant. But I'm afraid you're not the father.' There. It was out. Now they could get on with things.

Ray took the coffee-mug by the handle and took a long drink from it. 'Is this the part where I'm supposed to shout "Slut" and whack you across the face?' he said slowly. 'Would you care to explain?'

Tamzin looked uncomfortable. She kept the table and chairs between them.

'Well –' she began.

Ray wasn't finished. 'Because I've only read the Beginner's Guide to Infidelity,' he said. 'And I didn't enjoy it. But you seem to be working your way through the handbook. I thought you and I were an item, Tamzin.'

An item. Tamzin wished she didn't have a desperate desire to laugh. Ray was playing this scene like someone in an afternoon soap. It was almost as if he'd been waiting for the moment to trot out those lines.

'Of course we're an ... an ... item,' she said finally. 'And I've never been unfaithful to you. Well, not exactly –'

'Oh? So what was it – rape? Don't keep me in suspense.'

Ray got up from his chair and came towards her. Tamzin backed up against the sink. She picked up the breadboard and held it to her like a shield. She tried to remember what Luke's advice had been. At any point had he told her to run?

Ray stood over her, breathing. His blue eyes weren't fierce any longer.

Close up, they were puzzled. And hurt. Tamzin felt things getting away from her.

'Ray, believe me. I never meant to hurt you.' She heard her own voice sliding into soap opera now. 'I love you. I want to be with you. But, something happened ... a while back. When you were away on a shoot. Dammit, it's hard to explain.'

'I'm listening.'

Tamzin really thought he was. 'It was a one-off, ridiculous situation. It meant nothing to either of us. Well, not exactly nothing ... I mean ... Where are you going?'

Ray was at the door. He shrugged. 'I guess I just lost interest in your convoluted story, Tam. Let's say I just lost interest.'

He banged the kitchen door behind him. He banged the front door and then his car door too. Tamzin didn't move at first. She'd blown it, like she always knew she would. Hearing Ray roar off down the road, she wondered if she had lost him for good. She finished putting dishes in cupboards. She scraped bits of fish into Boris's bowl. It was midnight, but she knew she couldn't go to bed. Instead she picked up the phone and dialled.

'It's Tammy,' she said. 'We've got to talk. Can you come over?'

Tamzin and Davy had always got along well. Their own friendship had grown stronger for the fact that Fran and Tamzin were close. It was an easy, argumentative, loose bond. Tamzin thought back on the years as she waited for Davy's knock on her door. Scenes threw themselves upon her memory as film upon a screen. Some were grainy and indistinct, others sharp as glass. She saw Davy and Sophie at the school gate on Sophie's first day – a delicate, skinny child with worried eyes and a Free the Children bumper sticker on her suitcase. And Davy with his slow, hesitant speech pattern, just this side of apologetic ('We have got the right day, haven't we?'). She saw Davy in the recording studio, his hands moving confidently across the mixing desk, with dents in the thick curls of his dark hair where the headphones had been. She saw Davy with his shirt off at a one-day cricket match at the Wanderers, cupping hands to mouth and shouting 'Bowl at the furniture!' with uncharacteristic abandon. It had been such a good relationship all round.

Then there was Fran, telling her that Davy had left her.

And after that the night which she wanted to wish had never happened. Ray was away on a shoot. It was raining, quite hard, when she heard footsteps running up the path and a pounding at her door. Davy stood there, soaked through, rain running like tears down his face. She hadn't seen him since the breakup.

She pulled him inside. His hands were white and stiff with cold. He stepped around the flowerpot in the hallway positioned beneath a leak and stood shivering. He was dripping almost as much as the ceiling.

'For heaven's sake, David Phillips. Did you walk here?'

'It wasn't raining when I left.'

'Where's your car?'

'I lent it to someone for the evening. It's OK. I'm OK.'

In the movies, Tamzin would have had a roaring fire, or at the very least a bearskin rug and an old lover's dressing gown. Instead she could only offer a two-bar electric heater which filled the lounge with the unpleasant metallic smell of burning dust, and the now threadbare sleeping bag she'd lost her virginity on. She did have a bottle of reasonable wine, though, but first she made Davy take a hot bath. While he warmed up she put his sodden shoes in the warmer drawer of her oven. She was on her second glass of wine when he joined her in the lounge, draped in the sleeping bag. They sat on the floor and stared into the bars of the heater. Finally, Tamzin broke the silence.

'I'm sorry ... about ... you and Fran.'

'Mmm.'

'But it's good to see you. What brings you out this way anyway?'

Davy poured himself a glass of wine and topped up Tamzin's glass. The copper bracelet he wore on his wrist glowed hot and bright in the light of the heater. 'I suppose I needed to talk to someone. I picked a name at random in my little black book, and I'm afraid I got you, kid.'

'Skip the bullshit,' said Tamzin. 'We go back too far.'

But still Davy couldn't do it. Tamzin waited patiently, while he talked about Sophie, about the studio, about the songs. They finished a bottle of wine and she brought out another. It was past midnight when he told her, with a flippant, wry smile, about the side of him he'd always known about but never confronted. About the deceit and the lies and the sneaking around like a cheating husband. And finally he told her about Stanley, who had given him the courage and the strength to be honest. Honest with himself – which was as far as he'd been able to get. He still wasn't able to talk to Fran, or to anyone else about being gay. Making the break had nearly torn him apart. More than that he couldn't yet do.

Tamzin decided to take the practical approach while she digested the information. 'So Stanley you're sharing the flat with is –?' she said. She looked at Davy closely, but he seemed the same. After almost two bottles of wine he looked vulnerable and defenceless too, qualities which Tamzin had always found irresistible. She moved closer to him and they held hands and he put his cheek against her hair.

'The landlord of the block was a bit *hardegat*, you know, stubborn about the lease,' he said. 'Some owners of flats in Hillbrow still try to hide behind the old letter of the law. He wouldn't let a 'Coloured' man sign the lease, so it's in my name anyway. I did it for him as a favour a while ago and when we ... it seemed the most sensible thing to do.'

Then Davy began to cry and Tamzin, appalled, held on to him. She wondered what it must feel like to have made such a decision.

There was no doubt that he loved Fran and that she and Sophie were a big part of his life, the biggest part probably. But a relationship so fraught with danger must grow lopsided and topple eventually. Or so it would seem.

What happened after that Tamzin's mind was unclear on, whether because of the alcohol or because she had buried it in her subconscious where it wouldn't confuse her. Either way, she would never be sure. She did know that she initiated it, but she didn't understand why. To prove to the gay man that he wasn't really gay, that he only needed the right woman to show him? No, that was never it. She supposed if she were forced to analyse it, it was pure affection, closeness and sheer physical attraction (on her part, and not a little on his). Anyway, they had made love on the hard carpet in the lounge, and again in her bedroom. When she woke up with the first light of day, like any guilty lover Davy had gone. His tackies were still in the warmer, baked hard as clay. She wondered if he'd looked for them, and imagined him padding back to Hillbrow on his bare feet.

She had not spoken to Davy since then. Until now, with his baby growing inside her, when she could put it off no longer.

Stephan heard the telephone ring in the bedroom next door. He heard the low murmur of voices and a few minutes later footsteps in the hall as the front door opened and closed softly. He was wide awake. He lay with his arms folded beneath his head. It was after one a.m. and he wondered who had gone out and why. Was there an emergency? Should he get up? Beside him Carole stirred and turned over. She ground her teeth and muttered something in her sleep. They had been sleeping together for two weeks now, but this was the first time he had stayed over in the flat. Stanley and Davy were so easygoing and casual about him, he had at first been suspicious. Perhaps they were used to men in and out ... Then he had quelled these thoughts as unworthy, putting them down to his own insecurity. They were nice. They were his friends.

Stephan still felt a bit shell-shocked. His feelings for Carole, at first suppressed and confused with other feelings, had grown beyond anything he had imagined possible. It wasn't the colour part any more – he had ceased, almost, to be aware of it, and in the circles they moved in, it was never an issue anyway. Theirs was by no means the only mixed-race liaison. He'd had girlfriends, none serious (all white, said the ever-present voice in his head, sounding like a mixture of his sister and his mother), and the last thing on his mind when he got involved in the pageant had been a relationship, or in any event one which was likely to take a serious turn. Sure, he'd been hoping some of the glamour would rub off on him, perhaps one of the finalists even to have shown an interest. But he hadn't been ready for Carole.

He was still a farmer's son from the Free State. His father was a member of the AWB who had marched behind Oom Eugène in Welkom on Soweto Day. There was no way on earth they would ever accept Carole through the front door, and there was no way on earth he would take her home any other way. He knew he was a coward on this. He was afraid even to tell Ansie. The new South Africa hadn't even got to her yet – would it ever penetrate Soetwater?

Stephan heard the light going on in the kitchen. He got out of bed and pulled on his jeans. It was two a.m. Stanley was sitting on a stepladder against the wall, drinking milk from a cardboard carton. He was stark naked.

'Is there something wrong?' Stephan asked. He rubbed his eyes.

'No,' said Stanley. 'Davy got a call from a friend. It sounded urgent, but not desperate. Sorry if we woke you up.'

'No problem. I was awake anyway.'

'Sleeping in strange beds?' Stanley smiled. He held out the carton.

Stephan shook his head. 'Would it be OK if I made some coffee?' he asked.

'Go ahead,' said Stanley.

They sat at the table, talking, as an hour slipped past. Stanley switched on the radio and they listened to all-night music turned down low.

'It looks like my sister likes you,' said Stanley.

'I think you know the feeling is mutual,' Stephan said carefully.

'Carole has a history of falling for unsuitable men. I'm not warning you off – just warning you. Also, I can't ignore your background completely, although I'd like to.'

'I'm aware of that. Nobody more than I is aware of that.'

'Are you planning to stick around in Joburg, or what? Doesn't the farmer's son have to go back and claim his land?' Stanley smiled. 'That is, until it gets redistributed in the new dispensation. Joke –' he said quickly as Stephan frowned.

'Not funny,' said Stephan. 'If I did have any plans, I suppose they've changed now. Carole is in my life and I don't intend to leave her out of it from now on.' Stephan was amazed by his own words, but now that they were out he recognised that they were as true as anything he had ever uttered. Love, it seemed, even improved his fluency in English. Love. So that's what it was.

'Well,' said Stanley, yawning. 'Good luck. That's what I say.'

At half past three Davy came in. Stanley immediately got to his feet and went over to him. He touched him on the arm, an intimate, caring gesture that made Stephan look away. Davy's face was ashen. He didn't seem to notice Stephan there at all.

He took Stanley by the wrist and they went into their bedroom and closed the door.

Mbekhi finally turned up again. He phoned first and Miriam took the call. It came from a callbox and she heard nothing but a lot of loud background noise. She knew it was Mbekhi, although nobody answered her greeting. When the pips sounded she replaced the receiver. All she had said to him – which was all McBride had overheard on his way up the stairs – was 'It's all right. Come.'

It wasn't really all right, of course. McBride should have told Miriam that if he'd been thinking quickly. The convent was being watched day and night and the telephones had never been safe. The trouble was these days you didn't know quite who was bugging whom and who you were being watched by. In the old days the Security Police had been the spies and at least you had known where you stood with them. The unmarked car, the two gentlemen reading newspapers inside. Nowadays, what with the hit squad revelations and the spying upon spies from the inner core of the city councils down to the Murder and Robbery Squad up on the hill, it was all a bit confusing. What McBride did know, however, was that it wasn't safe for Mbekhi to be around here. He called Miriam up to his room.

'If Mbekhi is on his way here,' he told her, 'I need to see him.'

'Yes, Father.'

'*Is* he on his way, Miriam?'

'I don't know.' She looked up at him. Her face was clear and calm and uncompromising. 'If he comes I will send him to you. I need to know that my child is well.'

After lunch McBride took a nap on his bed. He left his door ajar in the hope of hearing Thabo coming in from school. He'd saved some barley sugar sweets for him from the chemist down the road. Before long, though, he was deeply asleep and when he awoke he found to his dismay that it was almost dusk. Clouds had gathered across the blue of the sky and hung low and damp over the garden outside. He could see Sister Joseph down in the courtyard hurriedly gathering in the washing from the line. She had a blue peg-bag round her neck and she plucked socks and pegs from the nylon cords with deft fingers. A sudden gust wrapped a large white sheet momentarily over her head and she beat at it wildly with her arms. McBride, smiling broadly himself, heard a small giggle and looked down to see Thabo beside him, peeping over the window-sill.

'That's the way, Sister. Don't let it get away from you now!' McBride called out cheerfully as Sister Joseph succeeded at last in subduing the billowing sheet. She scowled up at the window.

'If some people were down here helping before the rain comes down,' she called back, 'they might have clean sheets on their beds today.'

'Ah, but you're doing such a grand job, I wouldn't like to interfere.'

'Mbekhi's here,' said Thabo nonchalantly.

'Where?'

'Sleeping.'

McBride went down to Miriam's room. He opened the door softly. Mbekhi was lying on the bed with a blanket covering him, but he wasn't asleep. His eyes widened as the door opened, but he didn't speak or rise when he saw the priest.

'Mbekhi?'

There was no answer, just the eyes, black and intense, fixed on McBride's face.

'Are you all right?'

McBride closed the door behind him. He stepped across to the bed and sat down on the end. He put a hand on Mbekhi's shoulder and was startled to feel his body stiff and rigid as a board. He did not move and he did not speak. It was almost dark in the room, with the curtains drawn and the window tightly closed. There was a stuffy, musty smell which was not unpleasant. McBride was afraid. This was not the Mbekhi he knew. Something had gone terribly wrong here.

'Are you hurt?' he probed gently. 'Is there something I can do to help?'

'Leave him,' came a voice from behind him. Miriam stood

there with a tray in her hands. 'I have brought him some food and tea.'

'What has happened?' The priest stood up. He took the tray from Miriam and set it on her dresser. 'Has he told you what happened?'

Miriam shook her head. She bit her lip. They both looked down at the bed, where Mbekhi had turned away from them and covered his head with the blanket. 'He's not hurt,' Miriam said, 'on his body, but he does not talk. He needs to rest.'

'What do you mean, he doesn't talk?'

'He came here. He was shaking. Like he has a fever. I put him on my bed,' Miriam said simply.

'When?' asked McBride. 'When did he come?'

'Lunch-time.'

'And he hasn't spoken at all?'

Miriam shook her head. 'I must give Thabo his supper,' she said. 'Let Mbekhi sleep now. Later we will see.'

McBride had his supper with Miriam and Thabo in the kitchen. They sat at the wooden table and tried to talk. Thabo was tired and irritable. He wanted to watch TV but both the priest and his mother agreed that it was too late on a school night. Thabo sulked, then cried, then accepted not very graciously the substitute barley sugar. An hour went slowly by, with Miriam and Sister Joseph clearing up the kitchen and McBride paging through the evening newspaper. Then, 'May I?' he said, and hardly waiting for Miriam's barely perceptible nod, he went out to her room again. He found it wide open. The bread and tea had not been touched. The blanket was folded neatly on the bed and Mbekhi had gone again.

Twenty-One

Cassandra found herself in a movie queue in the shopping mall. It was ten a.m. She didn't even know what was showing, but she bought a ticket and moved to a back-row seat, in the corner. She curled her legs up under her. She tore the wrapper off a stick of mint flavoured chewing gum and put it in her mouth, feeling its roughness soften. She never bought chewing gum and her children were forbidden to have it. She hated the way it made breath smell, the way check-out girls in the supermarket moved their tooth-marked wads from one side of their mouths to another. Actually, she hadn't paid for this small packet. It had simply materialised in her bag after she'd bought her ticket.

Cassandra wasn't coping well with loneliness. She had heard not a word from Joel and she felt his absence acutely. She woke with it in the morning and it clung to her like a shadow all day. Mike was spending later hours at the office and playing squash more frequently with James. If he was at home for two meals a week it was a lot. But she was glad in a way. It left her free to spend the evenings in front of the television, not concentrating on the programmes, but glad of voices and people carrying on with their lives while she felt her own suspended in limbo. She waited like a schoolgirl for the telephone to ring. Once she had called Joel's number at home, but there was no reply. Another time she had left a message for him on his paging service but he hadn't returned the call.

Cassandra had stopped in at the bookshop where Fran worked on her way through the mall. She hadn't come in to work this morning, they said.

They weren't particularly worried or concerned. At the moment Fran was allowed to come and go as she pleased. She made her own hours. Cassandra bought a couple of novels and a biography.

The movie was about kick-boxing and the music score was deafening. Towards the end she found herself with a throbbing headache and an urgent need for fresh air and space. She felt dazed as she wandered out into the shopping crowds. She knew that if she didn't see Joel soon she was going to make a fool of herself. She'd go after him and plead. She'd grovel like a spurned mistress in a Victorian novel.

She tried on a skirt and blouse in a designer dress shop. She came out with a pair of stockings and a negligee, which she paid for, and a heavily studded black belt and silk scarf, which she didn't.

Today she had parked her car in a side road near the mall. As she turned into it, stepping carefully in her high heels over the uneven gravel, she became aware that she was not alone. Two young men squatted against the wall just in front of her car, while another two were strolling abreast a little way behind her. There was no one else in sight. Hers was the only car parked this far away from the public parking area of the mall. She put her head up and lengthened her stride. Her keys were in her hand. The squatting men were standing now. They watched her approach. They would probably ask her for money or offer to wash her car. She had words ready for them.

As Cassandra put the key to the lock, all four men were beside her.

'I'm sorry' she said, 'I haven't –'

She felt the key taken out of her unresisting hand and her bag pulled smoothly from her shoulder. Then she felt a hard object in her side and saw a screwdriver in the hand of the man closest to her. It was a small one, like one of a set her father used to have, with a see-through plastic handle. She thought fleetingly of kick-boxing and wished for an absurd moment that she'd paid more attention. And then she found herself being punched and kicked and thrown to the ground. She heard a tooth crunch and felt hot blood gush from her nose. She scrabbled to find her footing on the slippery bank of the road. By the time she managed to get herself to a sitting position, her attackers were a cloud of dust and spurting gravel at the corner of the road.

When she thought about it afterwards, it struck her as odd that even then, mugged and car-less in the northern suburbs, probably lucky to be alive, her first thought was of Joel, and her need, her only need, was of him. Finally, though, she had made her way back to the shopping centre and phoned Mike from the Village Bookshop. The manager had been kind and helpful. He had telephoned the police for her and made her tea. Her nose was tender and swollen. One of the shop assistants had gone out to the chemist and bought her painkillers. By the time Mike arrived to take her home the bleeding had stopped, but her face was crusted with dried, brown blood, except for the tracks where her tears had run down her cheeks – 'like the parting of the Red Sea', the manager had attempted to joke, as he guided her out of the shop with a solicitous hand on her arm. Normally, Cassandra would have stared him down with her haughtiest look, but in spite of her pain, she gave him a small smile and thanked him through her swollen jaw.

Mike called the doctor and he was at the house soon after they got home. He pronounced her nose not broken, only severely bruised. She had, however, lost two teeth. For the moment, though, he sedated her and left ointment and more painkillers.

A wide-eyed Selena was waiting for Mike at the foot of the stairs. 'The painter was here this morning,' she told him. 'To see the madam.'

'Oh?' said Mike. 'I thought we'd finished with him. He didn't say why he'd come back?'

'No, Master. He waited in the lounge for a long time. I made him tea. Then I went off for my own tea and when I came back inside he had left.'

'Well, thank you, Selena. I'll tell the madam he called.'

Mike was busy. He had to report all Cassandra's credit cards stolen. He had to call the bank and the insurance company. He had to start organising a car for her to drive. The next morning

Cassandra was still asleep when Mike left for the office. By the time he came home in the evening, she was sitting up and feeling better, but the painter's visit had completely slipped his mind.

Fran was released on Friday. It had not taken them long to get to the diary; she hadn't expected it to. Everyone seemed to know about it. She was thankful she'd had the foresight to take care of it. At least that was safe. She came home to a house of wilting plants and bad smells from the refrigerator. At least they hadn't made too much of a mess this time. Their search had been thorough, of course, but, she knew, fruitless. She had a shower and changed her clothes. She ate a bowlful of Sophie's Cocopops. She thought about her dead daughter and felt the pain drip out of the memory like blood from a wound. Everything had been for Sophie. The struggle was for Sophie and for children in South Africa like her. Fran had gladly given her life to the cause. There had been a purpose to it all with Sophie (and Davy) there. She told herself that that purpose hadn't changed. A just South Africa was still the goal, but somehow the impetus and the means had changed gear, just like Fran's energy and drive. She wished she could get it back, that pure feeling of commitment and vigour, the knowledge that what she was participating in was the best way. Her comrades told her that she needed time, that she shouldn't throw herself back into the deep end so soon. But time was what she had too much of, time to think and brood. Time to resent other people's children now, as well as their wealth and privilege, and their taking for granted that these things should be theirs by right. Fran knew how easy it could be to turn the cause into something personal and bitter, growing rank and choking like a weed. It was a trap she was determined she would not fall into. She wished she had stayed on longer in Botswana, with Mary and the children. There she never had any doubts.

At the bookshop they told her about Cassandra. Fran telephoned her straight away, but Cassandra was cool and diffident.

'It was good of you to phone,' she said through a blocked

nose. 'But it wasn't necessary. I'm all right.'

'Yes, well, I knew that,' said Fran. 'I just wanted to call, you know. To say how sorry I was. If there's anything I can do ...?'

'I'm fine,' said Cassandra. 'Thank you.'

'Well, if you're sure,' Fran said doubtfully.

'Oh, there is one thing.'

'Yes?'

'I wonder if you could tell the others there'll be no tennis today?'

Fran decided Jessica had been wrong about Cassandra. She wasn't having an affair. She wasn't any more relaxed than a snooker table. Cassandra didn't need anybody.

'Mbekhi is back again.'

McBride took off his glasses and laid them on his desk. He hurried down the stairs after Miriam and down to her room. Mbekhi was indeed back. He was sitting in a chair drinking a cold drink. He had a Coca-Cola Yo-Yo in his right hand and was doing intricate loops with it. Thabo sat at his feet watching his older brother with reverence.

'Can we have a minute alone, Miriam, please?'

Miriam nodded and took Thabo by the hand.

'Wait,' said Mbekhi. He held out the Yo-Yo and Thabo took it with a grin.

'He speaks,' said McBride.

Mbekhi smiled a half-smile. Today the room was bright with sunlight. It was hot and the November sun blazed out of a faded blue sky.

'I think,' said McBride, coming straight to what he felt was the point, 'that you, Mbekhi, are involved in something too deep for comfort. Am I right?'

'I'm sorry, Father, but you are wrong. I can look after myself. I have seen some bad things this last week and I needed some time to think things through.'

'What sort of things? Can you talk about them now?'

There was a tap at the door and Fran put her head round it. 'There you are,' she said to Mbekhi. 'May I come in?'

Mbekhi stood up and pulled out a chair for her. He clasped her hand briefly and McBride saw a fleeting look pass between them that he found curious for just a moment.

'Come in, my dear,' he said. 'Come on in. As you can see, the prodigal has pitched up.'

'Miriam's been worried about you,' said Fran. 'So have I.'

Mbekhi took a sip from his glass. 'I was just telling Father,' he said, 'about the road-block.'

'Ah, so you were picked up,' said McBride. 'We thought that was what happened to you. Your uncle phoned your mother. We were all worried when we couldn't find you this time.'

'What happened?' asked Fran.

'There were ten of us. Some were kids I know. My friend Tom Shabalala was one, others I never saw before. They took us in the van out into the veld.'

Fran frowned. 'Into the veld?' she said.

'Yes. I don't know where exactly. Other side of Soweto, I think. Further south.'

'And then?' McBride asked.

'Two police. They were laughing and talking big. In Afrikaans. They were saying how they had "done" the boys at Boksburg and now they were going to do us.'

'I didn't know you were at Boksburg, Mbekhi,' said McBride.

Mbekhi lit a cigarette. 'I was there. I recognised one of the men from that day. He was at the cathedral too.' He looked at Fran. 'I told you. The man with the thin face. He wasn't in uniform then, either.'

'Are you sure they were policemen?' McBride had not considered this possibility until now himself.

For a moment Mbekhi looked unsure. 'They talked like police. Looked like police.' He shrugged.

'What happened then?' Fran asked.

'They made us get out of the van on to the stones and grass. Then they started to beat us up, kicking, hitting us with bricks.'

'Mbekhi,' McBride interrupted. 'Were these policemen white or black men?' Immediately he regretted the question.

Mbekhi's eyes were sardonic. 'In the hands of a white or a

black man, Father,' he replied, 'a brick on the side of the head feels the same.'

'I'm sorry – go on.'

'Then it was over and they pushed us back into the van. Only there weren't as many of us this time. We left behind us three – three dead boys in the veld there.' Mbekhi stopped. He put his glass on the table beside the chair. He looked out of the window. 'Tom Shabalala was one of them,' he said.

McBride had been stopping up his pipe in his big, mottled hands. Now he sat holding it between his legs. He, too, looked out of the window and said nothing. He could see the blue sky, the green of the trees. It was a summer's day in South Africa – the 'new' South Africa, so long awaited. And what a pitiful legacy the country was reaping. There was more hatred now than ever before, more killing, burning, violence. It was hard sometimes to keep up one's hopes, or to maintain the voice of reason in the face of such bitterness, such anger. Or to believe that this was a necessary baptism of fire, that afterwards, when the smoke had cleared, the future could be rich and full and the energy constructive.

This is the day of atonement, McBride thought, the day of atonement for the whites who have had it so good for so long. 'What's past is past. Let us go forward to a new South Africa.' Who was it had uttered those smooth, shiny words – the State President, or Nelson Mandela? So easy for them. So easy. Let us forgive and forget. And when the people of the land said, No, let us not forgive and forget – who is going to *pay?* Then the people were not serious about peace, about sharing. They were obstructive, they were anarchists. They were not interested in coming to the negotiation table. And still, on the streets, in the fields around South Africa, every hand held a weapon at the ready, every face carried mistrust and betrayal in the eyes.

Mbekhi was a child of violence. He had known little else his whole life. His formative years had been dogged by boycotts and unrest. How then could one expect this boy and thousands like him to forgive and forget and move forward in one united South Africa?

'What happened then? Did they take you in?' McBride asked wearily.

'No, Father,' Mbekhi replied in a low voice. 'They dumped us on the highway outside Soweto.'

Twenty-Two

'Did you know Zinzi is learning to drive?' Gail Fleming and Ansie were making small-talk in the sun outside the school gates. 'I think it's wonderful, don't you?'

'Why wonderful?' said Ansie ungraciously. 'It's a free country.'

Gail glanced at her curiously. Then the children came running up, Petra and the twins together as usual. Petra asked breathlessly if she could have lunch at the Mokoenas' house.

'Their mother hasn't invited you,' Ansie said quickly, wishing Gail would move off.

'Yes, she has. She asked me this morning before school. Here she comes now. You ask her – *ask her*.'

Ansie was trapped between the hedge and her car. Zinzi panted up to them, her black face shining with perspiration.

'I wanted to ask you this morning,' she said, when she'd got her breath back. 'It would have saved you the trip, but you didn't see us as we walked along.' She smiled. She knew Ansie had seen them. Ansie hated this woman for making her feel so guilty. She wasn't by nature a mean person but Zinzi Mokoena somehow had the knack of making her seem so. Now that there was obviously no evading this situation, she bitterly resented her and she knew it must show on her face. Still, Zinzi clearly didn't expect her to refuse.

'How're the driving lessons coming along?' Gail interrupted. She was taking the Symons children home as Cassandra was still not well enough to drive the small new BMW Mike had given her.

'OK,' Zinzi said, and then to Ansie, as casually as if they had linked arms, 'Shall we go?' Holding Freda and Petra by the hands, she stood solidly by the door of Ansie's car. Ansie knew when she was beaten. She felt disturbed by the strength of her ill-feeling towards this impossibly cheerful woman.

They drove home in silence, pinned in by their seat-belts. Ansie kept the engine running outside the Mokoenas' house. Petra gave her a hard kiss on the lips through the window. 'Tara, Mama,' she said.

Zinzi, struggling to get out of the soft leather seat, put a hand on Ansie's arm for leverage. 'Will you come and have a cup of tea with me later on?' she asked.

The moist black fingers on her arm felt cool as putty. 'Well, yes,' Ansie said, knowing that to do otherwise would be churlish in the extreme. 'All right.' She let the big car slide forward with Zinzi's hand still on the open window ledge.

And then, of course, Ansie had to figure out what she could do to beat the mealie-bread. She considered a cop-out – a Swiss roll from the bakery or a packet of supermarket tennis biscuits. Either would certainly put Mrs Mokoena in her place. She even slowed down when she got close to the bakery but in the end it was good old Afrikaner pride which kept her foot on the accelerator, as of course she'd known it would.

By three o'clock Ansie's kitchen was thick with the smell of fresh-baked scones. Home-made jam, red as blood, shone in a dish on the heavy wooden table. Ansie split the scones with her fingers. She spooned ruby-red nuggets on to the melting butter in the centres. She followed this with a dense band of white cream whipped into fierce points. Then she was ready. She had risen admirably to the challenge.

Zinzi's living room was neat, but comfortable. Ansie, the afternoon visitor, sat with her knees together on the edge of the sofa. Zinzi complimented her on the scones, the jam especially. They asked each other about their husbands who, they discovered, were both in banking. This news irked Ansie more than she hoped showed. The children were playing computer games in the study and the electronic bleeps punctuated the erratic silences in their conversation.

All of a sudden, when Ansie felt the time had come when she could start to leave, there was an almighty bang from the stoep outside the living-room window. Ansie's hand flew to her mouth and the scone she'd been holding shot out of her fingers like a missile. It came to rest on the back of a chair where it clung like a scared, hurt thing, jam dripping bloodily from it. There followed a series of smaller, staccato reports and Ansie ducked her head down into her shoulders and put her shaking hands to her ears. Zinzi had whirled from the room at the first explosion and pulled open the front door with a crash. When all seemed quiet Ansie got up and crept to the window. Zinzi was at the garden gate with her hands to her mouth. 'FUCK OFF!' she shouted in a voice so big it must have echoed and bounced off the security walls all the length of the street. Ansie didn't know whether to be more shocked by the volume or the language. She could see no signs of conflict outside but an odd, acrid smell was in the air, a smell familiar but unidentifiable.

'Crackers,' said Zinzi placidly, coming back into the room. 'More tea?'

Ansie was bewildered. 'Crackers?' she said. 'Who's crackers? What's going on?'

'Sit,' said Zinzi. Ansie was peering nervously round the curtain again. 'Don't worry, they won't be back. Not today anyway. I guess they've used up their pocket money for the week.' She passed her a cup of tea and picked up Ansie's side plate which lay on the carpet. Then she explained about the firecrackers, the graffiti, the human and animal faeces on the lawn. The phonecalls and frightening noises in the night. She shrugged at Ansie's appalled expression. 'Don't worry,' she said again. 'It's nothing new. It will run its course and then we will be left alone.' She walked across the room to scrape Ansie's scone off the chair with the back of a knife. 'I feel better at least,' she said over her shoulder, 'to know that I have one neighbour I can call a friend.'

Deflated and disarmed, Ansie smiled vaguely at Zinzi's back and meekly held out her plate for the remains of the scone.

'With Ben there are two kinds of drunk,' said Jessica matter of factly. She and Fran were sitting out by the side of the swimming pool while her children played in the water.

'What d'you mean? Upright and all fall down?' Fran held out her hand for the sunblock and started working it into her skin.

'No,' said Jessica seriously. 'They tend to result in different behaviour patterns. It's quite interesting really. Andrew – I think Edwina's drowning! Turn her the right way up, please! It probably relates to the amount of alcohol he's consumed, but as I'm seldom with him when he's drinking with any serious intent, I can't substantiate that.'

'Go on,' said Fran.

'Well, first there's the aggressive mode. Fortunately, this isn't directed at me or the children, or not yet at any rate.'

'You mean he's just in a bad mood?'

'More than that. It's inanimate objects he gets cross with, particularly the children's toys, and especially if they're in his way as he comes stumbling through the house late at night.'

'Perhaps they remind him of his responsibilities as a father at a time when it's the last thing he wants to be reminded of,' Fran commented drily.

Jessica took her wig off and hung it on a branch of the lemon tree behind them. She was nearly completely bald now, and looked rather regal, Fran thought, like the queen from another planet in a Star Trek movie. 'I'd watch the sun up there, if I were you,' she said. 'Go on.'

'Well, the first time I noticed it was when I'd turned all the house lights off before going to bed. Actually, I'd forgotten that Ben was still out – it was about one in the morning – and I suppose I just wasn't thinking. Anyway, when he did come in it was pitch black of course and Andrew's roller skates were beside the front door. You should have heard the tripping and cursing.' Fran giggled. 'Those two skates came whizzing and buzzing down the floorboards like a sort of phantom skater in the night. They ended up crashing into Martha's dog basket in the kitchen. Ben was really mad.'

'Why didn't he just turn the lights on when he came in?' Fran asked.

Jessica was slipping into the water, slowly, inching downwards without a ripple. 'I don't know,' she said. 'I never thought about that.' She leaned against the side of the pool with her chin on her hands. 'Then there were other times,' she said. 'Shins, toes, banging into chairs not put back in their places. A lot of heavy hopping and very bad language. And once there was a bowl of fruit on the sideboard which he knocked over. I think he was trying to keep his balance. He was very drunk that time.' She chuckled.

'What?' said Fran. 'Why are you laughing?'

'It was like a nocturnal coconut shy,' Jessica said. 'The bananas and the naartjies were the worst. Ben just picked them up and threw them. All over the kitchen. Anna had to clean it up in the morning. God knows what she thought we'd been up to. There were all these brown, glutinous trails across the walls, like gross giant slugs had been there in the night.'

'Yuck,' said Fran. She got up and dived into the pool. Glenda and Andrew swam towards her and hung on to her shoulders, almost pulling her under again. 'It's cold in here,' she said. 'I don't know how you can stand it. Glenda – your lips are blue.'

'Mummy's took her head off,' said Glenda.

'I wouldn't leave it on the branch too long,' Fran said. 'Something might make a nest in it.'

Jessica climbed out of the pool and lay face down on the hot cement on her towel.

'What I can't understand,' Fran said, coming and sitting beside her, 'is what your role in this situation is. Do you just lie there and listen to Ben's crashing progress through the house or what? Don't you ever get up and light the way, as it were?'

'Ah,' said Jessica. 'The truth? I actually used to – but I don't do it any more ... '

'What?'

'Well, I'm ashamed to admit that I began to lay these, well, kind of traps, really, I suppose they were. I don't know that I did it on purpose or anything, not at first anyway. I didn't really leave the skateboard out on purpose; I just didn't bother to put it away that first time. And then … maybe I was just pissed off that Ben was coming home so late and always drunk, but I would leap up when I heard his car and turn out all the lights and then duck back to bed and listen.'

Fran looked at her sardonically. 'You didn't,' she said.

'You thought I was a nicer person, didn't you?'

'Tell me more.'

'Well, then I did start doing it on purpose, and sometimes it was quite spectacular, I can tell you. One of the best was the skateboard and the building blocks tower and the bag of marbles. That one woke the whole family. I felt sorry then and got out of bed to see if he was all right, but he wasn't a bit grateful. He just yelled at me, and at the kids, and we all crept back to our rooms. I had to take Edwina into bed with me, she got such a fright.'

Fran was speechless. She looked at Jessica with new eyes.

'I stopped doing it after the skittles,' Jessica said wistfully. 'He began to take it out on Andrew, and Andrew was very confused.'

'I guess the fun just went out of it,' said Fran sarcastically. 'Honestly, Jessica. You're very strange. What's the other kind of drunk?'

'Oh, you know, the maudlin number. Usually a bit earlier than the first kind. He comes in quite early, when I'm still up, reading or watching television or something. It's quite a standard pattern: the fumble with the key in the lock. The clumsy stumbling into the room. Then he stands directly in my line of vision, especially if I'm watching a programme on the box. You know the stance – legs a little too wide apart.'

'The hangdog expression.'

'Mummy-I'm-sorry-so-hit-me.'

'Does he make excuses?'

'A whole litany. I really wish he wouldn't bother. I stopped caring, or worrying, a long time ago. There was a time when I used to look at my watch and think about accidents, but that's long past.'

'Oh, Jess.' Jessica was looking depressed. She was making herself feel depressed. Fran wished she would stop.

'Sometimes then he tries to make love to me and that's worse than anything. He smells disgusting and can hardly ever get it up when he's in that state and if he does he labours away for half an hour mumbling pathetic rubbish into my neck.' She gave a short laugh. 'Until I could cheerfully stab him in the back with my nail scissors.'

'And now?' Fran said gently. 'How are things now?'

Jessica sat up and put her sunglasses on. 'I suppose I'm very naive,' she said. 'Or very stupid. But, you know, I thought that after this cancer was diagnosed, with all the treatment and everything, I thought ... '

'That he'd sharpen up a bit?'

'Yes, I guess so. Cut down on the booze, you know. I had this silly idea that it might help to bring us closer together, make us more of a family again. Stupid really.'

'Is Ben an alcoholic?'

'I don't know. If not, he's the next best thing. I suppose if I was a supportive, loving wife, I'd try to understand, to be there for him and all that stuff, but you know –'

'What?'

'I don't care. I don't care if he drinks himself to death.'

Fran couldn't find anything to say. The children were getting out of the pool and she got up and helped them to put towels round their shivering limbs. A sudden vision of Sophie in her polka-dot bikini, the top half riding way up above her flat pink nipples, hit her like a blow, and she shook her head to try to clear it. It was getting cool outside and there were shadows over the water in the pool.

'Let's go inside,' said Jessica.

They gave the children juice and biscuits and Fran made coffee for herself and Jessica. Jessica looked very tired but she clearly wanted to talk. 'Ben just can't come to terms with this,' she said, putting her wig back on. 'He can't even *say* cancer.'

'Perhaps you're being a bit hard on him,' Fran suggested. 'Give him time to get adjusted to it all.'

Jessica ignored her. She seemed almost to be talking to herself. 'You know what it is,' she said. 'I worked it out. Ben feels it demeans him in some way. Somehow I've deceived him. He chose a wife and the wife hasn't come up to scratch. I was flawed right from the start.'

Jessica spent a lot of time thinking about Luke, but she hadn't been able to bring herself to confide in Fran about him. She knew the danger of what she was doing. She knew that her self-esteem was at a low point, that her marriage was close to irretrievable breakdown, and that any man, attractive to her or not, who chose to make her feel good about herself was a potential trap she could willingly fall into. She knew all that. She talked it over with herself every day. And still she knew that with Luke it was different. It wasn't just that he found her attractive. She could tell that he did, God knew why. There was something more than that. It was the comfortable way they talked to each other, she supposed, the way he really listened to what she said. She'd always been a push-over for a good listener. And of course there was the way Luke was so honest with her about her illness and she really needed that. It was, ironically, her lifeline. Perhaps it was thinking about Luke, fantasising, knowing that it would probably never get beyond that point, that made her situation bearable. And the more Ben was out of the house the better. Which was why, when Ben came home from work and said he had to make a trip to Vereeniging and would be gone three days, Jessica felt positively uplifted. And why, when she was talking to Luke on the telephone the day Ben left, she let it slip that she would be alone in the house.

'Will you be all right on your own?' Luke asked immediately. 'Why don't you get Fran to stay over?'

'No,' she said. 'I'm fine. I like it on my own actually. It means the children are more relaxed and I don't have to cook.'

'I think I'd better come by and check on you,' he said lightly. It was the point of no return. They both knew that by the sudden silence on the telephone. It could have gone either way and Jessica held the ball.

'Come and see for yourself then,' she replied. 'Seriously. Why don't you stop by for a drink – that is, if it won't be a bore for you – ?'

He had come, but late. Jessica had had time to shower and to look critically at the hanging flesh on her bones. In the unflattering light in the bathroom her face was haggard and her skin without lustre. The patches on her skull made her look like a Belsen refugee. When he came he found her in tears. She stood at the door, holding it wide open like a challenge.

'It's no good,' she greeted him.

He smiled, bewildered.

'It's no good, I tell you,' she said. 'It's no good. I'm no fucking good. Look at me. I am completely and utterly without charm.'

Luke didn't laugh. He adjusted her wig, which was slightly askew. He pushed her gently inside and closed the door behind them. Then he took her in his arms and kissed her, just as he ought.

'I thought Wednesday was your chemo day,' said Fran.

'I changed it to tomorrow. I really need to talk to you about something. Fran, are you desperately busy today?'

'Never too busy for you, Jess. You know that. It's just that I'm dishing out pamphlets at a rally at lunch-time. I can't really get out of it. I haven't been pulling my weight lately and I've already got my car loaded up and everything.'

Jessica hesitated. 'Perhaps I can help?' she said. 'Couldn't I come along, or is it comrades only?'

Fran laughed. 'Of course you can come,' she said. 'With pleasure. I'll pick you up.'

It was a joint ANC-PAC youth rally in Soweto, aimed at getting the youth of the two factions together. The parties had expressed deep concern at the continuing violence raging in the townships around the country. Until a neutral peace-keeping force was brought in, Fran said, there would be no end to it.

Ideological polarisation was an added threat and desperate efforts were being made to heal the rifts.

Fifteen years in Johannesburg and Jessica had never been to Soweto. To her it had always been a smog- and smoke-filled place to one side of the highway. You were aware it was there, caught glimpses of it in the dip, but had no reason to visit it. Right now it was also a war zone and Jessica was nervous.

Fran drove swiftly and surely along the rutted streets. Taxis hurtled past them continually and she used her hooter all the time. The streets were filled with people and dust. Some turned to stare at the Morris and the two white women inside it. White people in the township were still an oddity, especially at the moment. Mostly the reaction was one of friendly surprise. Sometimes fists were raised in the ANC salute. The rally, heavily policed by ANC and PAC marshals, was held at a school stadium. Fran met up with some marshals and started distributing her pamphlets. Jessica helped her take them out of the car. She wondered what Ben would say if he knew where she was. It wouldn't be complimentary. There was some indifferent music, some impassioned speeches and much swaying and toyi-toying in the stands. Jessica didn't listen to most of the rhetoric; she was too busy looking about her nonchalantly and hoping she didn't look as out of place as she felt. Newspaper reports and no-holds-barred pictures sprang to mind: necklacings, informers set alight or beaten to death, crowd violence, clouds of tear-gas. Nor had she missed the burnt-out cars and oil drum barricades on their way in, though it had seemed neurotic to point them out to Fran.

The Morris looked safe enough parked on the edge of the playing field, but you couldn't be sure. She'd also heard about cars being hijacked to and from these events. She wondered what would happen to them if they had to make their way out of Soweto on foot. Fran seemed unconcerned, however, and she tried to take her cue from her. She also appeared to know almost everyone. Most of the time she spent talking to a young black boy she introduced to Jessica as Mbekhi. He looked familiar to her and after a while she recognised him as Thabo's brother, from Rosepark. It was ironic to think that he looked out of context here in Soweto, that she was more comfortable seeing him in white suburbia.

By four o'clock they were on the highway, none the worse for wear, making their way home through the afternoon traffic. There had been no sign of trouble. They were both hot and tired. Jessica felt a little faint too.

'We didn't get the chance to talk,' said Fran. 'Sorry – but you could see how it was. Shall we stop off somewhere for a drink?'

They found themselves at a bistro near the Dome. They ordered tall, cool glasses and Fran had a slice of cheesecake.

'It looks good, you know,' she said. 'The wig. I think we made the right choice. How does it feel?'

'Hot sometimes. And itchy. But I'm getting used to it. I take it off at night and Glenda brushes it with her Barbie brushes.'

'There's something bothering you and I'm making small-talk,' said Fran. 'What is it?'

'Ben's out of town for a few days,' said Jessica.

'And that's *bothering* you? Sorry – strike that.'

Jessica pulled a face. 'Believe it or not, I've been faithful to Ben since the day we married. Until last night. Last night I went to bed with Luke Stephens.'

'Oh,' said Fran. She signalled to the waiter for refills. 'You're a dark horse, Jess. How long has this been going on?'

'It hasn't. There isn't anything going on. Well, not really. At least not in so many words. It sounds so stupid. You know – I was attracted to him right from the day I accidentally went to him for a check-up and he discovered this whole thing. I didn't realise it was mutual, at least not for a while. And then last night he came over –'

'Did he know Ben was away?'

'I told him. I invited him. It was as blatant as that.'

'Why are you so edgy? Are you consumed with guilt?'

Jessica sighed. 'No,' she said. 'I'm not. But I think Luke was uncomfortable. He's happily married after all.'

'And he's a Catholic, don't forget,' said Fran. 'They don't do adultery as naturally as some.'

'What should I do?' said Jessica.

'What do you want to do? You'll have to see how Luke feels, I suppose.'

'And wait for "My marriage means more to me than a quick fuck with the likes of you"?'

Fran ignored that. 'Is this a doctor-patient obsession or is there more to it? Luke could get struck off the roll for this, I think.'

'I don't know what it is, but it felt pretty good.' Jessica chose for the moment to duck behind facetiousness.

'Well, I don't know what you want me to say. You're not stupid. You must have asked yourself all the usual questions. You've read the novels.'

'I know.' Jessica sighed again. 'I'm sorry. I think I just needed a sounding-board and you've always played the role so well.'

'Gee, thanks,' said Fran.

'Franny?'

'What?'

'Look at me, and tell me true: what could someone like Luke Stephens – or anyone else for that matter – possibly see in me? Wait –' Jessica held up a hand as Fran opened her mouth to speak. 'I see myself in the mirror – I'm well on the way to middle age, if I'm going to even get that far at the rate I'm going. I've got no hair. I feel so sick most of the time between one chemo session and the next I'm hardly a barrel of laughs at a dinner party. D'you think the man's some sort of freak or something?'

She looked so earnest that Fran burst out laughing.

'And don't give me any of that crap about seeing past all that into the inner me,' Jessica said crossly. 'Half the inner me's gone anyway, scraped out and thrown to the crows.'

Fran laughed harder. She got up from her chair and came round to give Jessica a hug. 'Oh, Jessie, you idiot,' she said. 'I bet Luke's wondering the same thing when he looks into the mirror in the morning. *His* bald patch is forever. Middle age has come and gone and he can't be too practised at dinner table repartee if he's been dining with Virginia all these years. Believe me, he probably can't believe his luck. He's found someone he can talk to, someone who doesn't always laugh at his jokes. It's rare in a relationship, you know.'

Jessica smiled wanly. 'I don't know why I'm doing this,' she said. 'I think it's death really, and the middle-age thing. How many shots can we expect to get at this kind of feeling in life, once we're married and everything seems so set? I'm not sure it's going to come along again for me, that's all. Whether it's a one-off, a fling – I don't know. I can't speak for Luke. For me, there might be more to it than that, and to be frank I don't know how I should handle it.'

'Well,' said Fran, 'you can rest assured that your agonising is nothing compared to Luke's at this moment. He's been married to the sugary Virginia for about twenty years. I think whatever happens you're going to have to be guided by him. Will you be devastated if he chooses his wife over you – they usually do, you know?'

Jessica thought for a moment. 'Yes,' she said. 'I suppose I might be.'

Sister Joseph had already locked up for the night when the banging at the front door sounded through the empty rooms downstairs. Father McBride was reading in his study. He heaved himself out of the deep leather armchair and shuffled in his bedroom slippers over to the window. His study looked down over the front garden and the covered porch at the convent's front door. All he could see were the trousered legs of three men. All were moving about restlessly. There was a white sedan car parked in the road outside. The loud knocking came again, followed by the sonorous tone of the bell.

McBride met Sister Joseph on the landing. She looked alarmed and carried a torch.

'I'll get it, Sister,' he said. 'Go on back to bed.'

She waited at the top of the stairs as the old priest walked heavily down the stairs, holding on to the banister as he went. His eyesight wasn't too good these days and the hallway was in darkness. She watched as he slid the chain out of its groove and turned the latch of the yale lock.

The men came straight to the point. They were looking for one Mbekhi Thekiso, apparently seen on the premises. He was wanted for questioning and under Section –

'Mbekhi Thekiso is not here,' McBride interrupted.

'Well, you won't mind if we take a look around, Sir, Father.'

McBride stood aside with a resigned sigh. He was fairly certain Mbekhi wasn't there. He'd been looking out for him all day and had suggested to Miriam that if she heard from him she should warn him that the convent was not a safe place for him at this moment. 'I think we should like some ID before we begin the tour,' Sister Joseph called imperiously from the top of the stairs, and the men raised their eyes to where she stood.

'Jirre Jee-suss!' hissed the shortest and stoutest of the three, taking a step backwards into his black colleague. They clutched each other, their eyes wide, until the spokesman for the group said something sharply to them in Afrikaans. Sister Joseph, standing in the deep shadow of the landing, held the light of the torch beneath her chin, like children do in Hallowe'en games. Her face was a ghastly waxy colour and her teeth long and pointed as she grinned ghoulishly on the group below. As the policemen scrabbled after their dignity, Henry McBride sank on to the bottom stair and sat there, helpless with laughter, his shoulders jiggling and his head shaking. He wiped his streaming eyes with a handkerchief.

The man in plain-clothes made an impatient noise with his tongue and irritably produced an identity document which McBride waved away feebly, trying to regain his composure.

The men trod through the convent, three ponderous Ghostbusters, their boots echoing on the wooden floors. They apologised gruffly when checking the nuns' rooms and gave them no more than a cursory glance.

Miriam and Thabo were awake and sitting side by side on Miriam's bed. Thabo was wearing his Ninja Turtle pyjamas and his soccer boots. 'I am sorry, Miriam,' said Sister Joseph, pushing past the men and sitting beside Thabo. 'These people are looking for Mbekhi.'

'Mbekhi's not here.' Miriam did not look up.

'There,' said Sister Joseph. 'Mbekhi's not here.'

The men ignored her. They moved warily about the room, looking clumsily beneath the bed and behind the door. The short fat man had the grace to look embarrassed. The man in plain-clothes had a swarthy face and thick black eyebrows. He smiled at Thabo, who stared back at him without blinking. Then he walked over to the bed and Sister Joseph tightened her grip on Thabo's shoulder.

'Teenage Mutant Ninja Turtles,' he said. 'My kids watch them all the time too. I bet it's your favourite programme, am I right?'

Thabo stared at him.

'Five o'clock, hey, after school. Every day the turtles. Michaelangelo, Raphael – was your brother here today, Thabo?'

At the mention of his name Thabo's eyes flickered to his mother's face, but he said nothing.

'Mbekhi comes to see you, am I right? Was he here today?'

'The child is five years old,' Sister Joseph said icily. 'How young do you start interrogating them? Perhaps you would like to use my torch?'

Henry McBride, who had stood blocking the doorway with his bulk, now stood aside and made a firm but polite gesture with his arm.

'Gentlemen,' he said. 'You can see that the boy is not here. May we all get back to sleep now?' Only a slight trembling of his heavy jowls betrayed the tightly controlled anger. The men moved towards the door, only the plain-clothes policeman pausing to stare at Thabo.

McBride escorted them off the premises and bolted and chained the door behind them. He turned off the porch light before they'd even stepped on to the path. Then he and Sister Joseph met in the kitchen and made cocoa for Miriam and Thabo. McBride took it through to them on a tray.

Twenty-Three

Jessica had been to chemo on her own. Luke wasn't there. Ben was still away. As the hours went by and Luke hadn't called, she felt her despair turn to a feeling almost of relief, as if the issue had been taken out of her hands. She didn't even debate it with herself as she usually did. Still, she did call Fran four times in one day until even Fran got impatient with her. 'The man's busy, Jess,' she told her. 'It doesn't mean anything. If you're so worried, why don't you call him?'

But Jessica couldn't bring herself to do that. The only reason a man doesn't phone, her mother had told her once insensitively at the end of a delicate romance in Standard Seven when she'd spent three nights bawling into her pillow, is because he doesn't want to. Jessica's mother saw no point in beating about the bush.

Ben came home and was quiet and sober. He helped Andrew make a kite. He cooked cauliflower cheese for supper when Jessica felt too ill to care. She watched him from the corners of her eyes as he moved about the house in his tartan socks. But she knew better than to be lulled. Ben had done this the last time he'd come back from a business trip. She knew the novelty soon palled. When she went to tuck Andrew in at bedtime she found a beer-can on the up-ended trunk he used as a bedside table. 'What's this?' she asked, prepared to be amused.

'I want to be like Daddy,' he said. 'That's my beer, but it's really Coke.'

Alone at home with Edwina on Friday morning, Jessica resisted the urge to call Fran again. She sat outside beside the pool. Life was almost back to normal. It was a hot day and

Edwina was flailing about in the shallow end with her armbands on. The chlorine in the water made her cough. Round and round she bobbed, burbling and coughing. Jessica sat in the shade, doing nothing, just watching her. Edwina always cheered her up. Then the telephone rang and she knew instinctively that this time it was Luke.

'Come,' she said to Edwina, tugging her unceremoniously from the water. 'You're not going to be a statistic.'

Anna had got there before her. She had been on her way out for a swim before doing the ironing, and she stood in the passage in lilac swimsuit and sunglasses, holding out the receiver. Anna loved to swim. She and Jessica used to do laps together before breakfast sometimes before Jessica got ill. She took Edwina from her mother, holding her out at arm's length, slippery and squealing. Jessica breathed in and out a few times, waiting for them to go outside.

It was Luke. He felt they should talk. He didn't want to talk over the phone. Could they meet at his rooms at four?

Jessica put the phone down and looked at it with distaste. Well. That was it, then. So cold, so professional. He was probably going to tell her that further tests had showed that she was clinically dead. And apologise, with a shamefaced smile, for getting carried away – it was all an embarrassing mistake and could she please change her doctor? Whatever he was going to say, Jessica thought, it was better than silence, and better to get it over with. She dressed with care. She had lost weight and the belt she put through the loops of her skirt had to be pulled in two notches tighter than the last time she'd worn it. She put on her red bikini G-string panties for luck, and noted that the sunburn on her shoulders was going a pleasing brown. She didn't look as ill as she felt.

Before she went out the door, Jessica phoned Fran on impulse.

'Luke called,' she said.

'Good,' said Fran. 'Can we all relax now?'

'He wants to see me. Now.'

'Even better.'

'Fran, I'm scared. What shall I do?'

'Play it by ear, I guess.'

'What if he says Marry me or I'll kill myself?'

'He won't.'

'He hates me. He despises me.'

'Jessica.'

'All right. I'm sorry.'

Fran was admirably patient. 'Goodbye, Jess,' she said, and hung up.

At four o'clock Jessica presented herself in Luke's rooms. There was no one else there. His receptionist was packing her bag and she looked surprised to see Jessica.

'Mrs T,' she said. 'I didn't realise you ... Doctor didn't say you had an appointment, it isn't in the book. He's cancelled all his afternoon appointments today, I'm afraid. I'm so sorry if you've come in all this way for ... '

'It's all right.' It was Luke, standing in the passage in his baggy white coat. 'No need to wait. I am expecting Mrs Tucker.'

They went into Luke's office together. They heard the outer door shut and the ping of the lift button which would take her down to the streets of Hillbrow. Sunlight streamed through the window on to a pot of flowers on the corner of the desk. Jessica watched a ladybird fan out its wings and walk down one stem and up another before either of them spoke. When they did, it was banalities, as she knew it would be.

'How're you feeling?'

'OK.'

'Sorry I haven't checked in on you. I've been –'

'– really busy. I know.'

In the silence the ladybird whirred past Luke's ear and out into infinity. Home to her children, if the nursery rhyme was to be believed. They were still standing. Jessica knew she would rather die than make the first move. She didn't know what move to make in any case.

'Look –' they both said together, and laughed uncomfortably. Jessica gestured to Luke to continue. She was fucked if she was going to make it easy for him. She sat on the chair at the desk and wished she smoked. Now was the time to toy with a cigarette packet, to search in her bag for a lighter. To blow a stream of smoke in his face.

'Jessica,' said Luke. 'The other night.' He looked tired, but he didn't turn away from what she hoped was her cool gaze. Jessica crossed her legs. Nonchalance was a good emotion to cultivate, she thought. It was an attitude which would stand one in good stead.

'The other night,' she prompted.

'Damn it – I don't know what to say.'

She couldn't believe it. The man wasn't prepared. Jessica blew a mental smoke ring, fat and round. Then she took pity on him, perhaps against her better judgement.

'It's called the cock-mind dichotomy,' she said.

'What?'

'The cock-mind dichotomy. It's very simple.' She crossed her legs again, saw him look and was glad of the vaseline she'd put on the dry skin of her knees as an afterthought that morning. 'Let's face it,' she said. 'We were good in bed and that's an experience you want to repeat – cock. But you know in your head it's useless to get involved with me because you're married and you want to stay faithful to your wife – mind. The cock-mind dichotomy.' She smiled thinly.

'Jesus,' said Luke slowly. 'Where did I get you from?' Then he put his head back and laughed.

'It's that funny?' Jessica said sourly. She felt the nonchalance wearing off. She began to regret helping him out. It was she, after all, who had been waiting by the phone, wasn't it? She was glad, at least, that he hadn't tried to touch her. She felt brittle as a twig, her bones light and porous as bamboo. If she cracked her knuckles like Tamzin did, would they snap off at the joints? The image was bizarre.

Luke said, 'Jessica. What happened the other night was –'

Please don't say 'Very special to me', Jessica thought.

'– incredible. And that's incredible in whatever sense you want to take it. I could hardly believe it was happening, although when I came to your house I felt ... I don't know. I felt that something would happen. But there's more to it than that, than just a sexual attraction. For me at any rate. It's everything else. It's flying kites, it's running barefoot on a beach, it's – If I were twenty years younger I'd be smothering you with flowers, going down on one knee –'

'And all that shit,' said Jessica. She cleared her throat. Her voice was breaking now too, not just her bones. 'Luke,' she said. 'What's your point? Why do I get the feeling that there's a But at the end of all this romantic tosh?'

Suddenly somebody was knocking at the outside door. They looked towards the passage.

'Shouldn't you see who that is?' said Jessica, when Luke made no move to get up. 'It could be someone with an axe buried in his skull.'

'I'm a gynaecologist,' said Luke.

'*Her* skull then.'

The knocking stopped. Footsteps receded. 'Lab result,' said Luke. 'They get delivered at this time of the day. They'll leave them downstairs. Where were we?'

'But,' said Jessica.

Luke's smile was a sad one. The older, wiser routine was coming up. It irritated Jessica. 'Yes, there's a but,' he said. 'You know there has to be a but.'

Suddenly Jessica didn't want to hear this part. 'Can I get some water?' she said abruptly. 'No – I'll get it.' She walked down the passage to the small kitchen, poured a glass of water and stood there for a few minutes, drinking it slowly. Then she walked reluctantly back to Luke's office and sat down again. 'Go on,' she said. She was bored. The ladybird was back, or was it another one? She wanted to go home to her children and the afternoon soaps on TV.

'I've never had an affair before, believe it or not,' said Luke.

'I believe it.'

'Have you?'

'No.' But I'm willing to try, she thought. The situation seemed to be slipping out of her grasp, not that it was ever within it. She wished urgently not to be there. She felt her armpits beginning to sweat.

Luke was meandering on. 'I suppose what I'm trying to say is: I don't know how it would feel, lying and cheating. Because that's what it comes down to, doesn't it? I don't think I do that kind of thing lightly.'

This was in danger of turning into a mindless discussion about the pros and cons of affairs. What had Helen Gurley Brown said in *Having It All*? If you're heading for an affair, for God's sake get on with it. It saves a hell of a lot on lunches. Jessica remembered Cassandra and the involuntary look of panic on her face when they'd had their discussion on the subject. She was sure now that Cassandra had been having an affair, and probably with Joel, but she was also pretty damn sure that the two of them hadn't analysed it to death to start with. Perhaps that was the only way to handle something so fraught.

Jessica stood up. She'd lost track of Luke's lecture. It was self-directed anyway, and disappointing. 'I'm going now,' she said. 'But before I do, these are my cards. One: I'm not in love with my husband. Two: I'll lie and cheat if that's the way you want it because, Three: I am in love with you. Do with it what you will.'

Do with it what you will. How on earth had she dredged up such a pompous phrase? Jessica felt embarrassed all the way down in the lift. She would never be able to face Luke again, she was certain of that, if of nothing else in her life.

She drove past the convent on her way home, hesitating when she saw the door of the church standing open. Then she accelerated with determination. It was hardly fitting to drop in for some guidance from above about adultery, was it? Even an asshole like she was knew that.

'It's a week to the night and there's a full dress rehearsal today. We'll probably go on till late.' Stephan put a small overnight bag beside the front door. Ansie was in the kitchen, making pastry. He heard her kneading the dough with loud thumps. These days she seemed to spend a lot of time in the kitchen pounding things. She looked up but not at him. Instead she spoke to the overnight bag skulking in her line of vision.

'You're working your way round to telling me you're staying out all night again.'

'You sound just like Ma.' Stephan knew he shouldn't have said it. He didn't want to fight with Ansie.

'She phoned last night. She wanted to talk to you.'

'Well. I'm sorry I missed her. Did you explain what I'm doing?'

'I don't know what you're doing.'

'*Ag, Ans. Wat gaan aan met jou*?'

'What's going on with *you*, Faan? We never see you any more. You know I don't like the friends you're making. They're turning you into a dope-*kop*.' Stephan laughed. Ansie laughed too. She did sound like her mother. She probably even looked like her mother, with her hair tied up and her arms coated with flour like joints ready for the oven. She took off her apron. Stephan came and put his arms round her. 'I'm just having a good time,' he said. 'I'm not turning into a dope-*kop*, I promise.'

Ansie looked sharply at the bag, which seemed to flatten itself slightly against the wall. 'Who have you been spending the night with then?' she said. 'Don't tell me it's all-night work.'

Stephan weighed up the situation rapidly. He settled for a half-truth. 'With the sound engineer and the keyboard player in the show. They have a flat in Hillbrow. We go out for a drink after rehearsals, to their place or to the Dome –'

'Ah,' said Ansie. '*Moffies*.'

After the rehearsal Stephan and Carole walked round Hillbrow looking for a place to eat. They chose pizzas and a table on the pavement. They held hands across white painted knotty pine while they waited for their order to be taken. Stephan's hand was a deep brown, Carole's ironically much lighter. She had very small hands and thin, tapering fingers. Her nails were long and varnished a pale, ice-cream pink. They matched the lip gloss she took out of her bag and applied, using Stephan's sunglasses as a mirror. Her tight curls were scraped back in an elastic band and a clutch of plastic pink dangling hearts. Stephan found her mesmerising. She took a pack of Beechies from her bag and offered it to him. He shook his head.

Hillbrow was full of strollers this early Saturday evening – window shoppers, hobos, black women selling crocheted tablecloths and wooden animal carvings; old white women with plastic shopping bags, standing indecisively at traffic lights. Children with hard, bare feet from the shelter down the road. It was a seething, restless hum of people in motion. Hillbrow spilled over with people, day and night.

Their pizzas came. Peperoni. Salami and olives. Carole asked for a Diet Coke. They sat without talking while they ate. Mostly, now, they spoke in Afrikaans. Stephan had noticed that Carole and Stanley lapsed into a mixture of Afrikaans and English whenever they were together. Afrikaans was their home language, Stanley told him with a wry smile. They came from Carnarvon in the Cape. Their father had been a musician, too, playing sax in a band in Sophiatown when he'd moved the family up to the Reef, before the bulldozers moved in. He'd been crippled with arthritis in his later years and had ended his days as a waiter at the Carlton Hotel in town.

'And your mother?' Stephan had asked Stanley at the Dome one night, late, after the pub had emptied and only the barman remained, wiping tables.

'She ran off with a white man,' he'd said, looking Stephan steadily in the eye. 'The last we heard from her she was in Harare somewhere.'

'How long ago was that?'

Carole and Stanley exchanged a smile. Stanley shrugged and pulled a gentle thread of blues from the piano. Davy was coming towards the raised platform they called the stage. He carried four polystyrene cups in his hands, and four hotdogs in paper serviettes, two beneath each arm.

'How long?' said Stephan.

' ... a rainy night in Georgia,' Carole sang softly. Stephan turned away and went to help Davy. Tomato sauce had leaked on to his shirt, a small bullet wound just below his heart.

'They want me back in Swaziland,' Carole said now. She licked the corners of her mouth with the tip of her tongue.

'What?'

'In Swaziland. At the casino, where I did a gig before. They want me for six months.'

'Six months,' said Stephan.

'Can I have another Diet Coke?' Carole asked.

Stephan watched as she sipped complacently through the straw. She smiled at him when she saw him looking and leaned over to kiss him on the cheek, as if what she had just said had not caused the earth to tilt a little awkwardly. He felt off balance. 'How does that leave us?' he said finally.

'What do you mean?'

'Well, I thought – you and me. You know.'

'We're together.'

'Yes, but –'

Carole pushed her plate aside. She waved to a girl standing in the doorway of a record shop across the street. 'There's Krista,' she said. 'She's Scandinavian. From Sydney.'

'Carole –'

Carole beckoned to the girl who darted through the traffic and came over to their table. She had white-blonde hair cropped like a man's and a tweed jacket with huge padded shoulders. Carole introduced them and Stephan stood up to shake hands. He pulled a chair out for her. 'Krista works in the record shop,' said Carole.

Krista smiled at Stephan. She had one gold tooth. He ordered more Diet Cokes and a beer for himself. He sat morosely to one side, while Carole and Krista talked. He thought about the farm for the first time in weeks. He shoved his overnight bag beneath his chair and held it between his heels.

Stephan hitched home from Hillbrow. When he walked into the house, Ansie was on the phone. She raised a quizzical eyebrow as he went past her to his room. 'That you, Faan?' William called from the lounge. Stephan did not answer. He closed his door and flung himself down on the bed, with his hands behind his head.

'DO YOU WANT YOUR CIGARETTES?'

'What the –?'

It was Petra. She was sitting on the floor in the corner of his room. She had his Walkman headphones on her head and her shrill, bright voice piped at him over the music. She picked up the packet from the desk beside her, shook a cigarette expertly half-way out as she'd seen him do and stretched towards him with a big smile. Stephan took the cigarette, shaking his head, chuckling. 'Got a light?' he said.

'WHAT?' Petra took the headphones off. 'You said I could listen,' she said defensively.

'Yes,' said Stephan. 'You carry on. I'm going to talk to your mother.'

Ansie was in the kitchen. 'You're always in the kitchen,' said Stephan. 'Come and have a drink with me. It's a beautiful evening. We can sit outside and look at the streetlamps.'

They sat in the deep shadow of the avocado tree. The sound of frogs came up from the darkness in the garden.

'I found one of those buggers in the swimming pool filter,' said William. He came out through the kitchen and sat on the steps. 'Did you eat, *boet*?'

'I had a pizza in Hillbrow.'

It was to Ansie's credit that she didn't ask Stephan what he was doing home. In fact, they didn't talk much at all, sitting out in the cool of the evening. Petra came out and crept on to Stephan's lap, where she fell asleep against the warm rhythm of his breathing.

'Who was on the phone just now?' William asked.

'Next door,' said Ansie with a graphic gesture.

'Oh?'

'She had a car accident this morning. Not serious. She's hurt her neck and has to lie still for a few days. She asked if I could take her children to school.' Ansie looked at William. His expression was guileless. 'That's all,' she said.

'I didn't say anything,' said William.

'It's not as if it's out of my way.' Ansie said.

On Monday morning she pulled into the Mokoenas' driveway and hooted outside the front door. There was no sign of movement. The house was asleep. She hooted again, a short, grudging toot. There was still no response. Ansie sighed and looked at the digital clock on the dashboard. No sense of time, these people. None. Africa time, they called it. She sent Petra to rap at the front door while she waited in the car. It was opened eventually by Freda and to Ansie's irritation she watched Petra slip inside and close the door behind her. Five slow minutes went by. Finally she went on to the porch and knocked. She tried the handle without waiting and went into the hallway. She called out to Petra. She called hello.

Zinzi appeared from an upstairs room. She was walking stiffly and was dressed in matching summer dressing gown and nightgown in wafting, silvery green. Her neck was held firmly in a surgical brace.

'*Liewe hemel*,' said Ansie. 'Why didn't you tell me you were badly hurt?'

'I'm not. It looks worse than it is.' Zinzi descended to the bottom of the stairs. There were sounds of chaos coming from the direction of the kitchen. 'The twins were getting their own breakfast. John had an early meeting. I suppose they're making a mess.'

They were. But it seemed that ProNutro had been consumed in more or less reasonable quantities and there was only juice spilled on the floor, which Petra, well-trained child, was cleaning up with a sink cloth.

'Come,' said Ansie. 'School. Leave this now, you'll only make it worse.' She turned to Zinzi who stood behind her like Nefertiti on a frieze. 'I'll be back a little later to help you get things straight. You don't have a girl, do you?' She could have bitten her tongue, but Zinzi didn't appear to notice the clumsy tactlessness. 'Don't try to do anything yourself. You should be flat on your back.'

Zinzi shuffled after them to the front door.

'What happened anyway?' Ansie asked her.

'It was a matter of a stop street,' Zinzi said.

'You didn't stop?'

'I was driving John's car. My feet got confused with the brake pedal and the juice.'

'*Liewe hemel*.'

'I got such a fright when I realised what was happening that

I stood so hard on the brake we skidded into some bushes and hit a tree. The car wasn't badly damaged and everyone else was OK. Just me – I got whiplash and tonguelash.'

'Tonguelash?'

'From my husband.'

They laughed.

On her way back from Rosepark school, Ansie went to the supermarket. She was planning to prepare and freeze a week's meals. She bought extras of everything. She spent the morning in her sun-filled kitchen, listening to the radio talk-shows and cooking. She fetched Petra and the twins at lunch-time and took them home. Zinzi was up and dressed and sitting on the veranda with a book, held at arm's length straight in front of her.

'I brought you some things,' Ansie said gruffly from the open window of the car. 'I was freezing stuff for us and thought you probably wouldn't be cooking –'

She carried the foil containers into the house on a tray and put them down. 'You shouldn't have done this,' she said, looking round the spotless kitchen. 'I told you I would give you a hand.'

Zinzi gave her an odd look. She seemed for a moment lost for something to say.

'You weren't sure I meant it?' said Ansie.

Zinzi nodded and winced.

Ansie looked at her with a steady, blue-eyed gaze. 'I always mean what I say,' she said.

Zinzi watched them from the porch, a twin holding on to each hand. The cardboard lids of the freezer containers had all been labelled clearly in large capital letters – Monday, BOBOTIE, Tuesday, LAMB STEW, Wednesday, FRIKKADELS – a whole week's worth of *boere* food. She wondered if Ansie was trying to tell her something.

Ansie felt like Meals on Wheels as she turned her car towards Cassandra's house. She had baked her a cake, feeling guilty that she hadn't been over to see how Cassandra was feeling. All these ailing people. The black gates were open and she drove up to the house. It seemed very quiet. She rang the doorbell but there was no answer. She walked round to the back of the house. The painter's van was there, but there was no other sign of anyone being at home. Then Selena appeared from her room in the courtyard.

'Is the madam not in?' Ansie asked.

Selena eyed her. She looked at the cake in its Tupperware cover. 'Uh uh,' she said.

'Oh,' said Ansie. 'Well.' She offered the cake. 'This is for her and the children. Will you tell her I called round?'

Cassandra was in bed with Joel. There were clothes all over the floor, the sign of hasty lovers, passion that couldn't wait. Her lust for this boy's body was unabated. He said nothing when she opened the front door to his ring, just stood there looking at her, smiling. There was no pretence, no need for niceties, the examining of paintwork. Cassandra did not even send Selena off on an errand this time. She did not care whether Selena suspected or even knew. She would give nothing away. It was not in her interests to do so.

Afterwards she told Joel about the assault and he kissed the bruises on her face. He held her head between his big hands and she breathed in the smell of him. It was these moments she knew she could survive on.

He did not stay long. He had to get to work. He'd left his boys on their own – the job down south. 'There's trouble in the township there,' he told her. 'The guys get a bit jumpy. They like to get home early.'

Cassandra wasn't interested. 'When can I see you again?' she said.

Perhaps Friday, Joel suggested. He'd have to see …

'I'm going away,' Cassandra said. 'Mike suggested a long weekend.' She grimaced. 'He thinks it will be good for me and the children. We're going down to St Lucia Bay. The company has a cottage there.'

Joel was putting on his clothes. 'When do you get back?' he asked. He took up Mike's hairbrush and pulled it through his long, tangled hair. Cassandra made a mental note to pull the blond hairs off it when Joel had gone. Shades of the bedroom farce, she reflected wryly.

'Sunday night,' she said. 'Shall we make it next week?'

'I'll call first,' said Joel.

Twenty-Four

Mary was on the telephone. The line from Botswana was full of static and loud crackling and Fran had difficulty in hearing what she was trying to say.

'They've found Gladys.'

'Oh, thank goodness,' Fran shouted back down the line. 'Is she with you?'

'No. She's dead. They found her body.'

'Oh, no,' Fran groaned. 'Mary – this can't go on. I'm not going to be responsible for this any more. I'm going to the press with the diary.'

'No, wait, Fran. They haven't given clearance yet. I'll talk to –'

'They're just being picked off one by one. If we'd known where Gladys was we could at least have warned her, but ... who can I talk to?'

There was more crackling and then abruptly the line went dead and Fran slammed the receiver down in frustration. Gladys Ntsonga had been an ANC cultural worker. Fran had known her quite well. They had been on a writers' workshop together a year or so back. She was a tall woman, statuesque, who wrote long narrative poetry and plays. She was also an up-and-coming theatre director and had a show on at the Market Theatre at the moment, which she had written and was directing and which had just won an award. When she disappeared without trace the actors had made their audience stand in silent tribute for up to fifteen minutes every evening before the performance began. It was rumoured in the press that Gladys's name was on the death squad list in the mysterious diary and she had immediately disappeared. The show had been getting mediocre reviews up till then, but suddenly the run was extended and every night the theatre was full. Full of white people taking their punishment, standing to attention in the obligatory period of silence to begin with, and hobbling through 'Nkosi Sikelel' i Afrika' at the end, awkward fists raised. Then they would leave, purged and sated. But of Gladys there was no word.

Fran walked to the café to buy a newspaper. She was jittery and tense. She couldn't go on like this. Political expediency or no political expediency, if she didn't get the go-ahead to give the diary to the press tonight, she would do it on her own. And to hell with everyone, the deputy minister included. She might once have seen the necessity of waiting for the moment of political advantage before using information to its fullest impact but there were lives, valuable lives, on both sides of the fence being lost without reason. The headlines brought her up short.

Amidst an unsubstantiated rumour of funds being channelled into hit squad activities as late as two months ago, the paper reported that Deputy Minister Johan van Rensburg had retired from active politics due to a deteriorating health problem. On the same page was a picture of ambulance men carrying a stretcher bearing the body of Gladys Ntsonga to the open doors of an ambulance. Gladys had been found lying face down in a polluted stream in the veld. Her hands had been tied behind her back with a length of razor wire. It appeared, although the autopsy would have to confirm this, that she had drowned.

When she got home, Fran put the paper aside and ran herself a hot bath. She lay in the water and tried to think. All she could see was Sophie as a toddler, when they had bathed together in the evenings. Sophie loved to wash Fran's feet. She would do them carefully, methodically soaping in between each toe and brushing Fran's toenails inexpertly with a small pink nailbrush. Then she would sit on the plughole as the water ran out, giggling as it sucked and glugged its way round her. *She would give up the diary. She would give it up tonight*. Still damp from the bath, she tried to get through to Botswana on the telephone but was forced to give up after a frustrating hour of cut connections. A call to the head office offered no better results. Someone would get back to her. 'But you never do … ' said Fran.

Still feeling uncertain and confused, and without Mary's sensible, reasoned guidance, Fran decided to go through Sophie's clothes to take her mind off the depleted list of names that was burning into her brain. She hadn't been able to bring herself to tackle this task until now, but she accepted that it was no use hanging on to a child's wardrobe when there were other, needy children who could use the things. She folded small dresses and put them in cardboard boxes. There were jerseys and tracksuits, and a nurse's uniform and cape, complete with name badge: NURSE PHILLIPS in Davy's clear print. Fran wondered that clothes so light could make her arms ache so as she packed and folded.

When she answered Jessica's knock, she was holding Sophie's pale blue blanket in her arms. Jessica went straight past her to the bathroom and Fran could hear her being sick. She emerged, pale and shaky, and lay down on Sophie's bed. 'Sorry,' she said. 'This is worse than morning sickness.' She leant up on an elbow and took the blanket from Fran. 'I used to have one of these,' she said. 'I had it until I was twelve and Jennifer Wilhelm came to spend the night.'

Fran smiled wanly. 'And how did Jennifer Wilhelm break the spell?' she asked.

'She walked in her sleep. But not just walked. She used to do things too. Her mother told us afterwards that she would put together whole puzzles on her bedroom floor without opening her eyes.'

'And the blanket?'

'When my dad came in to check on us before he went to bed that night, he found her sitting on the floor, cutting my blanket into pieces with my grandmother's nail scissors.'

'That must have been heavy going.'

Jessica sighed. 'My mother wouldn't replace it. I suppose it was wise, but I did miss that damn blanket. It went everywhere with me.'

'I wonder what it is that makes some kids need a security thing like that and others not? Do any of yours have blankets?'

'Not exactly.'

'What do you mean?'

'Well, Andrew and Glenda never did.'

'Edwina?'

'Edwina's something else. It's a bit embarrassing really. She doesn't have a blanket as such. Ed's got this thing about underpants. Especially Ben's. She trails around the house sucking her thumb and rubbing a pair of old undergutties against her cheek. Like some sort of midget pervert.'

Fran laughed. 'Chip off the old block,' she said. 'Want some tea?'

Fran asked about Luke and Jessica told her about their meeting. She told her she was trying, and failing, to put it out of her mind. Ben had been all fall down just about every night that week, too, so things were not looking too bright. Physically, she was more or less all right, except for the nausea and the depression, but she was managing. She was getting herself to and from chemo, although she wasn't supposed to drive. Luke hadn't been at the hospital for two weeks now and she supposed that was as it should be.

'You do sound bleak,' Fran said.

'I'm sorry. I suppose I'm battling a bit.'

'So am I,' said Fran. She said nothing of Gladys, the diary and the deputy minister.

It was three o'clock. Fran looked thoughtfully at the kettle, which was about to boil. She switched it off. She fetched a bottle of gin and two large glasses. 'How about a splash of mother's ruin?' she said. 'We haven't done this in a long time.'

'Got any lemons?' said Jessica. She knew she would pay for it later but it seemed appropriate.

They talked about Tamzin. Fran had noticed that she was very tense. She had also noticed her thickening waist, but when she raised the subject Jessica pleaded ignorance. Fran found this strange. Jessica knew most things about most people. But then Jessica hadn't been herself lately either. They all had their secrets.

*

'Talk of the devil,' said Jessica.

It was seven o'clock and raining. Tamzin stood on Jessica's doorstep decked out in a horrible see-through plastic mac and waterproof boots.

'That's indecent,' said Jessica, pulling her in out of the wet. 'Wipe your feet. Or better still, leave those things on the porch and maybe someone'll steal them. Can you stay for supper? I want to talk to you.'

They sat in the kitchen while Jessica made soup and toast for the children and then soup and toast for the two of them.

'Where's Ben?' asked Tamzin.

'Playing something,' said Jessica shortly. 'Squash, maybe – I forget. Or elbow-lifting. He's getting better and better at that. He'll earn his colours one of these days if his liver holds up.' She lifted the wooden spoon to her mouth and sipped cautiously. 'Shit, that's hot. ANDREW! GLENDA! C'M'NEAT!'

After the children were fed and sitting in a row watching television in their dressing gowns, Jessica and Tamzin sat on deckchairs beside the pool. The rain had stopped and the evening was warm. The leaves of the bougainvillaea glistened dark and wet all around them. Jessica lit a floating candle and pushed it into the pool with her toe. Little splashes of light broke up and formed again with the bobbing motion. They sat companionably and dipped toast soldiers into their tomato soup.

'Are you still living on a diet of fish fingers?' Jessica asked suddenly. She had been twice to supper recently with Tamzin and had been given the same fare. Tamzin was an enthusiastic and inventive cook as a rule. 'Fran knows you're pregnant,' she added.

'You didn't – ?'

'Of course not. But she's not stupid. Or blind. We were talking about you today. She brought it up, not me.'

'But you didn't confirm it?'

'I tried to change the subject, but frankly, Tammy, I don't like it. In fact, if you want to know the truth, I can't stand it. Fran's my closest friend in the world and I had a great deal of trouble looking her in the eye today. It's like the age-old thing of knowing your friend's husband is having an affair and not knowing whether to tell her about it or not. Only this situation is ten times worse. I'm sorry. You're going to have to do something or I'm going to explode.'

Tamzin looked crestfallen. She put her soup bowl down on the damp step beside her and looked away, across the pool. Jessica stood up. 'I'm going to put the kids to bed,' she said.

It started to rain again, very softly, a thin, misty tickle on Tamzin's arms and hair. She looked up and saw that the sky had clouded over and the moon was a faint, white shape riding high above the rooftops. She heard the clack of helicopter blades and saw two police helicopters, flying low with lights flashing, head north towards Alexandra township. Seven more dead in hostel clashes this morning, she'd heard on the car radio on the way over. She clasped her hands over the bulge of her stomach and felt the cool wet fabric of her dress beneath her fingers. There were drops on her eyelashes. They blurred her vision and soon small, snaking rivers went sliding past her nose. It began to come down harder and reluctantly she got to her feet and pushed the deckchairs under the shelter of the awning. The candle in the pool sputtered and went out. Tamzin found she'd been sitting on a pair of men's underpants and she picked them up and put them on the tray with the soup bowls. Jessica came out and held the door open for her. Gusts of wind lifted the striped awning and it flapped erratically against its supports.

'You're wet,' Jessica said.

'I found these outside. Ben's? Or someone more interesting's?'

'This one's current obsession,' said Jessica. She held Edwina on one hip. Her eyes were half closed in sleep. She held a pair of pants against her cheek. 'Those are her favourites,' Jessica explained. 'I think it's the bowler hat design. Ben likes them too, so it's a matter of who gets to them first.'

'Ah,' said Tamzin. She put the dishes in the sink while Jessica made coffee. 'I wish I hadn't told you,' Tamzin said to the taps. 'I should have known it would compromise your relationship with Fran.'

'Well, isn't it doing exactly that for you?'

Jessica took the milk out of the fridge. She paused, listening. 'There's Ben,' she said. 'Smart lad. He made it through the gates.' She splashed milk into mugs, picked a teaspoon up off the floor beside the dog baskets and absent-mindedly used it to spoon sugar into her coffee. Tamzin put a hand over hers. 'Not for me,' she said.

'You usually take sugar,' said Jessica. 'Is this since –'

'Since you just put three strands of dog hair and last week's boiled egg scrapings into yours.'

Ben put his head round the door. 'Tamzin,' he said. 'Jessica.' Then he walked away down the passage and they heard him trip and curse over Tamzin's boots which Andrew had been playing with and had left in the way.

'Here's my advice,' said Jessica. 'For what it's worth from someone whose life is so together I can afford to tell you how to run yours. First, you've got to tell Davy. Second, I think you should tell Ray the truth, and third, I think it's imperative that you tell Fran.'

'That's what Luke says.'

'Luke?' Jessica flushed.

'Luke. He's my doctor, remember?' Tamzin looked at Jessica curiously. 'Oh, yes,' she said. 'I'd forgotten. Is the patient still in love with the doctor or is the crush under control?'

'Yes. Don't evade the issue.'

'Yes what? In love or under control?'

'Under control,' Jessica said tersely. 'I wish you'd forget I ever mentioned it. I thought we were talking about you.'

'Sorry. Yes – Fran.'

'You have to tell her, you know.'

'I don't think I have the courage, Jess. I still feel so desperate about Sophie. She'll never forgive me for this. I don't think I could ever find the words to explain it to her.'

'And Ray? Are you going to tell him who the father is?'

'He called me today. Says he wants to talk.' She sighed. 'But I got one out of three: I told Davy.'

'How did he take it?' Jessica asked.

'Quite well under the circumstances. He was shocked, angry – at himself – at first. The first thing he asked, too, of course, was whether I had told Fran. He offered whatever support I need, financial, you know.'

'Will he acknowledge that he's the father? I mean, if you want it known?'

'He said he'll do whatever I want, but asked me, obviously, to understand his circumstances. Fran doesn't even know about him and Stanley yet, so to hit her with this so soon after Sophie – well, I don't know what it would do to her.'

Jessica frowned irritably.

'Fran's quite strong,' she said. 'Don't underestimate her. I think, frankly, she would rather *know* what's going on behind her back than have all these dark, ghastly secrets held from her, as if she were going to have a nervous breakdown the minute you let her in on them. Give her some credit, for God's sake. You know what I think? I think there's nothing anyone can say or do to her that will be more traumatic than losing Sophie. She's had the worst, losing her child. That's done, that's over. Fran will handle anything you throw at her. So Davy's gay. So you're going to have his child. She may not ever *talk* to you again, but she'll cope. You'll see.'

Ray and Tamzin went out to supper, late, after the evening's performance. It was Friday the thirteenth and Ray looked sombre.

He fidgeted with the salt and pepper cellars on the table. He poured small lines of salt carefully down one of the squares of the tablecloth, then took up a pinch between thumb and forefinger. Tamzin half expected him to snort it. Instead he threw it over his left shoulder, muttering. Tamzin was a little alarmed. Ray was always such a calm, organised person. He was the counter to her scattiness. She didn't like to see him so agitated. Perhaps it was best to humour him. She picked up a pinch herself and threw it over her shoulder, but discreetly, as if she meant it.

The watching waiter clearly felt it was time to interrupt. Were they ready to order, he asked, standing a safe distance from the table. Ray was playing with the blade of the knife and Tamzin was tearing her paper serviette into strips.

It was an uneasy meal. Ray asked Tamzin how she was feeling, but did not appear interested in the answer. 'I may be going to London,' he said, as they waited for the check.

'Oh,' said Tamzin.

'You could come too.'

'Oh,' she said. She had known for some time that the London stage was where Ray's heart lay, but she had not projected her thoughts any further. She took a peppermint from the bowl beside the cash till. Ansie had told her how she'd read in the paper about tests they'd done on certain substances in restaurants and how there was a high urine content on the peppermints they gave as you left. It was the men who went to the loo before leaving, apparently. Ray had just been to the men's room. He shook his head at the peppermint bowl. Perhaps he'd read the article too.

'Well?' he said when they were in the car. There was a stiffness about them, a formality Tamzin found stifling. It was as if they were talking to each other through the thick glass you saw in prison movies. Ray had not touched her all evening.

'I don't know,' she said. 'Is this something definite? I mean, are you booking your ticket?'

It wasn't definite. He hadn't booked his ticket. But it was a possibility and he thought Tamzin might come. She had never been overseas. He was acting as if she were a tourist, a handy companion to carry the guidebook. She'd be carrying a lot more than that, she thought. Like disposable nappies and teething syrup. Ray had not mentioned the baby all evening. She wondered for a peculiar moment whether he'd forgotten about it.

She decided to remind him. 'What about the baby?' she said bluntly.

Ray looked at her innocently. 'Give it to its father,' he said. 'You don't actually want it, do you?'

Tamzin stared straight ahead through the windscreen. Ray drove fast. The window was open and he beat a mindless thrubbing on the roof with one free hand. They skidded round corners, tyres squealing.

'For Chrissake,' Tamzin said, grasping the dashboard. All of a sudden she felt alone and strong and sure. Anger, too, was in there. She turned to look at his profile, Rasputin's profile, sharp nose and chin. He was very handsome, outlined in silver from the streetlights as they flashed by. She turned back to the windscreen and said: 'Davy Phillips is the father. Didn't I tell you?'

Twenty-Five

The pageant was by all accounts a dazzling affair. Spectacular girls, high-stepping, like circus horses with breasts, and suitably gaudy costumes. Sets that drew gasps from the audience. Miss Hillbrow accepted crown, sash, bouquet and kisses with the gracious smile she'd been practising all week, and thanked the organisers, the sponsors, her mother, grandmother and God without missing a beat. Dalene Diedrichs, Didi for short, and she signed her name with two little hearts over the i's.

Ansie accepted that she was very beautiful, if a little vacuous, but the expression on William's face – as on all the other men's she could see in their row – was equally vacant, so that had to tell you something about something.

Champagne and limp snacks in the foyer followed after the show. Stephan walked about looking dignified in his hired dinner jacket from Top 'n Tail. He'd removed the stud from his ear for the occasion. He introduced Ansie and William to the sound engineer, Davy Phillips. Ansie was taken aback. From Stephan's descriptions, she would never have made the connection with Fran. 'We know each other already,' she said. 'At least by sight.'

Stephan scanned the crowd for Carole. She looked stunning tonight, in shimmering peacock blue sequins, with thigh-length slits up the sides of her dress. Her hair was piled up on top of her head with a sequined band. Even her fingernails glittered. He could see her in the centre of a group of admirers with a glass of champagne in one hand and a cigarette in the other. About seven men were reaching at the same time for lighters and matches. Carole was laughing. He could see her tongue and teeth.

Ansie, too, was scanning the room. She watched Davy Phillips talking to the Coloured man who played the piano, the man with whom he shared the flat and, it appeared, his life. They stood close together. She felt sorry for Fran; it must be humiliating for her. No wonder she never talked about Davy. She also looked to see where Stephan's anxious eyes kept looking, to see which of the beautiful girls was the one he'd so clearly lost his heart to. She picked them off, one by one, like a sniper. Stephan was standing with the *moffies*. And then suddenly she knew. She came sauntering over to the small group, slim hips swaying like a tart, red lips smiling seductively. The siren and the sailor. Ansie let out a weak, involuntary moan.

'What?' said William. 'What is it?'

'Over there,' said Ansie. And then, knowing that William would never make the connection unless she spelled it out for him, she said dramatically, 'The Coloured girl. Stephan's having it off with the *meid*.'

William was intrigued, rather than shocked, as he should have been. 'Do you think so?' he said, a silly smile forming. 'Stephan never said.'

'Of course he never said. Do you think he's stupid? Can you imagine what Ma and Pa are going to say?' She all but wrung her hands.

'You don't know for sure, Ansie. What makes you think there's anything going on in any case?'

'He's holding her hand for one thing,' Ansie said drily.

The plan was to have a late dinner in town afterwards, which Stephan had arranged. Ansie had been looking forward to it. She had wanted to meet Stephan's new friends for herself, size up the competition. But now she felt sick and nervous. She wondered if it would be very rude if they excused themselves. She knew William would not hear of it.

They assembled outside the building. More introductions were made – Stanley Abrams, his sister Carole.

'*Jy't mooi gesing,*' said Ansie primly.

'*Dankie*,' said Carole. She planted another cigarette in her holder.

'Please don't smoke in my car,' said Ansie.

William kept an anxious hand on Ansie's knee beneath the table in the restaurant. He refilled her wineglass when she wasn't looking. She admitted grudgingly in the car going home that Stanley was a nice man, for a Coloured and a queer, but she hoped Stephan's choice of girlfriend was temporary, for all their sakes.

Stephan had forgotten his toothbrush. He opened the medicine chest in the bathroom and felt about to see if either Davy or Stan had a spare. He found some dubious looking pills and a bottle of old cough medicine. There was a whole shelf full of Rough Rider day-glo condoms. In the end he used his finger and some mouthwash he found on top of the shower.

In the bedroom Carole was taking off her make-up. Hers was the sort of dressing-table crammed with knick-knacks and souvenirs – small dolls and furry animals, coloured strings of beads looped over the mirror, and china cats with straw hats. There were photographs pushed beneath the glass top of famous singers and stars she'd met or worked with. 'All my love from Percy Sledge'. 'Doby Gray Loves Ya'.

Stephan was not by nature suspicious, but watching Carole tonight surrounded by men, he wondered for the first time whether he was, after all, anything more than a new conquest.

They made love, but half-heartedly. Carole was sleepy and not a little drunk. She turned over and curled up like a kitten in its basket. Stephan moulded himself to her back but lay awake till morning.

On Sunday afternoon Ansie found Zinzi where she'd seen her last: sitting on the stoep reading at arm's length. Her husband, John, was working on the computer inside. Petra played with the twins in the garden while Ansie made tea. She took mugs down from their hooks where she'd seen Zinzi put them. She opened the grocery cupboard, found teabags. 'If you make a list,' she said, coming out with the tray, 'I'll be going to Pick 'n Pay in the morning.'

It was a funny thing. As they sat outside in the shade of the veranda and their children played pig-in-the-middle on the grass, for the first time since she'd known Zinzi, Ansie did not feel in a hurry to get home. William was playing golf. Stephan had not yet come home. They did not talk much, but somehow the awkwardness was gone today. When they did talk it was about books and the school and township violence. Ansie all of a sudden found herself confiding her fears about Stephan's emotional attachment to an unsuitable girl.

'Why is she unsuitable?'

'She's Coloured,' Ansie explained. 'Although she seems like a nice girl. It's only ... well, Stephan's going to inherit the farm one day and –'

'I see what you mean,' Zinzi said. 'Your family could make things difficult for him.'

'Exactly,' said Ansie. You see, Zinzi understood.

Zinzi smiled.

'That's not to say,' Ansie went on, 'that this is a serious thing, and I hope it isn't. But if it were, well –'

'I take your point,' said Zinzi.

Irony was not something Ansie easily picked up in a situation. She washed the cups for Zinzi, waited while she wrote out a shopping list, and took Petra home in time for supper.

The house was in darkness when the Symons family got home that Sunday evening. They found it odd. Selena was expecting them back; she'd been given her instructions. And Selena could always be relied on. They soon discovered the reason. Mike went immediately to Selena's quarters. There was nobody there, no lights on either. The door was locked. Cassandra had a spare key on her ring and when Mike opened up, they both stood, dumbfounded. There was not a stick of furniture in the room. The bed had been lifted clean off the four bricks Selena used to elevate it from the floor for fear of the *tokoloshe*. Grey curls of dust lay exposed. The cupboard where she kept her clothes was gone too, and the dresser with the television set and her Bible. Even her potplants were missing.

'I can't believe it,' said Cassandra. 'I can't believe it.'

'Where's Selena?' the children said in chorus. Jason was holding the Coke bottle filled with sea-water they'd brought back from the coast for her. Rosalie's eyes were frightened.

'I'm going to call the police,' said Mike.

The house was still as a tomb. The heavy front door swung open on its hinges and their feet echoed on the wooden floor-boards where the small Persian rug had been. There was no sign of forced entry, no evidence of haste or panic. But their home had been picked clean – systematically, thoroughly and selectively. All the sound equipment had been taken, the television sets, the VCR, the microwave. Cassandra's and Mike's clothes and all their leather suitcases. The wall-hanging in the entrance hall and the monk's bench from the study. Cassandra's jewellery, her silver-backed hairbrush set, Mike's computer. Everything of value.

Cassandra sank on to a chair and put her face in her hands. 'I can't believe it,' she whispered. They were insured, of course, but it wasn't that. She felt violated. She wondered when they had come, who they were. Had they been watching the house, watching her and the children come and go? Had it been Selena who had let them in, willingly or unwillingly? Had they murdered her and taken her things too? Would she ever know?

Rosalie came into the study. 'Hah!' she said triumphantly, her sharp little face smiling with satisfaction behind her glasses. 'They didn't get everything. They didn't get Blue Doll.'

'Or the swimming pool,' Jason said, not to be outdone for observation. 'At least we can still swim,' he said. 'Can't we?'

Mike waited outside in the driveway for the police. He didn't want to be inside, where they'd been.

The police inspector was a serious, round man in trousers with turn-ups and braces. His team went to work on the routine examination and questioning, while he walked slowly round the house, hands behind his back. He nodded to himself, as if affirming something he had already suspected. He drew Mike to one side and pushed a pack of Gunston under his nose. He asked him if anyone had known they would be away over the weekend. No one other than his colleagues, and of course his domestic servant, Mike said. The inspector nodded. He cupped his hands to the match, passed it over to Mike. Mike didn't smoke, but he had taken a cigarette without thinking and it seemed foolish now not to put it to his lips.

'Have you had a carpenter in recently? A plumber?'

'No,' Mike said.

'Drains that needed attention? Rats in the ceiling?'

'What are you saying?'

'I've seen this one before. I've seen this bloke in operation. He's slick.' He declined to elaborate.

The inspector called Mike at the office the next morning. 'The name Cunningham mean anything to you? Or Bellingham?' the inspector said. 'Try Hunnicut?'

'Cunningham. Cunningham does. Joel Cunningham has just painted our house for us. Young chap. My wife said he was a medical student –'

The inspector chuckled, a wheezy, chesty sound. 'Medical student?' he said. 'That's a new one. He's good, I'll give him that. Well, he did a good job on your house, Mr Symons, on the inside, that is. Painted a purty picture for us.' He wheezed and coughed. 'A purty picture.'

Joel's prints had been all over the place. He had been out of gaol for less than six months after his last armed robbery conviction. He had a record a mile long. He was no more a painter and handyman than the inspector was. They were confident of an early arrest.

Cassandra took the news surprisingly badly. There must be some mistake, she said. It was quite likely Joel's prints were in the house. He'd had free rein when doing the job. If he was the thief wouldn't he have been careful *not* to leave prints? They couldn't prove it. They were using him as a scapegoat. They –

'Why are you defending him?' Mike asked tiredly. 'Anyone could see he was a hustler.'

'I –'

'They're going to bring him in for questioning anyway. If he's innocent, well – they'll let him go.'

For Cassandra the emotions came rapidly, sweeping over her like waves on a beach, steady and relentless: anger, betrayal, hurt, humiliation, disgust. She could go on and on. Ultimately, she was left with one stronger than all the rest. It was loss. It was simply loss.

It took them three days to find Joel. They found the Symons' microwave oven in the back of his van, but none of the other stolen goods, except for an emerald pendant in the pocket of his jeans, which Cassandra said was not hers. Joel was arrested and appeared briefly in court on Thursday afternoon. Bail was refused.

On Friday Cassandra went about the normal routine of her day in a kind of trance. Mike put it down to delayed shock, from the mugging, from the robbery, and from the knowledge that she had harboured, unknowingly, a gaolbird in their home, when he was possibly both armed and dangerous. She had had a lucky escape. This he kept telling her. Cassandra thought only of the front door key she had given Joel, telling him to wear it round his neck, next to his heart. She did not hear properly when people spoke to her and she could not sit still in one place for any length of time. Their doctor prescribed tranquillisers and sleeping pills. She took neither. When she was alone she wandered from room to room, thinking about Joel. She even for a moment considered visiting him in gaol to see for herself the mockery which must be there in his black eyes. Then she thought about his sick mother and the telephone calls, the flowers – how he'd probably even stolen those out of someone's garden. Our stolen moments, she'd called them once, she recalled with pain, after they'd made love. He'd smiled at the words, a smile that would melt your heart.

Cassandra considered cancelling tennis on Friday afternoon but changed her mind. She needed to hit tennis balls across a net with purpose and vigour. At least the patio furniture was still there. The table was bolted to the concrete.

Gail was thrilled. She grew quite animated with the horror of it. 'You poor, poor thing,' she said, many times over. She tucked

Cassandra's arm in hers and walked her through the house like an estate agent. 'If there's anything I can do –' She peeped into rooms, shaking her head, as if afraid of disturbing someone.

'They've gone actually,' Cassandra found herself saying through clenched teeth. 'The burglars have gone, Gail. It's OK to talk normally. They can't hear you.'

'You poor, poor thing,' Gail said, rolling her eyes at Jessica.

Tamzin and Jessica were more practical. They arrived together with cold drinks and plastic throwaway cups. 'We didn't know how much they'd left you,' said Jessica sympathetically.

Ansie brought brown bread sandwiches in a basket and an extra tennis racket just in case. And everyone had a story. They all knew someone who had been ripped off. Security alarms that were faulty. Armed response guards who took too long or never came at all. Security and crime were preoccupations of the northern suburbs. Residents took crime seriously.

'You had a break-in too, didn't you, just the other day?' said Gail, turning to Fran.

'Well –' Fran glanced at Jessica, but she was busy tying an elastic band round Glenda's ponytail.

'But that was different really, wasn't it?'

Fran had never worked out whether Gail was stupid or vindictive or both. She studied her now before answering, but Gail was the picture of guilelessness.

'They didn't take the television, if that's what you mean,' she said slowly.

'I didn't hear about this,' said Ansie. 'When was this? What happened?'

'Oh ... ' Fran thought if she was vague enough they might drop it. She hadn't reckoned with Gail however.

'Fran's house was rather thoroughly ... er ... searched, but I don't know that they found what they were after?' Gail arched an eyebrow.

Ansie looked about, clearly confused. There was suddenly in the atmosphere an imperceptible string of tension, of suspicion. Fran felt that she was on trial here suddenly, as if she were the perpetrator and not the victim. It was Tamzin who came to the rescue.

'Have they caught the guys, Cassandra?' she asked.

Cassandra shook her head. She felt tears spring unexpectedly to her eyes and she looked away.

'*And* they won't,' Gail said with satisfaction. 'They're professional. That's about the only area our black brethren *are* professional.' She laughed, taking Fran in with a sweep of long black lashes. She was so enjoying herself.

'Who said they were black?' It was Ansie. 'I don't think that's funny.' She turned to Cassandra. '*Were* they black? Did anyone see them?'

'Let's play tennis,' said Tamzin firmly. 'Aren't we supposed to be taking your mind off all this?'

It took Mike a few seconds to grasp that the reporter on the telephone wasn't talking about the burglary. The comment he was asking for was on a different matter entirely. For a few minutes he sat at his desk with the telephone receiver in his hand. His face was pale with shock. Slowly he replaced the instrument and leaned back in his chair. He swivelled the seat round until he was looking out of the window. Fourteen floors up and bomb-proof, the large expanse of glass faced south over the city and the pale honey-coloured mine-dumps beyond. The air was still today and a thick band of smog hung over the city centre like a pelt. Mike could hear the squeak and scrape of window-cleaning equipment on the floor below his. He watched as the rope swayed and braced with the shifting weights of the workmen. For a minute he fantasised that a Sunday paper photographer had bribed them to hoist him up to Mike's window to take more candid pictures. 'The moment before the exposé. Prominent businessman contemplates impending disgrace.' Perhaps he would hope for a picture of Mike as he jumped to his death rather than face the sordid facts.

The reporter's voice had had an odd, high pitch to it and just the merest trace of an accent he couldn't immediately place. Asked for his comments on the posh house of ill repute he frequented, Mike had been literally speechless. He had no comment to make, he had stammered out. None at all. There was, of course, the thin possibility that it was a hoax, but this thought gave him little comfort. He put his face in his hands. His skin was rough and dry. All of that day he spent alone in his office, refusing calls, seeing no one, alarming his secretary. He sent her out for bobotie and rice in a plastic container from the downstairs take-away at lunch-time and then threw the whole thing in the dustbin without touching it. The rest of the time he gazed out of the window, occasionally turning back to his desk and setting off his collection of executive toys. Cassandra added to this collection every wedding anniversary. They probably wouldn't have another one.

Mike's physical inertia concealed a feverishly working brain, back-tracking its way through the past weeks. The situation had a bizarre air of unreality, as if he had suddenly found himself in a B-grade movie. High-powered executive photographed with small-time hooker. Under-age hooker. *Under age?* Was there such a thing as statutory rape in this country, he wondered miserably. Whichever way he looked at it, Mike knew he could be in big trouble. The man on the telephone, bogus or not, had had all the facts. All except the name of Mike's winsome partner, the name he hoped, politely, Mike would like to supply. He wondered painfully what it would be like to go through a Sunday papers scandal. Perhaps he was about to find out. Me and Jeffrey Archer, he thought sourly.

He thought about Kerrin. Was it possible that she knew about this? That she had allowed it to happen? Had he been set up from the start? He realised that he really knew nothing at all about her. She was reticent about herself to the point of brusqueness, and their encounters were mostly silent and, on his side, almost apologetic affairs. She was light and pliant and practised. She did everything he asked her to do. Thinking about it, Mike groaned out loud and put his head on the shiny surface of the desk. It smelled of Mr Min furniture polish and reminded him of Selena and home. He wondered if Selena read the Sunday papers. He wondered where she was.

He thought of calling James Fleming. Perhaps he had had a similar call. Perhaps they were in this spot together. Perhaps – he let his hand fall and swivelled again to the window. Fat, white thunder clouds were gathering in the pale afternoon sky. The traffic on the flyovers was building up. Cars were already bumper to bumper on the freeway south towards Soweto and Sebokeng. They shimmered and flashed in the heat haze like a snaking silver river.

At five thirty he got abruptly to his feet, shrugged his shoulders into his jacket and left the office. He had to see Kerrin. He was too early. There were no other cars in the parking area. He drove three times round the block to make sure there were no press people lurking and then parked a little way down the street. Stella wasn't there and the bar was deserted. He asked for Greg, the pock-marked boy, but was told Greg was off sick. Then he walked back to his car and sat there, concealed as best he could behind the evening paper. He felt like a spy. Mike Hammer, private dick. Dick being the appropriate word and about to be private no longer.

For two hours Mike sat and watched the entrance to Thatcher's. He saw Stella return in her pink BMW and stagger to the back entrance with plastic Pick 'n Pay packets in each hand. As darkness drew in, a slow but steady stream of expensive cars moved through the gates. They were all about to get a rude shock come Sunday, Mike thought grimly. Word had obviously not reached them about the pending disclosures. Finally, just as he was about to start his engine, Mike saw her. Kerrin came walking along the pavement with a denim holdall over her shoulder. Her shoulders were bowed and she walked with her head down and her arms folded. The silky blonde hair was loose and shining softly in the fast fading light. As she drew level with the car she saw him and stopped. She stood waiting, saying nothing.

'I need to talk to you,' Mike said, leaning across to the passenger seat window. He opened the door and Kerrin got in obediently and sat with her hands in her lap.

'I'll get to the point,' Mike said. 'Somebody's been taking

pictures and they're going with them to the papers. Do you know anything about this?' When Kerrin looked at him, uncomprehending, he knew immediately that she didn't and his heart dropped. It meant that there was no way of retrieving the situation. He wondered who she really was and whether she had a family, too, whose lives were about to be changed as radically as his was.

'How do you know?' Kerrin asked. Her fingernails were bitten to the quick.

Mike told her about the reporter and how he had tried to call his bluff.

'Do you think it could be a hoax?' Kerrin asked, but without conviction.

Mike shrugged. 'I don't know,' he said. He didn't know what else to say. Still, in spite of everything, he still wanted to take Kerrin's warm, soft face in his hands and feel the young skin and the child's lips. In spite of everything. 'You'd better go,' he said roughly, and he leaned across her to open the door.

Twenty-Six

The newspapers were calling her 'Bonnie' and the police claimed they knew her real identity. Nevertheless, it appeared nobody could find her.

This time the attack was in Alberton, a white, mainly Afrikaans suburb of Johannesburg, and the target a four-wheel-drive truck belonging to Jurie Lategan, a known former death squad member who had been named during the commission of inquiry into their clandestine activities in connection with several assassinations of ANC and PAC members. The truck had been parked outside his home, where his wife and three children lay sleeping. It had taken the garden wall with it, as well as a rustic bridge over the fishpond on the lawn and the gnome with the fishing rod which had been sitting beside it. A neighbour four houses away had found two neat halves of a goldfish in his swimming pool. There was a picture of him and his fat daughter holding the unfortunate creature up for all the world to see.

In Alberton, two independent witnesses claimed to have seen a white woman on two separate occasions in the neighbourhood, both times in the Lategans' street. She wore a black beret, with tendrils of long hair wisping out from beneath it. The first time she had been on foot, in the company of a young black man; the second on her own in a blue car. She was rumoured to be the person responsible for the Krugersdorp hotel blast.

Fran studied the picture in the paper. It was another police artist drawing, with more detail this time, as well as a description of clothing, including shoes. She felt half paralysed with inertia. The moment's decisiveness the other day had faded out on her almost at once, leaving her feeling washed up on a remote and uninhabited shore. She felt completely alone. The diary had remained where it was and she'd had nothing but silence from all avenues of communication. The paltry bits of information which had been given to her for safe-keeping seemed suddenly of as little use as her own life. She felt she might as well throw them away. It was not like her to be so negative, but she told herself she had been through enough. Her support system had holes in it. There was a tide of power working somewhere underground that she was not a part of and Fran felt herself lost and treading water on the surface.

Still, the one thing that had eluded everyone so far, and the single thing which the police had used to deny the press's allegations, was the strongest card she held. The name on the cover of the diary. The name on the bank account into which the funds had been deposited. She knew who was the mastermind behind the deaths of her comrades and, if no one was going to do anything about it, she would do it alone and to hell with the consequences.

Fran dug deep into her meagre reserves of strength. She looked at the byline on the article in the newspaper, and she picked up the telephone and dialled.

Kelly thought for a long time about Pedro. She thought about him all through Geography and most of double Maths. She and Denise walked home together after school. Denise seemed troubled about something. 'Listen,' she said. 'What's this about a steakhouse we're supposed to be working at? Your mother phoned mine the other night. I had to cover for you. About something I don't know about.'

'I'm sorry,' Kelly said. 'I was going to ask you.'

'That's OK, but what's going on? I haven't seen you at all lately. You're never at the Sun any more. When did you and Pedro split up anyway?'

'Split up?'

They were taking a short cut from school through the dam and the gardens where the murdered kids had been found. They sat together on a bench in the sun at the water's edge. An ice-cream vendor came along the path, pushing his bicycle and ringing a bell. Denise felt in the pockets of her blazer.

'Split up?' Kelly's eyes were penetrating.

Denise looked at her. 'Uh oh,' she said. She rolled down her brown stockings and bared her freckled legs to the sun. She waved the ice-cream man over and he steered an obedient course in their direction. He was used to being summoned by peremptory white schoolchildren. 'As your one-time best friend I'd better tell you. I saw Pedro at the club with someone else the other night. Jackie was there and I asked her and she said it was Pedro's new chick and she's moved into the flat with them. I said what about you and she told me Pedro wasn't seeing you any more.' She pushed herself up off the bench, indolently, and went to meet the ice-cream man.

'Ice-cream, you scream,' he said, grinning and ducking his head.

'Yeah yeah.' Denise lifted the lid of his freezer and plunged her arm into the depths. 'You want?' She looked back at Kelly. 'Mint Crisp?'

Kelly shook her head. 'When was this?'

'I dunno. A week, ten days ago. Can't remember.'

Some small boys with crash helmets came rocketing by on skateboards and Denise started and jumped back. The ice-cream in her hand fell in a lump on to the path, splattering Kelly's legs with flecks of green.

'Oh fuck,' said Denise. 'Now look.'

The man and his bicycle moved hastily off. He rang his bell.

'Oh, what does he care,' Denise grumbled.

Instead of going home, Kelly walked on through the suburbs. She walked right past Thatcher's without looking up. She kept her eyes on the paving stones all the way into Hillbrow. There was no one at the flat. She walked on to the club. Pedro wasn't there.

'Everyone's looking for Pedro,' said the book-keeper. 'Mr Popularity today.'

'What a guy,' said Kelly.

'He was here,' the book-keeper said encouragingly. 'But then he left.'

Walking back through Hillbrow, Kelly discovered something she knew was probably quite important. She didn't care. She really didn't care that much at all. Walk away, the rhythm of her school shoes seemed to be telling her. Just walk away, Renee. She was tired and hot. She took the lift up to her father's consulting rooms and waited for him, paging through magazines. He looked startled when he saw her.

'Kelly,' he said.

'Can I get a ride home?'

On the way they even had a small conversation. Luke wondered whether it could be termed a truce or perhaps even a new beginning. He was encouraged and almost hopeful, but he did not ask what had brought her to Hillbrow, or why her eyes darted this way and that, as if searching for someone or something.

At home Kelly showered and changed. She declined to eat with her parents. It was Friday night and she was working at the steakhouse. They let her go without protest. 'Got your key?' Virginia called after her. She smiled at Luke.

Pedro was waiting for her in the shadows by the gate. He slid over to her, a square block of a man, a thug. He took her by the arm.

'You came to the club today,' he said.

Kelly felt detached from all this now. She was done. 'Let go of my arm,' she said politely. Pedro pulled her into the shadows with him. Then he let her go and she stood there, rocking on her heels.

'Why are you trying to ruin my life?' Kelly said. 'You've had photos taken. You've given them to the newspapers.'

'Sold,' Pedro said softly. 'The word is sold.' He smiled at her, amiably. 'Hey,' he said. 'It was an offer I couldn't refuse.'

Kelly folded her arms to stop herself shaking. She leaned against the wall, a diminutive and unconscious imitation of her ex-lover with the tattoos on his biceps. Snakeman on one and Hot Stuff on the other. It was thinking about those tattoos that got her through her speech. Although her voice came out low and sometimes shaky, she managed to get it all out. About the man called Mike who was decent, which was more than could be said for Pedro. About taking photographs through keyholes or however he did it. About trying to turn her into a whore. And about breaking up with her without even telling her. Well, he'd done her a favour actually. She was sick of clubbing anyway. He could swop her services with those of his new girlfriend.

Kelly stopped. She seemed to have run out of breath and bravado at the same time. Cars drove past them into the parking area beneath the trees, momentarily lighting them up in their beams, two figures on a frieze, graffiti. The smell of rotting jasmine was unbearable. It lay all around them on the pavement like dead grubs.

Pedro laughed and pushed himself off the wall. He pulled Kelly's head back by the hair and kissed her. His lips were very wet. 'I never took the pictures anyway,' he said, pushing her away. 'That's Greg's speciality, not mine. He's got the negatives if you want to have prints made for your album.' He began walking away, stepping backwards off the kerb, grinning. 'But I think you'll have to fuck him for them,' he said.

Kelly watched Pedro turn the corner. She bit her lip, trying not to cry. She was fifteen years old. She felt old and used. Soiled goods, was what her mother would call someone like her. She wiped her mouth with the back of her hand. She could see the silhouettes against the light of the pub window inside Thatcher's. She wavered, scuffing gravel with her shoes. A group of African women walked past her. 'Hello, siesie,' one of them said and they all looked back at her curiously. Still she hesitated. Then she sighed. It was worth a try. If she could get the negatives, maybe it was not too late.

The envelope was marked 'Personal' so it hadn't been opened. Mike's heart sank when he saw it was stamped with the franking machine of the newspaper group. He balanced it on the palm of his hand for a minute or two. It was not heavy. He took a perspex paperknife and sliced along the crease of the smooth brown paper. He reached inside and drew out the photographs. They were sharp and clear, not the indistinct, grainy blow-ups he'd anticipated having to use a magnifying glass on. In the top one he was even smiling, looking straight to where the camera must have been set. He had his navy-blue socks on with the small St Francis Bay yacht club anchors on the ankle bones. He had nothing else on at all. He was reaching an arm out to Kerrin on the bed, in a gesture that was difficult to interpret – half-teasing, half-supplication. He couldn't remember the exact occasion, whether at the time he was in the process of dressing or undressing. Kerrin was naked and she sat cross-legged on the bed, with her long, fair hair brushing her nipples. It was smooth and fell in straight sheets over her shoulders. Dressing, he must have been dressing. Kerrin always brushed her hair while he dressed.

The other pictures were as intimate but not so innocent. In each of them the photographer had done his or her job well. They made identification of the man and the girl making love quite straightforward, with no room at all for mistakes or fabrication. Mike laid the prints out, methodically, like playing cards, in a row on his desk. He looked at them thoughtfully. They were clearly not all taken on one occasion. Right beside the bed stood the dumb valet over which he hung his clothes. His fawn suit was there in one of them, in another his sports jacket, as well as what seemed to be the navy pinstripe – it would be, of course. He usually wore it with the yacht club socks. There would be no protesting to Cassandra that it had been a once in a lifetime fling, a night of drunken 'I didn't know what I was doing'. Here was a neat catalogue of infidelity.

Mike felt numb but not panic-stricken. He was the captain of the sinking vessel, with no course open to him other than to go down with his ship. Women and children first, he thought hollowly. He would be obliged to resign, of course. He couldn't begin to imagine the wrath of Cassandra's father. He thought about legal advice, an injunction against the paper. It would do no good though. Another unscrupulous rag would get hold of the story and it just needed one picture, one headline, for the damage to be done. A lawyer, a court case, would just prolong the agony and keep it in the public eye. It made no difference what he did. If he offered money, a thought which had crossed his mind, that would probably also come out in the press, besides which it would be a sure admission of guilt. Whichever way he looked at it he was doomed.

He turned the pictures over one more time. Kerrin was so perfect, so beautiful, he couldn't block the sudden jolt in his stomach as he looked at her. She belonged in an erotic movie. She was every menopausal man's fantasy. And, for a short while, reluctant whore, she had been his.

The telephone rang, as he knew it would. 'As you can see, Sir, the pictures are authentic. Perhaps you would like to let us have your comments now? If possible, if you have the time, that is, I wonder if you wouldn't let us have a short interview … '

'No comment,' said Mike, and put down the phone.

Twenty-Seven

'I found these on the gatepost. Some sort of signal perhaps?' Luke stood on the doormat, holding aloft a pair of tarty red knickers for all the world to see. Jessica, car keys in hand, uncharacteristically blushed and cursed her frivolous impulsiveness. Why she had had to pick the pair with Do It on the front, she couldn't now imagine. Edwina had gone for them in a big way. Ben's bowler hats had nothing on red lace.

'Gimme,' said Edwina, appearing out of nowhere and barrelling through Jessica's legs. She pulled herself up on Luke's trousers, leaving a Marmite handprint on his right knee. He dropped the panties into her hands.

'My spies tell me you've not been obeying doctor's orders. You aren't by any chance planning to drive yourself to the hospital, are you?'

'You can see I am,' Jessica said patiently, resisting the childish temptation to add What's it to you? Instead she said, 'What are you doing here?'

'Can we talk in the car? We'll go in mine.'

In fact they didn't talk very much at all. The chemotherapy department seemed an unlikely place for a lovers' tryst, but, they agreed, it was as good a place as any to start. Luke was calm and direct. He had been thinking and he thought, if Jessica felt she could, he could come to terms with lying and cheating. Something – call it fate, for the time being – had put him and Jessica in the same place at the same time and, well, chemistry had done the rest. None of the rational arguments, the all-night, mind-churning sessions, nor anything else, such as common sense, had had the slightest effect. It was just the suddenness of it, the unexpected blow to the side of the head that had caught him off guard.

Truly, Jessica thought fondly, women were more intelligent than men.

She sat with a needle in her arm while Luke went off to visit another patient on the same floor. Jessica wasn't alone today. There was a teenage boy having chemo with her. He looked rather strange with not a hair on his head and the palest of eyebrows, a bit like an unfinished sketch. He smiled across at her when he saw her looking at him. His mother was with him. She sat beside the bed reading a Tintin book and eating crisps from a packet. They crackled into the silence. She wiped her fingers on her skirt without looking up. Her lips moved as she read. Jessica suspected that she had the same pale eyebrows as her son, but hers were pencilled in in careful brown lines. They gave her a surprised look.

A nurse came in to check on them and behind her was Ben. Jessica started. 'Don't move!' the nurse said sharply.

'I tried to get home in time to bring you,' Ben said. 'But Anna said you'd gone already.'

'Luke came.'

'I'm sorry, Jess. I got delayed.'

'I didn't expect you, Ben, so it's OK.' Jessica felt sorry for him, an emotion which took her by surprise. It was as if they were old acquaintances, already living apart. Was that what was going to happen, she wondered. Luke came back and handled the situation like an old hand at adultery, although Jessica thought he seemed reluctant to shake Ben's outstretched hand.

Ben took her home. He had Anna make her tea, which she threw up immediately, as she knew she would. He had taken the afternoon off work and he played with the children in the pool while Jessica slept. It was the first time he'd done this since she'd been ill and she felt annoyed. He had to choose today to start playing the good husband.

When she woke up it was almost dark. She could hear the television on down the hall. She thought about Luke and wondered if she'd dreamed the whole thing. She considered calling him on the bedside telephone. A swift plunge into duplicity without looking back. It would be tricky, though, and Ben was still in the house. She wondered why he had done this today of all days. Why wasn't he out drinking? What was he up to?

It came with the boiled egg and fishpaste sandwich he brought her at seven o'clock. She set the tray aside, scarcely looking at it.

'Haven't you noticed that I can't keep anything down?' she said.

'I'm sorry,' he said, hangdog. What had he had for supper – humble pie? 'I do know that. I just thought, maybe –'

'Could you run a bath for me?'

He sat beside her on the toilet seat while she bathed until Jessica felt claustrophobic. Steam from the water was clogging her lungs. Finally, Ben began to talk. With each halting sentence, coated in self-pity, Jessica felt more and more depressed. He knew he had been a lousy husband and father, but he was going to make it up to her and the children. He knew that he needed help with his drinking. He accepted that it had become a problem and was out of control. His father had been an alcoholic – did Jessica know that? Jessica didn't and didn't care. She tried to focus on Luke but Ben was spoiling everything. He was telling her how he was going to book himself into a clinic just as soon as Jessica felt able to cope without him. (She let that pass.) Perhaps Luke Stephens could even suggest one?

He'd finished. So that was it. She realised he was waiting for her to say something.

'Pass me a towel,' said Jessica.

She went through to the bedroom and pulled on the old T-shirt she used as a nightgown. She knew she was not being kind. 'Just as long as you know what you're doing it *for*, Ben,' she called back. 'Don't make the mistake of doing it for me, for the kids or whatever. Sort yourself out for your own sake. For no reason other than that. That's the only way you're going to get it right.' Wasn't that what Anne Landers would say?

'I know,' Ben said, still humble.

'And for God's sake, get going now. I might be dead before

you know it and then you'll really have to cope.' She went back into the bathroom. Ben was still sitting on the toilet seat.

'I wish you wouldn't talk like that,' he mumbled.

'Is Mom going to die? Are you going to die, Mom? When?'

'Everybody's got to die some day, Andrew-eavesdropper. And no, I'm not going to die just yet if I can help it. And for Christ's sake blow that nose.'

Andrew was hurt. He took the tissue box. 'Anyway,' he said, 'there's someone on the phone for you.'

'Well, why didn't you say so – OK, I didn't ask. Who is it?'

'The doctor who was here the other night when Daddy was away.' Andrew had been asleep that night, hadn't he?

Jessica felt Ben's eyes on her as she wrapped a dressing gown round her. As the bathwater ran down the plughole he took a cloth and began slowly to clean off the ring.

'That is just so tacky. God. Tell me all.'

Fran and Jessica sat in the shade of Cassandra's patio, waiting for the others to arrive for tennis. Although she wasn't able to play, Jessica liked to go along with the children on Friday afternoons. She was unofficial refreshment organiser and dishwasher, now that Selena was gone ('Just took off,' Gail Fleming had taken it upon herself to tell them with relish. 'You think you know them and then – phwewt! Absolutely no sense of loyalty.') Cassandra was in the house on the telephone to the insurance agent for the third time.

'So you had breakfast first –?'

'Well, Luke did. It's still many happy returns with me. I can't keep a lot down – especially not just after a chemo session. Luke had muesli and croissants.'

'Bit of a wash-out for you then: no ice-bucket with champagne in your room? Were there roses at least, and a gentle breeze moving the net curtains about?'

'Oh, shut up. I'm not going to tell you any more. Wild horses wouldn't – hello, here's Ansie. She's brought Zinzi Mokoena along. Now there's an interesting bit of the new South Africa in the making.'

Zinzi had tackies and a white skirt, but no racket. Although her neck was no longer in its uncomfortable brace, she moved her head very slowly.

'I like to get the feel of the outfit before I get serious about the game,' she said. She had an infectious smile, with deep dimples identical to the twins'. 'Jessica and I will watch for cheating.'

They were quite a crowd today. The children played in the pool with much noise and splashing. Fran never got to hear about Jessica's and Luke's first real foray into infidelity.

Luke had booked a room at the City Lodge near the airport. It was a pit-stop for business people spending one or two nights in the city on company accounts. The rooms were basic. The lodge served only breakfast.

They had both felt appallingly shy. Struggling for conversation, Jessica imagined Luke was trying to convince himself it was just a breakfast meeting. Then she wondered for a ghastly moment if that was what it was and she had somehow misinterpreted it. She was also self-conscious for the first time about her body, though God knew Luke had seen her at her very worst, watching her retching and ashen. It was also difficult to feel romantic at eight o'clock in the morning after getting the children off to school and putting the dog blankets in to soak, and nearly electrocuting herself with the plug peering into a faulty steam iron while Anna stood by looking sceptical. In the end she found herself late and instead of carefully choosing what to wear, had flung on a severe skirt and polo-neck top, got Anna to help load up the car with old newspapers and two crates of empties for the deaf school which she might as well drop off as it was on the way, and raced along the highway to make love to Luke in a bland hotel room. She listened to the news on the radio like any ordinary commuter.

The room might have been austere and the vacuum cleaner out in the passage might have drowned out Luke's whispered endearments, but she liked to think it had been worth it. At least until Luke was hailed by one of his medical colleagues in the foyer on their way out.

'I can't do this,' Luke said to Jessica tightly as he walked her to her car. Jessica had just spotted a friend of Tamzin's too but she didn't like to mention it. 'I'm going to tell her. I'm going to have to tell Virginia.'

He was agitated. Jessica, though, was ready for this. An affair in theory was all very well, but what she was dealing with here, she recognised, was a severe case of Catholic guilt. Fran had warned her to watch for the symptoms. Fran had said they seldom left their wives, and if they did it was usually temporary, until their dirty socks had backed up.

'I want to come clean.'

Jessica felt a nervous giggle beginning in the pit of her stomach. She touched him on the arm and he looked around furtively. 'Luke,' she said. 'Luke. We had breakfast together, OK? Nobody suspected anything. The room wasn't bugged. Don't do anything rash now. We discussed all this, didn't we?' She straightened his tie and he flinched. 'Coming clean, believe me, is rash.'

They agreed not to see each other until the following week, until Ben, who had been true to his word, had booked himself into Rushmere clinic. Jessica had felt momentarily mean for encouraging him, to the extent of even looking up the telephone number for him, but had justified it by dismissing the ulterior motive in favour of the genuine need. She bought Ben a whole set of Wilbur Smiths which she tucked underneath his pyjamas in his suitcase.

Kelly told Virginia she had given up her job at the steakhouse. It was the first time in weeks that she had volunteered anything like information to her mother, let alone talked to her in sentences of more than two words. It was almost school holidays and Denise's family was going to Durban. They had asked her to go along and she thought she might – that was, if Virginia would let her. *If Virginia would let her*. This was another first. The thought did cross Virginia's mind that Kelly might be lying but she had the sense not to cross-examine her. Kelly looked sardonic. 'Her mom said she was going to call you,' she said.

Virginia said she would discuss it with Luke, but saw no reason why she shouldn't go. Kelly had been so troubled lately. It would probably do her good.

Luke, who had never so much as pulled a dandelion in the garden, came home from his hospital rounds and spent an hour watering the lawn and trimming the edges with the weedeater. When he came inside he set about fixing a dislocated handle on the kitchen door. Every time she wanted to talk to him he would slide out of range.

He ate almost nothing of her potroast at dinner. Virginia looked at him critically. He had lost weight, she thought. He never ate properly, except for breakfast. And even that he'd skipped that morning.

'Just another potato?' she coaxed.

'No,' he said. 'No, thank you.'

He did agree with her about Kelly. He, too, had been worried about her, the missing school, the general uncommunicativeness. He was relieved that she had stopped the steakhouse work. He had never approved of her being out so often at night and so late. She had rings under her eyes.

'It's a pity we couldn't make it a family holiday, the three of us,' said Virginia wistfully. 'But you're up to your ears, I suppose.'

Luke didn't reply.

'I do think we should try,' Virginia said, 'to be a closer family. Don't you?'

Cassandra had seen the posters of the lunch-time edition earlier in the day, but it was only when she had found two reporters and a photographer camped out on her patio that she knew the 'top businessman' caught with his pants down, so to speak, was Mike.

They took pictures of her pushing the children into the house. They waved small notepads in her face as she fitted the key to the lock. She closed the door behind her, putting the safety catch on the Yale lock. Then she went upstairs to Mike's secret drawer in his dressing room (perhaps the only private thing she hadn't told Joel about) and fetched his revolver. Her father had taught her to shoot on the mine-dumps south of Johannesburg when she was fourteen and she had become quite a crack target shooter in her twenties.

She pushed the bedroom windows wide, wide open and fired three shots into the air. The two reporters, who had been squinting up at the windows, flung themselves flat on the cement of the driveway with their hands over their heads. The photographer went into a low crouch and slunk behind a hydrangea bush. She could see his two-tone shoes sticking out and his camera lens inching cautiously forward again. She let off another shot for good measure. One reporter was beginning to leopard-crawl towards the safety of the porch, and he froze, whimpering.

In the deafening silence all round a dove fell heavily through the branches of the sneezing powder tree and thumped on to the driveway beside the maidenhair fern. Cassandra was too stunned to be appalled. She closed the windows and drew the curtains. Then she began to calm the children and reassure the dogs. After putting the gun away she looked outside again. There was no sign of the men. Only the dead bird, a wing raised like a last ditch cry of surrender, lay where it had fallen. She would no doubt read of this episode in the papers too, but at least some sort of satisfaction had been achieved.

The telephone rang and she pulled the plug briskly out of the wall socket without lifting the receiver. Whether it was Mike, the press or her father, she wanted nothing to do with it. She poured herself a brandy.

One of the small white dogs, its tail a blur of wagging, fetched the evening paper as he'd been trained to do. Cassandra opened it with resignation. Mike had a band of canine saliva across the back of his head and puncture marks in his shoulder. By the time he came home Cassandra had had time to think. He came to her uncertainly and she almost put out her arms, but they seemed to go lame on the arms of her chair. She felt drunk on brandy and outrage, but she could see he had been weeping, and that did not seem right to her. She took a moment to reflect that she had never seen Mike weep before.

'I tried,' he said, 'I tried to stop them.'

Cassandra said nothing.

'Where are the children?'

'Burying the pigeon I shot.'

'Ah.' Mike nodded vaguely. He lowered himself into a chair, gingerly, as if he was in physical pain.

'So,' said Cassandra. 'I gather these are not fake pictures.'

Perhaps it was true what they said about your parents. If you were one of the lucky ones, that was. That they would stand by you just because you were their child and they loved you unconditionally. Kelly had read that shit in a school set work once and had dismissed it with contempt. At the time Luke had been away at a conference in Montreal and Virginia had been on a hunger strike at Zwartland prison in sympathy with a rent boycott in an obscure township where she'd been running a soup kitchen. She'd had to spend a week with her father's senile aunt in Alberton. The boys in her class had put sandwiches in her desk for her mother. She thought she had tasted the worst in humiliation that time. But perhaps Thatcher's was about to top even that.

Luke and Virginia had not even registered at first that the pictures in the paper were her. Virginia was never interested in scandal. She never pored over telescopic images of Princess Stephanie naked on tropical beaches like everyone else.

And Luke read the political and economic stuff, and the sport. Kelly sat by, incredulous, as they swopped sections of newspaper over their after-dinner coffee, and her breasts with the neat little black censored patches over the nipples flashed across the living room as they turned oblivious pages. For one delirious moment she imagined getting away with it. If her parents didn't notice, maybe nobody else would. Maybe she could brush it off at school as an amazing look-alike. A twin sister separated from her at birth?

Luke had seen it.

He lowered the paper and looked at her. She tried but she found she couldn't meet his eyes. All she could see was Greg, heaving and panting on top of her, felt the acne scars on his back. She bolted from the room and was sick in the toilet. She crouched on her knees with her head in the bowl, choking and gasping. She felt her long hair being taken out of her face from behind. Luke had never struck her and she readied herself for his first blow. Instead his small, smooth hands took her hair and held it, stroking her head until there was nothing left in her stomach. She could not turn to look at him. She sensed not anger but immense hurt coming at her from behind like a smothering, dense cloud. Now was the time to fling herself into his arms and cry like a baby, begging forgiveness. She could do neither of these things. All she felt was an overwhelming need to injure herself, to bang her head on the cold, white porcelain of the toilet bowl, until it split like an egg, and spilled her brains, warm as porridge, into the antiseptic water.

Twenty-Eight

It hadn't been easy, but Fran had succeeded in getting her telephone number changed. She had also invested in an answering machine and now, whether she was at home or not, she kept the machine on to monitor her calls.

The papers had gone to town on the story. Pages of the diary had been reproduced in full and Van Rensburg's and his sidekick's signatures blown up and exposed. The government was severely embarrassed and censured by every country in the world, and once again, the delicate dance which they euphemistically called negotiations threatened to come off the rails. The best thing, though, was the picture of the man they called 'Die Waaghals' – the daredevil – now identified as Slabbert Joubert, the leader of the rogue death squad, ex-policeman, ex-CCB, who stood revealed, a small, burly man with a sizeable chip on his shoulder. Other members of his gang were exposed too, and a gallery of unsavoury-looking men appeared nightly in the press.

The police had had no option but to arrest Joubert and then, amid yet another indignant public outcry, they had released him on bail.

Fran waited for her knuckles to be rapped for ignoring orders, but absolutely nothing happened. The vitriolic calls continued, however, until she could stand it no more. That was when she had enlisted the help of the police in getting another number and now she sat stoically listening to the threats and obscenities until they almost ceased to bother her.

Fran felt Sophie's absence as keenly as ever. Instead of the pain and memories fading, it was like a reel of film winding backwards, with each image becoming fresher, sharper, more alive with each passing day. Sophie lived in her memory so fiercely she would wake up at night convinced she had heard her cry out from the room across the hall. One morning she made breakfast for her without thinking; another, she bought her a colouring book and new box of crayons. The parcel from her mother for Sophie's birthday, which had got lost in the postal system and arrived a month late, precipitated a fit of shaking which made her take to her bed and stay there for a whole two days. She took to sleeping with the one-legged tin soldier that had been Sophie's favourite toy, beside her bed. She slipped him into the cubbyhole of her car when she went out. Comrade Joe, Sophie had called him. Com Joe.

Sophie had been small-boned, like her, with fine, light hairs on her forearms. She sat with her knees together and asked questions in a slow, thoughtful way, and listened and digested when you answered her. Hours, sometimes days, later, she would pick up on a point she thought you hadn't been clear on. Without preamble, 'But if ... ' she would say.

Fran thanked God for her friends: for Jessica, with her intuitive compassion and humour, Tamzin's confused honesty, Ansie with her bluntness and generosity, and Henry McBride for all of those things. And Mary in Botswana, slow moving, slow talking, and so utterly dependable and available to her. She thought of her often when they weren't in direct touch, pictured her at the end of the telephone with Charity on her lap, or standing shading her eyes outside the door of her whitewashed farmhouse. Mary, perhaps like Laurike had been to her at one time, was a solid constant, a touchstone in Fran's life. It wasn't just the personal empathy between them, although that was strong enough. It was shared experience and ideals too, that counted for a lot. Mary had gone into exile in '76 and had been out of reach for a long while. She'd got married to Sam in exile too, and had her children in Lusaka. Then, finally, she had set up home in the dust and heat of Botswana. At least it was closer than Lusaka and Fran had been able to see her more often. Fran would have trusted Mary with her life. She'd taken Sophie in once, when Fran had been in detention, and kept her safe for six months. Davy had gone up every weekend to see her.

Fran wondered why Tamzin hadn't told her she was pregnant, and why Jessica, too, had tried to keep this from her. Perhaps because they thought it would upset her, with Tamzin nurturing a new life and Fran bereft of her own child. Perhaps because there was still a reticence between them which perhaps might never heal completely. Still, if Tamzin wasn't talking about it, there was a reason. Perhaps Ray didn't know yet, or maybe he didn't want a baby.

She and Tamzin met for pasta one night in town, at an oddly formal request from Tamzin. She skipped preliminaries and didn't even wait for the pizza bread. 'Fran, there's something I need to tell you,' she said.

Fran looked at her. Tamzin wasn't meeting her eyes. She seemed upset.

'Is it about Ray?' she guessed, finally, when nothing further seemed to be forthcoming.

'No. Well, indirectly. But that side of it doesn't affect you.'

'I'm lost.'

'I'm going to have a baby.'

'I gathered as much, but I still don't –'

'Davy's the father.'

They were playing loud Italian music in the restaurant. Sentimental love songs. 'O Sole Mio', with nectar dripping from the strings. A black waiter, Zulu gondolier, put steaming piles of white spaghetti before them with a flourish. He emptied the carafe of white wine into their two glasses, hesitating momentarily in front of Tamzin. 'Is mamma having wine?' he said. 'Is it not bad for the bambino?'

They both turned to him and Fran's icy-cool stare sent him slipping and sliding back to the kitchen. No more banter for table thirteen.

'Davy's the father?' said Fran. 'Davy? *My* Davy?'

'You're back-tracking,' said Tamzin. 'I can see you're back-tracking. Can I tell it to you properly?'

Tamzin told her story, while Fran ate her way steadily through her pile of pasta, not looking up except to drink from her glass. Her face was completely expressionless. She looked like someone eating a meal alone, concentrating only on emptying her plate quickly and efficiently. Tamzin talked valiantly on, focusing on the top of Fran's bent head. She left out the part about Davy being gay, although without it the thing made no sense. It was a puzzle with a piece missing. Jessica had agreed that that was the part Davy had to supply and if Tamzin had to force his hand, then so be it. She couldn't let the weeks slip by without addressing the problem of Fran.

'I wish you would say something,' she said, when she had run out of words.

'This,' said Fran slowly, 'has not been a very good year. Forgive me – I'm trying to get a grasp on this. You say you're not having an affair – how I hate that word – with Davy, that you've no intention of having even a relationship, other than friendship, with him. And yet you're carrying his child. Frankly, I'm not at all sure I know what's going on here. Did I miss something?'

Tamzin looked shrivelled. Even her hair was flatter on her head, subdued and cowed. 'I don't know,' she said, 'how better to explain it. A moment of loneliness, uncertainty –'

'Lust,' said Fran.

'– on both our parts. It wasn't premeditated or planned. It just happened.'

'It just happened.'

'I know it sounds trite. I'm –'

Fran put up her hands. 'Please. Just don't tell me you're sorry, OK? I accept it's difficult for you to tell me all this. That what you've done is an abuse of our friendship I think you know, so I won't point it out again. I also accept that you slept with my husband after he'd left me, so I suppose he was fair game. Frankly, though, I'm too weary to want to get involved with this, and if you're telling me just so that I can absolve you or something, please – go tell a priest. Don't come to me. Sure, I'm shocked. I don't understand. But you're going to have a baby and you're going to raise it and you're going to have years of struggle and joy ahead of you, if you're lucky. But, Tamzin, if you're thinking I'm not going to be able to bear the pain of seeing you with Davy's child when I've just lost the child I had with him, in a most brutal and untimely way, you don't know me very well. Just as long as you know what you're doing (and I doubt you do, if you want the truth), it's your life. I'm not going to castigate you. I'm not going to cut you out of my life either. In fact, don't look at me to punish you, because that's what it seems to me you're doing. Concentrate your head on that child in there. It's going to need everything you've got.'

Tamzin hadn't touched her food.

'Have you told Ray?' Fran asked flatly.

Tamzin nodded miserably. 'He has mixed feelings about it,' she said.

As transparent a lie as any, thought Fran, but she let it go. 'What about the school?' she asked. 'How are you going to manage? Are you going to be in a position to support a child? Don't count on a musician's income to see you through.'

Tamzin was close to tears now. Fran leaned across the table, forcing her to look up. 'You're choosing single parenthood, you know,' she said. 'I had a small taste of it. I wonder if you know just how hard that's going to be.'

They left the restaurant together and stood on the pavement for a minute before parting. As they moved off to their cars in different directions, Fran turned and called Tamzin's name. She took a couple of steps back.

'Does Jessica know about this?' she said.

Tamzin's expression had been answer enough, but Fran thrust that part of it away for the time being. There was a missing piece of the puzzle still, but she couldn't get a grip on what shape it was. There was more to this than Tamzin was telling her, and if Jessica knew the whole story, as she suspected she did, there was a reason why she hadn't told her. She would deal with Jessica later, but for now Davy was the only one who could enlighten her and if she was to have any peace, she would now have to know the truth.

Again she took the lift to his flat. She rang the bell. She tucked her hair behind her ears. Davy came to the door. He was wearing old rugby shorts, no shirt. She could hear music coming from what she presumed was probably the kitchen. She hadn't seen Davy for some time and she had steeled herself for the jolt in the stomach. Surprisingly, it didn't come. She looked at him curiously. He seemed smaller.

'Have you got a moment?' she said. 'It's important.'

'Is it Sophie?' he said. He closed the door behind her, kissed her on the cheek like an old friend.

She shook her head. She followed Davy into the living room. It was quite dark and cramped. There were cushions on the floor and wineglasses with dregs in them. Davy said, 'Can I get you anything? Coffee?'

Fran shook her head again. She tried to remember where it was she had wanted to start. 'Where's your ... girlfriend?' she said, amazing herself. Those words had never been in her head at all.

Davy looked startled.

'Carole. Doesn't she ... aren't you ... ' This wasn't what she'd come here for. What was the matter with her? *Our bedroom*. The cat and the window. She hadn't realised how solidly that phrase had stayed with her. *Our bedroom*. And clearly Davy was uneasy. He had never liked the direct approach. She could see he was stalling.

'It's all right,' she said. 'I'm sorry. It's not what I came to talk to you about anyway.'

'It isn't?' His relief was tangible.

'It's Tamzin. I believe she's pregnant with your child.'

The front door slammed. A voice called out 'Anyone home?' and Stanley Abrams sloped into the room. He looked from Fran to Davy. 'Hello, Fran,' he said. 'It's good to see you.'

'Stan – do you mind if –'

'Sure.' Stanley touched Davy on the shoulder and turned to leave the room. It was in that split second that Fran knew. She could never have analysed it; perhaps it was the familiarity of the gesture, the fondness that spoke of intimacy and not just male camaraderie, but whatever it was she knew with clarity that she had got it all wrong. Stanley was the missing piece. Of course he was.

'Cuntstruck.'

Luke was rocked. Such a word, flopping vulgarly out of Virginia's mouth, was like a belch from the Duchess of Kent presenting the trophies at Wimbledon. Virginia said things like 'Great Scott', occasionally 'Damn it', never anything stronger. At the moment she looked like a caricature of herself. Since the calls from the school principal, sundry long-lost family members and so-called well-wishers, she had taken to wearing bright red lipstick and strapless sundresses, and giving earnest interviews on adolescents to unscrupulous magazine reporters, who smiled behind their hands.

It was as if, in order better to understand the trauma of teenager-turned-hooker, she needed to get closer to the part herself. He wondered how 'jilted wife' would affect her dress code and whether the two roles would conflict. Her short hair, filing-cabinet grey, was a sudden mass of springy curls, courtesy of Salon Beth Joubert.

Luke cared deeply for Virginia. They had shared many years together and there was a bond there, stronger than any bitter words would break. Or so he imagined. He had intended only to suggest separation, to soften the blow (to make it easier for himself, his conscience said). He had decided he had no heart for adultery. Since Kelly's problems, it had seemed to him fairer to be honest – or as honest as he felt Virginia needed him to be. Virginia, though, had been on to him immediately. With the shrewd accuracy of a drunk no one takes seriously, she homed in on the core like a missile. 'You're having an affair,' she said. 'Let me guess: it's Jessica Tucker, isn't it? You fancy you're in love with her. But you're just a menopausal man, when you think about it. Cuntstruck, that's all.'

She was cutting the mould off a piece of cheddar cheese with strong hacks. Luke had denied nothing, although Virginia's choice of phrase made him wince. Feeling adolescent himself, he wished he could run away from home. Perhaps it would have been easier if it had been a twenty-year-old student nurse with a predictable body, instead of a bald woman in her thirties with three small children. And cancer. Perhaps it would have lessened Virginia's anger. She stood on the pedal of the kitchen bin. The lid shot open and green edges of cheese descended. Harshness was the weapon she chose after vulgarity.

'With any luck the bitch will die,' she said. 'And then perhaps we can go on with our lives.'

Luke moved out over the weekend. A colleague on long leave had a garden cottage which was standing empty. It was furnished in modern fashion, chrome and black, with standing lamps which looked like the Pink Panther without arms. The deal was that Luke would feed his tank of tropical fish. Luke had no trouble with that. He found it soothing to sit in the dark his first night and watch their eerie swimming. It gave him pleasure to see them dart to the surface with a flick of a tail to snip at the food sprinkled there. They flashed and shone and moved all the time.

Kelly came to see him on Saturday morning. She brought a six-pack of beers and they made shandies and drank them sitting on the lawn in the sun. Kelly was looking a bit better. She'd had a session with a therapist already, another colleague, who was sympathetic and practical. As a family they had handled the crisis quite well, in the circumstances, he thought. Kelly and Virginia were talking again. She told him they were thinking about moving away, maybe to Cape Town, at least for the holidays, maybe permanently. Virginia had a sister down there with teenage sons, Kelly's cousins.

Luke needed to see Jessica to get him back on track. She didn't even know he'd moved out. He called her. She was not surprised. 'Who's doing your laundry?' she asked, but she came over. She walked round the cottage like a cat, touching things, feeling the textures of cool leather and tiles against her bare brown feet. They made love only once and it was awkward and tender and coloured by guilt. They struggled to find the place where they had left off. They sat together and watched the fish and talked about Kelly. Jessica filled Luke in on the pieces about Mike Symons, or what she knew of that end of the story. Cassandra seemed to have vanished into thin air. No one could reach her, not even Tamzin. Her children were not in school and, as the term was almost over, probably wouldn't be again for the rest of the school year.

Luke was still talking about bringing things out into the open. If Virginia knew about them, Ben would discover it sooner rather than later. He was due to come out of the clinic at the weekend. Jessica had been to see him there and had found him playing table-tennis with a small Chinese woman who smashed at the balls as if her life depended on it. Why was it that table-tennis was considered so therapeutic, she wondered. She half expected Ben to be sitting weaving a basket the next time she went.

Jessica had had time to think while she was in the house alone, just her and the children. And Anna. Anna who had come in with her driver's licence the week before, borrowed the car and done the month's grocery shopping for Jessica, with only a small scrape on the front fender to show for it. They sat companionably in the evenings and watched TV. Anna wanted to move into the spare bedroom to keep an eye on things if Jessica took ill in the night, but Jessica wasn't ready for round the clock nursing care yet. Besides, there was Luke, and she was sure Anna didn't sleep as soundly as her children.

The thing was, Jessica liked having the house to herself. She stood in the living room and looked at the books on the shelves, the records in their holders, the cushions on the sofa that her grandmother had made for her. All the things that would have to be apportioned if it came to splitting up the home. She didn't think she could bear the effort it would take.

She thought her feelings for Luke were as strong as ever, but there was a shift in things that she didn't feel entirely ready for. Luke's decision had been made in panic. She felt pressured by the suddenness. Wasn't it always in times of stress that one clung to the minutiae of the familiar? She hadn't expected Luke and she hadn't expected that he would alter her life so radically.

If she thought about it honestly, she supposed that the role of mistress wouldn't be a bad idea at all. Was that downright immoral or, worse, amoral? She could see herself and Luke living on the touches, the looks, the City Lodge breakfasts. She wasn't sure she could see him sweeping up the leaves on her lawn.

Ben went to an AA meeting the evening he came home. He was quite pleased about it, before and after. He seemed to have found a purpose in life. He was starting to grow a moustache. He came up behind Jessica at odd moments and put his arms round her, with his hands on her breasts. Jessica pushed him away, pleading illness. She did, in fact, feel ill almost all the time. She spent hours on her bed. She had diarrhoea and headaches. Ben was still on leave and helped around the house. Finally, one evening he told her he was on a kind of probation from work, pending his doing something about his drinking problem. They had been sympathetic to an extent, she gathered, because of her illness and the trauma he was going through in coming to terms with it, but the ultimatum had come in the end: sort out the problem or no gold watch. He was trying. Jessica had to agree with that.

It was a warm evening and they were sitting out on the back patio beside the pool. Anna was doing laps in the darkness, snorting and grunting as she turned at each end. The telephone rang and she went in to answer it, wrapped in a towel.

'For you,' she said to Ben and he got reluctantly to his feet.

'Who was it?' Jessica asked, as Anna stood drying herself vigorously in the moonlight. Water gleamed on her brown shoulders.

'Woman,' said Anna.

Jessica had a funny feeling right then. It started in the small of her back and spread like a muscular pain across her shoulder blades. Anna said goodnight and left her sitting in the darkness. When Ben did not come back she knew she ought not to leave him inside too long on his own, but she couldn't bring herself to move. It was stupid but she hadn't thought of Virginia. Virginia was this grey area she didn't want to know about. She'd only met her once and Luke hardly ever talked about her. Now Virginia was on the phone pleading for her husband.

Virginia wasn't exactly pleading. She was just sharing the facts with Ben, as she saw them. For Ben, who had spent a cocooned weekend reading Wilbur Smith and playing table-tennis, not much of it made sense at first. It took him a minute or two to work out who the shrill-voiced woman on the telephone was, and another couple to get an inkling of what she was implying. By the time Jessica came inside with the empty coffee cups, he was slumped in a chair, pulling at the corner of his new moustache.

'I have no one but myself to blame.'

'Well. These things tend to get out of hand. There are so many people involved. It's not just the two starstruck lovers, I'm afraid.'

'I hate it when you're right.'

'It's not a question of being right. It's unpredictability. You work things out so that you can handle them, according to your own game plan. You know – keep it ticking along just as long as nobody gets hurt. I bet you could count on one hand the number of affairs like this where nobody gets hurt. There's no happy ending to this kind of stuff. I thought you knew that.'

Fran was blow-drying Glenda's dark hair. She wasn't sure that she ought to be talking frankly to Jessica at the same time, but Glenda was paging through a comic and Jessica looked as if she didn't care. She had grown spectrally thin. In shorts, the bones on her knees stood out like knuckles. She sat on the edge of the bed and bit her nails. Everything had gone wrong and so quickly. She had spent two days and two nights examining the whole sordid mess. She had never thought of herself as a selfish person, but now she supposed that that was what she surely was. She had met Luke, become obsessed with him, allowed him to know. And then instead of writing down a list of names like Ben, Virginia, Andrew, Glenda, Edwina, Kelly, and looking at them long and hard, she had gone straight in and ruined all their lives without a backward glance. Did cancer make a difference? It certainly didn't make it OK. Where had her sense of responsibility been when she invited Luke into her bed? Where had her brain been?

Now she was being forced into making decisions which a couple of months back she wouldn't have imagined ever having to make. Virginia wanted her husband back, Kelly her father. Luke was making do in what could only be described as a bachelor pad, and probably secretly resenting Jessica for putting him there. And Ben? Ben had gone on a binge and disappeared for two days. And all because of her.

Everywhere she saw the signs of age. Lying on her bed, she inspected the skin in the crook of her elbow. It sagged in a criss-cross of delicate lines. She had lines on her forehead, and small, permanent creases beneath her eyes. All her life Jessica had turned heads. Luke's was without doubt the last she could expect.

She and Fran had spent hours talking. Fran had come straight to see her after her visit to Davy's flat. When Jessica saw her on the doorstep she knew at once that the secrets were out and in spite of the expression on Fran's face, she felt a great and thankful relief.

'You knew,' Fran greeted her. 'You knew all along.'

'Well –' said Jessica, looking at Fran critically in the manner of a member of a bomb disposal unit circling a suspicious package.

Fran had not really been angry though. She was too stunned by first Tamzin's revelations and then Davy's, and she needed Jessica's practical comments and sardonic wit to help her deal with the situation. Jessica started to get into a 'You have to look at it from my perspective' conversation but Fran waved her away.

'I'm having enough difficulty looking at it from mine,' Fran said. 'This is going to take some getting used to.'

Jessica's problems were almost a diversion. They were so conventional it was a relief to discuss them. Ben had made no demands, she told Fran, given no ultimatums. He had retreated into the bottle like an injured genie and had simply stayed there, silent and unforthcoming.

Twenty-Nine

They'd had the Michael Jackson concert at Rosepark school. Thabo was the undisputed star of the show, Freda Mokoena's impressive Brenda Fassie impersonation notwithstanding. 'Why Tamzin can't put on a Christmas pageant like a normal nursery school, I don't know,' Gail was heard to say, but she was mollified by Simon, resplendent in Lincoln-green satin spines, giving a piercing rendition of 'Puff the Magic Dragon'– even if he did repeat the first verse three times and had to be forcibly removed from the stage.

Tamzin cleared up afterwards, helped by Petra and the twins, while Ansie returned the loaned wineglasses to the bottlestore. Not for Rosepark parents a traditional tea and cake afternoon; Tamzin's midday end of year cheese and wine party to help the mums and dads get through the concert had become something of a drawcard in itself.

Petra was a child come to life this term. She talked to Tamzin quite naturally and was almost affectionate where before she had stiffened or moved away when Tamzin tried to draw her into a group. Her English was improving, although she and the twins usually communicated in an effective mixture of Afrikaans and Xhosa. She would always be shy, though, it was her nature, and she would seldom, even now, actually initiate a conversation with an adult.

They cleaned out the lockers with damp sponges, collecting all the bits and pieces hidden in corners and behind cupboards and putting them in a Lost and Found box. Freda held up a pretty butterfly hairclip coated with dirt.

'Now who does that belong to?' said Tamzin.

Petra gave it a cursory glance. 'Sophie,' she said. She squeezed her sponge into the bucket.

Tamzin took the clip and rubbed it clean on her skirt. 'Sophie,' she echoed.

Her eyes filled with tears. She was so emotional at the moment, she'd even cried during 'The Farmer in the Dell', which they did every year. Last year Sophie had been the cheese. She knew she was pathetic but she couldn't help it. She slipped the clip into her pocket. She had a sudden vision of Sophie on the last day she'd been seen alive, hanging upside down on the jungle-gym, with her red hair almost sweeping the sand.

'The man in the white car took Sophie,' Petra said to Freda conversationally. She folded an abandoned blue jersey for the box, neatly, like adults do, with the sides turned in and the sleeves tucked away.

'What?' said Tamzin. 'What did you say?'

Petra looked apprehensive. 'Sophie went with him. The man,' she whispered.

Tamzin felt herself shaking. She sat on a chair and called Petra over to her. She came reluctantly, dragging her feet. Jonas was scaring Freda with a trick amputated finger. They ran screaming into the garden.

'Did you see Sophie get into a car?' Tamzin asked Petra carefully.

Petra shrugged and pouted.

'Did you see what the man looked like? Had you seen him before? Did Sophie go outside the gate to him or did he call to her? Have you ever seen the man again?'

Too many questions. She was playing it wrong. Petra looked as if she was going to cry. 'I don't know,' she said. 'I don't know.'

Tamzin didn't want to break the thread. It was tenuous at best. She tried to get control. 'It's all right, Petra,' she said. 'Don't be frightened. But why the – why didn't you tell me this before, when I asked everybody if they had seen Sophie go off anywhere?' She wanted to shake the child. Then she could see she'd blown it. Petra had retreated. Like a tortoise going into its shell, she could feel her sliding out of her grasp. It was no good pushing it. Tamzin let her go and she ran out after the twins. When Ansie came back she told her what had happened. Ansie was aghast. 'She's never said anything to us,' she said. 'I never asked her specifically, I suppose, but surely she would have –'

'Do you think she's making it up?'

'I suppose she could be. But Petra doesn't usually say things just like that. She tells lies like any other child when she wants to get herself out of a tight corner, but this sort of fabrication is most strange. Have you told Fran?'

'Not yet. I didn't think there was any point in alarming her, or getting her hopes up, for that matter, before I'd spoken to you, and tried to get a clearer picture. Perhaps you could bring it up again later on, when you're at home?'

Tamzin needed to talk to someone. She tried calling Jessica but there was no reply. Then she tried Ray and got his answer-phone. In the end she just finished clearing up the post-concert debris and waited for Ansie to ring.

But Ansie had no further light to throw on Petra's statement. All Petra would or could say was what she had told Tamzin: Sophie had got into a white car with a man – she did say he was a 'funny' man, but whether she herself had seen her go off with him, even Ansie couldn't establish.

She talked it over with William that night. William looked thoughtful. 'Do you remember,' he said, 'that night that second kid was found murdered? And we were watching the news on TV?'

'And Petra got hysterical talking about some *man*,' said Ansie. 'What was it she said – the same man. It's the same man. William, I'm getting the shivers.'

They had always suspected that Petra had a shadowy psychic streak. Ansie's *ouma* had it too. She used to predict things before they happened. She also used to be able to tell you what you wanted to know before you'd even asked the question. It would intrigue Ansie when she was a child.

'Perhaps we're jumping to conclusions,' said William.

The telephone rang and Ansie jumped. To her surprise it was Cassandra.

'I can't get Jessica,' she said without preamble, as if they had spoken just yesterday; as if her husband wasn't in the centre of the juiciest sex scandal in town. 'Or Fran. I just wanted to confirm tennis as usual tomorrow, and ask you to let the others know.'

'Tennis,' said Ansie blankly. 'Tennis as usual.'

'It was perfectly fine this morning.' Fran looked in exasperation at the Morris. Two sick coughs and that was that. That Jim had appeared at her elbow in the parking lot she knew was no coincidence. Since she had refused to see or talk to him, she knew he had been following her. She'd caught glimpses of his car in her rear-view mirror on the way to the bookshop that morning. And it was almost as if he had a permanent campsite in her garden. Like some cumbersome guardian angel, he never bothered to erase traces of his vigil any more and it still unnerved her, although he hadn't attempted to gain access to the house. She had told Jessica about it and her advice had been to go straight to the cops, the man was a loony. But Fran couldn't do it. This was Jim, still the boy next door. She decided so long as he didn't bug her, she would let it ride. Sooner or later he'd give up.

She looked beneath the bonnet of her car, wishing she knew what she was looking for – some loose wire perhaps, waving obviously at her, or a pipe with a clear leak that she could point confidently at when the AA man came. Instead she had Jim, in a woolly grey tracksuit on a sweltering Thursday afternoon, pulling up beside her.

He had a shocking cold and, by the looks of it, an overdose of sun. His nose was chapped and so were his lips. His cheeks, ruddy as apples, were peeling. White flakes stood out like dandruff. It was as if his face was falling off.

'It's probably your battery, Franny,' he said. He turned aside and coughed, doubling over. 'Sorry – I won't kiss you.'

You're quite right, you won't, thought Fran. 'You sound

awful,' she said. 'Are you taking anything for that?' She had a spanner in her hand, though what she was planning to do with it was anybody's guess – use it on Jim if it came to that.

'I'm all right,' said Jim.

'Do you have any jump leads?'

He shook his head. They were nowhere near a garage and Fran had a regional meeting in twenty minutes. She was reluctant to take the obvious offer, but couldn't think of an excuse.

'I'll take you,' said Jim.

'Oh, I don't –'

'It's no trouble. I'll wait for you to finish your meeting and then drop you off at home.'

'I can't possibly ask you to do that, Jim. You're ill, for heaven's sake. You should be in bed.'

'My mother died,' said Jim.

'Oh God,' said Fran. 'Oh God, Jim. I didn't ... when ... why didn't you – ?'

'I tried to,' he said. 'I called you five times.'

Fran recalled guiltily the blanket instruction she gave wherever she was: never put Jim Walton's calls through to her.

'I'm so sorry,' she whispered. 'I was fond of your mother.'

There was no further argument. Jim held the door open for her and she moved to the passenger seat like an automaton. 'We had the funeral last week,' he said. 'Just a couple of her bridge friends. No one else.'

They drove in silence. 'Look,' said Fran, making a quick, she knew unwise, decision. 'Take me home to my place. You go in and put your feet up and have a sleep or something. If you'll let me use your car, I can still make my meeting, and pick up something for you from the chemist on my way back. I won't be more than an hour. I bet you haven't been eating or anything.' Why was she doing this? Last time she had let Jim into her house he had practically tried to rape her. He would only take this as encouragement. He was smiling at her now. She recoiled from his cracked, reptilian lips.

Driving to the ANC offices, she rationalised her act by reasoning that Jim really was sick. He had flu or bronchitis or something. He would no more be capable of jumping her in the state he was in than she was of ever responding to his attentions. She was safe. She could dose him up and put him in Sophie's room for the night. It would be all right.

When she got home later on, with Med-Lemon and cough mixture in a brown paper bag, Jim was asleep on his back on Sophie's bed. His mouth was open and his breathing was restless and uneven. She could see the sheen of perspiration on his forehead from the doorway. She walked gingerly into the room and drew a light blanket over him. She left the medicine, with spoons and cold water, beside the bed where it was within easy reach, and tiptoed out again. On impulse she turned the key in the door, locking him in. She was getting paranoid. What if he wanted to pee in the night? She unlocked the door and left the hall light on. When she went to bed herself she turned the key in her own door and secured the window too, just in case. It was ludicrous, she knew, but it felt better that way.

In the morning Jim was still feverish and he coughed incessantly. 'You ought to see a doctor,' said Fran, not very enthusiastically. He was sitting up in bed, sipping at the mug of tea she'd brought him. She stayed in the doorway, looking at him over the rim of her cup.

'No,' said Jim. 'I don't want to bother with all that. It's just a cold.'

'Well, look,' Fran said, not really wanting to get involved in calling doctors when she herself had a full day. 'Why don't you stay here, in bed, today? There's plenty to eat, drink, whatever. I don't think you should be thinking of going in to work.'

'I'm on leave. Compassionate leave.'

'Oh.' He really knew how to do it. 'Well, you could probably do with some bed rest in any case. You've been through a lot lately. I'm really sorry.'

Fran brought him fruit juice and toast. She asked if he wouldn't mind lending her the car so that she could get to work. She had left the Morris in the car-park, where it would be safe under the eye of the security guard, but she needed to sort out the battery problem. If Jim was going to stay put, it wouldn't inconvenience him too much. He waved her away. 'No problem,' he croaked.

She should have gone home at lunch-time to check on him, but couldn't bear the thought of it. He came to the telephone, though, sounding half asleep. He was fine; he'd made tea. He was going to sleep the rest of the day. Fran should go ahead and enjoy her tennis.

They had all been amazed by Cassandra's sudden confirmation, as if nothing had happened. As if she hadn't just dropped out of sight for days. True, the scandal had all but died down when the principal players had steadfastly refused to be interviewed, but it was still *there*, like a great big exclamation mark. The press had finally got dispirited and switched their attention to the other house of ill fame. It was offering better news anyway: they had come up with a Northern Transvaal fullback family man called Stokkies Malherbe, and a discount king married five times.

Fran asked after Ben as soon as Jessica arrived. He was all right, said Jessica; he was pretending nothing had happened. 'I think he hopes it will all go away if he goes on acting normally,' she said.

'And how do you feel?'

'Exhausted. Unnerved. Luke's spending all his time with Kelly. I think she's having some kind of breakdown.'

'Has he moved back home?'

'Surprisingly, not so far. And Virginia's talking of taking Kelly and going to live in Cape Town. The fresh start routine. I think Luke would be relieved. I know I would be.'

'But where does that leave you? Have you decided what to do yourself yet?'

'I can't. I can't even think coherently, much less act it. I'm just trying to get through the days without slitting my wrists or throwing up in public places. Not always in that order.'

Cassandra, statuesque and bronzed, nevertheless seemed brittle around the edges. She invited no sympathetic noises and so she received none. Jessica was not used to brushing things under the carpet, other than household dust, especially not lately, when her own dirty laundry was a matter of such interest to her immediate circle, but even she didn't say anything. If that was the way Cassandra wanted it to be, they would play tennis and drink tea and Rome and the townships and the *Sunday Times* could all burn to the ground.

Ansie arrived with Petra. She told them about her brother Stephan's relationship with Carole Abrams. She wanted advice or ammunition. Zinzi had suggested that she not interfere, that it would work itself out one way or another, and any advice Ansie wanted to offer should be kept firmly buttoned inside her lip. Still, it was difficult. Ansie was used to speaking her mind. Stephan refused to discuss it with her, though, and he spent most nights away from home, preferring to sleep at Carole's flat in Hillbrow. She looked discreetly at Fran, who had a peculiar look on her face. Fran gave her a small, crooked smile.

'It's a strange world,' she said. 'People will form relationships with the most unsuitable people, won't they? People you would never have expected would have anything in common find their way to each other in the most unlikely ways. Here we are, in such genteel surroundings, playing tennis in our whites, for God's sake, as if ... as if this is what one does. And yet, somehow, we're all entangled in the same ball of string, messy and full of knots, but connected in some way. We're all pulling at our own particular bits, getting further and further caught up. And still there are things we can't talk about.'

Everyone was stunned. They had never heard Fran talk this way before. They all knew what she was doing, widening the gap, but some secrets stay close to the chest, even when they're not secrets any more, and no one took the bait. Like pegs on a washing-line, close but not touching, they bobbed in the wind. Like a secret spy-ring and the need-to-know principle.

It was very hot in the garden and the children flopped around the adults on the patio after tennis, drinking Cokes out of plastic mugs. Petra and Glenda were playing ludo on a cardboard board. The edges curled in the heat. Edwina, as yet unseen, was playing with dried dog turds.

'Where's your car?' Tamzin asked Fran suddenly. 'I didn't see it.'

Fran looked sheepish. She glanced at Jessica. 'I borrowed Jim's for the day,' she said. Jessica looked at her pointedly. 'The Morris packed up yesterday and he helped me out. I let him stay over at my house last night.'

'You *what*?' said Jessica.

'It's OK. He's in bed with flu. And I locked my bedroom door.'

'What's the matter?' said Ansie. She was looking at Petra, who had sprung to her feet and was standing, white faced, on the grass in front of them. 'Petra?' She looked nervously at Tamzin. Neither of them had yet said anything to Fran about Petra's odd statement yesterday. There hadn't been the right moment. Petra ran to her mother and buried her face in her shoulder.

'Petra?' said Tamzin, getting up. 'What is it?'

'The car.' Her voice was muffled but the words sent a chill up Tamzin's spine. Petra pointed a finger behind her in the direction of the driveway where Jim's white Cortina was parked.

Petra was pacified, the police were called, and Fran sat, carved in marble, completely white and rigid, like a dead person. Her fingers had to be prised off the edge of the chair. They were ice-cold and stiff, like a swimmer who's stayed out in the ocean too long. Even her lips were blue. Jessica, panic-stricken, called Luke who came at once and gave her a shot and put her to bed in Cassandra's guest room. Jessica sat beside her, stroking her hair, while they waited for Davy. The police had been swift and thorough. A hairclip, the twin of the one Tamzin had found in the classroom, had been discovered under the mat of the front seat of Jim's car. Jessica thought of Jim, lying in Sophie's bed, sniffing and wheezing, dosing himself with the medicine Fran had bought for him, and she felt light-headed with rage. A check had revealed Jim's record with the Child Protection Unit: two terms in gaol for child abuse, one of attempted rape. And a long period in Valkenberg under observation. All in Cape Town, before his reappearance in Fran's life. Those 'lost' years, when she and Jim had not been in touch, he was making a name for himself as a schizophrenic and a paedophile. Jessica felt she could have torn him apart with her bare hands.

When Davy arrived, she left him alone with Fran. Cassandra, amazing Cassandra, had made all the children hotdogs and had them corralled in the TV room. She had bathed Edwina and found a nappy and a change of clothes in Jessica's bag. A large pot of tea and a plate of anchovy toast was laid out in the dining room. Nobody had left, except the police, and they all sat at the dining room table, not speaking, like mourners at a wake. Luke was holding Jessica's hand and no one showed any surprise. She slumped against him wearily, and he bent his head to kiss her. It was a tender, unselfconscious moment, where a knot in the ball of string slipped itself loose.

Tamzin, as Fran would do endlessly in the days that followed, was reliving Sophie's last moments. How trustingly Sophie would have gone off with Jim, her mother's friend, on whatever pretext. What would he have said to her? Would a four-year-old, no matter how often she was told never to go off with anyone without first checking with her mother or teacher, question the authority, the confidence, the familiarity of harmless Uncle Jim?

Cassandra, meanwhile, studied Luke from the end of the table. She looked hard for traces of the beautiful features of the child who had so seduced her husband, but found none. All she saw was a small man with delicate hands and thinning hair, who looked inexpressibly tired. That he was more than Jessica's doctor was very clear, and she was surprised to feel nothing more than a mild envy. Could infidelity be catching? The numbness which had beset her ever since Joel's defection was still partly there, rather like novocaine wearing off gradually after a session at the dentist. She saw these things through a kind of haze. They didn't touch her at all. She and Mike were helping each other through, and for the first time in a long, long while, they were close to finding something that seemed like it might be worth salvaging. She did not want, for the moment, to look further than that.

Later that evening, when it seemed there was nothing left for anyone to do, one by one they all took their leave. Tamzin kissed Davy and held him close for a minute. How naturally things gained perspective in the light of the day's revelations. They would all cope, each in their own way.

Ansie helped Cassandra make up another bed in the guest suite for Davy. She called his flat to let Stanley know what had happened, and got Stephan.

It was like a black comedy. As she turned away from the telephone, it rang and she picked up the receiver.

'Cassandra, is that you? Sorry I missed tennis today, but I got the message too late. Did I miss any good gossip?'

'Hello, Gail,' said Ansie, smiling to herself. 'It's Ansie. I'll let Cassandra know you called. And no, no *skandaal* today, I'm afraid. Maybe next Friday.'

Ray called Tamzin late that night. She'd forgotten the message she'd left on his machine. So much had happened, so much emotion had been waded through, she felt disorientated when she heard his voice. This was someone from way back, from before. It was quite nice to feel herself being pulled from another direction. She told him what had happened, about Jim. Tentatively, she suggested he might come over if he wasn't too tired. He wasn't and he did. They talked till the early hours and it was almost good again. Having made her peace, as it were, with Fran and with Davy, Tamzin was reconciled to her new role. Ray didn't make her feel defensive this time. She felt they were on equal ground.

'I'm on holiday,' she told him, with surprise. 'I can sleep in and indulge myself. It's been a very long term.'

It would soon be Christmas and then another new year. And a whole lot of different changes to turn her life upside down again. There were plans to be made for the school.

'Tammy,' said Ray. 'Come with me. Come to London.'

Tamzin was tired. It had been a draining day. This was not something she felt she could make a rational decision on at one in the morning. Although she had thought about it before, and the prospect did attract her in many ways, she couldn't quite ever get a hold on why Ray was asking her. Marriage was not a word which came up in any serious discussion and it didn't seem to be on the agenda now, either. And besides, was that even what she wanted? Would marriage to Ray give security to her and her baby? And was that kind of security that desirable after all? She felt better able to control things if she was in charge. And she didn't know anyone in London. All her friends were here. Luke was here, and Davy. Fran and Jessica. Her life was full enough.

'I'll think about it,' she said, ever the coward. 'You don't need an answer right away, do you?'

Ray stayed the night and Tamzin curled in to his body warmth and slept more soundly than she had done in weeks. In the morning they made love and watched the sky lighten in the east. It was going to be another hot summer's day. A day to go swimming.

'Where does Cassandra live?' Ray asked over breakfast. 'Is she far from here?'

'Why?' asked Tamzin.

'I want to go over and see Davy. I feel we need to talk to each other again. He could probably do with a friend right now.'

Tamzin looked dubious. Her Minnie Mouse nightshirt was pulled tight across her stomach. The material stretched Minnie's face into a lewd smile.

'What's the matter?' Ray looked puzzled.

Tamzin hesitated. 'Nothing,' she said. 'Only ... well, did I mention Stanley at all?'

Thirty

Never in her wildest moments would Jessica have imagined Ben to be the suicidal sort. Suicide was a weak man's answer. Pansies pulled heaters into bathwater and dived head-first off buildings. Real men faced their problems and overcame them. So when Anna came running into her room at five in the morning, brandishing Jessica's wig and demanding that she put it and her slippers on, Jessica thought she'd lost her mind. She had taken a sleeping pill the night before and had been right at the bottom of a very heavy sleep. She seldom woke early these days, and certainly not in the school holidays. Ever since Virginia's phonecall Ben had been sleeping in the spare room, so Jessica was not even disturbed by his morning preparations for work.

Fuzzy with sleep and confused by Anna's noise, Jessica stumbled after her down the passage and out through the kitchen door to the garage. Ben was dozing in the car with his head against the window.

'Keys,' Anna said to her fiercely. 'Where are the spare keys, Ma?'

'Ben?' said Jessica.

'Keys!' yelled Anna.

Then Jessica saw the children in the back seat. They were all asleep. Glenda had her Flopsy Bunny, Andrew, Thomas the train. Edwina, curled on the front seat, was clutching the red knickers. Only then did she become aware that the engine of the car was running and only then did she see the piece of green hosepipe lying where it had been yanked off the stationwagon's exhaust pipe. She turned in fright to Anna and ducked just in time as Anna's hefty black arm heaved a brick through the windscreen and lunged for the keys.

How they pulled the children from the car she didn't know, but it must have been before she fainted because when she came to, there were men in white coats closing the doors of an ambulance in her driveway and Anna was slapping her wrists and trying to force brandy between her teeth.

Her children were all alive. They had not been in the car very long before Anna, always an early riser, had come through the garage on her way to put the garbage out on the pavement for the morning's collection. Had Ben decided to take that way out the previous night when Jessica and the children were asleep, they would all have been dead by morning.

Jessica was heavily sedated and spent the day and a night in the hospital where Andrew, Glenda and Edwina were under observation. Fran called Luke and he came to the hospital and sat beside Jessica's bed with her, with his head in his hands. Fran refused to leave, even to eat, and when Luke had to go back to his rooms, Fran kept vigil by herself. She was there at the bedside when Jessica woke up. And it was she who told Jessica that Ben was dead.

'I didn't –' said Jessica. 'This wasn't –'

'I know,' Fran said.

Jessica struggled to a sitting position. 'The kids?' she said.

'They're fine. They're all fine.'

'Oh, Christ. Oh, Franny, what have I done?'

Fran had no real words for this. Instead she pulled Jessica to her and held her and they sat, forehead to forehead, in the hospital room and waited for a signal so that their lives could begin again.

Perhaps something close to good had come out of it all. Fran had discovered that whether or not Davy was her husband and lover, he was, and always would be, her friend. And if that sounded unbelievably nauseating, she didn't care. It was the only kind of one-dimensional emotion she felt she could deal with. She had stayed on at Cassandra's house for a whole week, while Davy and Mike had taken over. They had removed all traces of Jim Walton from the Kensington cottage, right down to the Med-Lemon sachets which were thrown out with the trash, and a biscuit tin in the pantry. It was less easy to erase Jim himself from her mind and there was the court case which they would somehow have to get through. But Davy had come out of this with a strength and sureness Fran could only marvel at. Davy, who liked to take his insecurities and weave them into music, had hardly left her side. It had needed only a sign from her for him to talk about Stanley, about being gay, and about his years of sexual dilemma. Fran found it easier to understand than she would have thought possible a few months before. They talked about Tamzin and the baby, too, without finding it too great an obstacle. There really was something therapeutic about communicating openly. After weeks of holding herself in, Fran allowed Davy to take the lead.

She had tried to explain it to Jessica, in the few days before Ben had decided to play God. Jessica was typically tart. 'I'm happy for you, Fran,' she'd said, when Fran had been out to supper with Davy and Stanley. 'I can imagine what it must be like: sort of not losing a husband but gaining a brother-in-law.'

Jessica was dithering. The strain of living with Ben's refusal to address the situation in their own home was beginning to take its toll. The only time he had mentioned Luke was to tell Jessica he understood her desire to have a fling – he was not without guilt in that area – but she would know when enough was enough and he was prepared to wait it out. In the meantime an alternative specialist could be found so that when she broke it off, that would be the end of it. He had never mentioned Luke's name again. He went back to work, he stayed off the booze, and he went to AA meetings. While he was out in the evenings, Jessica would go over to Luke's house and hate herself for it in the mornings. Ben had given no outward indication that his patience was running out, but the autopsy revealed a body clogged with alcohol and barbiturates. He had left no note, no written accusation.

*

Tamzin, Fran and Davy were there when Jessica and the children came home. Anna, wiping the corners of her eyes with her apron, embraced them one by one. She lifted Edwina from her car seat and held her on her hip. Edwina squirmed and twisted her head around, trying to see her mother. She could not bear for Jessica to be out of her sight. Andrew and Glenda ran inside and went immediately to the television.

'Well,' said Jessica drily, looking round at her friends, 'if there really is a link between stress and cancer, no amount of fucking chemotherapy will help me now.'

Tamzin burst into tears.

It was spitting with rain. Gusts of wind whirled about them, pulling at their clothes and hair. Jessica steadied her wig. The sky was a threatening grey.

'We'd better get inside,' said Davy.

Later he and Fran went off together and Tamzin stayed with Jessica. She read the children a story and then she and Jessica watched a movie on television. She told Jessica about Ray and how she had decided not to accept his offer. Jessica tried to seem interested but her eyes were red with fatigue. When Tamzin, too, had gone, she walked heavily into each of the children's rooms in turn. They were asleep, safe and warm in their beds. She picked Edwina from her cot, a dead-weight with her plump legs dangling, and carried her to her own bed. She put her arms around her, pulling her in close to her body. They lay, unmoving, until dawn broke and Jessica drifted into sleep.

She woke to find Anna in the room, moving about quietly, humming a Christmas carol. She was putting away the ironing. Jessica watched her without moving. Anna came to a stop at the open door of the cupboard she and Ben shared. She held a pair of Ben's shirts, freshly ironed, by their hangers. She seemed uncertain as to what to do with them. She stood there for a long time while the rain fell outside the open window. 'Anna,' Jessica said softly.

Anna turned around and Jessica saw she was weeping. She made a helpless gesture with the hangers.

'What do I do with these now?' she said.

*

It was Tuesday evening. Ansie and William were addressing Christmas cards. They had a good assembly line going: Ansie would write the message, William address the envelope, and Petra lick stamps and slide the cards in. Ansie usually got this chore done in early December, but nothing this year was going much according to plan.

Stephan came into the lounge. 'Have I missed supper?' he asked cheerfully. He picked Petra up and whirled her round the room. 'How's my girl?' he said.

'I left some food for you in the warmer,' said Ansie. She looked at him suspiciously. 'Why are you so happy?'

'I'm going to Swaziland,' Stephan said.

'Hey, that's nice.' William looked up. 'What's in Swaziland, *boet*?'

Ansie had a fair idea, but said nothing.

Stephan looked at her nervously. She feigned indifference. 'Go get your supper,' she said.

When he came back she looked at him over the top of her glasses. 'Just don't tell us you won't be here for Christmas. We're all going down to the farm together, remember.'

That had been the original plan, yes. But things had changed.

'You'll have to go without me,' Stephan said after a pause. 'I know Ma will be disappointed, but there'll be other Christmases.'

'Disappointed?' William chuckled. 'She'll cut you out of her will, *swaer*.' William was the original innocent. Vibes swung by him like bats with radar.

'So what's in Swaziland?' Ansie said casually, refusing to be drawn, or not yet. She could feel herself working up to it.

Stephan took a breath. He cut vigorously at his quiche. 'Well, Carole's doing a gig there. We're driving up together on Friday –'

'This Friday?' It was Ansie's coldest voice, pure iced water. She signed her name with a flourish at the foot of a reindeer, then took off her glasses. Petra was ready with the envelope. She held out her hand.

'I've got the money I earned from the pageant,' Stephan said. 'It'll be a holiday.'

'Your life is a holiday,' said Ansie, caustically.

'Ans,' said William.

She turned on him, talking through her husband to her brother. 'It's too much, William,' she said. 'He knew we were going to have a family Christmas on the farm. It's really important to Ma and Pa. They're expecting all of us. What am I going to tell them?' That was the real issue, wasn't it? They all knew that.

'That your brother's run off with a Hotnot could be your opener,' said Stephan. He put his fork down. Petra stopped in mid-lick. 'Don't talk about me as if I'm not here,' he went on. 'I think it's time we got this out in the open. I happen to be in love with Carole –' Ansie clicked her tongue unattractively '– and the fact that she's so-called Coloured is neither here nor there.'

'That's where you're wrong,' Ansie interrupted. 'It's both here *and* there. You only *think* you're in love with her and believe me, she's not in love with you. A woman can tell these things. You're going to make a fool of yourself with this girl, Stephan. And what's with this lefty language – "so-called Coloured". A Coloured's a Coloured and there's nothing wrong with that. It just won't work, that's all. What future is there for you with her? What can you offer her in the end? So you're going to university. But in your blood is the river of Soetwater, Stephan. You'll go back to the land, to your inheritance. But you won't take her with you, you know that as well as I do. It won't work, not in your lifetime or mine. There is a time for knowing your place.'

'This is the new South Africa ... ' Stephan began, verging on petulance.

'Ag, new South Africa *se voet*!' said Ansie. 'In Hillbrow maybe. But it's not going to reach the *platteland*. Not ever.'

Deadlock. Stephan finished his meal. Ansie piled the cards up irritably and left the room. William was contemplative. So this was how families got divided, he realised. When issues were too big for compromise.

*

Stephan hitched a ride into Hillbrow. Carole wasn't expecting him but he needed to talk to her, to get things back into perspective. She hadn't been all that enthusiastic about him going with her to Swaziland. She was afraid he would be bored. She would be spending much of her time in rehearsal and her evenings performing. What would Stephan do? This was a six-month gig, after all. Stephan thought she was sweet and thoughtful to worry about him. He could take care of himself, he told her. He would find things to do. He might even find a job there. University could wait. He had to get his priorities right.

He rang the bell at the flat. Nobody came. He looked at his watch, undecided. Finally, he heard the shuffle of footsteps and Stanley pulled open the door. He was yawning, rubbing his eyes.

'Hey,' he said.

'I'm sorry, Stan,' said Stephan. 'I know it's late, but I need to see Carole. Can I come in?'

Stanley held the door open. 'Sure,' he said, 'but Carole's not here. She left this evening.'

'What do you mean?'

'For Swaziland. She's got this gig there, remember? She must have told you. I know she's forgetful, but she's not that bad.'

'But it's Friday she's leaving. We're going together.' Stephan looked bewildered. Stanley put an arm round his shoulder.

'Listen,' he said. 'Let me tell you about my sister.'

Thirty-One

It was the week before Christmas. Ansie had been baking like a fiend: mince pies, Christmas puddings, Christmas cakes. Petra had stirred until her small arms ached. She and the twins had scrubbed the five-cent pieces with toothbrushes until they shone. Turns had been taken to drop them into the spicy-smelling mixing bowls. Wishes were made. Ansie had baked Christmas cakes for all her friends. She and Petra spent the afternoon delivering them. The Mokoenas got the biggest one, as well as a batch of mince pies. The day before they were due to leave for the farm was a full and busy one. Ansie marched straight into Zinzi's kitchen with a tray covered in foil. Petra came on behind, weighed down by a basket of presents – games and puzzles for Freda and Jonas, books and strawberry preserve for Zinzi, computer games for John.

The Mokoenas were not going away over the festivities, and had offered to keep an eye on Ansie and William's house. 'Feel free to swim whenever you like,' said Ansie.

'What's the latest on Stephan?' Zinzi asked.

Ansie could not prevent the small smile, the well-what-did-I-say expression. 'Poor Stephan,' she said. 'His heart is a little bruised, I think, but he's coming to the farm with us after all.'

Stephan had not really told his sister the full story. He hadn't told her about the floor manager at the casino called Ernst, which was a confidence Stanley had shared with him. Nor about the ring he'd blown most of his savings on, with the engraved hearts and initials: ST and CA, wonderfully entwined. His practical sister would have latched immediately on to Chantelle Ackermann as a helpful solution, she of the solid thigh and single eyebrow from the neighbouring farm. He had explained instead how he and Carole had decided in the end that she should go on ahead and he would join her in Swaziland in the new year. But the words had lacked conviction and Ansie had been as tactful and supportive as she could be under the circumstances. She could not wait to get to the farm, to get Petra out under acres of uninterrupted sky and into a brown-water dam where you couldn't see the bottom, where the crabs and frogs hid in the cool summer mud. Where there were horses to ride, grandparents and aunts and uncles to fuss over her, and cousins to roam the land with. She wanted to see the bloom in her child's cheeks, to allow her to forget the hours of stressful interrogation and the man in the white car. On Soetwater it would be easier to put those things behind them.

John had bought Zinzi a car for Christmas. It was black and fast and had air-conditioning and a CD player. Zinzi took Ansie for a spin round the suburban streets. They put the hood down and the music up and felt like a couple of teenagers on a joyride. 'Slow down,' Ansie shouted. She held on to her hair which was whipping back off her forehead in the wind.

In the evening everyone assembled at Zoo Lake for Carols by Candlelight. Tamzin had started the tradition when she started Rosepark, and it had become the event which officially marked the end of the school year. They were all there: Fran had come with Thabo Thekiso and his mother. Jessica was there with her children, Cassandra and Mike with theirs. Gail was there with Simon and the Barkers and the Mokoenas came together. They spread blankets on a grassy slope, slightly to the edge of the crowd. Edwina was fascinated by the coloured fountains in the lake and kept tottering down to the water's edge. They lit their candles as the service began.

It was a warm, still night. Tamzin looked up at the sky. A few kilometres out of the city they might have been able to see the stars, but the glow of a thousand candles in amongst the trees was magical enough. She felt the baby turn and jab with an arm or a leg and she smiled; she loved the sensation.

Last year Sophie had been there too, sitting in the warm hollow of her father's crossed legs. She had dropped off to sleep without anyone noticing and her candle had fallen over and burnt a hole in Jessica's sleeping bag. Ben had scandalised everyone by bringing out a six-pack and snapping open a can in the opening bars of 'O Little Town of Bethlehem'. Tamzin wondered if anyone remembered that, and how she and Jess had got the giggles. Was anyone else thinking back to last year like she was? Ray had been there too, singing in his pleasant, deep baritone. Had Cassandra been part of the group? Yes – she'd been there but she hadn't sat with them, preferring her smart folding chair and mohair knee rug. Tamzin looked across to Jessica who was sitting on the edge of the blanket in an anorak with the hood on. She sat hunched over, fidgeting with the fringe on the blanket, not singing, not looking up. Half-way through the service she saw her bend over and whisper to Fran, then get up and walk away into the black shadows of the surrounding bushes. She looked enquiringly at Fran, who mouthed 'It's OK' and drew Jessica's children in closer to her.

Jessica was waiting for them at the car when the service ended. She declined coffee at Tamzin's with the others. 'I'm tired,' she said. 'My body is tired.'

'Will you be all right?' Gail asked.

'Yes. Thank you. I'll be fine.'

On the way over in the car Mike took Cassandra's hand. 'Did we go to this thing last year?' he asked.

'I did,' she said. 'You were working.'

'Ah yes. You went with the girls – made a night of it. I remember.'

Cassandra said nothing. The girls. This time she really had been with the girls. It felt good. She held on to Mike's hand. His flesh was warm and smooth. Even his wedding band was warm. 'Wouldn't it be nice to be going on holiday somewhere,' she said. 'Just to get away, right away? A white Christmas maybe like, when was it – '84?'

They had made no holiday plans this year. They hadn't felt like a family. Mike pulled up outside Rosepark. 'Ray's here,' he said. He sounded pleased. He and Ray had become quite friendly during the week Davy and Fran had spent with the Symons after Jim Walton's arrest. Ray had been in and out frequently, spending long hours talking to Davy. Mike, who had taken sudden, recommended leave until the new year, joined them at the poolside. He cleaned leaves and dirt from the surface with net and pole. They talked about all sorts of things, and they played backgammon.

Ray was in good spirits tonight. Tamzin was grateful and relieved, after their last confrontation when she had told Ray that she would rather have her baby here at home than in London like Ruth amid the alien corn. Ray had been relieved, too, and they had agreed to keep in close touch and review the situation when their lives were more settled. She would be taking on two new teachers for the school but, as hers was the hands-on approach to pre-school teaching, she wanted still to make herself available to the children and their parents. She wasn't ready yet to leave.

She and Ray had reached a new level of understanding. She would miss him and he her, but whether they would get back together again neither of them was foolish enough to predict. It would be frightening to have the baby on her own, she knew that, but her friends were here, her support group. She would manage well enough.

Anna had left all the house lights on, as if she wanted to spare a home-coming Jessica any dark, morbid corners. Only at Jessica's repeated insistence had she reluctantly agreed to take an evening off at all. The children had fallen asleep on the back seat, a jumble of arms and legs. For a moment Jessica looked at them in terror, the relaxed helpless limbs, their faces calm in sleep. She stood with her hand on the car door handle, suddenly struck immobile with fear. She had been unable to cry for Ben and it was not tears which threatened now, but anger. But it was an impotent anger which made her stand there, in the light from the street, unable to go forward or back.

'Let me,' said Luke. He stepped out of the shadows and took the keys from her. He reached out to her and she let him hold her and talk to her until, like a sleep-walker, he was able to guide her into the house. He carried the children inside, one by one, and put them in their beds.

Jessica was sitting where he'd left her, hood up, bag over her shoulder. 'Edwina's probably wet,' she said gruffly.

'She'll last,' said Luke.

He went to the liquor cabinet and found whisky and glasses and poured an inch into a glass for Jessica. She drank it down like medicine. Luke sat and warmed her hands in his.

'Do we still love each other?' Jessica asked. 'Is it possible that we could have fucked up so badly just because of that?'

'Don't,' said Luke.

'I'm going to have to find a job.'

'It will be good for you.'

'I can't do anything. I haven't a skill in the world. Except perhaps wrecking marriages. I do that pretty well.'

Luke said nothing. He held on to her hands. He kissed her knuckles.

'Bet you I don't qualify for medical aid, not with my record.'

'Will you stop, please.'

'You've never seen me maudlin, have you?' Jessica stole a sly look at him. There was a trace of a smile on her face. He wanted to blow on it, like a draught on a small flame, to warm it into life. He thought, given time, he could do it.

Thirty-Two

'Father?'

It was Mbekhi. McBride knew the voice like his own. His breathing came roughly out of the darkness. 'Yes, Mbekhi,' he said.

'I need to talk. Are we safe here?'

McBride smiled to himself. He supposed that the confessional was safe enough, although you never knew. He heard confessions on Thursdays and Saturdays as a matter of routine, but this afternoon was quiet. It was summer holidays now and the convent schoolgirls had all gone home to enjoy the sins they would admit to next term.

'I think so, Mbekhi. What's on your mind?'

Mbekhi was not a Catholic and to McBride's knowledge had never made an official confession to a priest. He was a little puzzled. Mbekhi could as easily have come to him in his study if he wanted to talk in private and in confidence. As Mbekhi told his story, however, he realised that it probably wasn't chance that had brought Mbekhi here, seeking the darkness and sanctuary of the cloth. Also, Mbekhi was clearly more comfortable with the grid and the veil between them, which prevented them having to look into each other's eyes. Mbekhi was not kneeling though; he was not a penitent. He stood with his back against the wall, the position he had adopted for most of his young life. Haltingly at first, the words came, then gradually more fluidly until McBride could hardly keep pace with him. He spoke of personal revenge which had got in the way of his judgement. Of the man they called 'Die Waaghals' and of his friend whose picture had also been in the papers.

'He was the man at the cathedral, Father,' he said. 'And at the rally in Alex.'

And he was the man responsible for the road-block and the death of his friend. Now, however, Mbekhi had abused his position of trust as a soldier of the struggle, acting without authority, without licence. The papers had talked about Die Waaghals's business front in the centre of town, a small photographic shop specialising in identity document pictures and drivers' licences. It had been easy, too easy.

Mbekhi fished two startled-looking pictures of himself out of his pocket for McBride to see. The priest pulled the curtain aside, stuck out a hand and took them. He held them up in the gloom, as if expecting them to offer him, Investigating Detective McBride, some vital clue. He gave them back.

'Are you telling me what I think you're telling me, Mbekhi?' he asked.

'Yes, Father. I have made the front pages of the papers too many times in the past weeks, but all in the course of my duties.' His voice dropped to barely a murmur. 'This time it was an act of the heart, not my head. Tom Shabalala was my closest comrade.'

McBride sighed. His wooden chair creaked as if in sympathy. 'Go on,' he said.

'I came straight here. I want you to telephone. Here is the number.'

McBride wasted no time. The call was made, the area cleared. When the limpet mine went off, it injured no one, although the small shop and the one next door were badly damaged. This time the police were at the convent almost simultaneously. There had been no time for a callbox and McBride was expecting them. He could tell they were pleased. All along they had been on the right track. Now they had his voice on tape there was no disputing the evidence. They didn't even ask for Mbekhi this time.

Thabo watched curiously from the garden as McBride got into the police car. As they drove off he waved tentatively. 'See you later, Father,' he called.

Fran was alone in the ECC office. Since the blast that had nearly taken off her legs, they had moved into the building next door. It was amazing, really, how neatly tenants could find excuses to vacate the premises when the neighbours were suspect. These offices were nice; lighter, airier.

Most of the volunteer people were away on their Christmas holidays. She was catching up on the admin, for which nobody else seemed to want to take responsibility. She had the January newsletter to prepare, too. She made herself a cup of coffee and stood with it at the window overlooking the park. It was dusk, the twenty-third of December. Tomorrow was Christmas Eve. Fran fervently wished she were in some foreign country where they didn't celebrate Christmas, where it would be a normal kind of day. She wasn't altogether sure that she would ever enjoy Christmas again. She had to steer her mind away from last Christmas and the one before that. She had had plenty of invitations. Davy and Stanley were driving up to Swaziland and had urged her to join them: free accommodation, good cabaret. She knew Davy had been torn. He wanted to be with Stanley, but he also knew that their first Christmas without Sophie was going to be hard. But what was the use? Moping around, remembering the cross-eyed fairy on the tree, one of a batch made at Rosepark in a frenzied rush because Tamzin had got carried away with the Octopus's Garden project and had forgotten about Christmas decorations.

'Davy's got his own fairy this year, don't forget,' Jessica had said. She was getting back to her old self. She and Luke would probably spend part of Christmas together, but Jessica's parents were going to be there and the children were going to Ben's parents for some of the time too. Jessica didn't think any of them were ready for Luke yet. Tamzin and Ray would be spending the day together; the Symons had flown off suddenly to the Seychelles and the holiday house Cassandra's father had bought them as a surprise.

Fran knew she shouldn't spend the day alone and she didn't intend to. The Malans' house was as close to a home as she could possibly want and she had chosen to have Christmas with them, where she could curl up in a corner of their rambling house and read and eat and sleep. It was the obvious thing to do and she was looking forward to it. François would be there too, her neglected godson. She wanted to spend time getting to know him.

She turned back to her desk. As she did she caught a glimpse of movement at the door and Mbekhi Thekiso slipped through the glass doors into the office.

'I didn't mean to startle you,' he said.

'Mbekhi. What are you doing here? I hear your name everywhere.'

Mbekhi came straight to the point. 'I have no transport,' he said. 'I'm sorry. Will you help me?' He was out of breath, as if he had run up four flights of stairs – which he had.

'Oh God, Mbekhi. You really shouldn't be here. It's asking for trouble.'

'I saw your car,' Mbekhi said pointedly.

Fran thought quickly. She knew, though, that she really had no choice. A comrade in trouble was a comrade who must be helped. 'OK,' she said. 'But get the hell out of here. Go to this address –' she wrote swiftly on a yellow Post-It pad and put it into his pocket '– and I'll pick you up in half an hour. I need to make a couple of calls, but I can't make them from here.'

Mbekhi swallowed. 'Thank you,' he said softly. 'I didn't like to do this, but –'

'It's OK. Just go. You'll have to walk. It'll probably take you about half an hour in any case.'

Mbekhi slipped down the stairs again and she saw him jog along the street and into the park. She felt annoyed and elated at the same time. She didn't go home. Instead she drove swiftly to Jessica's house where she borrowed an overnight bag and some of Jessica's clothes. 'They'll be long on you,' Jessica said, standing by critically.

Fran pulled a face at her.

'Mind telling me what's going on? This is all very unorthodox and MI5.'

'Sudden change of Christmas plans,' said Fran. 'I haven't time to go home. I'm picking up a friend and taking him to Botswana rather urgently.'

'Will you see Mary?'

'I'll spend a couple of nights there. Listen – do me a favour. Can you call the Malans and let them know? They're expecting me, but they'll understand.'

Jessica looked dubious. 'I suppose you'll want to take this?' She held up the diary.

'Thanks, Jess.' Fran took it from her and put it at the bottom of the bag. 'I think it will be safer back over the border.' She shoved a T-shirt and two pairs of shorts into the bag. 'Can I take that shampoo?'

'Be my guest,' said Jessica. 'It's no bloody good to me. Want the conditioner too?'

Fran gave her a hard hug and a kiss. 'Take care,' she said. 'Happy Christmas, Comrade.'

Fran had done this route many times before. With the Morris newly restored, they made good time. They talked sporadically, but Mbekhi was nervous and restless. He kept turning to look behind them. He made Fran nervous too. 'We'll get there,' she said. 'Don't worry.'

They stopped for petrol and Kentucky at about ten o'clock, then drove on a little way and pulled into a lay-by to rest. 'Have you brought nothing with you?' asked Fran.

Mbekhi was in shirtsleeves and sandals, no socks. He shook his head. The smell of fried chicken filled the car. Fran rolled down the window. She turned on the radio. 'I want to catch the news,' she said. 'See what's happening in Alex.'

But it was the Botswana raid that was the main news story of the day. Their suspected involvement vehemently denied by the South African Police, the assassins had struck at midnight, a full-scale assault, it seemed, with hand grenades and AK-47s. The occupants of the house didn't have a chance.

It was believed that the notorious terrorist 'Bonnie' was the main target. She could now be named: Mary Elizabeth Peterson, for a long time sought by the police anti-terrorist units, and the prime suspect in a series of terror attacks in Johannesburg over the past months. Her husband, known activist Sam Peterson, in exile for thirty years, was also believed to have died in the hail of bullets, as were their two children.

Mbekhi passed a hand over his face. He put a chicken bone, picked clean, back in the red and white striped box, and he placed the box beside his feet. He did not look at Fran while the rest of the news was read. Neither of them made a move to turn off the radio. They sat together, facing out into the pitch dark of the countryside, right through the weather report and two Phil Collins' songs, without saying a word. Occasionally the powerful beams of trucks using this little-used road would light them up as they passed. Fran looked at herself in the mirror on the sun visor. The face she saw there in the moonlight was haggard and old. The eyes were dark pits and the mouth scored deep by tension. She thought about the last hot nights she had spent in Botswana, smelt the herbs on the barbecueing fish in its tinfoil jacket and remembered the radio hanging from the branch of the tree. And how she had thought about how simple and pure life seemed to be out there in the country, untainted and whole. She reached out a hand and touched the mirror with a finger. Then she started the engine and moved the car slowly on to the tarmac.

'Do you want me to come with you?'

Fran shook her head. The sun was bright and hot and she squinted up at Mbekhi standing on the road beside her window. 'You go on,' she told him. 'I'll be all right.'

They shook hands through the window, a strong three-way clasp which neither of them broke at first. Fran put her free hand over Mbekhi's. 'When I get back,' she said, 'do you want me to see your mother and brother?'

'Thank you,' Mbekhi said. 'Thank you, Comrade.'

When Fran arrived at the farmhouse, it was already early evening. Her shirt was sticking to her back and her feet slipped on the pedals of the car. It was desperately hot, the sky almost white, as if all the colour had been bleached from it during the day. She had anticipated a cordon, a police presence, press. But there was nothing, no one that she could see as she approached along the pitted road, with grey dust, fine as powder, rising from her wheels and filling the air. A small black boy ran to open the gate for her, as if she was a visitor with people to visit. He raised a clenched fist. 'Viva,' he said. He was all of about six years old.

'Viva, viva,' Fran murmured to herself, her eyes on the

house, scanning the area around it for signs of life. They had lived a pretty isolated existence out here, she reflected. It was miles from the nearest school or store. Mary had been lonely sometimes, especially when Sam was away.

It looked like any old, abandoned building. The windows were smashed. One wing all burned out. The door hanging crookedly open. Fran got out of the car and leaned against its side. She didn't need to go inside. The little boy had followed her. He squatted a short distance away, watching her, like a clay child risen out of the earth. There was no other dwelling within sight. She walked over to the trees at the side of the house, stepping carefully on bare feet, looking out for the sharp *duwweltjies* – little devils – fallen from their vines in the sand. The swing-seat was there. There was one plastic cushion on it, at head level, and a Scorpio coffee mug beside it on an upturned log. Had Mary been a Scorpio? She couldn't think. She sat on the seat and leaned back, looking at the house, swaying softly. Knotted round one of the supports were the beads she had given to Charity the last time she'd been here. Small hands had wound them round and round in impossible knots, never to be unravelled. She began working them loose with her fingernails.

The child had crept nearer. He was looking beyond her, at something or someone behind her head. She turned listlessly and saw a woman standing some distance away. She did not seem surprised to see Fran, but she stayed where she was. She had a white enamel basin in her hands, filled with green mealies. She looked at the house, then at Fran. She put the basin down carefully, securing it between tufts of grass. Making a wild sweep with her arm in the direction of the house, she said, her words carrying clearly on the hot air: 'All.' And again, 'All.'

The evening star, the star of the east, was a bright beacon in the cobalt sky. Fran, neither wise man nor shepherd, turned her weary, dust-coated car towards it and drove in second gear back the way she had come. She had looped the cheap necklace of wooden beads over the rear-view mirror. Faded by the relentless weather, they hung there, swinging and bouncing with the rhythm of the road.